THE NOSFERATU SCROLL

"What do you want with me?" Marietta said, her voice trembling with fear.

"You'll find out soon enough," the man snapped. "Now, do exactly what we tell you, or—" He triggered the Taser again, then pointed to the house. "Go up there," he ordered.

Marietta stared around her, at the small island with its grass-covered slopes, clumps of bushes and occasional small trees, and at the house itself. Beyond it lay the waters of the Venetian lagoon. A surge of pure terror coursed through her body as she realized she was beyond help.

"I have a friend," she said desperately. "I was on my way to visit him. When I don't arrive, he'll call the police."

The man with the Taser smiled at her, but it was not a smile of amusement. "I've no doubt he will. The police will never find us, or you. And even if they did," he added, "it wouldn't make any difference, because you're not the first."

Marietta stared at him, and then she screamed.

"Feel better now? Get moving. We have people waiting for you."

Marietta gasped for breath and stared round again, looking desperately for anything or anyone that might offer her some hope. But there was nothing.

THE
NOSFERATU
SCROLL

JAMES BECKER

WITHDRAWN

A SIGNET BOOK

SIGNET
Published by New American Library, a division of
Penguin Group (USA) Inc., 375 Hudson Street,
New York, New York 10014, USA
Penguin Group (Canada), 90 Eglinton Avenue East, Suite 700, Toronto,
Ontario M4P 2Y3, Canada (a division of Pearson Penguin Canada Inc.)
Penguin Books Ltd., 80 Strand, London WC2R 0RL, England
Penguin Ireland, 25 St. Stephen's Green, Dublin 2,
Ireland (a division of Penguin Books Ltd.)
Penguin Group (Australia), 250 Camberwell Road, Camberwell, Victoria 3124,
Australia (a division of Pearson Australia Group Pty. Ltd.)
Penguin Books India Pvt. Ltd., 11 Community Centre, Panchsheel Park,
New Delhi - 110 017, India
Penguin Group (NZ), 67 Apollo Drive, Rosedale, Auckland 0632,
New Zealand (a division of Pearson New Zealand Ltd.)
Penguin Books (South Africa) (Pty.) Ltd., 24 Sturdee Avenue,
Rosebank, Johannesburg 2196, South Africa

Penguin Books Ltd., Registered Offices:
80 Strand, London WC2R 0RL, England

Published by Signet, an imprint of New American Library, a division of Penguin
Group (USA) Inc. Previously published in a Transworld Publishers edition. For
further information contact Transworld Publishers, a division of Random
House, Ltd., 61–63 Uxbridge Road, London W5 5SA, England.

First Signet Printing, February 2012
10 9 8 7 6 5 4 3 2 1

To Sally. For always and for everything.

Acknowledgments

No book is ever the work of just the author: it's invariably a team effort. In this case, the original spark came from the talented team at Transworld, and specifically from my dedicated and forceful editor there, Selina Walker. She liked the idea of Bronson and Angela mixing it with the undead, as a departure from their usual haunts of dusty caves, ancient manuscripts and clay tablets. My brilliant agent, Luigi Bonomi of LBA, liked the idea as well, and we all thought Venice was pretty much the ideal location for the story. Throughout the writing process they both offered invaluable insights and suggestions, all of which improved the book immeasurably.

PROLOGUE

10 May 1741
Krumlov Zamek, Český Krumlov, Bohemia

"Open it."

The torchlight gave the priest's face a haunting, almost satanic, quality, an impression reinforced by the chamber in which he was standing. It was a small underground room in the castle, located in the same part of the building as the cages that held the wolves. Four flickering torches were mounted in sconces, one on each wall, but they failed to drive away all the shadows.

A sturdy table stood in the center of the room, and on it lay a large, ornate, black wooden coffin, the closed lid divided into two parts and hinged on one side, the other edges secured with screws. The coffin had arrived from the Schwarzenberg Palace in Vienna two days earlier and had immediately been carried into St. George's Chapel in the castle. There, the upper section of the coffin had been opened to allow the mere handful of mourners who had appeared in the building to see the thin, white face of the body inside.

The princess had come home for the last time.

Masses for the immortal soul of Princess Eleonora Elisabeth Amalia Magdalena von Schwarzenberg had been held all over Bohemia, but few people made the journey to the vast castle—which wasn't a single structure at all, but a complex of huge yellow and gray stone buildings roofed with red tiles—that stood on the north bank of the Vltava River.

It was here that her burial was about to take place, and there were preparations—important preparations—to be made.

Four servants had carried the coffin down from St. George's Chapel. Now one of them moved forward in response to the priest's instruction and removed the handmade iron screws that secured the upper part of the lid. His task done, he stepped back.

"No. Take all of them out," the priest ordered.

The man looked surprised, but obediently removed the remaining fastenings that held down the lower section of the lid. As he worked, he glanced back at the priest, wondering why the man who'd so publicly shunned the princess while she was alive was now so concerned with her dead body.

The priest's name was Bohdan Řezník, the surname meaning "butcher," and in truth he looked as though he would be more at home in a bloodstained apron than in the plain, dark brown robes he habitually wore.

When the body of the Princess Eleonora Amalia had been delivered to the castle, one of the escort party had walked down into Krumlov town, found Řezník at his home and handed him a single folded sheet of parchment. The document bore three separate seals, one of them the distinctive double-headed eagle mark of Karel VI, King of Bohemia, the current ruler, and a member of the Habsburg dynasty, which had governed the country since 1526.

The instructions contained on the parchment were unambiguous, and made perfect sense to Řezník. He'd noted with satisfaction that his orders had been prepared by Dr. Franz von Gerschstov, Eleonora Amalia's preferred physician, and a man whose other, less well-known, qualities struck a chord with Řezník.

The servant removed the final screw, and stepped back from the coffin once more, awaiting any further instructions the priest might issue.

"Swing back the lid," the priest said, and watched as two of the servants did so, to reveal the whole interior of the coffin.

"Now leave me with her. You may return in half an hour."

Only when the door of the small room had closed behind the men did the priest step forward. He walked across the flagstone floor to the coffin and looked down with distaste at the slight figure of Eleonora Amalia. Her hands were placed demurely on her breast, the right hand resting on the left, her wasted body clad in a long white dress, her small feet bare.

Řezník felt in the pocket of his habit and pulled out a folding knife with a black wooden handle. He'd spent several minutes the previous evening putting a fine edge on the dark steel blade.

He made the sign of the cross and muttered a prayer— not for the immortal soul of Eleonora, but for himself, asking for forgiveness and divine protection for the actions he now had to take. He lifted the princess's hands and laid her arms at her sides, then snapped open the knife. Řezník inserted the blade under the neckline of the dress and in a single fluid movement ran the knife all the way down to Eleonora's feet, slicing through the layers of material. Then he peeled aside the two cut halves of the dress and looked down at her naked body. The skin that had been so white in life was now mottled and discolored, with livid brown and purple marks where the initial stages of decay had taken hold.

But that wasn't the most noticeable feature. What held Řezník's attention was the crudely stitched cut that ran from between the princess's small, wrinkled breasts down to her pubis.

Her nakedness offended him, but he had his instructions. His expression of distaste deepened as he again used his blade, this time to slice through each of the rough stitches that held the skin and flesh of her abdomen closed. Then he put down the knife, inserted his fingers into the wide incision and with little difficulty pulled apart the two sections of dead tissue. He was looking for one thing, one single object in the chest cavity, and in seconds he knew it wasn't there—which was as it should be. But Řezník had been ordered to make absolutely sure before the burial took place.

He nodded in satisfaction, wiped his hands on the front of his robe and stepped back from the open coffin. Then he walked across to one corner of the chamber, where another, much smaller and very plain wooden box was propped against the wall. Řezník was a strong man, and he picked up the box with little effort. He carried it across to the table, placed it next to the princess's coffin and lifted off the lid.

Then he strode back to the wall of the chamber and picked up a leather bag, the contents of which clattered metallically as he carried it over to the table. He placed the bag on the floor, opened it and took out three substantial leather straps, which he positioned under the open box, spacing them equally along its length.

He reached into the larger casket, picked up the mortal remains of Eleonora Amalia and dropped the body unceremoniously into the smaller box. Before he placed the lid in position, he took a small vial of clear liquid from his pocket and sprinkled the contents over the corpse, muttering a prayer as he did so. Then he took a hammer and a handful of nails from his bag, and drove a dozen of them firmly through the box's lid, securely sealing it to the base. To complete the process, he knelt down and tightened each of the leather straps around it.

Řezník took a deep breath and then, grunting with the effort, he lifted up the small wooden box and maneuvered it into the larger coffin. It would have been easier to wait until the servants returned, but his instructions had been clear—when they returned to the chamber, he was to have sealed the coffin for the last time. Nobody must ever know what he had done. He closed the lid and started replacing the screws.

When the servants knocked at the door a few minutes later, Řezník had finished securing the lid and was standing beside the coffin, waiting for them.

"We leave the castle at eight," he said. "Ensure that the carriage is ready and everything has been prepared by then."

A few minutes before the appointed hour, Řezník strode into the castle courtyard. Night was already falling, and the expansive open space was in deep shadow, the only illumination coming from the fitful flames of the torches mounted along the walls.

A black-painted carriage, its doors bearing the device of the Schwarzenberg dynasty, stood waiting in the center of the courtyard. Two black mares were already hitched to it and tossing their heads impatiently in black-plumed headdresses. The driver, also dressed in black, stood beside the vehicle. As Řezník had instructed—his absolute authority conferred by the parchment he still carried—all of the castle's servants, wearing the darkest clothes they possessed, were standing silently on one side of the courtyard to bid their mistress a last farewell.

Řezník walked across to the carriage and looked into the rear section, behind the seats. The coffin was already in place, the gleaming black wood marred in two places by the leather straps that held it in situ, a precaution against the jolting the carriage would experience on the rough and unmade road that ran from the castle to the church of St. Vitus, where the princess's body was destined to rest for all eternity. Řezník nodded in satisfaction: all his instructions had been followed to the letter. Finally, he clambered up onto the carriage, the driver joining him a few moments later.

For a couple of minutes nothing else happened, and then the castle clock struck eight. As the first peal of the bell echoed around the courtyard, the servants standing beside the large wooden gates stepped forward, released the bolts, and pulled them open. Only then did the driver tap the reins lightly across the broad backs of the two mares. Obediently, the horses stepped forward, their hooves clattering on the uneven stones of the courtyard, and the carriage began to move, creaking gently as it did so.

The funeral cortège, if that word could accurately be applied to only a single carriage containing two men and one corpse, passed through the wide gateway and out of the castle. The sight that greeted the two men outside the walls was both spectacular and sad: the road that wound away from the castle was lined on both sides by silent and unmoving figures, each holding aloft a flaming brand. Indeed, from the castle gates, it looked as if a thin double ribbon of fire was stretching out in front of the carriage, illuminating the final route that the princess's body would take.

Řezník glanced at the first few figures as the carriage drove slowly past them. Some of the torchbearers had been drawn from the local villagers, but the others, and perhaps the majority, were men and women of the cloth: monks and nuns who had been summoned by Řezník so that their piety and righteousness might lend a certain dignity—and protection—to the proceedings. Each of them bowed his or her head in respectful supplication as the carriage passed, and then made the sign of the cross.

And as the carriage trundled slowly past the silent ranks, the torchbearers extinguished their burning brands in metal water buckets that had been placed beside each of them specifically for that purpose. The moving end of the ribbon of fire marked the position of the carriage, while behind it darkness again reclaimed the land.

An impartial observer might have wondered at a funeral for a princess of the Schwarzenberg dynasty being conducted in such a manner. It was unusual enough that the presiding clergyman should be just a village priest rather than a bishop or some other high Church official, but even more surprising was the complete absence of a single member of the Schwarzenberg family, or any representatives from the other aristocratic families to which

the Schwarzenbergs were linked or related. Even Eleonora Amalia's son Joseph was missing.

It was as if the only people who had any regard or respect or affection for the princess were the peasants and
villagers of Krumlov itself, but even that impression was
false. The local men and women lining the route and
holding the torches aloft had been ordered to do so by
Řezník, on pain of punishment.

About twenty minutes after leaving the castle, the carriage drew to a halt outside the open doors of the Church
of St. Vitus. Řezník climbed down from his seat and issued a series of instructions. The straps holding the coffin
in place were released, and the heavy wooden box was
hoisted onto the shoulders of six powerfully built monks.
They carried the coffin into the church and placed it on
a wooden trestle that had been prepared and positioned
in front of the altar.

The service was short—about as brief as Řezník could
make it—and almost all the pews in front of the pulpit
were noticeably empty. The only people sitting in the
church were wearing the habits of monks and nuns, summoned like the torchbearers before them. Once his duty
was done, Řezník stepped down from the pulpit to super-
vise the actual burial.

It might have been expected that, as a Schwarzenberg,
the princess would be laid to rest in the family vault, in
St. Augustine's church in Vienna, but Eleonora had been
denied that privilege. Instead, Řezník led the way into a

small side chapel where a large section of the flagstone floor had already been removed and a deep grave dug, a grave that had been lined with a clay-based concrete. The six monks lowered the casket to the floor, where three substantial ropes had been placed in readiness. Then they each seized the end of one of the ropes and lifted the coffin off the floor, moving awkwardly in the confined space around the grave, and maneuvered the casket over the hole. Slowly they lowered the coffin into the waiting void.

Řezník murmured a few last prayers, and then ordered the handful of official mourners out of the church. The final rituals were to be witnessed by as small a number of people as possible.

Řezník stepped to one side of the chapel and picked up a crudely fashioned wooden ladder, which he carried over to the side of the grave and then lowered into it. He gestured to the monks, who silently descended into the pit. Řezník held a torch over the void so they could see what they were doing. Stacked along both sides of the grave were a number of heavy flat stones. Working under the priest's direction, the monks picked these up, two men to each stone, and placed them carefully on the flat top of the black wooden coffin, in a double layer.

Řezník inspected their work carefully from the top of the grave, and ordered them to climb out again. Their next task required all the considerable strength the monks possessed. Řezník had already arranged for a rough wooden arch fitted with a heavy-duty pulley to be positioned inside the chapel to allow a single heavy slab to be laid across the top of the open grave to seal it completely. Even with this mechanical device to assist them, it still took almost half an hour before the slab was positioned to Řezník's satisfaction and, despite the cool evening air, the sweat was pouring off the faces of the six men.

But still they weren't finished. Řezník permitted them a short break to recover their strength, then supervised the disassembly of the wooden arch, the component pieces of which they stacked against the sidewall of the chapel. Once that had been completed, he instructed them to drag three heavy sacks containing soil, taken from the cemetery outside the church, across to the slab that now covered the tomb. They upended the sacks and spread the contents into a single even layer over the slab.

Now, finally, the monks' work was almost over. They replaced the flagstones that had been removed to allow the hole to be dug, but left enough space directly over the grave for the gravestone itself, a slab that Řezník had had prepared by a stonemason in the village the previous day. Two of the monks picked up the stone and lowered it carefully into position.

Řezník stepped to the end of the gravestone and lowered his head in prayer for the last time, the six monks who had assisted him kneeling on the flagstone floor beside the tomb.

Moonlight speared in through one of the chapel's side windows and the beam played silently across the freshly cut and very simple inscription in the stone. The words made no mention of Eleonora Amalia's family name or her aristocratic status. It didn't even include the Schwarzenberg coat of arms. On the specific instructions of Řezník, who had himself simply been following the orders he had been given by the men who had prepared the parchment, the inscription simply listed the first name of the princess, and the date of her death:

Hier liegt die arme Sünderin Eleonora bittet für sie.
Obut die 5 Mai A1741.

*   *   *

With the body of Eleonora now safely consigned to the earth, Řezník had two more tasks to perform. The carriage was standing outside the church, the driver waiting for him. Řezník climbed up onto the vehicle and instructed the man to return to Krumlov Castle.

The gates were still wide-open, but the courtyard was now virtually deserted. Only three men waited for Řezník's return and the orders they expected him to issue. The priest stepped down from the carriage and walked across to them.

The men were all wearing tunics that identified them as servants of the Schwarzenberg dynasty, and two of them were armed with short swords, the scabbards buckled to their belts. It was these two men whom Řezník approached first.

"It's time," he said. "Do it now. Kill them all, and dump the bodies in the forest."

The men nodded, turned on their heels and vanished inside the building.

Řezník turned to the third man. "Show me the painting."

The servant led Řezník into the castle and to a long gallery, at one end of which hung a life-size portrait of Eleonora. The priest stared at the princess's pale face for a few moments, his lip curling in disgust.

"Lift it down," he ordered.

Once the painting was leaning against the wall, Řezník took his folding knife and opened it. He drove the point of the blade through the canvas to the left of the princess's head and hacked downward in a vertical line. He repeated the operation on the right-hand side of the image as well, then sliced a horizontal line above the head to join the two cuts. He seized the flap of canvas that now fell forward, and started to cut along the last remaining side.

As his blade began cutting through the painted image of Eleonora's neck, the mournful howl of an animal echoed through the vast old building.

The man beside Řezník glanced round in alarm, but the priest ignored the interruption. He completed the final cut through the canvas and stepped back, holding the painted image of the princess's head in his left hand. He looked around and then stepped across to the nearest sconce in which a torch burned brightly. Taking it down, he held the flames to one corner of the square he'd removed from the painting. The canvas was heavy and the paint thick, and for a few seconds it merely smoldered. Then the fire took hold and it flared suddenly, the flames a kaleidoscopic mix of colors as the pigments in the paint were consumed by the heat. Řezník dropped the final corner of the canvas to the floor and watched as the last of the flames flickered and died.

"Are there any other pictures showing that woman?" he demanded. He couldn't even bring himself to speak her name.

"That was the last one. All the others have been destroyed."

Řezník nodded in satisfaction. His work was done. The princess was buried in what amounted to an unmarked grave, and he had done his best to expunge all traces of her life, all reminders of her presence, from the castle.

Without a backward glance, he walked out of the gallery and a few minutes later passed through the double gates that secured the courtyard of Krumlov Zamek. He knew he would never enter that cursed and wretched castle again.

He just hoped that he had done enough to stop the contagion before it took hold in the district.

But in that regard, Řezník was mistaken. Over the next few years he would officiate at nearly a dozen burials that would require him to use his peculiar and arcane knowledge, though none of these would involve another member of the aristocracy.

And on his own deathbed, nearly twenty years later, he would finally acknowledge the truth he had shied away from for all those years.

Because what happened in the months and years after the burial of Eleonora Amalia proved to him beyond doubt that she was not the source of the plague, as Řezník had always believed, but simply another victim.

1

Present Day

"This truly is a spectacular place," Chris Bronson said, looking back at the city of Venice.

It was the first day of November, and he and Angela were standing side by side in the stern of a crowded vaporetto that was ferrying them from the Fondamente Nuove stop on Venice itself across the lagoon to the Isola di San Michele—the island of St. Michael—to take part in the celebrations known unofficially as the Festival of the Dead.

There was a stiff breeze blowing from the southeast, sufficiently strong to create dozens of white horses that surged all around the vessel, but the boat carved an arrow-straight wake through the choppy waters. The lights of the city were just starting to pierce the late-afternoon gloom, a gloom made more pronounced by the patches of mist that were forming over the water.

Venice looked almost like a huge and improbable cruise ship, floating silently in the cool and shallow waters of the lagoon.

"I thought you'd like it," Angela said, taking his arm to steady herself. "I wasn't expecting this wind, though. Is it the sirocco?"

Bronson shook his head. "No. It's the wrong time of year. The sirocco only blows in the spring and summer."

"Well, I was hoping for a warm and balmy evening—a kind of last gasp of summer, if you like—but this feels more like the onset of winter."

"It is November, you know."

Angela shivered slightly. She was wearing a pair of black trousers (she'd guessed that a skirt would be much less practical for climbing in and out of vaporettos during the evening), a white blouse and a kind of woolen tunic that Bronson had incautiously referred to as a cardigan, only to receive a loud sigh at his manifest lack of fashion sense. Over this, she was wearing a midnight blue silk coat. Bronson liked it; it brought out the color of her eyes. He could see now that it couldn't be very warm.

Bronson had always regarded fashion as an easy way of separating large sums of money from gullible men—and even more gullible women—who were foolish enough to believe the rubbish spouted by the self-appointed fashion "experts." He invariably dressed for comfort and practicality, selecting a shirt by opening a drawer and picking up the one that lay on top of the others. He chose trousers, socks and underwear using the same simple and, to him, foolproof system. His only concessions to fashion were that he normally wore dark colors, usually blues and blacks, and had never owned a pair of white socks. This evening, he had chosen a dark checked shirt, slightly faded blue jeans, and a pair of black sneakers. And his leather jacket was proof against even the strongest wind the Adriatic could produce.

Angela buttoned her coat, and snuggled closer to Bronson. "With your love of Italy, and all things Italian," she murmured, "I'm really surprised that you've never been to Venice before."

"I know," Bronson replied. "For some reason, I've spent my time on the west side of the country. So I know Rome, Florence, Pisa and Naples really well, but this is the first time I've ever visited the Adriatic coast. And it really is stunning."

It had all been Angela's idea. There had been an unexpected reduction in her workload at the British Museum, and for the first time since the start of her employment there she had found herself with almost nothing to do. She was a ceramics conservator, and spent most of her working day either trying to reassemble ancient pottery shards into something that resembled a recognizable vessel or writing reports and assessments for the benefit of other people who were trying to do pretty much the same thing.

And this lull in her workload had coincided neatly with the dates of Bronson's final week's leave for the year. Her ex-husband had planned to do little more than sit around at his home in Tunbridge Wells, watch a bit of television and, if he could summon the energy and enthusiasm, tackle a handful of DIY jobs that he knew needed doing. When Angela had suggested spending the week exploring Venice instead, Bronson had thought carefully about his choice for nearly a second and a half before agreeing to go with her. It was, he thought now as he put his arm round her, absolutely the right decision.

"OK," he said, smiling down at her, "you're the historian. So what, exactly, is the Festival of the Dead?"

Angela rested her head against his shoulder. "Do you really want a history lesson?" she asked.

"I like hearing you talk, especially when you're talking about something that really interests you. And you know I'm never tired of hearing about Italy."

"Actually, it's not really *Italian* history," Angela began, "because the date—the first of November—comes from a really old pagan festival, and is celebrated throughout most of Western Europe. Yesterday was, of course, the last day of October, or Halloween, which as everyone knows has always been associated with death and the supernatural. But what's less well-known is that it's only ever been a kind of taster, a precursor, if you will, for the main event—Allhallows or Hallowmas, which is today."

"I thought it was a kind of saints' day," Bronson objected. Angela nodded. "If you talk to a Christian, especially an Anglican or Roman Catholic, he or she will tell you that today is All Saints' Day, a day that celebrates

God and all his saints, both known and unknown, so the Church can cover all the bases. But it's a little more complicated than that, because the early Christian Church was desperate to try to stamp out all competing religions, especially all pagan rituals and celebrations. They couldn't simply ban pagan festivals because they feared that people would still observe them in secret, so they did the next best thing: they hijacked them.

"Sometime in the early seventh century, Christians began celebrating All Saints' Day on the first of November. In 835 A.D. Pope Gregory IV officially authorized the festival, and it's been celebrated ever since. Allhallows was once one of the four greatest and most important festivals in the pagan calendar, but most Christians today have never heard of it, because the Church has done such a good job of changing the original purpose and meaning of the celebrations.

"And, just to ram home the fact that November the first was a Christian celebration, the Church also created another festival day on the second of the month—All Souls' Day, which is a celebration to help cleanse and purify the spirits of the dead. And you'll find similar crowds out on San Michele tomorrow, because the Venetians celebrate both days."

"But surely the early Christians weren't celebrating death?"

Angela shook her head. "No, not death, but the dead themselves. Allhallows was intended to help people remember the dead, and to say prayers for the souls of the departed. Interestingly, it's not just in Western Europe that you find this kind of celebration. Over in Mexico they have a Day of the Dead, which is also on the second of November, and that's a kind of combination of an ancient Native American tradition and the Catholic All Souls' Day. The people there decorate their homes with fake skeletons, visit cemeteries to clean and tidy the graves of their deceased relatives, and even leave offerings of food and drink for various wandering spirits."

"And I suppose the Venetian Festival of the Dead is something similar?" Bronson asked.

"Exactly, but over here they don't so much tend the graves as wander about the cemetery carrying lighted candles and chrysanthemums. Those flowers have become firmly associated with burial ceremonies in Italy, and it's a very bad idea to offer a bunch to anyone who's still alive. But, being Italy, it's become a social event, too, especially for locals—and because we're here in Venice, I thought it would be interesting to come along."

"So we'll be spending the evening in a graveyard. How nice!" Bronson turned his back on the city they had left and looked ahead at the Isola di San Michele, colloquially known as the "Island of the Dead" because it was simply a huge graveyard.

He'd read that the idea of using one of the islands in the Venetian lagoon as a graveyard dated back to 1807, when Venice was conquered by Napoleon and was suffering under a French occupation that virtually bankrupted the city. Burial on Venice itself was deemed to be unsanitary, so the neighboring island of San Cristoforo della Pace was selected for the task. When that proved inadequate in size, the narrow canal that separated San Cristoforo della Pace from the larger San Michele was filled in, during 1836, and the combined island became known simply as San Michele. For a very short period the island was also used as a prison, but afterward reverted to solely being a graveyard, which still held some very famous corpses. The bodies of the dead were transported across to the island from Venice on special funeral gondolas.

The edge of San Michele lay only a couple of hundred yards from Venice itself, but the vaporetto stop was at the most northerly point of the island, right beside the Chiesa di San Michele, one of the earliest Renaissance churches in Venice. Bronson could see it now, its stark white Istrian stone standing out in the gloom, and marking it out from the mellow colors that characterized most Venetian architecture.

A couple of minutes later, the vaporetto was stationary alongside the jetty, and the gangway had been opened. The passengers surged off the vessel and started making their way toward the entrance. Bronson and Angela were in no particular hurry to leave the boat, so they waited in the stern until almost all the other passengers had left. Then they too stepped onto the jetty and followed the rest of the crowd, who, noisy and gesticulating, seemed to be getting in the mood for the evening ahead.

"The wind's dropped, which is good news, but it's getting a bit murky," Bronson said to Angela, pointing at the blanket of fog that was descending fast. They had seen patches of mist forming over the water after they'd left Venice, but what lay in front of them was more like a real pea-souper. Within minutes, visibility was reduced to just a few yards, and they were glad that the path itself was visible, though the family in front of them was still making enough noise that following them was very easy.

Angela shivered again. "You're right—it's quite spooky now. And this mist is exactly the right atmosphere for an evening in a graveyard." She took a map of the island out of her pocket and smoothed it out.

"Well, as long as we can find our way back to the jetty and the boat, I'm not bothered," Bronson said. "But I certainly wouldn't fancy spending the night out here. Do you see that kind of yellow glow in the mist over to the left of us? Shall we head toward it?"

Angela looked in that direction as well, and nodded. "It's probably from all the candles people are carrying."

They were now catching up with the people ahead, who had walked along the semicircular path that curved around in front of the church, and had then turned down another path that seemed to be leading in the opposite direction.

"Where are they going now?"

Angela looked down at the map. "This path takes us over toward the center of the cemetery, and also toward some of the older areas. One slightly odd thing about this graveyard is that, these days, the bodies are removed after about ten years. They're buried in the usual way in the ground, with the grave marked by a slab or headstone, but because this graveyard serves the entire population of Venice, space is pretty limited. So once the body has been reduced to bones, it's exhumed and the skeleton stored in an ossuary, or bone box. Apparently, there's an exhumation timetable posted near the entrance."

Most of the more modern graves they were passing displayed photographs of the occupants, and almost all of them had been decorated with fresh flowers, giving the graveyard a strangely colorful appearance despite the gloom.

Even through the fog, Bronson could tell that the cemetery was huge, a vast expanse of ground studded with ancient vaults and individual tombstones, some standing erect, others either deliberately placed flat on the earth or having presumably fallen at some point over the centuries.

Walking through one of the older parts of the cemetery, they paused at intervals to look at some of the inscriptions. These varied from the simple to the flowery: from just a name, date of birth and date of death, to elaborate verses written in Italian or even Latin, to glorify or justify the life that had ended.

Angela had been right about the source of the yellowish glow. Almost every person they passed—and there seemed to be literally hundreds—was carrying a large candle, and the combined mass of tiny flames was giving the heavy mist a distinctly yellow or orange color.

"So what do we do now?" Bronson asked.

"It's a shame we didn't think to bring any refreshments," Angela replied, pointing at the people milling around them. Many were carrying bottles or flasks, and a few had even brought wicker picnic baskets with them, others clear plastic boxes containing food.

Angela had been absolutely right: it was obvious that Hallowmas or the Festival of the Dead was a major social and family event. Men, women and children were wandering around the graveyard, obviously determined to enjoy their evening in the somewhat unusual surroundings.

"Well, I've got a bar of chocolate in my pocket if you want to share that," Bronson said, passing it over.

Angela snapped the bar in two and handed back one section. For a few moments they just stood there, enjoying their impromptu snack and soaking up the atmosphere.

"It's strange, isn't it?" Angela asked, after a minute or two, looking around at the noisy and cheerful crowds.

"What do you mean?"

"Here we are in a graveyard, walking above the decaying bones of hundreds or even thousands of long-dead citizens of Venice. This should be a place of sorrow or somber reflection, but actually we're in the middle of a huge party."

Bronson grinned at her. "That just goes to show the importance of atmosphere. In those old Hammer films you used to be so fond of, the director would try to get the audience quivering expectantly just by showing them a couple of polystyrene tombstones with some fake mist swirling around them, while some suitably spooky music played in the background. And here we are, surrounded by the real thing, and everyone's really happy, laughing and joking. The dead aren't bothering them at all."

But then, in the distance, they both heard a distant howl, the sound so faint that the animal—which Bronson presumed was an Alsatian or some other breed of large dog—clearly wasn't anywhere near the Isola di San Michele. "What the hell was that?" Angela asked, her face white and strained in the darkness.

"It sounded like a hungry German shepherd," Bronson suggested. "But don't worry—it's a long way off and not about to rip out our throats."

Angela laughed out loud, then stopped as the sound of a solid thump echoed from somewhere nearby, and a scream of pure, undiluted terror cut across the noise of the revelry with the awful finality of the fall of a guillotine blade.

2

On the Island of the Dead, the mist was thick, and visibility was reduced to a matter of only a few yards. To complicate things further, it was difficult to identify the direction from which the first scream had come. But by now, Bronson and Angela were surrounded by people in a hurry, and who seemed to be moving south, toward the center of the island. So Bronson and Angela headed in the opposite direction, to where they thought the commotion had occurred.

Moving aside to avoid the sea of people rushing straight toward them, they threaded their way between the tombstones and, moments later, found themselves facing a group of men and women who were standing in a rough circle, staring at one of the larger tombs.

Bronson's police training kicked in, despite the fact that he was about a thousand miles from his home beat. He switched to Italian and pulled out his British warrant card—he knew it would mean absolutely nothing to anybody there, but it would give him a thin veneer of authority while he found out what had so alarmed everyone in the cemetery.

"Police. Let me through. . . . Police officer," he kept repeating, waving the warrant card like a talisman as he pushed his way through the unmoving crowd, Angela following just a few feet behind him.

Almost reluctantly the people parted to allow him passage. Unusually for any group of Italians, they were almost silent, staring in fascination at something on the ground in front of them. And then Bronson reached the middle of the group, and could see precisely what had sparked the general exodus from the area.

The Festival of the Dead was in some ways a misnomer. The revelers who traveled to the cemetery were not there to celebrate the dead, but rather to celebrate the lives and memories of friends and relatives who had passed away. Absolutely the last thing they expected to see in the cemetery was an actual body. But that was the sight that now confronted Bronson.

And it wasn't just any corpse.

"Fascinating," Angela breathed as she stopped beside him and looked down at the tomb. "Though I can't believe this was the cause of so much panic in the crowd."

Bronson took a couple of steps forward to study the tomb.

It was clearly one of the older burial chambers in the cemetery, an oblong stone box about four feet high and topped by a flat stone slab. The sides were carved with symbols or scenes, but the old stone had weathered so much that it was difficult to make out exactly what was depicted, while the slab on top bore faint and virtually illegible marks—presumably an ancient inscription that gave the name and date of death of the occupant.

Bronson didn't know exactly how it had happened, but one of the sides of the tomb had cracked into three pieces and then fallen out, and in doing so had dragged the upper slab of stone with it. That must have caused the sound they'd heard, he thought. And now the previously sealed box was open to the elements, and the body inside exposed to view for the first time in what he guessed was at least a hundred years.

Unsurprisingly, the remains were mainly skeletal. Parts of the coffin had survived, but only as fragments of wood along both sides of the corpse. A few wisps of rotted cloth still clung to the long bones of the legs, and part of the rib cage was encased in leathery, dark brown skin. In short, the corpse looked almost exactly as one might expect a body to appear if it had been buried in a wooden coffin inside a sealed tomb for more than a century. Except in two respects.

Above the rib cage the neck terminated in a single shattered vertebra. The head of the body, which, like the rib cage, was still partially covered in skin, and even had a few tufts of white hair clinging to it, was positioned centrally between the bony feet. That was unusual enough in itself, but to add a further layer of the macabre to the scene, the mouth of the skull had been levered open and a thin half brick jammed firmly between the jaws.

For a few seconds, Bronson stared at the desiccated—
and desecrated—corpse; then he glanced sideways at Angela. "What did you mean when you said 'fascinating?'"
he asked.

"I'll explain later," she said. "This is something I've
heard about and read about, but I never thought I'd actually get to see an example of it."

She opened her handbag, pulled out a compact digital
camera and started snapping pictures of the scene before
them. She moved closer to the corpse, and took several
shots of the severed neck and the head with its bizarre
mutilation.

There was a further commotion behind them, and
Bronson turned to see two uniformed carabinieri approaching. Behind him, Angela was still snapping away,
recording the scene.

The two carabinieri looked closely into the open tomb.
One of them crossed himself and muttered something
that could have been a short prayer.

"Your name, please, signor?" the other officer asked.

Bronson pulled out his passport and gave it to him.

The officer wrote down Bronson's name and passport
number, handed back the document, and then asked, in
halting English, what he was doing in Venice. Bronson
replied in fluent Italian that he was on holiday with a
friend. They had heard shouts and screams from the vicinity of the tomb and had come to investigate. He also
produced his warrant card and explained that he was a
British police officer, and his former wife—the woman

who was still taking pictures of the open tomb behind them—worked for the British Museum.

The policeman glanced at her. "And why is she taking so many pictures of that skeleton?" he asked.

Bronson raised his voice slightly, and repeated the question to Angela, in English.

"It's not actually the bones I'm interested in," she replied, "but these pottery vessels in the tomb. They've been broken, but I think they were probably intact when they were put in beside her."

"How do you know that the skeleton is female?" Bronson asked.

"The pelvis is fully exposed, and the male pelvis and female pelvis are very different in shape. This skeleton is definitely that of a woman."

Bronson translated what she'd told him to the police officer.

"It's very strange, what's happened to that body," the Italian said. "Perhaps it was done by vandals, a couple of centuries ago."

"What will you do with it?" Bronson asked.

"Eventually, I expect we'll bury it again, but for the moment we'll have to take it into custody. Our orders in this kind of circumstance are quite clear. It's the body of a human being, and because it's skeletal we will need to get a forensic pathologist out here to inspect the scene and ascertain its age. Then we'll transport it back to the mortuary for examination, just in case any kind of crime has been committed."

"Well, whoever did that to her head is certainly guilty of a crime."

Privately, Bronson thought that transporting the body to the local morgue was a complete waste of everyone's time and effort, but he fully understood the position of the carabinieri. Police forces in Britain had similar regulations governing the handling of both corpses and skeletal remains. It was not unknown for murderers to conceal the bodies of their victims inside existing graves.

A few of the onlookers had started to drift away, many of them taking pictures of the tomb and its occupant as they left, but others, curious at the presence of two police officers beside an ancient open grave, were beginning to appear.

"I don't know if it would be of any help to you," Bronson said, "but my partner is an expert on pottery. If you have a problem dating the burial—if the inscription on the tomb can't be read, I mean—then she can probably help by analyzing those pottery shards."

"Thank you for the offer, Signor Bronson. Which hotel are you staying at?"

Bronson told him, as Angela finally finished her photographic record and stepped forward to join him.

The second police officer was already speaking into his radio, organizing transport for the forensic pathologist from Venice out to the Isola di San Michele.

While they waited for the boat to arrive, Bronson and Angela provided the two carabinieri with brief written statements of their recollection of the events of the evening.

Almost half an hour passed before three new figures emerged from the mist, accompanied by one of the police officers who had gone to the vaporetto stop to wait for the boat. One carried a collapsible stretcher, another a black body bag and the third, a gray-haired, stooped man in his fifties, carried a large plastic equipment box. Quickly, they donned gloves, plastic overshoes and white coveralls. The older man—the pathologist, Bronson assumed—stepped forward and looked at the grave and the corpse from a few feet away. He gestured to one of the men who'd accompanied him to take a series of pictures, and stepped back to talk to the carabinieri who were still waiting by the grave. Then he moved forward again and examined the skeleton closely, before issuing further instructions and peeling off his protective clothing.

The two men with him transferred the remains of the corpse from the shattered tomb to the body bag, taking particular care with the head to ensure that the brick remained in place. They also removed all the pieces of broken pottery. Finally, they used flashlights to scan the interior of the tomb to make sure they hadn't missed any last small bones or fragments, placed the bag on the stretcher, and vanished in the direction from which they'd arrived, accompanied by both police officers.

"Is there anything else you want to see?" Bronson asked Angela, watching as the short procession vanished into the mist.

Angela shook her head. "No. I think I've got enough.

Those pottery shards are interesting and unusual, and I'd like to take a proper look at them, but in a laboratory, not out here on-site. Actually, there was something much more interesting than them in that grave." She patted her pocket, and smiled at him, her eyes shining. "And unlike the pottery, which, of course, I had to leave in situ, I've got it with me."

3

Marietta Perini stepped off the vaporetto at the Accademia stop on the southern side of the Grand Canal and walked briskly north across the Ponte dell'Accademia toward central Venice. Her route took her through the dogleg shape of the Campo San Vidal and on into the Campo San Stefano, one of the biggest squares in Venice, second only to the Piazza San Marco. Both squares were busy with people: old men with small dogs on leashes, women with children in carriages and strollers, Venetians returning home after work, or just couples and families strolling around with one another. Church bells rang out across the Campo San Stefano, sending peals of sound across the open space, almost drowning out the buzz of conversation from the cafés and restaurants that lined the square.

Everywhere and in all directions, people walked and talked, arms flying in extravagant gestures as they illustrated some point they were trying to make.

Marietta paused for a few moments by the monument

in the center of the square. Known irreverently to Venetians as the *Cagalibri* or "book-shitter," it commemorated the life of the nineteenth-century writer and ideologue Nicolò Tommaseo, his studious career represented by the large pile of books positioned just behind him, and which had given rise to the statue's nickname. As usual, there was a pigeon sitting on his head, and the colorful organic decoration that had been applied to the statue's head and shoulders suggested that this was a favorite perch for some of Venice's innumerable feathered residents.

Over to one side of the square was the reason Marietta had not continued straight across toward her destination. She had a weakness for ice cream, and just a few yards away was one of her favorite *gelaterias*. She glanced at her watch, checking she had enough time, then gave way to temptation, strolling across and choosing a large cone, into which the smiling, dark-haired waiter inserted three balls of ice cream in her choice of flavors.

Then she walked on, taking small and delicious bites from the top of the cone, and savoring each morsel, moving it around her mouth with her tongue before finally swallowing it. She moved slowly across the square, concentrating far more on what she was eating than on where she was going or on her surroundings.

Marietta was completely unaware that two men were following her, and had in fact picked her out even before she'd boarded the vaporetto at the Arsenale stop on the east side of Venice.

She wasn't a random target. The two men had been

sent out that evening to find her, and her alone. One of them was holding a folded sheet of paper in his hand. On it was a full-face photograph of their quarry, plus her address, and details of the company for which she worked. And there was a very specific and compelling reason why she had been chosen.

As she left the Campo San Stefano, Marietta took one of the narrow streets to the right, and almost immediately the press of people reduced, and she found herself walking along with just a handful of other pedestrians.

Then she took another turn, moving farther and farther from the crowded thoroughfares and closer to her destination: her boyfriend's apartment near the center of the old city. And only then did she wonder if the two men were following her.

Marietta didn't feel concerned, not at first. Venice was a crowded city and it was almost impossible to walk down most of the streets at any time of the day or night without finding other people there. But when she took another turn, and the men continued to follow her down this narrow—and conspicuously empty—street, she glanced behind her again and then quickened her pace.

Immediately, both men started running, and in a few seconds they had caught up with her. One of them slammed Marietta back against a wall. She opened her mouth to scream, but then collapsed to the ground when the second man produced a black pistol-like object from his pocket, pressed it against her stomach and pulled the trigger. The Taser sent a charge of more than one hundred thousand volts through her body, rendering her senseless for a few minutes.

This was all the time the men needed. One of them swiftly applied an adhesive gag to her face and lashed her wrists together with plastic cable ties, while the other man unzipped the bulky bag he was carrying, and pulled out a folded lightweight carpet—an old, but still very effective, way of concealing a body. He dropped it flat on the ground, and, working together, they rolled the girl's unconscious body into it. In moments, the bigger of the two men had hoisted the carpet onto his shoulder, and the two of them walked down the street toward one of the canals that penetrated central Venice from all sides. The other man took out a small mobile phone and spoke urgently into it.

When they reached the bank of the canal, they stopped and peered to their right, toward the junction with the encircling Grand Canal. A dark blue speedboat was heading toward them, a single figure at the controls. The vessel came to a halt at the landing stage in front of the two men. The driver climbed out, holding a mooring line that he wrapped around a vertical wooden post, and held the boat steady while the two men embarked in it. Then he released the rope and climbed back aboard himself, swung the boat around in a half circle and headed back the way he'd come.

The bundle in the carpet began moving, and one of the men unrolled it just enough to reveal the girl's terrified face. He held the Taser in front of her eyes and squeezed the trigger. A vicious high-voltage spark leaped between the two electrodes with an audible crackle.

"Shut up and lie still," he hissed in colloquial Italian, "or I'll give you another dose of this."

Then he flipped the end of the carpet back over Marietta's face.

"You need to be careful with that thing," his companion murmured. "Hit somebody too often with it and you can kill them. And we need her in prime condition."

"I know, but all we need to do is keep her quiet until we get into the lagoon. Then she can scream and wriggle about all she wants to, because it won't make any difference."

At that moment, the powerboat swung left into the Grand Canal and heeled over as the driver opened the throttle and increased speed.

4

Venice is a stunning and amazing place, Bronson thought, but it also has a lot of problems.

Possibly the most beautiful city in the world, it is spread over a total of one hundred and seventeen islands set in a shallow lagoon, and its population of around sixty thousand lives in a maze of streets so confusing that even natives of the city can still get lost in them. And, although it possesses some of the most outstanding architectural jewels in Italy, arguably in the world, the vast majority are slowly and inexorably sinking into the mud of the lagoon as their wooden foundations yield to the enormous weight of masonry pressing down on them. Many buildings have been abandoned; many others will suffer the same fate without very extensive—and very expensive—renovation and recovery work.

It is perhaps therefore not surprising that hotels in Venice are a long way from being the cheapest in the world.

Angela had made the booking over the Internet, and had managed to find a small hotel tucked away in the Cannaregio district, to the north of central Venice, which wasn't charging anything like the rates demanded by some of the more central establishments. To be fair, the rooms were small and cramped, there was no elevator, and the only views available from any room were of the walls of the adjacent buildings or the street outside. But, as she'd explained to Bronson, the whole point about being in Venice was to get out and see the city, not lounge around in a hotel bedroom all day, so in her opinion the views were much less important than the price.

They'd caught a vaporetto back to the Fondamente Nuove stop from the Isola di San Michele a few minutes after the two carabinieri had left with the pathologist, but Angela had stubbornly refused to show him what she'd taken from the grave until they reached the hotel.

The narrow streets were dark and silent as they walked toward their hotel, the only noise the lapping of the water in the canals beside them. There was something about the atmosphere Bronson didn't like, and it was a relief when he saw the lights of the hotel lobby shining brightly in front of them.

"Right, Angela," Bronson said, once they were safely inside their room, "what was it in the tomb that's got you so excited?"

"What we saw back there was the tomb of a vampire."

For a few seconds, Bronson just stared at her. Then his face creased into a smile, and he laughed. "Of course it was," he said. "Now, stop messing around and tell me what you really mean."

Angela smiled back at him. "I'm being perfectly serious," she said. "Or, to be absolutely exact, the people who broke into that tomb about a century and a half ago were being perfectly serious."

"A vampire? But you and I both know that vampires don't exist. Just like werewolves and krakens and golems don't exist. They're the product of myth and legend, nothing more than that."

"*We* know that, here and now in the twenty-first century. But it wasn't always that clear-cut, you know."

"But I thought Bram Stoker more or less invented the vampire myth when he wrote *Dracula* in—what, the late nineteenth century?"

"No," Angela said. "Nobody knows exactly when people first started believing in vampires, but it certainly predates the Middle Ages, and possibly dates back a lot further than that, maybe as early as the Assyrians. There's also some suspicion that vampirelike creatures were believed to exist in the countries surrounding the Mediterranean basin as early as five thousand B.C., and one of the ancient Egyptian gods—Shezmu—had what you might call vampirelike habits. He was the old god of execution, slaughter, blood and wine, and often killed people by decapitating them, putting their heads in a wine press and drinking the blood that came out."

She paused for a moment to collect her thoughts, then spoke again. "If you search the literature, belief in vampires, or creatures that act in some way like vampires, seems to be endemic. Almost every culture, on every continent, has some kind of a legend of this type. And that includes places you wouldn't normally expect, like Australasia and China, and even Mexico and the Caribbean.

"And it wasn't actually Bram Stoker who first wrote about it. In eighteen sixteen, almost a century before Stoker, Lord Byron was holidaying near Lake Geneva with friends and suggested they each write a ghost story. Byron came up with the idea of a tale about a vampire, and one of his friends, in fact his personal physician, a man named John Polidori, picked it up and expanded it. This was the first time a vampyre—he spelled the word with a 'y' instead of an 'i'—had appeared in a piece of fiction written in English. But nearly a century earlier, in seventeen thirty-two, the word 'vampyre' had first appeared in print in Britain, but then the word was being used as a political symbol."

"How come you know so much about vampires?" Bronson demanded.

Angela grinned at him. "I read a lot," she said. "Anyway, what I was going to say was that even as late as the first millennium, the world was still a very mysterious place, and people were looking around for explanations for natural phenomena that we now understand perfectly. They still believed that prayers to a god or spirit, or even a sacrifice, were absolutely necessary to ensure the rising of the sun or a good harvest, and the end of winter was still greeted with relief and celebrations. That was the kind of climate in which belief in vampires first arose, when superstition and belief in supernatural events and beings were the norm, not the exception."

"But a bloodsucking creature of the night? Where the hell did that come from?" Bronson objected.

"Nobody knows. It's been a part of the folklore of Europe, and especially of central Europe, since records began. But it's possible that this kind of creature was first assumed to exist as a reasonable explanation for something that otherwise made no sense."

"Like what?"

"Postmortem changes to a body, for instance. If for any reason a grave was opened a short while after the burial had taken place, the people who looked at the corpse wouldn't have understood what they were seeing. There might well be blood in and near the mouth, and the hair and nails would have grown, and the body would appear to be plump and well nourished. Medical science now knows exactly why these strange effects occur. After death, blood may be expelled from all orifices, not just the mouth, as a normal part of the decay process. The receding skin can make the hair and nails of the corpse appear longer, and the gases created by decomposition will bloat the body—you know that."

Bronson nodded. As a policeman, he'd grown used to seeing corpses in varying stages of decay.

"Now put yourself in the position of somebody who's just opened a fresh grave. You see a corpse that looks well fed, with hair and nails growing, and with blood on the mouth and face. Knowing nothing about what is actually happening inside the dead body, the most reasonable explanation might be that the corpse isn't a corpse at all, and that somehow it's managing to escape from the grave at night and is feeding on the blood of living things, hence the blood around its mouth. And if somebody in the neighborhood is suffering from anemia or consumption or some other wasting disease, you might also conclude that that person was the victim. Even the unexplained deaths of cattle or sheep might be attributed to the actions of a vampire.

"And that's probably all it would take for the legend to be born. As far as I know, nobody knows exactly when belief in vampires first started, but it quickly spread all over Europe, and was concentrated in Hungary and the Slav countries in the early eighteenth century. It was probably those legends that Byron, and later Bram Stoker, picked up on. And we do know that the word 'vampire' itself was derived from the Serbo-Croat word *vampir*, and it entered the English language through either French or German, probably also in the eighteenth century. It's also true that many of the other Slavic and middle European languages, like Bulgarian and Croatian, had very similar words to describe the same phenomenon. But the actual root of the word probably comes from the Old Russian word *upir*, which was first recorded in the eleventh century."

"And what about crucifixes, garlic and a stake through the heart?" Bronson asked.

"You can thank Bram Stoker and *Dracula* for that," Angela said, "though I suppose the crucifix and the stake do make some kind of sense. A body arising from the grave to feed on the living is obviously demonic, and people might well think that such a creature would be frightened away by the symbol of the Christian religion. Driving a stake through the chest would destroy the heart and prevent it from circulating the blood, and that would kill the vampire as well. There's another theory that impaling it with a stake would pin the vampire's body to the earth and stop it moving."

"And garlic?"

"I've no idea, but garlic was supposed to be a cure, or at least a preventative, for the plague, so there might be a link there. Actually, garlic's been renowned as a deterrent against vampires in almost every culture that has legends about the creatures, but nobody seems to know why that should be. And before you ask, I'm fairly certain that vampires being destroyed by sunlight, not being visible in a mirror and not casting a shadow are all either creations of Mr. Stoker's imagination or embellishments added by later writers."

"Are you saying that vampires were linked to the plague?" Bronson asked.

Angela nodded. "At one time, almost everything was linked to the plague. The Black Death arrived in Europe in the middle of the fourteenth century, and nobody had the slightest idea what caused it. All they knew was that it was incredibly contagious, and that once you'd got it, it was effectively a death sentence. Wild theories abounded about the possible cause, everything from an unfavorable alignment of the planets to earthquakes that released foul air from the interior of the earth, and even a kind of ethnic cleansing orchestrated by aliens."

"You're kidding."

"I'm not. There were numerous reports of evil-looking, black-clad figures standing at the edges of towns waving a kind of wand that emitted a noxious fog, and anyone that the substance touched subsequently died of the plague. The accounts sound remarkably like descriptions of men wearing protective suits dispensing a chemical or biological weapon through some sort of pressurized dispersal system. Witnesses described the strangers as acting as if they were scything, swinging the wand from side to side, and it's actually that image which gave us the expression 'the grim reaper.' "

"Your breadth of knowledge never ceases to amaze me," Bronson said.

Angela smiled at him. "Well, history is my thing," she said. "It's the minutiae, the details, which have always fascinated me. In some countries, particularly in Germany and Switzerland, the Jews were blamed for the plague, and records show that there were several massacres in which they were rounded up and killed, sometimes by being burned alive. Religious zealots believed the plague had been sent by God, and for some time flagellation became a popular cure. Traveling bands of flagellants roamed Europe, flogging themselves in the name of God, and in many cases very efficiently helping to spread the plague at the same time.

"Perhaps the most common belief was that it was somehow caused by a miasma, by corrupted air, which harks back to that grim reaper image, and many of the preventative measures put in place were intended to combat this, to try to purify the air that people were breathing. So houses were washed with scented water, timber that was known to give off a pleasant smell, like juniper, was burned in fireplaces, and people carried garlic and vinegar to ward off the contagion. But, bizarrely, other people believed that the plague was spread by vampires, and extraordinary measures were taken to try to combat this."

"So we've come full circle," Bronson suggested. "We're back to the woman in the grave."

"Exactly," Angela agreed. "The death toll from the Black Death was simply enormous. For obvious reasons, no accurate figures have survived, but it's been conservatively estimated that in some towns where the plague took hold, as many as half, sometimes even two-thirds, of the population died. This meant that individual burial of bodies was simply impossible. The dead were tossed into huge communal graves—plague pits. But for anyone suspected of being a vampire, special precautions had to be taken, to avoid the vampire feeding on the other victims buried alongside it in the pit. And perhaps the commonest preventative measure was to jam a brick between the vampire's jaws.

"Two or three years ago, right here in Venice, a plague pit was discovered and excavated, and one of the skulls from a female skeleton was recovered intact, with the brick still jammed into her mouth. That body dated from the sixteenth century, because although the Black Death was at its height in Europe in the fourteenth century, there were recurrences of the epidemic right up to the eighteenth century, and mass graves have been found that date from this whole period."

"Do you think somebody believed that the woman in the grave we saw tonight on the Isola di San Michele was a vampire, and applied an ancient remedy to ensure that she would stay dead and buried? So why did they also cut off her head?"

"That was another traditional way of killing a vampire. Because they sucked blood from their victims, removing the head from the body would prevent them from feeding."

"So in her case it was a kind of belt and braces—the brick in the mouth and decapitation."

Angela nodded. "Yes," she said, "but actually, it's a bit more complicated than that."

"What do you mean?"

"According to legend, most vampires were heretics, criminals or victims of suicide, and in most cases such people would be denied burial in a Christian graveyard because of religious sensibilities. The tomb that cracked open was quite an expensive burial chamber and, as far as I could see, she was the only occupant. If she had been suspected of being a vampire in life, even if she came from a wealthy and aristocratic family, she would probably have been buried in an unmarked grave on unconsecrated ground. That's the first point.

"The other thing that struck me was that the vertebrae in her neck had crumbled when it was smashed. I'm not a forensic pathologist, obviously, but that suggests to me that the body was already at least partially skeletonized when the head was removed."

"So you think she was just buried in the usual way, and then several years later somebody decided that she might have been a vampire, cracked open the tomb, and did their best to ensure that she would stay there for eternity."

"That makes sense," Angela said, "except for three things. Did you notice anything odd about the grave?"

"You mean apart from the decapitated body and the skull with the brick rammed into its jaw? No, not really."

Angela sighed. "Almost every tomb I looked at on that island had either a crucifix inscribed on the slab covering the grave or a separate stone cross standing at one end of it. That grave had neither, and that's unusual."

Bronson looked puzzled, but didn't say anything.

"And the remains of those pottery jars we saw in the grave suggest something slightly different about the original burial," Angela went on. "I have a feeling that she probably *was* buried as a vampire, but by people who didn't find that concept in any way offensive, a kind of vampire cult, if you like."

"Really?"

"Yes. I think those jars were deliberately smashed when the grave was opened later. Pottery was never normally placed inside Christian tombs, but if it had been, in a sealed environment, it should have remained intact. The fact that those jars—there were at least two of them—were broken suggests a deliberate act. And why would a pair of sealed pottery vessels be placed in a tomb? To me, the only thing that makes sense is that they were there for the benefit of the dead woman. And if they thought she was a vampire, they would probably have contained blood, most likely human blood. I'd love to get my hands on them and analyze what's left of the contents."

"Are you serious?" Bronson asked, startled. "A vampire cult?"

"They're not unknown," Angela said, "though I'm not aware of any operating in Venice around the time our woman was buried. The inscription on the lid of her tomb was badly weathered, but I did take a few pictures of it, and I'm pretty sure the year she died was eighteen twenty-five. At least that bit of the inscription was still legible. And I'm guessing that the grave was opened again before the end of the nineteenth century, and that the ritual killing of the vampire inside it took place then."

Bronson leaned back and stretched. The chair he was sitting in was cramped and really too small for him. "It seems to me that you're deducing the existence of an entire—and pretty bizarre—secret society on the basis of a few bits of smashed pottery and one crumbled neck vertebra on a two-hundred-year-old skeleton."

"No, there's something else." Angela reached into her handbag, and pulled out a small, heavily discolored black object, which appeared to be bound in leather. "This was lying under the body," she said. "I think it was originally inside a wooden box, probably placed under the coffin, but over the centuries both the coffin and the box rotted away. I spotted what was left of the box underneath the skeleton, but when I touched it, the wood crumbled away to nothing and I saw this."

"So now you're a grave robber," Bronson said.

"I trained as an archaeologist," Angela replied, "and 'archaeologist' is just a polite word for a tomb raider. It's what we do. And if I hadn't picked it up, it would have either been sealed up again in the grave or taken by some tourist who would have no idea what it was."

"And what is it?"

"I think," Angela said, "it's a kind of diary."

5

The dark blue powerboat was speeding through the inky darkness of the Venetian night, heading south, past San Clemente, toward a small island situated some distance from its nearest neighbor.

This island covered only three or four acres, and was dominated by a large and impressive Venetian mansion, a five-story edifice in gray stone that sat at its highest point. Directly below the house was a substantial stone-built jetty capable of berthing perhaps a dozen powerboats. At first sight, the jetty seemed ridiculously large, but the lagoon provided the only means of access to and from the property.

Four other vessels were already secured to the buoys that edged the jetty, but the driver of the blue powerboat had plenty of space to maneuver. He brought the boat alongside the landing stage, put the gearbox into reverse, and expertly stopped the vessel close enough for one of the other men to step ashore. In moments, both mooring lines were secured and the engine shut down.

The driver assisted his two passengers in manhandling the rolled carpet onto the jetty, where they lowered it to the ground.

"I think she can walk from here," one of the men said, unrolling the carpet and pulling Marietta Perini to her feet. The man with the Taser checked her wrists were still securely bound, ripped off her gag, then aimed the weapon at her and squeezed the trigger. The girl shrank back as the evil blue spark jumped from one electrode to the other with an audible crack.

"What do you want with me?" she said, her voice trembling with fear.

"You'll find out soon enough," the man snapped. "Now, do exactly what we tell you, or—" He triggered the Taser again, then pointed toward the house. "Go up there," he ordered.

Marietta stared around her, at the small island with its grass-covered slopes, clumps of bushes and occasional small trees, and at the house itself. Beyond it lay the waters of the Venetian lagoon. Pockets of mist were drifting over the surface, driven by light breezes. She looked at the pitiless faces of the three men who had abducted her from the city of her birth. A surge of pure terror coursed through her body as she realized she was beyond help.

"I have a friend," she said desperately. "I was on my way to visit him. When I don't arrive, he'll call the police."

The man with the Taser smiled at her, but it was not a smile of amusement. "I've no doubt he will, and I'm sure the carabinieri will make all the right noises and do their best to reassure him. But we left no clues, and nobody saw what we did. It's as if you simply vanished from the face of the earth. The police will never find us, or you. And even if they did," he added, "it wouldn't make any difference, because you're not the first."

Marietta stared at him, and then she screamed, a cry of terror that stopped only when the last vestige of breath had been driven from her lungs.

"Feel better now? Get moving. We have people waiting for you."

Marietta gasped for breath and stared round again, looking desperately for anything or anyone that might offer her some hope. But there was nothing.

6

"A diary? You mean a *vampire* diary?" Bronson asked. "Are you serious?"

"I've only had a very quick look at it," Angela said, "but as far as I can tell it contains a list of dates and events, which is pretty much the definition of a diary, I suppose."

"So what are these events? If they're written in Italian, you'll probably need my help to translate them."

"Actually, I won't," Angela said, "unless you've added Latin to your repertoire of languages. At the time this burial originally took place, Latin was still being used as an international language, and it remained the language of classical scholarship right through the eighteenth and nineteenth centuries. Even today some documents and treatises are composed in Latin, and of course it's still the official written language of the Roman Catholic Church and the Vatican."

She leaned forward and handed the book carefully to Bronson.

"Our woman was buried in the first half of the nineteenth century. If she came from an educated and aristocratic family, which she probably did if her tomb is anything to go by, she might well have spoken Italian or a local dialect in daily life, but she would certainly have been able to read Latin, and probably would have used it for all her letters and written communications. Frankly, I'd have been amazed if the language in the book was anything other than Latin."

"So what have you translated so far?" Bronson asked.

"I haven't had time to do more than glance at a few of the pages. But I've already found several references to blood, to its healing and rejuvenating properties, and in a couple of places there are descriptions of rituals that seem to involve drinking blood. I really think this might be a vampire's diary."

Bronson groaned. "Does this mean that our sightseeing holiday is now going to be replaced by the two of us sitting in this hotel room translating a two-hundred-year-old diary, written by someone who thought she was a vampire?"

Angela grinned. "Of course not. This is just a curio. Nobody knows we found it, and it's frankly of little or no interest to anybody except someone like me, or an historian specializing in that period of Italian or Venetian history. It's pretty fragile, so what I will do is scan the pages into my laptop so that the text will be preserved, even if the book falls to pieces. Then I'll take it back to London and work on it in my spare time. As far as I'm concerned, we continue with our holiday just like before."

She looked across at Bronson. "Speaking of which," she added, "isn't it about time we had something to eat? That bar of chocolate we shared on the island seems like a long time ago."

Bronson glanced at his watch and nodded. "You're absolutely right. I feel a bowl of spaghetti coming on. That family restaurant on the corner might still be open."

"Good idea," Angela said, standing up. "I'll just nip down to reception and see if I can borrow their scanner, and then I'll be ready to go."

7

Marietta Perini walked slowly toward the double wooden doors set into the front facade of the gray stone house. Her senses were acutely sharpened by the terror coursing through her, and she noticed that the ground-floor windows, on the right-hand side of the entrance door, were brightly illuminated. Through the old glass, she could see a pair of elegant chandeliers, brilliant clusters of cut glass studded with tiny electric lights. And she could also see figures in the room, perhaps three or four men in elegant evening clothes, moving about and talking and drinking.

She took another couple of steps toward the doors, then felt a tug on her arm.

"Not that way," one of her captors snapped, pointing instead to a stone path that ran around the side of the house.

Marietta turned down the path, wondering about the scene she'd glimpsed inside the spacious salon. It looked to her like an upmarket reception, a social evening, or maybe even a group of wealthy men enjoying an aperitif before sitting down to a banquet.

But that didn't square with what was happening to her. The men who had abducted her in Venice were malevolent, evil, she was certain. Though it didn't make sense, perhaps they were nothing to do with the elegantly dressed men in the salon she was walking away from. Maybe the people inside the property could be her salvation?

Marietta took a deep breath and screamed her heart out, a shriek of agony and terror that bounced off the walls of the house.

As she had hoped, the sound clearly penetrated the windows of the lighted room, and, as she looked back, all of the men turned to stare at her. A couple of them even walked across to the tall windows and looked out, straight at her.

One of her captors seized her and turned her to face the house, so the people inside could see her more clearly. The two well-dressed men by the window smiled at her, and one nodded approval. Then the man holding her started to laugh. In that instant, the terrified girl knew she was beyond any help, any hope of rescue.

She stared around her. Surely somewhere there was a place to hide, to get away from the three men behind her. But even if by some miracle she could manage to elude them, she would still be a prisoner on the island.

But she had to try.

Taking another deep breath, Marietta stepped off the path and ran for her life.

She heard a muttered curse, and then the sound of the men behind her. Almost immediately, one of them grabbed at her shoulder, but she ducked and swerved, and the man lost his grip.

Her bound wrists were a greater impediment than she'd expected, and in seconds she lost her footing on the uneven ground and tumbled sideways. Before she could even try to get to her feet again, the men reached her. Two of them grabbed her by the arms and pulled her upright.

"I told you what would happen," said the man with the Taser, his face dark with anger.

"Be careful," one of the others warned. "She needs to be unharmed."

The man adjusted something on the Taser, then took a step forward. "Hold her still," he instructed, menace in every syllable.

Marietta shrank back. "No, please, no, don't," she whispered.

The man looked into her eyes and smiled slightly as he rested the twin prongs on the thin material of her blouse.

Then he pulled the trigger.

Marietta had never felt such agony. It seemed as if every nerve ending in her body was on fire, or bathed in acid. She lurched backward, and would have fallen but for the restraining hands of the other two men.

The man in front of her kept the trigger of the Taser

pressed for what felt like minutes, such was the pain surg-
ing through her, though in reality the current could have
flowed for only a matter of one or two seconds, possibly
even less than that. Finally, mercifully, the agony stopped,
the men released her arms, and Marietta slumped to the
ground.

They gave her a couple of minutes to recover her
senses, then jerked her back onto her feet and marched
her toward the rear of the house. This time they were
taking no chances. One man walked on either side of
Marietta, gripping her upper arm. There was no way she
could free herself from their grasp even if she had had the
energy or the strength to do so. In any case, the last
charge from the Taser had left her nerves jangling and
screaming, and she knew that if her arms were released,
she would probably not even be able to walk unaided.
Running was out of the question.

The path ran beside the house, then curved around in
a circle toward the back door of the building. Marietta
assumed this was their destination, but instead she was
led toward another, smaller structure hidden behind the
house. It had also been solidly constructed of gray stone,
and just one glance was enough to tell her that it had
once been a small church or chapel. Most of the steeply
pitched roof was missing, but all four walls were still
standing, and looked to be in a reasonable state of repair.
Strangely, even the old wooden church door was still in
place, and both the windows in the end wall contained
stained-glass panels.

One of the men lifted the latch on the door and swung it open, the well-oiled old hinges making no sound. Marietta was pushed through the doorway into the open space beyond. Above her head, about half of the original supporting timbers for the roof were still in place, a dimly visible skeleton, showing black against the evening sky.

The men led her down what was once the church's central aisle, and across the space where the altar would have stood; a few broken slabs of stone were all that remained of the original structure. She was marched across to the far side of the building and shoved against the wall. The man behind her stepped over to one side, and Marietta briefly lost sight of him as the other two stood beside her, blocking her view. Then she heard a faint rumbling sound, and a section of the wall a few feet away from her swung open like a door. The third man reappeared, reached into the black opening in front of her, and clicked a switch. Naked bulbs sprang into life, illuminating a narrow spiral staircase that curved down to the right.

Marietta stopped dead. She'd always loathed cellars and any other sort of underground space. It wasn't just simple claustrophobia, though this was a part of it. She'd always thought that a cellar smelled like a tomb.

"Keep going," one of the men ordered.

"No," Marietta said.

She felt the twin prongs of the Taser pressing into her back, and knew she would do anything to avoid suffering that pain again. Fighting back tears of terror and frustration in equal measure, she stumbled forward, and started down the stone staircase, the sound of her footsteps echoing off the walls.

It wasn't a long staircase—for obvious reasons, deep cellars were almost unknown in Venice and on its islands—and after about twenty steps the staircase ended at a flagstone floor. Again, one of the men clicked a switch and a single bright light came on at one end of the room, enabling Marietta to see her surroundings.

It was a long and wide cellar, possibly extending to exactly the same floor area as the ruined church building that stood above it. By the foot of the staircase was a cleared circular area, in the center of which was a large oblong stone table, looking something like an altar. Marietta guessed that it was positioned directly below the broken altar in the church above. When she looked at it again, she realized that it wasn't a perfect oblong, because it had a small square extension in the middle of one of the two shorter sides, and at each corner a hole had been drilled through the stone. Behind that table was another table, also made of stone but much smaller.

Along one side of the cellar were four short stone walls that extended from the floor up to the low ceiling and created a line of small, open-fronted rooms that had possibly been used as storerooms originally. The three men led Marietta into the first of these and hustled her across to the back wall. There she saw a rough wooden bed covered by a thin mattress and, bolted firmly to the wall above it, a new steel ring. A single metal handcuff dangled from the ring on the end of a metal chain.

The men pushed Marietta onto the bed. One of them reached into his pocket and pulled out a small pair of pliers, which he used to sever the plastic ties holding her wrists together. The moment he did so, another man snapped the handcuff around her left wrist, chaining her to the wall. It didn't matter that there was no door to her room. She would not be leaving.

"Please, no," Marietta shouted after the men as they walked away. "Don't just leave me here. Please."

Moments later the light clicked off, and she was left in the stygian blackness and utter silence of the cellar.

For several minutes Marietta just sat motionless on the hard mattress, eyes wide, willing them to adapt to the dark, to allow her to see something, anything. She sought a glow, a chink of light—something, however small, to provide her with a frame of reference. But there was nothing. Not even the faintest scintilla of illumination penetrated the blackness.

She gave way, and for a few minutes sobbed out of fear and frustration, but then she started to pull herself together. She tried to slide the handcuff off her wrist, but it was clamped too tightly. She tugged on the chain attached to the ring in the wall, but it was new and strong, and the ring was completely immovable.

When she finally accepted that there was no way she could get free, she set about exploring her immediate surroundings. Before the light had been extinguished, she'd seen the wooden bed, but hadn't noticed anything else. Now she walked to the limit of the chain, and then, with her right arm stretched out in front of her, she moved first left and then right, feeling her way through the blackness. All she found was empty space, and the cold and damp stone walls of her underground prison.

As she walked back to the wooden bed, her shoe hit something beneath it, and she bent down, her fingers probing. Moments later, she realized it was a metal bucket shoved under the bed, the purpose of which was fairly obvious. There was even a half-used roll of toilet paper on the floor beside it.

For a few minutes, she sat on the edge of the bed, trying to make sense of what had happened to her, and listening intently, alert for the slightest sound.

And then she heard a noise. Very faintly, and from somewhere at the far end of the cellar, it was like a distant whispering of several people, a sound that seemed to be getting slightly louder, though Marietta wasn't even sure of this.

"Who's there?" she yelled at last, in as strong and determined a voice as she could muster.

There was no response, except for a slight and temporary reduction in the volume of the sound, which then continued just as before.

Marietta listened again. What was it? Where could it be coming from?

With a sudden start she realized what it was.

And then she screamed.

8

The following morning, Bronson and Angela lingered over breakfast. Sitting at a corner table in the hotel's small dining room, surrounded by the remains of their meal, they were trying to decide where to visit next in Venice. They'd already been to some of the principal attractions in the center of the city, and had spent an expensive but pleasant afternoon wandering around the Piazza San Marco, climbing to the top of the Campanile to take in the spectacular views that that vantage point offered. In fact, they both decided that they preferred the much smaller Piazzetta San Marco, the open space that lay on the south side of the piazza, near the Doge's Palace, and which served as a connection between the piazza and the waters of the Grand Canal.

"How about Murano?" Bronson suggested. "Glass-making has always fascinated me. According to this guidebook, the demonstrations there are free, and that's not a word you normally associate with Venice."

"That's this island here, isn't it?" Angela asked, pointing at the map in her own book.

Bronson nodded. "Yes, though it's actually a group of six islands, not just one. And apparently there are lots of interesting little shops and boutiques there which you can have a root around in. We can take a number forty-one or forty-two vaporetto from the Fondamente Nuove stop, and it's not that far away—the next stop after San Michele, in fact."

But a few moments later, it became obvious to both of them that they weren't going to be able to visit Murano or, at least, not that morning.

The dining room door swung open, and the hotel receptionist peered inside. Spotting Bronson and Angela, she pointed them out to somebody waiting just outside. A moment later, two Italian police officers walked in, and crossed briskly to the table where they were sitting.

"Signor Bronson?" the first officer asked.

From the insignia on his uniform, Bronson guessed he was the equivalent of a sergeant, and the other man probably a constable. He nodded.

The officer pulled out a notebook, flipped through it until he found what he was looking for, and glanced at something written on the page.

"I understand you speak Italian," he said, and Bronson nodded again. "Where were you last night?"

"What?"

"I asked where you were last night," the police officer repeated.

"I understood what you said," Bronson said, "but I don't know why you're asking me this."

"There was an incident, and we are trying to establish the movements of anybody who might have been involved. It's routine."

Bronson didn't like the sound of that. In his experience, whenever a policeman assured a suspect that a particular line of questioning was "routine," it usually meant that it was anything but.

"What sort of incident?" he asked, deciding to play along. He knew he had absolutely nothing to worry about, whatever the "incident" might be. "I was here, in this hotel, after we got back from the Isola di San Michele. Then we went out for a late dinner, probably at about nine, and returned to the hotel just after eleven. We were in our room all night until about an hour ago, when we came down for breakfast."

The carabinieri officer noted down Bronson's answer, then looked at him again. "Can anyone substantiate your account, Signor Bronson?"

"I paid for the meal at the restaurant with a credit card," he replied, "so that will establish where I was between about nine and eleven. After that, Angela and I were together, and as far as I'm aware nobody else saw us after we came back to the hotel."

The officer frowned, and Bronson could tell that his answers hadn't satisfied him.

"If you can tell me what incident you're talking about, and the time it took place, we might be able to help."

The officer shrugged. "There was a break-in at the mortuary last night, and some damage was done."

"What's he saying, Chris?" Angela asked.

Bronson briefly translated what the officer had just told him.

"Somebody burgled the mortuary?" Angela sounded incredulous. "Why on earth would anyone want to do that?"

"Was anything taken?" Bronson asked. "And when did it happen?"

"We think the break-in occurred at about two or three in the morning. No valuables were stolen, as far as I know, apart from a camera."

"Then I have no alibi," Bronson said, "except that my partner is a very light sleeper, and if I had got up and left the room, I'm sure she would have heard me. What damage was done?"

"You saw a corpse, I believe, on the Isola di San Michele, at the Cimitero Comunale?" Bronson nodded. "Whoever broke into the mortuary removed its head, and scattered all the other bones and pieces of pottery, as if they were looking for something. And they stole an expensive digital camera."

Bronson leaned forward. He'd guessed that it had to be something to do with the events of the previous night; otherwise he could see no possible reason why the Italian police would want to question him.

"It wasn't us," he said firmly. "If you want to search our room, you're very welcome to do so. We've got nothing to hide, and absolutely no reason to steal an ancient skull or take a camera."

The Italian officer shrugged again and closed his notebook with a snap. As he did so, his radio emitted a static-laden squeak, and he turned his head and pressed the transmit button to respond. For some reason the radio reception in the hotel wasn't particularly good, but despite that Bronson was able to make out a few phrases of the message that the carabinieri control room was passing. One in particular seized his attention: "there's been another, but we've found this one." Taken in isolation, this phrase seemed innocuous enough, but it clearly meant something more to the sergeant, who immediately gestured to his companion to leave the room.

"How long will you be staying in Venice?" he asked Bronson.

"For the rest of this week."

"Good. We may need to speak to you again."

"So what the hell was all that about?" Angela demanded, when they were once again on their own.

"I've no idea," Bronson replied, "but I intend to find out."

"Where are you going?"

"I'm going to follow those two. Something's going on, and it must be linked to that corpse we saw in the cemetery last night."

9

Marietta Perini woke with a yelp of fear as something brushed across her face. Her eyes snapped open. She rubbed desperately at her cheeks, but whatever had touched her—a fly or spider, or whatever it was—had disappeared. The rattle of the chain that secured her left wrist to the wall, and the impenetrable blackness that surrounded her, only confirmed her terror. The nightmare of her dreams was her living reality.

She ran her hands over her body, checking that no other insects were anywhere on her skin or clothes, because she now knew the source of the noise that had so alarmed her the previous night. It was the sound of dozens, maybe hundreds, of tiny pointed feet moving across the flagstone floor and along the walls. The cellar was alive with cockroaches.

She had screamed at the realization, and had immediately lifted her feet off the floor and onto the mattress, away from what she'd felt sure was a plague of insects heading toward her. And then she'd heard a louder, more pronounced scurrying noise, and she'd screamed again.

Cockroaches were bad enough, but that noise had then convinced her that there were also rats or mice down there with her in the darkness.

Within minutes, the sound seemed to have spread all around her, and she'd created a terrifying mental image of tens of thousands of cockroaches swarming onto the bed and all over her, and rats gnawing at her flesh. But actually, the reality had been considerably less traumatic. She'd continued hearing the insects and the rodents scurrying about, but not one creature had touched her or climbed onto the bed—yet.

She hadn't expected to sleep, because of her fear and loathing of the other residents of the cellar, but the air down there was cold, and eventually she'd pulled an old and smelly blanket—the only piece of bedding provided— over her, simply to keep warm. And within a few minutes she'd drifted off into a fitful sleep, from which she had awoken, shivering and terrified, at intervals during the night.

Marietta had no watch on her wrist, but she guessed it was midmorning, and she was ravenously hungry and really thirsty. She'd had nothing to eat or drink since the previous afternoon, and her throat was parched and dry.

She consoled herself with the thought that if her captors had intended to kill her, they would probably already have done so. And that meant that they wanted her alive. But why? It couldn't be for ransom—her family wasn't rich, and she had no money of her own. There must be something else. And if they didn't want her to die, they would have to feed her.

Even as that thought gave her some slight comfort, she heard a grating and rumbling sound as the door at the top of the spiral staircase was opened, and the cellar lights snapped on.

Blinking in the harsh illumination, she stood up, shivering and waiting. Alone. And very frightened.

10

Bronson picked up the compact binoculars and small digital camera that he'd brought down from their room in readiness for their day of sightseeing. He slipped both instruments into the pockets of his leather jacket.

"Are you sure about this, Chris?" Angela asked.

"I'm afraid so," Bronson replied with a rueful smile. "Look, while I'm out following those two carabinieri, maybe you could have a look at the pictures you took of the grave. See if anything strikes you as being odd, apart from the decapitated body and the brick, I mean. It might also be worth trying to find out the name of the woman in the grave."

He glanced through the window at the street outside, where the two policemen had stopped for a few moments. Bending down, he kissed Angela lightly on the lips, and then strode across the dining room and walked out of the hotel.

The two carabinieri were on foot, of course—Venice

being a car-free zone—and were walking northeast along the street from the hotel, turning right at the end, and then left. It looked to Bronson, who was following about fifty yards behind them and taking frequent glances at the street map of Venice he'd picked up at the airport, as if they were heading toward the edge of the lagoon. This suspicion was confirmed when the two men walked onto the jetty by the Fondamente Nuove vaporetto stop. There he saw a police launch waiting for them, the engine running and two other officers already on board.

Although Bronson guessed that he would look just like any other tourist in the anonymous throngs already crowding the streets, he hung back, waiting for the vessel to depart. As soon as the sergeant and constable were sitting down in the launch, the driver freed the mooring line and gunned the engine. Bronson took out his binoculars and watched the vessel and its passengers. Once it had cleared the other water traffic that was maneuvering near the vaporetto stop, the boat swung around to the left and headed northeast, accelerating across the lagoon toward the northern end of the Isola di San Michele—in other words, pretty much as he'd expected.

About ten minutes later, shortly after the police launch had reached the jetty on the island, in fact, Bronson boarded a number forty-two vaporetto and began the same journey himself.

The Isola di San Michele was reasonably large, about five hundred yards by four hundred yards, he guessed, and very popular with visitors to Venice, so he didn't anticipate any particular difficulty in remaining unobserved once he got there.

He stepped out of the vaporetto onto the jetty more or less in the middle of a group of German tourists, and headed toward the part of the cemetery where they'd found the broken tomb the previous evening.

That was his first surprise. The tomb was covered in a heavy green tarpaulin, which was lashed down and held in place with a couple of orange polypropylene ropes. Clearly the authorities had decided to shield the broken structure from prying eyes. And there was no sign of any police officers. Whatever the carabinieri had come over to the island to investigate, it was obviously nothing at all to do with that grave.

Bronson looked around the vast cemetery, and over to one side he finally spotted a handful of police officers clustered around another grave. Feeling somewhat like a ghoul, he headed that way himself, taking a circuitous route so as not to make his approach too obvious.

Standing at the edge of the group of tourists that had gathered at the site, Bronson pulled his camera from his pocket, held it unobtrusively by his side and aimed it in the general direction of all the activity. The camera was equipped with a powerful zoom lens and had both still and movie modes, so he pressed the button that would provide him with a video record of what was going on.

The carabinieri had erected a temporary screen on the far side of the new grave. This, like the broken grave of the previous night, was another stone box with a slab covering the top, but as far as Bronson could see, it was completely intact. Instead, the police officers' attention was directed toward the ground beside the tomb. As he watched, a man wearing a set of white waterproof overalls, cap, gloves and rubber boots, and carrying a large plastic toolbox, emerged from behind the screen. He paused for a moment to exchange a few words with a couple of the police officers, then walked over to a patch of grass on which several other cases had been left. Bronson had been involved with enough serious crimes to know what the man's job was, and then, as the white-clad figure turned slightly toward him, he recognized the man as the same forensic pathologist who'd traveled out to the island the previous night. And that, he knew, meant that another body had been discovered.

If any confirmation was needed, it followed just moments later, when two men dressed in civilian clothes, and carrying a black body bag and a collapsible stretcher, walked behind the screen.

A few minutes later they emerged, carrying a zipped body bag on the stretcher. Before they moved away, however, one of the policemen halted them with a gesture, and unzipped the bag just far enough to allow him to see the head of the victim.

Bronson lifted the camera higher, pressed the zoom button and tried to get a close-up shot. A tumble of blond hair filled the LCD screen, but it looked as if the face of the girl—and the victim was obviously a young woman—was invisible. Several of the tourists standing near him were also using their cameras, snapping away, and one of the carabinieri shouted angrily at them.

Bronson stepped back and tucked the camera into his pocket, a flush of embarrassment warming his cheek. He'd never liked the salacious attitude of the public—and especially of the British press—about accidents and crime, and he didn't much like the feeling of being on the other side of the crime-scene tape, of being one of the morbid spectators.

And, he admitted to himself, he was probably just wasting his time. He had no idea whether the girl who was being carried away from the tomb had died by accident or from some other cause. About the only thing he was sure of was that it had nothing to do with the ancient mutilated corpse they'd seen the previous evening.

Turning away, he walked quickly through the graveyard toward the Cimitero vaporetto stop. He would go back to Angela, he decided, and they would resume their holiday and try to forget all about the vampire's tomb and the dead girl he'd just seen.

But as the vaporetto cut through the waters of the lagoon, a part of what he'd overheard continued to nag at him. The radio broadcast to the sergeant had included the phrase "there's been another." This could mean only one thing: the blond-haired girl hadn't had an accident; she had been the victim of foul play. And she hadn't been the first.

11

"Sit down," the man holding the Taser instructed.

Marietta knew she had to obey, so she nodded meekly and backed toward the bed.

"What do you want?" she asked, fighting to keep her voice level, to sound unafraid, despite the abject terror that had her nearly paralyzed. She'd tried running; she'd tried fighting back. Neither had done her any good at all. The memory of the bolts of electricity she'd endured from the Taser still seared through her brain. She would do anything—almost anything—to avoid experiencing that agony again.

"You'll find out soon enough," the man said, his voice indifferent, almost conversational. He gestured to the other man who'd accompanied him into the cellar, and who was carrying a laden tray. "Breakfast," he added shortly, and instructed his companion to place the tray on the floor well within Marietta's reach.

She eyed the food hungrily. She was absolutely famished, but for the moment she didn't move. She remembered reading somewhere that hostages—and to quiet her escalating terror she'd decided that she was, for whatever reason, a hostage—stood more chance of surviving their ordeal if they could establish some kind of rapport with their captors. With no other options, this seemed to be the only viable course of action she could take.

"What's your name?" she asked.

The man with the Taser looked at her. "My name is not important," he said, "and I don't think you'll be around long enough for us to become friends."

His words, and the light, almost careless manner with which he said them, sent a chill through Marietta, but she forced a smile onto her face. "My name's Marietta," she said.

"I know. Marietta Perini," the guard replied.

Marietta felt a lurch of despair. She'd rationalized that perhaps she resembled someone else, that she'd been snatched by mistake, and that once her captors realized their error, she'd be released unharmed. The guard's matter-of-fact statement meant that she'd been abducted for a specific reason, and she didn't like to think what this reason might be.

"Eat some food," the guard instructed, pointing at the tray.

"When I've finished," Marietta said, "could I please wash?"

"I'll have a bucket of warm water brought down, with some soap and a towel. Anything else?"

"Yes. Can you please, please, leave the light on, at least while I'm eating? Just to keep the rats and insects away."

The guard nodded; then he turned on his heel and walked out, his companion following.

The moment Marietta heard the cellar door slam shut, she picked up the tray of food and attacked it ravenously. There were bread rolls, butter and preserves, a small plate of ham and cheese, a large glass of water, a cup of black coffee, two cubes of sugar and a plastic container of milk. She needed the water more than anything else, and drank it all in moments, then slowed down, taking her time over the rest of the meal. She ate every scrap, then poured the milk in the coffee and drank that. She didn't put the sugar in the drink, but hid the cubes under the mattress, as a pathetic reserve, just in case they didn't bring her anything else to eat or drink for the rest of the day.

She scanned the tray for the last time, to see if there was anything she'd missed, or if there was anything on it that she could use as a weapon or a tool to try to free herself. But the only utensils she'd been given were a plastic knife, fork and spoon, and none of them would be of the slightest use to her. She replaced everything neatly on the tray, walked forward and put it down on the floor where it had been left.

About half an hour later, the guard reappeared, carrying, as he'd promised, a bucket of warm water, and with a towel draped over his arm.

Marietta sat silently on the bed as he lowered the bucket to the ground, and stepped forward to toss the towel onto the mattress beside her. Then he fished in his pocket and pulled out a small wrapped bar of soap—the kind found in budget hotels all over the world—and another small packet, both of which he placed on the towel.

"There's a toothbrush and toothpaste in that," he said, as he backed away to pick up the breakfast tray.

"Can you uncuff me so that I can wash?" Marietta asked, even though she knew her request was futile.

The guard shook his head. "Not a chance."

In a couple of minutes, Marietta was alone again, but at least now she felt a little better. She'd eaten a decent breakfast and had enough to drink, and she was sure that once she'd washed her face and hands—and that was about all she was going to do—she'd feel a lot cleaner as well. And being able to clean her teeth was a bonus.

She dragged the bucket over to the bed and first brushed her teeth, while the water was still clean. Then she unbuttoned her blouse and slid it down her left arm and onto the metal chain so that it was out of her way. She unwrapped the soap and washed herself as best she could, her chained left wrist restricting her movements more than she had expected.

Then she retrieved her blouse and got dressed again. All she could do then was lie on the bed and wait for whatever the day might bring.

At least the cellar light was still on, and she'd not seen any sign of the cockroaches that she'd heard the night before. They were still there—she knew that, because she could hear an occasional rustling sound from the walls—

but for the moment the light seemed to be keeping them at bay.

There was another thing about her captors that surprised her. Despite the brutal way she'd been grabbed from the street in Venice, they had treated her quite well since she'd arrived on the island. She'd anticipated physical abuse, maybe even rape, but apart from being manhandled after they'd shocked her with the Taser, none of them had so much as touched her.

But that wasn't all. What bothered her most was their air of superiority, of detachment. It was almost as if they felt they were above the law, as if they knew that the authorities wouldn't, or couldn't, touch them. She had the feeling that no matter what they subsequently did to her, none of the men believed they would suffer for it. And Marietta found this more frightening than her captivity itself.

Worse still, it suggested that she was a disposable asset in their eyes, a person of no consequence. Which meant that—short of a miracle—she was never going to get off the island alive.

12

A stocky, middle-aged man, his black hair showing the first subtle shadings of gray at the temples, walked out of the elegant building situated a short distance from the Piazza San Marco and turned north, heading for the Campo Santa Maria Formosa. It was a sensible place for a meeting, away from the more usual haunts of the tourists who still thronged the city, and with several cafés and bars where two men could sit together quietly and exchange confidences. In fact, Carlo Lombardi had not the slightest intention of saying very much at all: he was going to the square to receive information; important information, he hoped.

The call he'd taken in his office about a quarter of an hour earlier had been the first important break they'd received in the case—assuming, of course, that the man who had telephoned the police station really did know something of value about the multiple killings of young women that were currently plaguing the city.

Lombardi shook his head as he strode down the street, casting off his doubts. The caller was clearly well-informed, because he had already mentioned one fact about the series of murders that had never been released to the press, or publicized in any way at all. Whoever he was—he'd told Lombardi to call him "Marco," a common enough Italian name and almost certainly not his true identity—he had at least one piece of information that was known only to the perpetrators and the police. If he hadn't been involved in the killings himself, then it was at least probable that he had been a witness to them.

In any event, he was somebody that Lombardi, as the senior investigating officer in charge of the case, needed to talk to. "Marco" had told Lombardi that he would only meet him alone and face-to-face in a public area, and the Campo Santa Maria Formosa had seemed as good a spot as any. And Lombardi was going there alone and on foot, as he'd been instructed, just in case the man was mounting surveillance of the streets between the police station and the square. But that didn't mean that their meeting would go unobserved.

Lombardi had already dispatched a dozen police officers to cover the eight or so exits from the Campo, and four more to position themselves with parabolic microphones and high-resolution still and video cameras in a couple of the buildings that lined the square, to record the meeting.

"Marco" would find it easy enough to get to the Campo

and to the café he'd selected, but he would find it much more difficult to leave afterward.

Lombardi's orders had been absolutely clear: the man he was going to meet was to be arrested as soon as he left the café.

The senior police officer didn't hurry as he walked up the Calle Drio la Chiesa, allowing his men plenty of time to get into position. He turned left past the Museo Guidi, still closed after proving too expensive to run, then right again, following the west bank of the canal toward the square.

Carlo Lombardi had been born in Venice and prided himself on knowing every street and alley and canal in the city, and he believed he'd covered every possible way out. He was quite certain that once "Marco" walked into the Campo Santa Maria Formosa, he would only leave the square in handcuffs. And, at last, they might finally have a break in the case that had been both puzzling and alarming Venetian police officers for the previous two years.

He still remembered that dreadful afternoon when he'd responded to a call from one of his senior inspectors, and had traveled in a police launch out to the Isola di San Michele. He had stood over a shallow pit behind a line of trees and looked down onto the white and waxy naked body of a twenty-year-old girl, apparently dumped there only a few hours earlier. Her eyes had been wide-open, though already discolored by the actions of insects, attracted by the faint smell of decomposition. As Lombardi had stared down at the body, he'd heard a faint buzzing sound, and then a couple of blowflies had emerged from the girl's open mouth, where they'd doubtless been laying eggs. Other flies were clustered around the left-hand side of her neck.

Lombardi had looked at the inspector, his eyes questioning, but the man had simply flapped a handkerchief beside the girl's neck to drive away the insects. And then he and Lombardi had stared down at the fatal wound, its edges raised and ragged, which marred the perfect white skin of the corpse.

The results of the subsequent autopsy hadn't been a surprise. The girl had died from loss of blood—exsanguination—which had pumped out of the wound on her neck. There was also clear evidence of restraints: the marks of ropes or straps around her wrists and ankles. And she'd been raped, raped violently, several times, her genital area marred by heavy bruising. The body had yielded no useful clues to suggest where the girl had died, or any indication of the identity of her killers. Despite the evidence of rape, traces of lubrication within her vagina meant that the rapist, or rapists, had used a condom; and the body appeared to have been thoroughly washed after death to remove any pubic hairs or other trace evidence.

The one slight oddity revealed at the postmortem was the contents of the stomach. Very shortly before she died, the girl had ingested about a quarter of a liter of milk.

That in itself was unsurprising, but extensive bruising to the lips and the inside of her mouth suggested she might have been force-fed the liquid, which was unusual. But the analysis of the milk itself provided the biggest surprise, because the pathologist hadn't been able to identify the animal from which it came. All he could tell Lombardi was that it wasn't from a cow, sheep, goat or any other farm animal he was aware of, nor even from a human female. It simply wasn't in the database.

There were, of course, a lot of animal species in which the female produced milk to nourish her off-spring, and testing the samples removed from the dead girl's stomach against every possible mammal would have been a lengthy and very expensive process—and probably ultimately pointless. So Lombardi had told the pathologist not to bother, because it was already clear that the milk hadn't contained any form of drug, and had in no way contributed to the girl's death. It was just a curious anomaly.

Lombardi was quickly convinced that she had been the victim of a kind of ritualized murder, and he'd vowed there and then that he would bring the perpetrators—and there were obvious indicators that several men had been involved—to justice.

Since then, there had been other disappearances of young girls, usually between the ages of eighteen and twenty-five. Some of the bodies had been found, but in other cases the girls had simply vanished without a trace. The recovered corpses bore the same indicators of a hideous death as the first corpse: evidence of multiple rapes and exsanguination through severe wounds in the neck.

And in every case, a small amount of the unidentifiable milk had been recovered from the victim's stomach.

Lombardi mused on this as he walked along beside the canal. As was so often the case with investigations into serious crimes, the Italian police had been plagued by the usual crop of nutters who wanted to confess to the murders, or to produce convincing—to them—evidence that the killer was the man next door or the pope or the American president or even a visiting alien. They'd talked to most of them, just in case they were involved in some way, but they were quite satisfied that none of the people they'd interviewed had had anything to do with the crimes.

But the thing that had convinced Lombardi that "Marco" could help him with the murders was the single sentence the man had said during his telephone conversation: "I know about the milk."

Nobody, apart from the pathologist and the senior carabinieri officers investigating the murders, had been told what had been found in the victims' stomachs. Now they had a potential witness, or perhaps even a member of the group responsible for the killings, who was prepared to talk to them. This, Lombardi knew, could finally break the case wide-open.

By now he was walking toward the end of the street. The last part of his journey—a right turn over one bridge and then an immediate left turn over another—would take him into the southern end of the Campo.

Then somebody grabbed his arm and swung him

round, and Lombardi found himself looking into the hostile eyes of a man he was sure he'd never seen before.

"Who are you?" Lombardi demanded, casually loosening his jacket so that he could reach his pistol more easily.

The stranger smiled slightly and slid his hands into his jacket pockets. "I'm Marco."

"But we were supposed—" Lombardi began.

The other man shook his head. "By now you'll have plainclothes officers and uniformed police forming a nice tight circle around the Campo, and probably a surveillance unit or two watching the café. If I walk into the square with you, I'll only leave it with my hands cuffed behind my back. And that's not a part of my plan at all."

"And what is your plan, Marco?" Lombardi asked, relaxing slightly.

"You don't need to know that." The man's voice was almost haughty, his manner arrogant, as if he were talking to an inferior. "All I want to do is give you a message to take to your colleagues, because we think you're getting a little too close to us. And that must stop."

"So what's the message?"

"This," Marco replied. Shifting his right hand slightly, he pulled the trigger of the compact semiautomatic pistol he held concealed in his pocket.

The nine-millimeter bullet, fired at almost point-blank range, plowed through Lombardi's stomach, driving him onto the ground, his hands clutching at the wound. The sound of the shot echoed deafeningly around the street, and the few pedestrians in the vicinity stopped dead and stared in horror at the scene being played out in front of them.

Unhurriedly, Marco walked a couple of paces forward to where Lombardi lay writhing and screaming on the ground, and looked down at him.

"You should have stuck to what you're good at," he said, "which is catching common criminals, and left us to get on with our important work."

He pulled the pistol from his pocket, and almost casually fired two further shots into Lombardi's chest. Then he turned and strode away, tucking the pistol out of sight as he did so.

Behind him, Lombardi's legs twitched a couple of times in his death throes. And then he lay still.

13

"Any luck?" Bronson asked, opening the door to their hotel bedroom. It was early afternoon, and Angela was sitting near the window in the pale sunshine, frowning at her computer screen.

"That really depends on your definition of luck," she said. "Rather than trying to tackle the diary, which I thought might take me a while because my Latin is probably a bit rusty, I decided to do the easy bit first. I thought I'd start by trying to trace the family history of the woman in the grave."

"And did you?"

"Well, you know that I photographed the slab that covered the tomb?" Bronson nodded: she'd photographed everything in sight the previous evening. "When I looked at the pictures, even blown up on the screen of my laptop, almost the entire inscription is illegible. Absolutely the only thing I can make out for certain is the date of the burial, which was eighteen twenty-five, and I actually read that when we were in the cemetery last night."

"That slab looked very badly weathered to me," Bronson said. "In fact, I suggested to one of the carabinieri officers that you might be able to assist with dating the grave by looking at those shards of pottery we saw in the tomb."

Angela shook her head. "No, you misunderstood me. The slab was weathered, I agree. That's not surprising, bearing in mind it's been sitting out there, exposed to the elements, for nearly two hundred years. But that wasn't why I can't read the name on the gravestone. The letters have actually been chipped off, probably with a hammer and chisel, because I can just about make out the marks of a steel tool on the stone."

"You mean it's been vandalized?"

"Unless Venetian vandals are better equipped than their British counterparts, probably not. To me, this looks like a determined attempt to obliterate the name of the woman in the grave."

"Could you make out any part of the inscription?" Bronson asked.

"I thought her surname began with the letter 'P,' but I couldn't even swear to this with what I found on the tomb. There's a short gap where none of the stone has been chipped away, which I assume was the space between her first name and her family name, and in one of my photographs you can just about see the upper half of the letter carved into the stone. But it could also be the letter 'R,' 'B' or even a 'D'—not much to go on."

"Can I see it?"

Angela turned the laptop so that Bronson could see the screen easily.

The display showed a grayish stone, the surface marked with patches of lichen in faded reds and greens. On the right-hand side of the frame was a faint semicircular mark, barely visible, with a straight line on the left-hand side of it. It looked like the upper part of the letter "P." Above and around the marks, several parallel scratches could be seen.

Angela pointed at them. "You can't see it terribly well in this picture," she said, "but that area is lower than the surrounding stone, and I think those marks were left by the chisel that hacked away that piece of stone."

"So why didn't the person who did this chip off the rest of the letter?"

"They did," Angela said shortly, "or they tried to. Most inscriptions on masonry use a V-shaped cut to form the letters, and that was done here. The upper part of the letter was removed, and what we're seeing in this picture is the deepest cut made by the mason's chisel, the very bottom of the V-cut that formed the letter. This is the only picture that shows it, and I think that was just luck. The camera angle meant that the flash just managed to pick it out."

Angela looked away from the screen and up at Bronson. "And where did you get to? You've been gone for hours."

"I know. Oddly enough, I went back to the Isola di

San Michele. I followed those two carabinieri to the edge
of the lagoon, where there was a police launch waiting for
them. I watched them head out to the island; then I
hopped on a vaporetto and followed them."

"They went back to the grave, you mean?"

"That was my assumption too, but they went to a different part of the cemetery because another body had
been found there. A fresh corpse, I mean, not another old
burial."

Bronson explained to Angela what he'd seen, not
mentioning the video and still images he'd taken at the
scene, because he was, in truth, still a little embarrassed
about what he'd done.

"So that's an entirely separate crime," Angela said.

"Actually, I don't even know if it was a crime. All I saw
was the body of a girl with long blond hair being carted
off, presumably for forensic examination and an autopsy.
She could easily have been the victim of accidental death.
All I saw, really, was her hair."

"So the fact that her body was on the island, not far
from the broken grave, is just a coincidence," Angela
said, looking skeptical. "You think that the two incidents
are entirely unconnected."

Bronson paused. "As far as I can tell, there's no link
between the two apart from their location. But there is
one thing that intrigues me, something I overheard when
that police sergeant received the radio message."

"I guessed you'd heard something when you decided
to follow them."

"The dispatcher, or whatever they're called in the car- abinieri, said that 'there's been another, but we've found this one.' Then the two officers went straight out to the island. To me, that suggests young women have been disappearing, and only some of their bodies have been recovered."

Angela sighed, got up from her chair and stretched. "In other words, it rather looks as if there could be a se- rial killer operating here in Venice." She turned to Bron- son. "And you want to investigate, don't you?"

Bronson stood up too and put his hands on her shoul- ders. "I'm not going to get involved, I promise. I'm just interested in what's going on. Just like you're interested in that vampire diary or whatever it is."

Angela smiled gently. "Touché," she murmured. "So what are you going to do about it?"

"Nothing much. I thought I might just check the ar- chives of the local newspaper and see if I can spot a pat- tern. That's all. And what about you?" he added. "Have you gotten anywhere with that thing yet?"

Angela gestured toward the small black leather-bound volume lying on the desk next to her laptop.

"Not really. It's in pretty poor condition, as you might expect. I still think it was put in the grave underneath the coffin when the woman was buried. That makes the most sense, especially if the people who buried her, her family or her friends, accepted her for what she was."

"That she was a vampire, you mean?" Bronson said.

"Well, to be accurate, she was a woman who believed

she was a vampire, which isn't exactly the same thing. But to honor her memory, as it were, they buried her diary with her, and those two small pottery jars as well. I still think they most likely contained blood, intended to sustain her. They probably just thought they were humoring her last wishes."

"But later on, somebody took her claim to be a vampire a lot more seriously, and they had a very different attitude to her."

"Exactly. It was someone who obviously believed absolutely in the vampire myth, and was probably appalled to think that the body of such a creature should be buried here in Venice. They went to enormous trouble to obliterate her name from the tomb, and to desecrate her body, to kill her off if she was a vampire, at the same time."

"So what have you found in the diary?" Bronson asked.

"I've only had a quick look at some of the early pages," Angela replied. "But the exciting thing is that I now know her name, because on one of the first pages she's explained the purpose of the book. The translation of one phrase she wrote is 'the record of the life of Carmelita Paganini,' and that ties up with the remains of the letter 'P' I deciphered on the slab over her grave. I also tried to see if the lengths of the obliterated words from the slab more or less matched that name, and they do."

Bronson picked up the book and opened it carefully, but the closely written text meant nothing to him. It was obvious that Carmelita had used different types and colors of ink over the years, because on some pages the writing was as clear and sharp as if it had been done the day before, while on others the ink had faded to a gray or reddish shadow.

"Be careful with it, Chris," Angela said, taking it back from him. "It's very fragile."

"I suppose you're using the scanned images," he replied, "because the writing on some of these pages is virtually illegible."

"Oddly enough, because I could adjust the sensitivity of the scanner, the images in my laptop are a lot clearer than the original text. So, yes, I am working on the computer, and not from the book."

Angela glanced at her watch. "Why don't we go out for a bite of lunch now? And then I'll do a bit more work on the diary, and you can amuse yourself digging around in some newspaper's morgue, looking for clues, just like a real detective."

"I am a real detective," Bronson protested faintly, "but that's a good idea. I'll just see if I can find out anything, just to satisfy my curiosity, and then we can forget about it. And tomorrow we'll go back on the sightseeing trail."

14

"Officer down! Officer down!"

"Get an ambulance! Right now!"

The cries of shock and alarm rang through the Campo Santa Maria Formosa and the neighboring streets. The officers who'd been deployed on the stakeout at the café were at the scene in seconds. But by then, the well-dressed assassin had vanished into the crowds, leaving behind his grisly handiwork.

Within minutes the area was swamped by police officers and paramedics, and two ambulance launches were moored in the canals closest to the scene of the shooting, their engines rumbling quietly. But the reality was that they were too late. They were all a lifetime too late.

Inspector Filippo Bianchi approached the scene at a run, his identity card held in his left hand for all to see.

"Who in God's name is it?" he shouted.

The uniformed carabinieri officer stationed some distance from the scene swung around as the senior officer approached. He recognized him immediately, and shook his head. "It's the chief inspector, sir," he said. "It's Lombardi."

When he heard that name, Bianchi stopped in dismay. Around him, uniformed police officers, paramedics, technicians in civilian clothes and others wearing white coveralls milled about the scene. The obvious focus of their attention was the area right beside the edge of the canal. Temporary screens had already been erected in a rough square to protect the crime scene, and to hide the body from the curious glances of the Venetians and tourists who were passing down the opposite side of the canal, and looking over at the scene from boats and gondolas.

Inspector Bianchi was a solidly built man in his fifties, his fine aquiline features now darkly suffused with anger and disgust. As he walked closer to the body, several of the men nodded greetings, but none spoke to him. Their mood was clearly both subdued and very angry.

Carabinieri officers, like policemen everywhere, accept the inherent dangers of their job. They are on the front line, the thin blue line that separates the criminal elements from the law-abiding citizens in their country. And in Italy there has always been the added menace and complication of the Cosa Nostra, the Mafia—the criminal organization that many maintain still holds the real power in the country. As many prominent officials have found to their cost over the years, Mafia godfathers are always prepared to remove—permanently—anyone who they believe is getting in their way. Judges, politicians, and, of course, police officers, have all paid the ultimate price for their desire to uphold the rule of law.

But Carlo Lombardi had not been involved, as far as Bianchi knew, in any anti-Mafia operations, at least not in the five years he had known him. Lombardi was Venetian born and bred, had spent all his working life in the city, rising to become one of the most senior officers employed there. And most of this time, all he and his men had had to deal with was the usual spate of bag-snatching and pickpocketing, as criminal elements at the very bottom of the ladder preyed upon Venice's annual influx of tourists. "Bottom-feeders" was the way Lombardi had usually referred to these criminals. They were an irritation, not a threat, and rarely targeted any of the local people.

And never, in Bianchi's experience, had any one of these "bottom-feeders" carried a firearm. But now, Chief Inspector Carlo Lombardi lay dead in the center of the screened-off area, three bullet holes in his body, and his dark blood staining the old stones on which he lay.

A plainclothes officer looked up as Bianchi came to a stop beside the feet of the dead man.

"A bad business, Filippo," the officer said.

Bianchi nodded. "What happened, Piero? Any witnesses?"

"He was executed. That's what happened," Inspector Piero Spadaccino replied angrily. "He was shot down in cold blood, right here in the middle of Venice. It looks like the first bullet hit his stomach, because of the position of his hands. And either of the second two in his chest would have been enough to kill him. The doctor thinks both those bullets probably went through his heart. I tell you, Filippo, this looks to me like a gangland killing."

"Any witnesses?" Bianchi asked again.

Spadaccino nodded. "Several," he replied shortly. "None of them saw the first shot, though they all heard it. A medium-caliber pistol, probably nine millimeter. That took Lombardi down, and they all turned to look. Then the killer walked over to him, lying here on the ground, said something to him, and then fired the other two shots. An execution; nothing more, nothing less.

"All the witnesses describe a man in a dark suit with black hair, dark eyes and a tanned complexion, no distinguishing features. About the only point of interest in the descriptions is that a couple of people said the man was very casual—no hurry, no sign of stress. He just walked over, shot the chief inspector and then walked away. One man told me he actually thought it was part of a film, and he spent a few seconds looking around to see where the cameras were. I've got my men taking full written statements from the witnesses now, and obviously we'll do follow-up questioning as well, but I don't think any of them will be able to give us a photofit for this guy, or pick him out of a lineup."

Spadaccino paused, and he and Bianchi both looked down at the crumpled figure lying on the stones between them.

"You worked with him, Filippo," Spadaccino said softly. "What the hell could he have gotten himself involved with that could have led to this? I mean, was he investigating organized crime?"

Bianchi shook his head. "Not that I'm aware of."

In fact, Inspector Bianchi had a very good idea who had ordered the assassination of his superior officer. The trouble was, if he said anything, the plan he was working on would probably come to nothing. And now the endgame was so close, he couldn't take that chance.

For the moment, all he could do was wait.

15

Bronson had visited various newspaper morgues in Britain over the years, and he was all too familiar with the unmistakable smell of musty newsprint that seemed to infuse such places, even those that had embraced modern technology to the extent of installing microfiche machines.

The Venice newspaper office had taken a step further into the twenty-first century, and had scanned all their previous copies into a series of hard drives that were accessible through a couple of PC terminals. The newspapers printed more than twenty years earlier had simply been scanned as images, and searching through those would be a laborious process, just like searching microfiche records. To find anything relevant among those copies would really require a fairly accurate date, so that the appropriate edition could be inspected.

But the articles and stories in the more recent newspapers had been stored as text files, as well as images, which meant that Bronson was able to search for a specific word or phrase. He really had no clue when any other young women's disappearances had been reported—or even if there had been any such disappearances—but, because of this facility, he was able to carry out extensive and detailed searches without much difficulty.

The results were generated almost immediately, and he printed out the relevant stories as each one appeared on the screen in front of him. Within a matter of minutes, Bronson realized that there had been a spate of disappearances from Venice and the surrounding area, including a couple of girls who had been reported missing from the mainland. The only common factor, as far as he could tell, was that no trace of most of the young women had been found—in fact, only two bodies had turned up. It was as if the other girls had simply vanished.

The Italian police, of course, had been informed, and had carried out interviews with friends and relatives of the missing girls, but with no clues, and without any bodies to analyze and investigate, there was little they could do. It was even suggested that the girls might have become romantically involved with somebody, or that perhaps they had just run away.

These suggestions irritated and angered the parents involved, who all believed that, even if their daughters had eloped or run off, they would still have written or telephoned to confirm that they were alive. The continued lack of any form of communication from any of the young women was distressing for all concerned, but there was still little that the police could do, simply because they had nothing to go on.

Bronson totted up the total number of disappearances, and realized that at least a dozen girls had vanished over the previous eighteen months, six of them recently. Prior to that, there had been reports of a couple of women who had gone missing, but in both cases there appeared to be good reasons for them to have left their families. And both had later reappeared, alive and well. So unless there was something about these twelve girls that the journalists had failed to report, it looked very much to Bronson as if a serial abductor, who was almost certainly a serial killer as well, was operating in Venice. And operating with impunity.

This was interesting, but that was all, because Bronson knew that if he could deduce this from reading a handful of newspaper articles, the Italian police, who would have had access to those same articles plus all the other reports relating to the disappearances, must have come to exactly the same conclusion. And perhaps, if the body found in the cemetery on the Isola di San Michele was that of a girl who had disappeared—and a very recent edition of the local paper reported another disappearance the previous week—the police would now have plenty of clues to work with. In Bronson's experience, the dead could speak, and often produced a wealth of information about the manner in which they'd died, and sometimes a lot about their killers as well.

Almost as an afterthought, he did another search of

the archives, this time looking for articles on a totally unrelated subject—the vandalizing of graves. He was somewhat surprised to discover that there was plenty of information in the back numbers of the newspaper about this as well. Again, he printed a series of articles so that he could read them at his leisure back at the hotel.

What he'd found surprised him so much that he decided to run a third search, which produced a single result. It had nothing whatsoever to do with Venice, but Bronson took a copy of this as well. You never knew, he thought, what information might prove valuable. Especially when it related to vampires.

16

"It'll be dark in three or four hours," Angela objected. "Are you sure you want to go back there again today?"

They were back in the hotel room, the newspaper printouts Bronson had obtained spread across the bed.

"I'm not bothered about the dead girls," Bronson said. "Investigating those disappearances is a police matter, without question. It's nothing to do with us. But these other stories I found, about the vandalized graves out on the island, are really interesting. I just thought I'd like to go over there and see what sort of damage had been done, and also find out the age of the tombs that had been targeted."

"Why?" Angela was already putting on her boots, Bronson noted, and had selected a heavier coat for the journey across the water.

"It's your talk about a vampire cult that's got me interested. I was wondering if all the graves were from the nineteenth century, and if their occupants were all female.

I'd also like to know if the tombs were opened, or if the vandals had sprayed graffiti on them, for instance. Was it genuine vandalism, or were the people involved trying to open the graves because they were looking for something?"

Angela smiled. "Oddly enough, I want to go back to the Isola di San Michele as well, but for a completely different reason. While you were out, I translated some more of the Latin text in that book, and there's a reference in it that I'd like to look at." She pointed at the black leather-bound book. "In fact, there are several references to the same thing. According to that diary, somewhere in the graveyard, in the 'tomb of the twin angels,' as the writer calls it, is the 'answer.' Now, I haven't got the slightest idea what she means, but I'd be very interested in finding out."

"Right, then," Bronson said, zipping up his leather jacket. "Let's go."

A few minutes later they walked out of the hotel and turned north, toward the vaporetto stop. Angela had her handbag slung over her shoulder, while Bronson was carrying her laptop bag. She had insisted on taking her computer and the diary with them while they explored the cemetery, just in case she needed to refer back to the Latin text.

Ten minutes after they'd left, a man appeared at the reception desk, produced identification that showed he was a senior carabinieri officer, and demanded to see the hotel register. He explained that it was just a routine check, as part of a confidential statistical analysis that the Venetian authorities were carrying out into hotel occupancy by non-Italian guests.

The receptionist handed over the register without comment.

The carabinieri officer made some notes, thanked the receptionist, and then left the building.

A little more than half an hour after that, two middle-aged Italian men, both wearing business suits and carrying briefcases, marched straight into the hotel lobby, deep in conversation, and climbed the stairs to the upper levels. The receptionist didn't recognize them, but there were a number of new guests at the hotel, and he assumed that the men were new arrivals.

Once they were out of earshot of the reception desk, the two men fell silent. At the top of the stairs, they walked down a corridor and stopped outside one particular room. While one of them watched for any sign of movement, the other man removed a small jimmy from his briefcase, slid the point between the door and jamb, and gave a hard shove. Moments later, they were both inside.

They left the hotel about fifteen minutes later, still talking together and still carrying their briefcases. Again the receptionist ignored them.

17

Without a watch, Marietta had no idea of the time, or even if it was day or night. She'd been given another tray of food about three or four hours ago, just bread, ham and cheese and a cup of coffee, which she presumed was her lunch. Since then she'd neither heard nor seen anyone or anything. Despite being terrified about her predicament, she was also thoroughly bored.

Her other problem was the cold. The cellar was obviously damp, the walls moist to the touch, and the very air chilled her bones. The only way she could keep warm was by sitting on the bed and wrapping the blanket around her.

Hours later, she heard the rumble of the cellar door opening again, and the guard reappeared with another tray, which he placed on the floor near her bed. A waft of even colder air seemed to swoop down the staircase, reducing the temperature in the cellar still further. Marietta guessed that it was already late afternoon, and the temperature was dropping.

She didn't move, didn't speak, just watched as he swapped the trays round and turned to leave. Then, as he started walking away toward the spiral staircase, Marietta heard a sound that chilled her even more than the cold of her surroundings. Through the open door to the ruined church above the cellar, she suddenly heard a loud and mournful howl.

Somehow she knew it wasn't a dog, an Alsatian or anything like that. There was something different about that noise, something that caused the hairs on the back of her neck to rise. It sounded almost primeval, an ancient human nightmare come terrifyingly to life.

And it was close—really close. Definitely somewhere on the island.

"What's that?" she demanded, as the guard continued to walk away from her.

He stopped, turned around and looked back at her, a malicious grin working its way across his face. "Just one of our little pets," he said. "A playmate for you, perhaps, a bit later on."

"But what is it?" she asked again. "A wolf?"

"You'll find out," the guard said. "But if I were you, I wouldn't be in too much of a hurry to meet it."

A few seconds later, the cellar door rumbled closed and Marietta was alone once more with her thoughts and fears.

At first, she ignored her meal and just sat on the bed, looking across the cellar to the base of the spiral staircase. Over and over again, in her mind, she replayed the sound she'd heard, and the guard's thinly veiled threat.

She was never going to escape from this island. She knew that with a kind of dull certainty that settled in her mind like a cold and heavy weight. There was no hope for her.

Marietta toppled onto her side, pulled the filthy blanket over her head, and let the tears flow.

18

It was late afternoon, and once again the Island of the Dead was shrouded in shadows as the sun sank slowly toward the western horizon.

"Let's start with your vandalized graves, Chris," Angela suggested as they walked away from the vaporetto stop. "What do the newspapers say about them?"

Bronson shrugged. "Like most newspaper stories, they're heavy on sensation and light on details. According to the best report, two graves were interfered with on one night, and they were very close to each other, down at the southern end of the cemetery."

"So let's make a start there, then."

They walked between the ranks of tombs down to the south of the island, looking at the names on the graves as they passed them. Bronson spotted an area where most of the tombs appeared somewhat older than the majority.

"This report also says that one of the graves was over

four hundred years old," he said. "Those graves over there look pretty old to me."

Despite the enormous number of tombs, it didn't take them that long to find the first of the two graves the newspaper claimed had been attacked by vandals. It was a similar structure to the one Angela had taken to calling the "vampire's grave"—another stone box topped with a flat stone slab that bore the name and dates of the deceased entombed within.

"Here it is," Bronson said. "That's the name that they give in the paper."

For a few moments they both stared at the structure in front of them.

"I don't know about you, Chris," Angela said, "but I don't see much evidence of damage. In fact, it looks untouched."

"You're right." Then Bronson noticed something, and pointed at the base of the slab covering the top of the grave. "I think somebody lifted off that slab," he said. "Look, the cement holding it in place is fresh. You can see that clean line running all the way around it."

Once he'd pointed it out, the new cement was very obvious. And when they found the second tomb, it was precisely the same story, except that on this grave the slab had obviously cracked when it had been levered off, and the repair work on the damaged slab also included a couple of metal pins to hold the two sections of it together.

"Well," Bronson said, "I think it's obvious that we're not looking at the work of your average vandal here. Both of these graves were opened by people who were clearly searching for something, and I'll bet that if we located all the other tombs that have been attacked, we'd find the same thing. The other point that strikes me is that both of these graves date from the early nineteenth century, so they're about the same age as your vampire's tomb."

"Which does make you wonder what, exactly, they were looking for," Angela said. "There's not likely to be a hell of a lot left inside a two-hundred-year-old tomb, unless the grave was sealed completely, or they used a lead coffin. Do you want to try to find any of the other graves mentioned in the newspaper stories, or are you satisfied with what you've seen here?"

"No, I'm happy that we know what happened, even if we don't know why. These graves were opened by people who were looking for something specific. Let's try to find the twin-angels tomb you're interested in."

"The book describes it as the 'tomb of the twin angels,' so presumably we're looking for a grave that's marked by a couple of carved stone angels," Angela said, looking around at the mass of tombs that surrounded them. "The problem is that the two most common symbols on all these graves are the crucifix and angels, single or multiple. I suppose we just have to hope that there's something very obvious about the one we're looking for."

"And if we find it?" Bronson asked. "Are you planning another session of grave robbing?"

"I'd just like to find the tomb to prove that my translation of the Latin is accurate. I mean, this is just an intellectual exercise, not a treasure hunt or anything like that."

"Why don't we split up? That way we can cover more ground. Just make sure we don't get too far apart. We don't want to have to spend hours tramping around here looking for each other."

"It's not that big a place, Chris," Angela pointed out. "And what we're looking for is quite specific. Because of the date of the diary, the tomb has to be dated no later than about eighteen hundred, maybe eighteen ten, and because the diary uses the expression 'twin angels' every time the topic is mentioned, I think the carving will be of two identical angel figures, not just two different stone angels on the same grave."

"OK," Bronson said, and turned to his right. "I'll head over this way."

For the next hour or so, they both looked at a wide variety of graves, all of which exhibited some of the characteristics they were searching for. In all, they found more than a dozen tombs that were about the right date, and that were decorated with the stone figures of angels.

But it wasn't until they looked in a section of the graveyard that appeared to be the most neglected that Angela thought they might have found the one referred to in the diary.

In one corner of this area she spotted a sarcophagus-type tomb. Unlike most of the others they'd looked at, which had carved stone figures surmounting them, either as part of a heavily ornamented top slab or as a separate piece of monumental stone, this grave had a fairly plain slab covering the top of the sarcophagus, and there was no immediate sign of any angelic carvings. But then she looked at the foot and saw an incised carving that depicted two angels side by side, their limbs entwined, one virtually a mirror image of the other.

"Is this it?" Bronson asked, walking over in response to her wave.

"It's the most likely, I think. The two angels are identical, and it's obviously a really old grave."

Angela stepped forward and looked at the letters and numbers on the top of the slab. The stone was quite badly weathered, but most of the inscription was just about legible.

"The date of the burial was July, seventeen eighty-three," she said. "The name is a bit more difficult to read, but I think the surname is Delaca. I can't make out the first name at all, except that it begins with the letter 'N.'"

Angela took a notebook out of her handbag and recorded the information she'd found on the slab.

"I'll do a bit of research on the Web," she said, "and maybe check one or two genealogy sites. I might be able to find out something about him or her." She looked closely at the tomb, at the joints between the stones, and shook her head. "It doesn't look to me as if anybody's touched this grave for decades, maybe even centuries.

Perhaps the 'answer'—or whatever Carmelita Paganini was referring to—isn't actually in the grave, but visible outside it."

"You mean there might be something in the inscriptions themselves?" Bronson asked.

Angela nodded, took out her digital camera and took pictures of the tomb from every angle, trying to ensure that the images showed the inscriptions and symbols carved into the stone as clearly as possible.

"Are we finished here?" Bronson asked finally. It was beginning to get chilly and he didn't like the way the shadows were starting to lengthen between the graves.

"Yes. Let's go back to the hotel," Angela replied. "I'll do a bit more work on the translation when I have time, and see if I can find out anything else about this 'answer' our diarist talks about."

"And I suppose you can do that once we get back to England, so tomorrow we can start our holiday again?"

Angela nodded in agreement and laced her arm through his as they walked back toward the entrance to the cemetery.

They'd gone about fifty or sixty yards when Bronson suddenly stopped and looked around.

Angela looked at him inquiringly. "What is it?"

"Can you smell something?"

"Sorry?"

"It's foul and unpleasant—and I have a horrible feeling I know what it is."

For a second or two, Angela looked at him. "We are

standing in the middle of a graveyard," she reminded him.

"I know. But even in a cemetery you shouldn't be able to smell a decomposing corpse. That's why bodies are buried in coffins—to keep everything inside." Bronson glanced around. "I think it's coming from over there," he said, gesturing over to the right of the path they were following.

He stepped off the path and walked slowly through the graves. "It's definitely stronger over here," he called out.

"I can smell it now," Angela confirmed, joining him.

The odor faded slightly as they passed a line of tombs, and they turned around to retrace their steps.

"That might be it," Bronson suggested, pointing at an old grave. "You see the corner of it? A section of the slab has broken off."

They walked over to the sarcophagus-type structure that Bronson had indicated, and with every step they took, the smell grew stronger and more offensive. Angela took a handkerchief from her bag and pressed it against her nose, but it made little difference.

The stone box that comprised the grave was about eight or nine feet long, about four feet wide and roughly the same height. The slab covering the top had obviously cracked in one corner and that section of the stone had fallen onto the ground beside the tomb. Bronson stepped closer to the opening that had been created, then retreated.

He coughed a couple of times, trying to rid his lungs of the stench of decay, then turned back to Angela.

"I left my camera back at the hotel," he said. "Can I borrow yours?"

"You're going to photograph a rotting body?" Angela looked shocked.

"Don't you see? This is an old grave, so the body should have decayed into nothing years and years ago. Whatever is causing that smell is very recent. We've got two choices. Either we slide the slab off the top of the grave, which is something I really don't want to do, or I point your camera into the tomb through that hole in the corner and take a picture of the interior. If it's just a cat or some animal that's crawled in there to die, we can forget all about it. But if it's something else, we'll be able to tell exactly what it is from the image, and then, if we have to, we can make a call."

"You think there's a fresh corpse in there, don't you?" Angela asked, and Bronson nodded. "Right, here's my camera."

Bronson took it from her, walked back to the tomb, aimed the lens through the hole, and pressed the shutter release. There was a sudden explosion of light as the flash was triggered. It took the camera a couple of seconds to process the image, and then a picture of the interior of the tomb appeared in full color on the small LCD screen.

Bronson turned away from the tomb, and handed the camera back to Angela.

"Oh, my God, Chris," she whispered, her face turning pale.

Bronson nodded grimly, took his mobile phone from his pocket and dialed 112. They needed the emergency services, fast.

19

"Signor Bronson, we meet again." The carabinieri sergeant looked at Bronson appraisingly. "You seem to be making something of a habit of being at the scene of desecrated tombs."

"It's only happened twice," Bronson objected.

"Apart from some simple vandalism over the past few years, there have only been two cases that I know of where graves in this cemetery have been desecrated. The first one was yesterday, just over there"—the sergeant pointed—"and when two police officers arrived on the scene, the first person they spoke to was you. And now you've called us to report this one as well. That's two in two days, and the only common factor, Signor Bronson, seems to be you. That's what I call a habit."

Behind the sergeant, about half a dozen police officers were in attendance, as well as numerous other people wearing civilian clothes—Bronson presumed they were crime-scene technicians, the pathologist and staff from the mortuary.

"In your call"—the sergeant referred to his notebook—"you said there was a dead girl in the tomb."

Bronson shook his head. "No, I didn't," he said. "I actually told the operator there were three dead girls."

"Three?"

Bronson nodded.

"So you looked into the grave?"

"As a matter of fact, I didn't. I haven't got a flashlight and I wouldn't have been able to see anything inside the tomb without one. Instead, I used a digital camera with an automatic flash."

Bronson reached into his jacket pocket, pulled out Angela's camera, switched it on and found the photograph he had taken through the crack in the lid of the tomb.

The sergeant muttered something under his breath. The image was pin-sharp, and the flash had driven away the darkness inside the grave, and recorded forever the appalling scene inside it.

Clearly visible in the picture were the stone base and sides of the tomb, and the remains of a very old coffin, most of the wood disintegrated and rotten. Mixed in with the wooden fragments were a few tattered scraps of cloth and, at one end of the grave, the leg bones of a human skeleton. But it wasn't this evidence of an ancient burial that had transfixed the sergeant. It was the three naked female bodies that were lying on top of the disintegrated coffin, one on top of another, their corpses already bloated and discolored as the disintegration of their tissues accelerated.

The sergeant looked at the picture on the LCD screen for a few moments longer, then handed the camera back to Bronson. He turned away and addressed the men who'd arrived in response to Bronson's call, issuing orders and instructions.

Temporarily dismissed, Bronson walked a few paces to where Angela sat on the ground, her back resting against a gravestone. He sat down beside her and took her hand. She looked pale and shaken by what she'd seen.

"Why did whoever killed those girls dump their bodies here?" she asked.

"That's easy. Where's the best place to hide a body?"

"In a graveyard?"

"Exactly. And that's what happened here. If the corner of that slab hadn't cracked and fallen off, they might never have been discovered."

"So can we go home? Back to the hotel, I mean?" Angela asked.

Bronson shook his head. "Not yet. We'll have to make statements, obviously, and my guess is that the investigating officers will want to speak to us before they'll let us leave."

He looked across at the tomb, which was now isolated behind a perimeter of tape to prevent anyone approaching it. Several tripod-mounted floodlights had been positioned around the scene, illuminating the grave in the evening darkness. A technician, wearing white coveralls and latex gloves and with slip-on booties covering his shoes, was standing just outside the tape, carrying a powerful digital camera. As Bronson watched, he shot at least a couple of dozen pictures of the grave from various angles, moving around the perimeter to do so. Then he ducked under the tape, took several close-up shots of the tomb from all sides, then finally stepped closer still and took several more shots of the interior through the gap in the slab.

"Why don't they just take the slab off the top?" Angela asked.

"They will, of course, but first they'll want to gather as much information as they can about the scene. There might be footprints around the grave, though that's a bit unlikely on this surface. They'll want to dust the slab for fingerprints, and thoroughly examine the immediate vicinity of the tomb for any possible clues—objects the perpetrators might have dropped, fibers from their clothing, tool marks on the slab, all that kind of thing. They'll probably just be wasting their time, in my opinion, because they've no idea how many other people might have passed this way since the bodies were dumped here, and of course last night was the Festival of the Dead, when the number of living on the island probably outnumbered the dead."

"You think those poor girls were left here before the festival yesterday, then?"

"Judging by the condition of their bodies, I do. And I think if there are any clues to be found, they'll be inside the tomb, and probably on the corpses themselves. But until the officer who's been appointed to lead this investigation arrives here, they certainly won't open the grave."

The carabinieri sergeant walked back to where Bronson and Angela were sitting, a uniformed constable following behind him.

"This officer will now take a written statement from you, Signor Bronson, and from your companion," he said.

About ten minutes after Bronson had read and signed his own statement, and had translated into Italian Angela's much shorter statement—which basically corroborated what he had said—and she had signed it in her turn, another half dozen men arrived at the scene, one of whom was immediately approached by the sergeant.

The two men talked together for a few minutes; then the sergeant pointed toward Bronson and Angela. The other man followed his glance, and nodded. Then he walked across to look closely at the tomb, the sergeant following. Even from where Bronson was sitting, perhaps twenty yards away from the tomb, the smell of putrefaction was unpleasantly strong, and he wasn't surprised at the expression of distaste on the senior officer's face as he moved forward to the hole in the slab and peered inside, a small but powerful flashlight in his hand. Then he stepped back and walked briskly away from the grave.

Bronson and Angela seemed to have been temporarily

forgotten, and although Angela wanted to get back to the hotel, Bronson was keen to stay, at least for a few minutes more, and watch the recovery of the bodies. And, as he pointed out, they hadn't yet been told that they could leave.

The Italians were working in much the same way as English police officers would have done in the same circumstances. Once the tomb was opened, the photographer moved forward again to record the scene. He was followed by several of the investigating officers and a man Bronson thought was probably the pathologist. Only then was the first body lifted out of the grave and transferred immediately into a body bag.

Bronson used Angela's digital camera to record the operation.

"What are you doing?" she muttered in disapproval.

"I'm making a record of what's happening," he replied. "Just in case."

"Just in case what?"

"I don't know, but this is a peculiar situation we're involved in, and having a photographic record seems to be a good idea."

With the first body removed, more photographs were taken, and then the operation was repeated to lift out the second corpse, and then the third. Once all three body bags had been closed, the unpleasant smell began to dissipate, and several of the Italian officers removed their face masks. Further checks were run on the tomb, and it was carefully searched for any other possible clues.

"I'll ask the sergeant whether we can go now," Bronson said at last.

With Angela beside him, he walked around the taped-off tomb and approached the investigating officers.

"Is there anything else you need from us?" Bronson asked in Italian.

The sergeant glanced toward the more senior carabinieri officer. "Inspector Bianchi?"

The officer glanced at Bronson and Angela, looked as if he was going to speak, and then shook his head.

"You've both made statements," the sergeant said, turning back to Bronson, "and we know where you're staying, so that's it. Just try to keep away from graveyards for the rest of your time in the city. We really don't need any more bodies."

"I'll try," Bronson promised.

On the way out of the cemetery, they passed the vampire's tomb and Bronson noticed immediately that the position of the ropes had changed. Obviously the site had been disturbed.

Motioning for Angela to wait, he stepped across to the grave and lifted the base of the tarpaulin so that he could see inside the tomb. The few bits of wood from the coffin that had survived the passage of time were scattered around. There was even evidence of digging in the soil around the grave, and marks on the stone that suggested it had been hit by some hard metallic object, perhaps a hammer or a chisel.

Bronson dropped the tarpaulin back into place, and then rejoined Angela.

"What is it?" she asked.

"Somebody has searched that tomb," Bronson replied. "And I think we both know what they were looking for."

20

The hotel management had been most apologetic. They had no idea when the thief had broken into their room, or how he had managed to get past the reception desk without being challenged.

Actually, Bronson thought that getting past the receptionist desk would be the easiest part of the operation, but he hadn't said that to the duty manager who'd met them in the lobby with the unwelcome news.

They couldn't stay in their original room, obviously, because the door would no longer lock, or even close, so they'd been given a slightly larger room on the floor above instead.

The following morning, at breakfast, Angela was subdued, but clearly angry.

"Yesterday was horrible," she announced, as they finished the meal. "Do you really think that it was a random break-in?"

Bronson shook his head. "No, and nor do you. I think

most robberies in hotels are carried out by the staff, because they're the people who've got access to the room keys. Breaking down the door is rare, and it seems far too coincidental that our room was the only one in the building to be targeted."

"So you think they were looking for the diary?"

"That seems the simplest explanation, yes."

"So what are we going to do about it? Should we give the book to the police?"

"Definitely not. They've got their hands full, according to what I read in the local paper this morning. One of their most senior detectives was killed yesterday, gunned down in the street on his way to meet an informer. And in any case I'm not sure how interested the carabinieri would be in a two-hundred-year-old diary written by some woman who thought she was a vampire. In fact, I'm not sure why anybody, apart from perhaps a social historian, would have the slightest interest in it." Bronson shook his head. "But the reality is that somebody seems desperate to get their hands on it."

"Do you think it could have anything to do with the bodies of those three poor girls you found in that tomb?"

"Frankly, no," Bronson replied, "apart from the coincidence of the two graves being quite close together. I don't see what link there could be between a woman who's been dead for two hundred years and a serial killer operating in Venice today."

He drank the last of his coffee. "So what would you like to do today?" he asked. "And, before you tell me, we'll be sticking together. I'm not prepared to risk you being targeted because somebody wants that diary."

"That's what I was going to suggest as well," Angela said. "We'll take the diary and my laptop with us again. And something else struck me about this attempted robbery—"

"I have a feeling I know what you're going to say," Bronson interrupted. "The only people who knew that we had been at the scene of that first vandalized tomb were the carabinieri. I talked to two of them in the cemetery that night, and then two other officers appeared here at the hotel the following morning. As far as I know, nobody outside the Venetian police force has any idea who we are or how we're involved."

"Exactly. And that doesn't exactly fill me with confidence." She sighed. "I still wish I knew why somebody wants that diary."

"I might have a theory about that as well," Bronson said, and reached into his jacket pocket to pull out a folded sheet of paper. "I found this story in the newspaper archives, in the international news pages. Apparently there was some kind of a road improvement scheme on the outskirts of a Czech town called Český Krumlov. When the workmen dug up a piece of land as part of their road-widening operation, they found an early-eighteenth-century grave containing eleven bodies. That's not unusual, but what puzzled them was the way three of the corpses had been buried.

"According to this article, bodies were usually laid to

rest lying in an east-west direction, but these three had been positioned so that they lay from north to south. And one skeleton had been treated in exactly the same way as the body we saw in the grave on the Isola di San Michele: it had been decapitated, the skull placed between its legs, and a stone rammed into its mouth. All three of the skeletons had been pinned to the ground with heavy, flat stones, and another one had a hole in the left side of the chest directly above where the heart would have been, which was consistent with the sternum having been pierced by a sharp object. The article doesn't actually say that it was a wooden stake, but that's pretty obviously what they think did the damage."

Angela nodded, staring at the picture that accompanied the story. "It sounds like a typical vampire burial. Quite a few of these have been recorded, most often from places like Czechoslovakia and Hungary."

"And there's an interesting postscript to the story you've got in your hand. In the last paragraph it says that they took the skeletons to Prague, but before the remains were transported, somebody broke into the building where they were being kept and stole several bones from each body. Someone seems to be collecting vampire relics—those bones in Czechoslovakia, the head from the grave here in Venice—and they're obviously after that diary as well."

"You're talking like there's some kind of vampire conspiracy," Angela said, smiling.

"Well, it's the only explanation that seems to fit the

facts. Look"—he leaned forward across the table—"you and I both know that the vampire myth is exactly that—a myth. But I'm beginning to think that there are people right here, in this city, who not only think vampires are real creatures of flesh and blood, but who are actively trying to collect relics from them. And maybe they're even trying to become vampires themselves. It bothers me."

"You and me both," Angela said. "You really think there are people who are that deluded?"

"Well, somebody's certainly collecting relics, and they're doing it now. That's unarguable."

Angela shivered. "I'm beginning to think that coming to Venice for a holiday was a really bad idea. We might have had a quieter time in Transylvania, the way things are going."

Half an hour later, they left the hotel together, and made their way through the streets toward the city center. They'd decided to walk first over to the Piazza San Marco, and then explore the Castello district, before picking up a vaporetto from the Celestia stop that would take them back to their hotel.

Bronson was very aware of their surroundings as they walked through the narrow streets of the Cannaregio area, but he saw nobody who concerned him.

They crossed over the Grand Canal into the Santa Croce district on the Ponte degli Scalzi, which literally translated as the "bridge of the barefoot monks" and was one of only four bridges which spanned the Grand Canal. Suddenly, the door of one of the tall houses that lined the street was pushed open directly in front of them and a man stepped out. He was so close that Bronson and Angela had to step quickly over to the left to avoid walking into him. The man turned toward them, his face and voice full of apology.

But even as Bronson tried to wave aside the man's explanation, he was suddenly aware of two other figures emerging through the open doorway behind them. He reached out to try to protect Angela, but before he could pull her to him, something crashed into the side of his head, and he fell senseless to the ground.

21

Marietta Perini stared in horror at the cockroach climbing up the wooden leg of her bed. It was almost the size of a rat, easily the biggest insect she had ever seen. She lay still, clutching the filthy blanket in both hands, paralyzed with terror, because that was just the vanguard of the attack. From the other side of the bed, by the stained concrete wall, dozens of enormous insects were climbing up toward her. She could see their probing antennae above the edge of the mattress, could hear their feet scratching as they drew closer to her.

Then the first cockroach reached her feet and, with a sudden spurt, ran straight under the blanket, heading for her bare legs. She felt the insect's horny carapace rubbing along the side of her calf, felt the movements of its legs as it moved up her body, but she simply couldn't move an inch. Then a tidal wave of cockroaches swept across the edge of the mattress, heading straight toward her, and finally she found her voice.

She screamed, the noise echoing off the walls of the cellar, and suddenly found she could move. She threw the blanket from her body and jumped off the mattress onto the floor, the chain attached to her left wrist wrenching her arm back as she did so.

And then she woke up. For a few seconds she stood stock-still, panting with terror, eyes wide as she stared around her, looking at the nightmare that had become her reality. There were no giant cockroaches, of course, but there were three or four of the insects scuttling about on her bed.

With an expression of disgust, Marietta flicked them off with the blanket, and checked the mattress and her clothing carefully before she got back onto the bed. She hadn't expected to sleep at all, her mind whirling with images of insects and rats, and whatever that nameless creature was that she'd heard howling the previous night, and what sleep she'd gotten had been restless and disturbed, punctuated by vivid and disturbing images.

Then her thoughts shifted, changing direction, and an image of her boyfriend's face swam into her mind. He would be worried sick about her. He had always been possessive, perhaps too possessive, forever wanting to know where she was, where she was going and whom she was with. In the past she'd found it slightly irksome—she was, after all, a liberated Venetian woman—but right then she thanked her stars for Augusto's personality. He would, she knew, have tried to contact her, to call her mobile, when she hadn't arrived at his apartment that evening as they'd arranged. Then he would have called her parents, and after that he would have raised the alarm.

Somewhere out there, beyond the island, the search would already have begun. People—a lot of people— would be out looking for her by now; of that, she was certain.

She thought of her parents, sitting in their small apartment at the northwestern end of Venice, near the railway station, worrying about her, wondering where she was and—knowing them as she did—probably fearing the worst. More than anything else, she wished she could see them again, or at least talk to her mother one last time. But that, she knew, wasn't going to happen.

Tears sprang to her eyes, and she wiped them away angrily, because she'd just heard the cellar door rumble open. She didn't want to show any sign of weakness, of emotion, to her captors. It wouldn't make any difference to her fate, but keeping up her calm facade gave her something—some tiny bit of pride and strength—to hang on to.

One of the guards stepped into the cellar and walked across to her, a plastic tray in his hands.

"Why are you keeping me here?" Marietta asked, as the man lowered the tray to the floor and turned to walk away.

"You'll find out," the guard snapped, as he'd done on every previous occasion. But this time, as he turned to leave the cellar, he looked back toward her for the briefest of instants with something like pity in his eyes, and added a single bleak sentence that drove all other thoughts from her mind. "You'll find out tonight, because we've just found the second one."

22

Bronson opened his eyes, and immediately closed them again against the glare of the sun. For a few seconds he had no idea where he was or why the side of his head ached so appallingly. When he lifted his arm to touch his skull, his hand came away red with blood. He levered himself up onto one elbow and opened his eyes again. For the first time, he became aware of a small group of people surrounding him, their faces grave with concern. Two men were kneeling on the ground beside him. One was repeatedly asking him something, while the other was trying to help him up into a sitting position.

Bronson reached again toward the injury on his head, then suddenly realized that he couldn't see Angela. This drove all other thoughts from his mind, and he staggered clumsily to his feet, staring around him.

"Gently, signor," one of the men said. "You've had a bad fall. We've called for an ambulance."

But Bronson wasn't listening. Angela was nowhere in

sight, and a sickening realization dawned on him: the men who had attacked him had taken her. He quickly took stock of his situation. He didn't know exactly how long he'd been unconscious, but it could only have been a matter of minutes.

"There were some men with me," he said to the man standing closest to him, "and a woman. Did you see where they went?"

"No. I only saw you lying on the street."

Bronson stared at the building from which he'd seen the man emerge, seconds before he'd been attacked. Shaking off the restraining hands of one of the men, he walked somewhat shakily across to the door, and tried the handle, but it was locked. That, too, was unsurprising.

For a few seconds, Bronson tugged at the handle in impotent fury, and then his rational mind reasserted itself. The one place in Venice where Angela certainly wouldn't be was inside that building. He had no doubt his attackers had dragged her inside as soon as the assault had taken place, but she'd have been within its walls only long enough for them to subdue her, and then they'd have taken her to some other secure location. Both the streets and buildings in that part of Venice were narrow, and many of the houses ran from one street to another. By now, she could be in any building or even on a boat, heading for another part of the city or out to one of the islands.

"The ambulance boat will be here soon," one of the men said. "You need to have that wound examined."

Bronson shook him off. His head ached, but already the bleeding seemed to have diminished, and he was fairly certain there was no serious damage. In any case, he had other priorities.

Until that moment, he had thought they'd been dealing with two unrelated sets of incidents. A person or group of people obviously wanted the vampire diary that Angela had lifted from the tomb on the Isola di San Michele, and there appeared to be a serial killer operating in Venice. Now the appalling possibility hit Bronson like a hammer blow: suppose, just suppose, that the serial killer and the man looking for vampire relics were one and the same.

And now Angela might be in his clutches.

Bronson knew that scenario didn't really make sense. Virtually all documented cases of serial killers showed quite clearly that they invariably worked alone, or at most as a pair. And the attack that had just occurred had involved three people—the decoy, the man who'd opened the door right in front of them and distracted Bronson, and then the two men who'd emerged from the building behind them.

The much more likely probability was that Angela had been grabbed because she had the diary, and once they'd taken that from her, the chances were that they'd let her go. Rationally, Bronson knew this made sense, but that didn't help calm his almost frantic worry for her safety.

Now that he was on his feet, and able to talk, several of the people in the group started to drift away. But a couple of the men remained behind. For the briefest of instants, Bronson wondered if they'd actually been a part of the attack, but then he dismissed the idea as ridiculous. If they had been, there was always the chance that he might recognize one of them.

Again, Bronson shrugged off their concerns. He needed to call the police and find Angela. The sound of an approaching ambulance siren on the canal galvanized him into action. He knew his head wound needed treating, but this was very much a secondary concern. He picked up the padded bag containing Angela's laptop—at least he still had that—which had dropped from his shoulder when he was attacked, and walked away from the scene as quickly as he could. The moment he was around the corner, he took his mobile phone out of his pocket and called the police.

Ninety minutes later, Bronson was at the Ospedale Civile—the local hospital in the Castello district—sitting on a hard chair, his hands gripping the armrests, as a young Italian doctor closed the cut on the side of his head with metal clips. When he'd arrived at the hospital, his wound had been cleaned, the hair around it cut off and that section of his scalp shaved. A couple of shots of local anesthetic had been pumped into the torn and bruised skin, and then the metal sutures applied. Stitches, apparently, were rarely used these days, the metal staples—at least, that was what they looked and felt like to Bronson—being the preferred way of closing up a wound.

The emergency operator had been more interested in the attack Bronson had suffered than in Angela's disappearance, but Bronson's insistence and concern had finally convinced her to connect him with an officer in the carabinieri. Bronson had given the man a brief description of Angela, and had explained the circumstances of the attack.

It helped that Bronson knew the ropes. He'd provided the best possible description he could of the man who had stepped out in front of them in the street. Unfortunately, though, he had seen him for only a matter of seconds, and his description—a man of medium height, average build, with dark hair, wearing glasses and dressed in a light gray suit—would probably fit several hundred men in Venice. And as for the men who had carried out the attack, he could offer no description at all, except for his impression that they were both about his height—around six feet tall—with dark hair.

Frankly, Bronson couldn't care less about the three men. His only interest in them was as a possible route to finding Angela. The officer, who'd met Bronson at the Ospedale Civile and ensured his injury had been attended to as quickly as possible, had taken careful note of his description of Angela, and had radioed it to the dispatcher for immediate dissemination to all carabinieri officers in Venice and on the mainland.

"We'll find her, Signor Bronson," the officer said reassuringly, closing his notebook.

"I'm sure you'll try," Bronson snapped. "But what

worries me is the number of young women who've vanished from the streets of Venice over the last few months, women who've left no trace, and who've never been seen again."

The officer seemed surprised that Bronson knew what had been happening in the city.

"That isn't confidential information, is it?" Bronson said sharply. "I checked the local newspaper archives, and about a dozen girls have disappeared over roughly the last eighteen months. And you can add another one to that total if you count the girl who vanished a couple of days ago, and one more if you include Angela. I want her found," he added, his voice cracking with the strain, "before some maniac dumps her body in a tomb on the Island of the Dead."

The officer looked even more surprised. "How do you know about that?" he asked.

"I was the one who found them," Bronson said shortly. "Now, you know precisely where and when my partner was abducted. I know Venice has a lot of buildings, and a hell of a lot of places where a person could be hidden, but it's also quite a small city. So please, please, do your best to find her for me."

Bronson's eyes had suddenly filled with tears, and it wasn't just because of the doctor driving home the final staple into his scalp.

23

Marietta had barely touched the meal her captor had brought down for her at lunchtime. All she could think of were his last words. What lay in store for her that night? She felt physically sick with dread, her body numb with fear.

When the cellar door rumbled open sometime later she absolutely knew that something out of the ordinary was going to happen. She still had no weapon to defend herself, nor any form of protection; all she could do was what she had done almost every time any of the men had entered the cellar: she sat very upright on the edge of the bed, staring toward the base of the spiral staircase, and waited to see who was coming toward her.

Whoever it was seemed to be carrying something heavy, because she could hear the confused sound of footsteps clattering down the stairs, rather than the measured tread she had grown accustomed to.

A sudden piercing scream, obviously a woman's, tore

through the still air of the cellar, and Marietta jumped. Then she heard a cracking sound that had become only too familiar—the sound of a Taser being discharged—and the scream ended as suddenly as it had begun.

Moments later, the guard and one of the other men who'd abducted her stepped into view, dragging the unconscious form of a young woman between them. Neither man so much as glanced toward Marietta as they hauled the body past the end of her open room.

Because of her restricted view, Marietta couldn't see where they took her, but the sounds she was hearing suggested they had entered the cell right next to hers. There was a dull thud, which she presumed was the noise of the men dumping the unconscious girl on a bed, followed by a clanking sound and a click—the handcuff being secured around the girl's wrist.

After a few seconds, the two men reappeared, and the guard stopped for a moment at the entrance to Marietta's room.

"You've got company at last," he said, an unpleasant sneer on his face. "She's the one we've been waiting for. Now we can get started."

24

For about twenty minutes after the men had left the cellar, the only sound Marietta could hear from the adjacent room was a dull moaning. The girl, whoever she was, had clearly reacted badly to being shocked by the Taser, and was taking a long time to recover.

Eventually the girl's breathing grew more regular as the effects of the high-voltage current she'd experienced subsided, and Marietta could hear her starting to move around on the bed. She left it another couple of minutes, then called out to her.

"Who are you?" The girl's voice was tremulous, racked with fear and uncertainty.

"My name is Marietta Perini. Who are you?" She echoed the girl's question.

"I'm Benedetta Constanta. Where am I?"

"Didn't you see where they brought you?" Marietta asked.

"I was just outside my apartment when a man walked

up and fired something at me. The next thing I knew, I was in some ruined church. I started fighting and struggling, and they shot me again."

It sounded as if Benedetta had taken a lot longer to recover her senses than Marietta, or maybe the men who'd taken her had used a higher voltage in the weapon.

"They snatched me in just the same way as you, but I was conscious for most of the time," Marietta said. "We're on an island out in the lagoon, but I've no idea what it's called. It's not very big, and I think the only buildings on it are a house and the ruined church that you saw. We're in the cellar under that church."

"But what do they want with us? Have they—you know—attacked you?"

Benedetta didn't use the word "rape," but Marietta knew that was exactly what she was thinking.

"They haven't touched me," she said, trying to keep her voice steady. "They've fed me regularly, and brought me warm water and soap so I can wash. But the nights are the worst—it's very cold and dark, and I . . . I keep hearing things. . . ."

"How long have you been here?"

"About two days. I think it's Wednesday today, and I was on my way to see my boyfriend in Venice on Monday evening when I was attacked." Marietta wrapped her arms around herself to stop the shivering. "He'll be wondering where I am. What happened—"

"What do they want from us?" Benedetta interrupted harshly.

Sitting on her bed on the other side of the old stone wall, Marietta shook her head. "I don't have any idea," she said, rubbing the tears from her eyes. Her voice broke as her mind vividly replayed the last words the guard had spoken. "But I think we're going to find out very soon."

25

Bronson had been discharged from the hospital, and was walking slowly back toward Cannaregio. He was conserving his strength, because the attack—both the physical assault and the sheer shock of the event—had left him feeling weak and unsteady.

And as he walked, he looked everywhere, desperately searching for some sign of Angela. He knew that what he was doing was essentially pointless, but he did it anyway. Whoever had snatched her, and whatever their motive, he was certain that she was now either hidden inside a building somewhere in the city or being held on one of the dozens of outlying islands. The chances of her still being somewhere on the streets of Venice itself were nil. But still he kept looking.

It took him well over an hour to get back to their hotel, because of his slow progress and the meandering route he'd taken. When he arrived and walked into the lobby, the receptionist gave him a somewhat startled look, her attention fixed on the white bandage and thick pad that covered one side of his head. Bronson ignored her and went slowly up the stairs.

He paused for a second in the corridor outside their room, hoping against all odds that somehow Angela had managed to escape and that she'd be waiting for him inside. But as he pushed open the door, he saw at once that the room was completely empty.

The rooms in that hotel didn't have minibars, and he knew that consuming alcohol wasn't a particularly good idea after what he'd been through that day, but at that moment all he really wanted was a good stiff drink. He put down the laptop bag, took another look round the room, locked the door and then walked back down the stairs to the hotel bar. He ordered a gin and tonic, and took the drink over to a corner table by one of the windows that offered a view of the street outside the hotel.

He took a long swallow of his drink, and gazed through the window at the pedestrians strolling by, at the Venetian businessmen mingling with the press of tourists, cameras raised to faces that were partially obscured by hats and sunglasses. Bronson stared at the throng, searching vainly for Angela.

After a few moments, he took out his mobile and stared at the screen for what felt like the hundredth time that day. There were no missed calls, no text messages.

His head told him that the Italian police would be doing everything they could to find Angela, and that the only thing he would achieve by calling them would be to raise their level of irritation. His head knew this, but his heart didn't agree, and almost without thinking, he dialed the mobile number he'd been given—as a courtesy and simply because of his job—by the investigating officer.

The ensuing conversation was short and fairly brusque. Yes, all carabinieri officers in the area had been given a description of Angela and a copy of her passport photograph. Yes, an officer would leave Angela's passport at the hotel reception desk later that day. And, finally, yes, he would definitely be the first to know if and when they found a trace of her.

Bronson ended the call with a sense of immense frustration. He wasn't used to being on the other side of a police investigation, and the lack of any hard information was difficult to handle. He was sure that the Italian police were searching for Angela, but how many men had they deployed? Were they checking cars and trains leaving Venice? Had they detailed men to check the vaporettos and gondolas and the privately owned speedboats that buzzed up and down the canals and across the lagoon? Were they searching the outlying islands? He had no answers to any of these questions, and he knew that the carabinieri officer would refuse to tell him, just as he, Bronson, would be unwilling to answer similar questions from a member of the general public in Britain under the same circumstances.

He finished his drink and sat for a few moments, his head in his hands. Then he roused himself. Getting drunk wouldn't help find Angela, nor would moping around the hotel. Walking the streets looking for her would achieve nothing, because he knew she wouldn't be there. But he had to do something, something constructive, something that might help the police effort. He toyed with the idea of visiting some of the quieter canals, just in case the abductors hadn't yet smuggled her out of the city, but a moment's thought showed him that that idea would also be a waste of time. Venice wasn't that big a city, but there were miles of canals, and he wouldn't be able to cover more than one or two of them.

That started a new train of thought. One thing he could do was to ensure that he was as mobile as possible.

Standing up, he walked out of the bar and across to the reception desk. The pretty dark-haired girl who'd checked them in was on duty, and gave him a welcoming smile as he walked across the lobby.

"Signor Bronson, what happened to your head?" she asked, looking with concern at the bandage around his skull.

"I had a bad fall; that's all," he said, deciding not to tell the staff what had happened to Angela.

"Can I help you with something?"

"We'd like to explore the canals. Is it possible to hire a speedboat for three or four days?"

"Of course. It will take me a little while to arrange, because this is a popular time of year in Venice, and I may have to try several hire companies. Will you be taking the boat outside the city? Into the lagoon, I mean."

"I might, yes. Does that make a difference?"

"Only to the type of boat. If you're going into the lagoon, you'll need one with a more powerful engine. Please leave it with me, Signor Bronson, and I'll see what I can find. Will tomorrow morning be soon enough?"

Bronson would have preferred to get his hands on a boat right away, but he replied, "Perfect. Thank you."

He waited while the girl noted down details of his credit card, gave her a smile that was completely at odds with the inner turmoil he was feeling, then walked back up the stairs to their room. He hadn't done much, but already he felt better, simply knowing that by the morning he would be able to navigate his way around Venice reasonably quickly.

He lay down on the bed for a few minutes, his eyes wide-open, staring at the ceiling. What could he achieve? he wondered. Yet again, he replayed the events of the day, trying to remember any clues or indications that might help the carabinieri narrow the search. But he came up with a blank.

Then something struck him. Because the gang of men had grabbed Angela, they would now have the vampire's diary in their possession. Could there possibly be any information contained within it that might suggest where they were likely to go next? If, for example, the diary mentioned another grave, and if the people who'd snatched Angela were hunting for relics, he could suggest to the police that they could mount a watch on that location.

It was thin enough, but as far as Bronson could see, it was the only useful thing he could do.

He got up from the bed, took Angela's laptop out of its case, and plugged the power cable into the wall socket. Angela hadn't switched off the computer, and as soon as he opened the lid, the system resumed operating. A screen saver appeared, and when Bronson touched the space bar to clear it, a dialog box popped up requesting the input of a password. He hesitated for a few moments, then typed "SealChart" into the space, and pressed the enter key. Angela always used the same password—the name of the church in Kent where they'd gotten married—and Bronson felt a sudden lump in his throat as the system accepted the password.

Angela, he thought. I can't lose you now, not after everything we've been through. I'm going to find you if it's the last thing I do.

26

Marietta jumped as the dull rumble echoed through the cellar; she knew what that noise meant. She moved to the edge of the bed and sat there, waiting. This time it sounded as though more than one person was descending the stone spiral staircase.

"What is it?" Benedetta sounded terrified, and Marietta didn't feel much better.

"It's the door at the top of the stairs. Someone's coming," she replied, not taking her eyes off the opening that marked the base of the staircase.

The sound of footsteps drew closer, and then two men stepped into view. Marietta could have wept with relief as she saw the guard approaching her carrying a towel and a metal bucket, the contents of which steamed slightly.

The guard went straight over to where Marietta sat, and placed the bucket on the floor in front of her.

"Wash yourself," he instructed curtly, then turned and left.

The other man, who had presumably delivered a bucket and towel to Benedetta, followed him from the room.

"What do we do now?" Benedetta asked, her voice trembling with fear.

"We do what they tell us," Marietta said.

Ten minutes later, the guards returned, carrying two bundles of white material, one of which they tossed onto Marietta's bed, the other one onto Benedetta's. One of the men removed a key from his pocket and the Taser from another, and then stepped forward.

"Give me your left hand," he said. "I'm going to release your handcuff so you can get changed. If you try anything, you'll taste the Taser again. Do you understand?"

Marietta nodded. "Get changed into what?" she asked. "What for?"

"You're to put on that white robe I've given you and get ready for the ceremony. Take off all your other clothes. All of them—your underwear as well. And then wash your whole body again. You have to be clean."

Releasing her handcuff, he stepped back. "Now, get on with it," he snapped. "We haven't got much time. The ceremony must begin on time."

27

Bronson was no further forward. He was unfamiliar with Latin, and had spent most of that time reading through Angela's translations of the pages of the diary, looking for something—anything—that might give him a clue about what had happened to her. He looked at the computer screen, his gaze unfocused, as he mentally relived the events of the previous two days, and the macabre mystery that they had become embroiled in. The desecrated tomb; the vampire's diary; the dead girl in the cemetery; the three corpses jammed into the grave; the burglary of their hotel room; and, finally, the attack on Bronson himself and Angela's abduction. Running through the sequence of events, two things immediately stood out.

First, the desecrated tomb and the vampire's diary were clearly important, very important, to somebody in Venice. The only reason, he was convinced, that he'd been attacked was so that the group of men could grab the diary, and they'd needed to get him out of the way first. But what he still didn't understand was why they had taken Angela as well.

Then he remembered his conversation with the carabinieri officer in the cemetery on San Michele. He'd mentioned to the Italian that Angela worked for the British Museum and, actually, that might provide some kind of a motive. Because of the burglary at the hotel, Bronson was fairly sure somebody in the Italian police force had leaked the information about where they were staying. Maybe her kidnappers had also learned that she was an archaeologist, and believed she could help them translate the text in the diary.

It was a stretch to reach that conclusion, but why else would anyone want to kidnap an Englishwoman who spoke almost no Italian? Bronson immediately felt better, because it suggested an alternative to the only other reason why Angela had been kidnapped: that she'd been grabbed by a serial killer who was operating in Venice. And that was a possibility he simply wasn't prepared to face.

The second factor that seemed obvious to him now was that the Isola di San Michele, the Venetian Island of the Dead, was inextricably linked with what had been going on in the city.

This set Bronson thinking about the four dead girls whose bodies had been found in the cemetery, and he decided to take a look at the pictures he'd taken out on the island, to see if there were any visible clues on the corpses. As he transferred the images from his camera onto the laptop—Angela had already downloaded all the still images and video films from her digital camera onto the hard drive—he acknowledged the possibility that he'd been trying to avoid ever since the attack, that the girls had been killed by the same people who were accumulating the vampire relics.

Setting his misgivings aside, Bronson concentrated on the images that were now appearing on the screen of the laptop. When he'd taken the video of the police recovering the body of the first girl on the island, he'd been trying to use the camera as inconspicuously as possible. The inevitable result was that the video was jerky and frequently didn't actually show the scene he'd been trying to capture.

He watched carefully as the two men emerged from behind the temporary screen carrying the body on a stretcher, and then saw a police officer step forward and unzip the body bag. The dead girl's tumble of blond hair filled the screen as Bronson had used the camera's zoom lens to focus on her face. For the briefest of instants he saw her forehead, her open left eye—at the moment of death, the eyes don't close serenely the way they do in the movies, but remain open and staring—the side of her face, her cheek and part of her neck.

Something struck him about what he was seeing, and he wound the movie sequence back to the point just before the police officer unzipped the body bag. Then he ran it forward in slow motion. This helped clarify what he was seeing, but he still couldn't be certain. So he ran it again, this time advancing the video film frame by frame.

Three of the frames offered him the clearest possible view of the dead girl's face, and he examined each of them carefully, enlarging one particular section to study it more closely.

The girl's skin was marred, almost freckled, by dark marks, which Bronson guessed were either dried blood or earth from where her body had been dumped; the skin itself was mottled with the first signs of decomposition. But there were several marks that he didn't understand, but which filled him with unease.

Bronson closed down the video and searched the hard drive until he found the pictures that he'd taken with Angela's camera of their discovery of the three dead bodies in the cemetery and the subsequent events.

The first image he opened was the shot he'd taken through the hole in the slab over the grave. It was, by any standards, an extremely gruesome picture. The image showed the stone sides of the grave, the ancient coffin lying on the floor of the tomb, and the naked and decaying bodies of three young women dumped on top of it. Unsurprisingly, given the circumstance in which the picture had been taken, it was a little out of focus, and the flare of the automatic flash meant that some parts of the scene were so brightly lit that little or no detail was visible. But the upper corpse, the girl who'd been put in the grave last, was reasonably clear. Bronson enlarged the part of the picture that showed her head and neck, and studied it closely for some minutes. Then he sat back in his chair and shook his head. What he was seeing just didn't make any sense.

In both the images he enlarged, he'd found what looked like the same type of injury: on the sides of the girls' necks puncture marks stood out. He frowned. When any animal—a dog, a cat or a human being—bites, both the upper and lower jaws are involved. If it's small enough, the object being bitten will have marks on both sides.

The twin puncture wounds used by Hollywood directors to portray the bite of a vampire are impossible to make unless the vampire's mouth is capable of entirely encircling the neck of the victim, something that is at best extremely unlikely. In fact, any creature with jaws the approximate size and shape of the human mouth, whether equipped with oversize canine teeth or not, would leave bite marks on the side of a human neck completely unlike the neat twin puncture wounds of the classic vampire mythology.

The most likely shape of such a wound would probably be two semicircular marks made by the jaws, probably with deeper wounds where the longest teeth would have sunk into the flesh. And if the bite was delivered powerfully enough, quite probably the skin and flesh might be bitten through to leave an almost circular wound. And that, Bronson realized, was exactly what he was staring at in these photographs.

It looked to Bronson as if the people who were col-

lecting vampire relics were far from the bunch of harmless
nutters that he and Angela had assumed. Whoever they
were, they'd clearly moved a long way beyond just collecting old books and ancient bones.

The girls in the cemetery might have been enthusiastic
members of the group, for whom it had all gone badly
wrong. But Bronson doubted it. He thought it was far
more likely that they were innocent victims on whom the
vampirists—for want of a better description—had been
feasting.

The very idea was manifestly ridiculous, but Bronson
couldn't doubt the evidence before his own eyes. And
what he'd seen on those images lent a still-greater ur-
gency to his search for Angela, because he now had no
doubt that she was in the clutches of a group of people
who had killed at least four women already, and would
presumably have no qualms about increasing that tally.

28

Getting washed when the only equipment at hand was a bucket of lukewarm water and a small bar of soap was difficult enough. Doing so standing up in front of a stranger—a man—who was staring at her body with unconcealed lust was one of the most unpleasant experiences of Marietta Perini's short life.

She began by trying her best to conceal her private parts from his gaze, but quickly realized that this was impossible. Eventually she just ignored him, never looked in his direction, and pretended that she was alone. When she'd finished and dried herself, the guard nodded his approval.

"Very good," he said. "Now put on the robe. Don't bother with any underwear. You're not going to need it."

Shaking with fear, Marietta pulled the robe on over her head; then her captor snapped the handcuff back around her wrist, securing her to the wall of the cellar once again.

Then he walked out of the room to the adjoining cell, and repeated the operation with Benedetta, who initially refused point-blank to take off a single item of clothing. But her resistance ended moments later when the crackle of the Taser told its own story. When she'd recovered she washed and put on the white robe, but Marietta could hear her sobbing in terror and fury as she did so.

As soon as Benedetta had finished dressing, the guard turned to leave the cellar. But before he could walk across to the foot of the stone spiral staircase, another sound intruded into the relative silence of the cellar. Somebody, or something, was coming down the steps, but the noise sounded more like a kind of slithering than footsteps.

Marietta stared across the flagstone floor, trying to see who it was. Then she noticed that the guard seemed incredibly uncomfortable, almost scared. He'd moved back until he was almost standing against the wall opposite, and he, too, was staring fixedly toward the entrance to the cellar.

Then a figure entered the chamber. Clad in an all-enveloping black robe, the hood pulled forward to obscure his face, hands invisible in the long sleeves, the new arrival moved a few feet forward and stopped.

Marietta was immediately conscious of a sharp and unpleasant odor, and then a feeling, a sudden and completely irrational feeling, of abject terror. Never before had she felt that she was standing in the presence of such unremitting and undiluted evil. And she knew that, whoever it was, he was staring straight at her. She could feel his eyes, still invisible under the hood, roaming up and down her body.

The figure turned toward the guard and asked a question, his voice soft and sibilant, the words inaudible to the two girls. The guard took a couple of hesitant steps forward, pointed at Marietta and then spoke.

"That is the Perini girl, Master," he said. "The other one is Constanta. She has the strongest bloodline. Both are linked to Diluca."

The figure looked back toward the two girls, and appeared to nod, although the large hood made it impossible to see a definite movement of his head. Then he glided—that was the word that sprang unbidden into Marietta's brain—across the floor and into Benedetta's cell. There was a sudden high-pitched scream, followed by the sound of terrified sobbing.

A few moments later, the figure reappeared, and Marietta caught a glimpse of his left hand as he moved past the open entrance to her cell. It was only fleeting, but just enough for her to see he had unusually long fingernails and white skin mottled with age spots.

The figure pointed back to Benedetta's cell, and said something in his soft voice. The guard nodded, but didn't move until the hooded figure had crossed to the cellar doorway and vanished.

Marietta was the first to find her voice. "Who was that?" she demanded.

"It's probably better that you don't know," the guard said. "It's better that no one knows."

*   *   *

"Are you OK?" Marietta asked, as soon as he'd gone. "What did that man do to you?"

For a few moments Benedetta didn't respond. Then she spoke again, her voice tremulous with fear and loathing.

"He just touched me; that was all. He ran his fingers down my cheek, but his hand was like ice, freezing cold, and his breath—his whole body—simply reeked."

"I smelled something too," Marietta said, shuddering at the recollection, "but I didn't know what it was."

"He smelled like rotting flesh, as if he had gangrene or some hideous disease. It was all I could do not to throw up when he got close to me. And before that, the guard stared at me the whole time I was getting washed. I've never been so terrified in my entire life."

"That's all he did, though? He didn't do anything else to you, did he?"

"No. But I have a horrible feeling that all that's about to change. I think he's been told not to go near us, in case he sullies us. We've been saved for some kind of special event, haven't we? And it's going to happen tonight. Why else would we be told to wash and dress in this stupid outfit? Oh, God, Marietta. I don't want to frighten you, but somehow I don't think we're going to see tomorrow."

29

Angela came to slowly. Her head was throbbing, and when she tried to move her hands she couldn't. Unaccountably, they remained by her side, as if she was held by some kind of restraint. There was something tied around her thighs as well, and she could feel a pad or bandage wrapped round her head and covering her eyes.

She could sense people around her, could hear figures moving and talking in a language she didn't understand. For a few moments she assumed she must have had some kind of accident and was in hospital. That would explain the noises, certainly, but she had no recollection of how she'd gotten there.

What had happened to her? She remembered being in the hotel, remembered leaving the building and walking down the streets with Chris at her side. Then her memories became more confused. There had been a man, and a door suddenly opening right in front of them. And then something else had happened but she couldn't clearly remember what. There had been other figures, men crowding around her, a dark room or maybe a passageway, then nothing.

Where was Chris? And where was she, come to that? Angela suddenly went cold as the realization finally dawned on her. She wasn't in any hospital. She was somewhere far, far worse.

The murmur of voices around her ebbed and flowed. The only thing she was sure about was that they were speaking Italian. She recognized the musical cadences of the language, if nothing else.

Then she felt hands doing something to the bandage that was wrapped around her head; moments later the pad was lifted away from her face and she opened her eyes.

High above her was a white ceiling, decorated with elaborate cornices and moldings, and with a large electric chandelier providing brilliant illumination. It was the kind of ceiling you might expect to find in the drawing room of an English country house. But the one thing she was certain of was that she was a long way from England.

She seemed to be lying flat on her back on a wide sofa, her wrists tied with lengths of cord; and cord was wrapped around her upper thighs too: a simple and effective way of immobilizing her. Standing in a rough circle around the sofa were about half a dozen well-dressed men, all looking at her and talking quietly together. Their expressions were neither hostile nor threatening: they simply looked down, regarding her as though she was a strange life-form they'd not previously encountered, which Angela found far more disturbing than blatant aggression would have been.

"Who are you?" Angela asked, her voice cracking with tension.

But the men just continued to look at her, with no hint of understanding in their faces.

Angela tried again. "Where am I?"

"You're on an island in the Venetian lagoon," a new voice replied in accented English, and the circle of men parted to admit another figure.

He was, like the other men in the room, smartly dressed in a dark suit. He looked as if he was about forty years old, with the dark hair and complexion that characterized many Italians. His features were regular, unmemorable, almost pleasant, but his eyes were cold and dispassionate as he approached her.

She looked up at him, fixing her attention on the man simply because he appeared to be the only one in the room who understood—or at least the only one who spoke—English.

"What island?" she asked.

"Its name isn't important. It's a private island in a secluded part—a very secluded part—of the Laguna Veneta."

"What do you want with me?"

"Your help, at least to begin with."

"What kind of help?" she asked.

"Professional, of course. You and your husband re-

moved a book that was not your property." He held up
the fragile leather-bound diary Angela had taken from the
old tomb on the Isola di San Marco.

"I'm not sure it's anybody's property," Angela said,
more annoyed now than scared. "The grave we found it
in was about two hundred years old, which means anything in it cannot possibly belong to anyone living today."

"I'm not going to discuss the legal status of the pos-
sessions of a corpse with you," the man snapped. "We
have spent a considerable amount of time and money trying to find this book, only to have you walk off with it."

Angela struggled to sit up, then realized it was impossible. The man issued a brief instruction, and two of his
companions removed her bonds and helped her to lean
against the back of the sofa.

"Why was it so important to you?" Angela asked.
"And who are you, anyway?"

"You don't need to know that."

Suddenly, Angela realized she had no idea where Chris
was or what had happened to him on the street.

"Where's Chris?" she asked, the pitch of her voice rising as anxiety swept through her. "The man I was with.
I'm not going to do what you want until you tell me what
happened to him."

The man smiled then, but it wasn't an expression of
reassurance, rather a look of mild and disinterested
amusement, the kind of look an indulgent parent might
bestow on a wayward child.

"I've no idea where that man is right now," he said. "I

don't even know whether he's alive or dead. When my men left him, he was unconscious—he had taken a nasty blow to the head. That might have been enough to kill him, or caused brain damage, or perhaps only given him a really bad headache. Frankly, I neither know nor care. It simply doesn't matter."

"It matters to me," Angela snapped.

"Well, it won't for much longer. We know that you work for the British Museum in London and—"

"How do you know that? How do you know that I work for the museum?"

"We have our sources. And that's the only reason you're here. You must have looked at the book you took from the tomb. If you did, you'll know why it's important. Now you'll supply us with a translation of what it says."

Angela shook her head. "I'm not a linguist," she said. "I work with ceramics. And in any case, that book is just a diary."

"How do you know that," the man asked mildly, "if you can't read Latin?"

"OK, I'm fairly familiar with Latin, and I did translate some of it. But what I said is true: it's just a diary."

The man shook his head. "That book is far more than just a diary. The first section is a chronicle of events, yes, but that isn't the part we're interested in. It's the last dozen or so pages—what's written there is very different."

"I didn't do more than just look at that section," Angela pointed out.

"Well, now you're going to translate all of it."

"Why? What could possibly be so important in a two-hundred-year-old diary? Important enough to justify all this?" Angela made a sweeping gesture to encompass the entire house and whatever lay outside the building.

"We're looking for something."

"I guessed that. What?"

"A source document. A document that's older, hundreds of years older, than this diary. Twelfth century, in fact."

Despite her situation, and her worries about Bronson, Angela felt her pulse quicken. Once history grabbed you, it never let go, and ancient texts had always held a special fascination for her.

"What document?" she asked.

An expression that could have been a smile flickered across the man's face. "We don't know what it's called, but we do know that it exists. Or at least that it existed."

"How do you know?"

"Because we've seen copies of copies of different parts of it—many of them to some extent contradictory. We believe that this diary might tell us exactly where to look for the original."

Angela frowned. "I don't understand. This diary—or whatever you want to call it—was written by a woman almost two centuries ago, and has been locked up inside her tomb since she died. How can you possibly know it contains information about this other document?"

"We've always known about the diary. We just didn't know where it was. The Paganinis were somewhat notorious in Venice, and we've studied the family archives. Carmelita Paganini's tomb was the next place we wanted to search, but we didn't know where it was."

"It looked to me as if somebody had erased her name from the slab covering the grave," Angela said.

"Exactly. Carmelita was an embarrassment while she was alive, and even more so when she was dead, at least to some members of the Paganini dynasty."

"The brick in the mouth? They thought she was a vampire?"

"A primitive attempt to destroy her, but completely pointless. Carmelita Paganini wasn't a vampire—she just thought she was. She spent her life trying to achieve that nobility, but it's clear she never managed it. The crumbling bones in her grave are proof enough of that."

"*Nobility?*" Angela asked.

The man smiled again. "That seems to us to be an entirely appropriate term to use when referring to a higher form of life, to something superhuman."

Angela opened her mouth to deliver a sharp retort, but then she glanced around at the other men and thought better of it.

"So this source document," she asked instead. "What do you know about it?"

"We don't know its name, so we just call it 'the

Source.' It was written in the early twelfth century, apparently by a lapsed monk who lived in part of the country that's now called Hungary."

"It was called Hungary then as well," Angela pointed out. "It's one of the oldest countries in Europe."

The man shrugged. "Whatever. We've found several references to it in various archives, and some of them talked about a book written by Carmelita Paganini. According to one contemporary account, she'd not only seen the original text, the source document itself, and incorporated some of the passages into her diary, but also knew where it was hidden. That's why we've been so keen to find it, and why you'll now assist us by translating Carmelita's diary."

"And why should I help you?" Angela said. "You've attacked me on the street and kidnapped me. What makes you think that I'll do anything to help you?"

"I'm sure we can persuade you. I think you're right-handed," the man replied, "so we'll start with your left hand."

Angela stared up at him, her blood turning to ice. "What do you mean?" she demanded.

"Let me show you," the man replied. He turned to one of the other men and issued a crisp instruction in Italian.

After a few moments the second man returned, carrying a jar perhaps six inches high and three or four in diameter, fitted with an airtight lid. It looked to Angela like a small version of one of the old Kilner jars her mother had used years ago for preserving fruit. Inside it was an almost colorless liquid in which several small pale objects were submerged.

"What's that?" Angela demanded.

"I suppose you could call them souvenirs," the man said, moving the jar closer to Angela's face. "You're not the first person we've needed to—what shall we say?—*motivate* to assist us with the translations and other matters."

For a few moments Angela stared at the objects inside the jar uncomprehendingly; then she recoiled with a gasp of disgust. What she had first assumed were some kind of vegetables—carrots, perhaps, or parsnips—were actually the severed joints of human fingers.

"Every time you refuse to do what we ask, we'll remove a part of one of the fingers on your left hand," the man continued. "You won't bleed to death, because we will cauterize the wound with a soldering iron. One of my men particularly enjoys doing the amputations. He uses a pair of bolt croppers if he's in a good mood. But if you annoy him, he'll do it by clamping your finger between a couple of pieces of wood and using a hacksaw. That takes longer, and there's a lot more blood, but he doesn't seem to mind that."

Angela tore her horrified gaze from the revolting contents of the jar and looked up into the man's face. "You utter bastard," she muttered.

The man shook his head. "Abuse won't help you," he said. "In fact, nothing can help you now. You've seen our faces, and we simply can't afford to let you tell anybody else what you've seen."

For a few seconds Angela just sat there, numbly digesting the explicit threat. Because this was the point. She *had* seen their faces, and she knew with a terrifying sense of certainty that she would never be allowed to leave the island alive.

The man—whoever he was—had just casually delivered her death sentence.

30

The cellar door rumbled open, the light snapped off and the door closed sharply. Benedetta gave a little cry of shock and surprise.

Marietta shrank back onto the bed. It was the first time the light had been switched off since the morning after her arrival, and the action alarmed her.

For a few seconds the only sound in the cellar was the breathing of the two girls; then Benedetta gave a low moan. "What's going to happen to us?" she murmured, her words barely audible. "I'm so frightened. Why has the light gone off?"

"I don't know," Marietta replied, a tremor in her own voice.

A few minutes later they heard the familiar rumbling sound as the stone door at the top of the spiral staircase was opened again.

"Somebody's coming," Marietta said. "They'll put the light on before they come down."

But she was wrong. They heard the sound of footsteps, several footsteps, descending the stairs, and saw a flickering glow that grew brighter with each passing moment. Then a figure walked into the cellar.

He was clad in a very dark robe, tied at the waist with a cord, a hood covering his head. It was a foul parody of a monk's habit, but Marietta had no doubt his thoughts were anything but godly. The man held a lit candle in his right hand, and the flickering flame cast a fitful light over his features. Staring at him in horrified silence, Marietta made out a large, bulbous nose, a heavy jaw and dark, sunken eyes.

Then she looked behind the man and saw that he was simply the first in a procession of figures, perhaps a dozen in total, all dressed in the same dark hooded robes, and each carrying a large candle. The tiny, dancing yellow flames—the only illumination in the room—cast an eerie glow over that end of the cellar. The third man in the line was also carrying an ornamented wooden box, about the size of two shoe boxes, and apparently not very heavy.

From her doorless cell, Marietta had a good view of what they were doing. The line of men—and she was sure that they were all men—filed slowly from the staircase entrance over to one end of the cellar, where they formed a circle around the stone table positioned there. For a few seconds nothing happened; then the figure holding the box took a pace forward, lowered it carefully onto the table and stepped back again. The other figures stood in silence, waiting expectantly.

A familiar rumble echoed through the cellar. The door at the top of the stairs was closing. Then Marietta heard another sound, and literally shook with terror. The slithering noise coming from the spiral staircase could mean only one thing: the man who had so frightened both her and Benedetta was coming back into the chamber. Moments later, he appeared in the cellar, and a pungent odor suddenly filled the confined space.

The figure paused, looked over toward the cells where the two girls were imprisoned, then made his way toward the hooded men, who each bowed low as he passed.

The man took up his position at one end of the circle, looked around at his companions, then raised his left hand in a casual gesture toward the man who'd been carrying the small box. He, in turn, bowed low again, stepped forward to the table, and carefully lifted off the box's lid.

That action seemed to act as a catalyst for another of the men, who left the circle and walked behind his companions, lighting another half dozen or so large candles mounted in freestanding candlesticks, each about five feet tall, illuminating the table, and allowing Marietta to see more clearly. His task completed, the figure returned to his place in the circle. Then four of the other figures moved, each removing what looked like a length of rope from his robe, and stepped forward to thread it through one of the holes driven through the four corners of the table. Then they too moved back into position.

Marietta found the silence that had accompanied these

actions unnerving. Clearly, the men were following a well-rehearsed and predetermined sequence of actions. No orders or instructions needed to be given, because every man knew his place and what his function was.

The man who had carried the box down the stairs now reached into it and extracted what looked almost like a deep soup bowl, which he placed on the table in front of him. He then took out a short object with a rounded end and placed that inside the bowl. As he did so, Marietta heard the characteristic sound of stone striking stone and, rather to her surprise, realized that what she was looking at was a mortar and pestle.

The figure closest to the box raised both his arms high above his head, and Marietta could sense the anticipation from the other men around the table.

Slowly, he lowered his hands, put them inside the box, and took out a small, round object, brownish in color. This he lifted high above his head, holding it aloft for a few seconds, then replaced it on the table directly in front of him.

Suddenly Marietta saw exactly what it was. The vacant pits of the eye sockets, the twin vertical lines marking the position of the nose, and the white line of the teeth were unmistakable. The object they appeared to be worshipping was a human skull.

What happened next was even stranger. The man holding the skull took a pair of pliers from the pocket of his robe and used them to snap off a small piece of bone, which he lifted up and showed to the assembled group.

Then he placed it in the mortar and began to grind it up, the noise of the operation echoing around the room.

After a few minutes he removed the pestle and handed it and the pliers to the man standing beside him. Then he picked up the mortar with both hands and lifted it high above his head, and as he did so the other men around the table bowed their heads. Next, he walked round the circle to the man who'd been the last to arrive, the apparent leader, bowed low and showed him the mortar. The man looked closely at its contents and inclined his head, whereupon the man holding the mortar bowed again, walked slowly back to his original position and placed the object on the small stone table behind him, a table that Marietta had noticed when she'd first entered the cellar.

Now the atmosphere changed, and an almost palpable thrill of excitement, of anticipation, seemed to emanate from the silent figures. The hooded ringleader bowed his head briefly and stepped back from his position. All of the other men bowed in turn, and stepped back, away from the table. Then the hooded man hissed a single instruction, which Marietta heard clearly: "Bring the first girl."

Two of the men bowed, left the group and walked toward the cells where Marietta and Benedetta were being held. Marietta retreated as far as she could and gripped the wooden head of the bed firmly with both hands, determined not to give up too easily. But the men ignored her and entered Benedetta's cell.

The other girl howled in fear, her scream echoing around the cellar. Marietta half expected to hear the crackle of the Taser, but the two men simply manhandled the girl out of her cell. As they dragged her, wriggling and screaming, past the open entrance of Marietta's cell, Benedetta stared with terrified eyes at her fellow captive, begging her to come to her rescue. But Marietta could do nothing for her.

The two men stopped at the table, holding Benedetta firmly by her wrists and upper arms. Two other men stepped forward, one in front of the girl and the other behind her, and seized hold of the white robe she was wearing. Simultaneously, each man tugged the material, and the two halves of the garment parted, leaving Benedetta completely naked.

There was a sudden collective intake of breath from the men surrounding the table as they saw Benedetta's naked body for the first time. She was, Marietta saw immediately, very beautiful.

Trembling, Marietta felt the seams of the robe she was wearing. They were thick and bulky, and when she pulled at one, it emitted a characteristic ripping sound. She realized that the seams were made from Velcro, precisely so that the robe could be torn apart in this fashion.

Marietta looked back at the scene in front of her. Benedetta was screaming even louder now, the sudden shock of being stripped naked adding immeasurably to her terror. But the other participants in the ritual were proceeding in silence, their movements measured and organized, despite the girl's yells and struggles. Benedetta was forced forward until she was standing at the end of the table. Then the men turned her round until her buttocks were pressing against the stone. Two other men stepped forward and grabbed her ankles, and then she was lifted bodily and deposited in the center of the table and held there, squirming helplessly.

Then the reason for the ropes on the table—which Marietta could now see were actually leather belts— became obvious. Working with practiced ease, the men holding Benedetta in place swiftly lashed the belts around her ankles and wrists. In seconds, the girl was strapped down on the table, spread-eagled across it, as helplessly as a butterfly pinned to a display board. But still she writhed and screamed, tugging helplessly at her bonds.

The dark-robed figures standing around the table gave no sign that they could even hear her. They just looked down at her struggling naked body, the flickering light from the candles they still held giving their features a demonic cast.

Another two men stepped forward and stopped one on either side of Benedetta's head, which Marietta suddenly realized was resting on the small stone extension, the extension that she'd noticed when she'd first seen the table. And suddenly the purpose of the table was all too clear. One of the men held Benedetta's head still while the other strapped a leather belt around both her forehead and the stone, and then cinched it tight to prevent her from moving.

Yet another man approached the table, a funnel and a small bottle held in his hands. He walked across to Bene-

detta's head, placed one hand on her chin to force her
mouth open, and pushed the funnel between her teeth.
Then he removed the stopper from the bottle and poured
a white liquid into the funnel.

Benedetta coughed and choked, but only when the
bottle was empty did the man remove the funnel and step
back.

Immediately, the girl started to scream again, spitting
out some of the white liquid. But then the man who'd
tightened the belt around her head produced a pad of
white material, positioned it over her mouth and secured
it in place with adhesive tape.

Terrified and nauseous, Marietta simply couldn't take
her eyes off the scene in front of her: the wriggling, helpless figure of a girl she barely knew, and the cold and
haughty appearance of the men—and she'd now counted
thirteen of them—who surrounded her. Men who were
about to do something unspeakable to their innocent victim, and Marietta feared that she, too, would have to
endure the same fate within minutes.

With Benedetta's cries now reduced to little more than
a whimper, the silent figures drew closer, so close that any
of them could have reached out and touched her body.
But clearly rape was not their objective, Marietta thought.
That, at least, was a small mercy. Then even that assumption was shattered when the hooded man issued another
quiet instruction to the man on his right, and he, in turn,
pointed at two of the silent, robed men.

One of them bowed in response, handed his candle

to the man next to him, then stepped out of the circle and pulled his robe over his head. Underneath it, he was naked apart from his sandals, and Marietta could see immediately that he was completely prepared for the act he was about to perform. He folded his robe to form a pad, placed it between Benedetta's legs as a cushion for his own knees, pulled on a condom, climbed onto the stone table, lay on top of the girl and thrust himself into her.

Then the second man removed his robe as well, opened a small packet and took out a condom, clearly waiting for his turn on the table with the girl.

Marietta could hear Benedetta's muffled howl even through the gag, but then her attention switched to the hooded man, who had moved for the first time since he'd joined the others at the table, and watched him walk over to the girl's head. Behind him, another man followed, carrying what looked like a large white ceramic bowl. Marietta noticed that the attention of all the men around the table was not on the girl, but instead on what their leader was about to do.

She strained to see what was happening, but the old man bent down and his body completely blocked her view. What he did next provoked another agonized moan from Benedetta.

There was almost complete silence in the cellar, just the rhythmic pounding of the naked man riding Benedetta on the stone table, and her muffled cries of pain.

Then Marietta heard a new sound, a kind of sucking noise.

And then, as the hooded man moved to one side and half turned toward Marietta, she recoiled in shock. Even in the gloom of the cellar, illuminated only by the flickering light of the candle flames, she could clearly see the long pointed canine teeth gleaming white in his open mouth. They had to be false, inserted in his mouth for the ceremony; they just had to be. Marietta's brain wouldn't accept any other explanation.

For an instant she thought he had a beard, and then realized, with a further jolt of terror, that the dark, almost black, discoloration covering his chin and the sides of his mouth was fresh blood.

At last Marietta saw the appalling fate that awaited her. On the right-hand side of the other girl's neck was a round wound, and her blood was flowing freely from it into the bowl beneath.

Marietta couldn't help herself. She threw back her head and let loose a scream that was deafening in its intensity, a howl of absolute terror and utter dismay. The men turned as one to look at her, even the one lying on top of Benedetta, and their leader responded with an angry gesture.

One of the group walked swiftly over to Marietta, grabbed the front of her robe at the neck and ripped it forward and down, the seams parting instantly to reveal her naked torso. He pulled out a Taser from his pocket, held her around the throat so she couldn't wriggle free, placed the electrodes of the device between her breasts and pulled the trigger.

A surge of current ripped through her body, sending her limbs into spasm, and a moment later she slumped backward and fell to the ground unconscious.

31

Bronson had barely slept a wink. Every time he'd closed his eyes, a horrific full-color image of Angela, blood streaming from a ragged wound in her neck, had flooded his consciousness. Just after six in the morning he gave up, climbed out of bed and got ready for whatever the day might bring.

He was keenly aware that there was nothing useful he could do. Angela's fate was completely in the hands of the carabinieri, and what really bothered Bronson was that he was certain somebody in the police force was leaking information to whoever had taken her. But there was nothing he could do about that, either, because in Italy he had no official standing, and he was familiar enough with the labyrinthine ways of Italian bureaucracy to know that registering a complaint would achieve absolutely nothing, except to make any further cooperation with the carabinieri almost impossible to achieve.

As far as Bronson could see, the only thing he could

do was again study the book Angela had retrieved from the tomb on the Isola di San Michele, and hope he could identify something in it, some clue, that would help him find her. He didn't know much Latin, although he recognized that the Italian language he loved so much had been derived from it. But Angela had downloaded a Latin-English dictionary from somewhere on the Web, and he supposed he'd be able to use that to translate some of the entries in the diary.

He switched on Angela's laptop, checked the signal strength on his mobile phone, and left his room, locking the door behind him.

He was the first guest to step into the dining room for breakfast. He wasn't hungry—he rarely had much of an appetite in the morning—but he knew he ought to eat something. He poured himself a cup of coffee and picked up a couple of croissants from the buffet, then carried them over to their usual table, and ate them while he stared through the window at the early-morning bustle. Then he drank a second cup of coffee before returning to their room.

The first thing he did was to read all the notes and translations that Angela had already prepared. He'd done the same thing the previous day, but nothing of importance had struck him. Then he started looking at some of the Latin sentences on later pages in the book. As Angela had said, most of the text seemed to consist of diary entries, but toward the back of the book he found a separate section that looked rather different. There were no dates or times or places listed, only paragraphs of closely written Latin text.

Bronson looked at these paragraphs for a few minutes, picking out the odd Latin word that he recognized, then decided it probably was worth trying to make a reasonable translation of the text. But he'd barely even begun when his mobile phone rang.

For an instant his heart pounded with anticipation. Could it be Angela, calling him to let him know she'd been released by her captors?

"Chris Bronson," he said.

There was a pause and then a heavily accented voice spoke to him in English. "Signor Bronson. My name is Filippo Bianchi, and I'm a senior Venetian police officer. I may have some bad news for you."

"Tell me," Bronson replied in Italian, sitting down heavily on the bed.

"I'm sorry to have to tell you this, but a body has just been found," Bianchi replied, switching to his native language, "and it matches the description you gave of your former wife. We would like you to come to the police station in San Marco, which is near the mortuary, to identify the corpse."

Time suddenly seemed to stop, and Bronson had the bizarre sensation of the room closing in around him, constricting his chest and driving the breath from his body. For a few moments his mouth opened and closed, but no sound emerged. A loud and continuous beep sounded in his ear.

Then he regained control and took a deep breath. He realized he was clutching the phone so tightly that his fingers were pressing down on some of the keys. He released his grip slightly, and the beeping sound ceased. He gazed at the wall opposite, a tumble of emotions coursing through him.

"Give me the address," he said, and noted down what Bianchi told him. Then he ended the call.

For a few seconds, Bronson sat motionless on the bed, his mobile phone still in his hand. This really couldn't be happening, he told himself. Angela simply could not be dead. Their week's holiday in Venice—a simple break from the routine of England—had turned into a nightmare that seemed as though it would never end.

Then he roused himself. He didn't want to go to the police station or the mortuary, but he knew he had no choice. Opening his map of Venice, he quickly found the location of the police station. He slipped the map into his jacket pocket and headed back down to reception.

Ten minutes later, Bronson stepped into the red-painted powerboat the hotel receptionist had arranged for him, started the engine, put it into gear and steered it away from the side of the canal.

It was still fairly early in the morning, and the water traffic was light, though as usual the streets around the canals were crowded with pedestrians, many of them obvious tourists. Less than a quarter of an hour after he'd set off from the hotel, he moored the boat in a canal about a hundred yards from the police station and walked slowly over to the building, subconsciously delaying the moment of his arrival there, as if that could possibly make the slightest difference to the outcome.

The mortuary was in an adjacent building, and Bronson was led there by Bianchi himself, who'd been waiting for him near the reception desk in the station. Bianchi was a bulky, heavily built man in his midfifties, and Bronson recognized him at once—he'd been the senior investigating officer who'd appeared on the Isola di San Michele to investigate the three dead bodies that he and Angela had found in the tomb there.

It wasn't the first time Bronson had visited a mortuary, though he'd never before been in the position he was in now. Normally, he was the presiding police officer, waiting for an anxious relative to confirm the identification of the body lying under a white sheet. He saw immediately that the Italians did things in much the same way as the British.

The viewing room was cold, much colder than the air-conditioned chill he'd experienced when they'd walked through the doors and into the mortuary, but it wasn't just the chill in the air that made Bronson shiver. It was a small oblong space, three walls painted white and the fourth entirely invisible behind a deep purple curtain, behind which he knew would be the fridges that held the bodies. A large but simple crucifix adorned the wall beside the door, and a row of half a dozen uncomfortable-looking metal and plastic chairs lined the adjacent wall.

He registered all that as soon as he walked in, but what gripped and held his attention was the sheeted corpse lying on a trolley directly in front of him, in the middle of the room.

Bianchi strode across to one end of the body and positioned himself there, a mortuary attendant beside him. Bronson stepped closer to the trolley.

"Are you prepared, Signor Bronson?" Bianchi asked.

Bronson took a deep breath and nodded.

The police officer gestured to the attendant, who released a safety pin from the sheet covering the body, and gently pulled back the material that covered the face of the corpse.

Bronson noticed the hair first. Blond and about shoulder-length, the way Angela normally wore it. Then his gaze moved slowly down her face, noticing the closed eyes, small nose and wide, generous mouth. He took a step closer to the trolley, to the midpoint of the dead body, and for a long moment stared down at the woman's pale face, her skin white and waxy.

"Signor Bronson, can you confirm whether or not this young woman is your wife?" Bianchi asked quietly.

Bronson looked up at the police officer and the silent, unsmiling mortuary attendant standing next to him.

"Yes," he said. "I can."

32

Marietta awoke slowly in the darkness of the cellar. For a few seconds she had no recollection of where she was, but then she moved her left arm and the rattle of the chain and handcuff brought the hideous knowledge flooding back.

Instinctively she glanced down at her wrist, but her watch had been taken, so she had no idea what time of day or night it was. The last thing she recalled was the surge of current from the Taser, a bolt of electricity so powerful that she'd lost consciousness. But she also knew, because of her previous experiences with the weapon, that she recovered quite quickly from it. So something else must have happened to her afterward, because the cellar was now still and quiet and absolutely dark, and she couldn't see any sign of the silent and malevolent figures who'd so terrified her.

And what of Benedetta? The last image, burned indelibly into her brain, was of the girl strapped down on the table, one man violently raping her while another collected the blood pouring from the wound on her neck. Had she survived? Or was she lying dead, her body even then growing cold on the stone table, or on the rough wooden bed in the adjacent cell?

"Benedetta?" Marietta whispered. There was no response. She repeated the name, raising her voice. Still there was no reply. As the echoes of her calls died away, a deep silence fell once again. It sounded as if Marietta was entirely alone.

Tears filled her eyes, and panic gripped her as she remembered the way Benedetta had suffered at the hands of their captors. And with that memory came a sense of confusion. Because they'd both been prepared for the "ceremony," Marietta had assumed that, once the men had finished with Benedetta, she would have suffered the same fate.

She reached up and felt her neck, her sensitive fingertips tracing the skin on both sides. It felt bruised. This didn't surprise her—the memory of the man with the Taser grabbing her throat was still very vivid—but she could feel no evidence of a wound or any other damage. And she knew that she hadn't been violated. So when they'd finished with Benedetta, they hadn't come for her. Why not? And why had she remained unconscious for so long?

With her right hand, Marietta gently explored her body. She was naked—the white robe must have been ripped off after the Taser hit her—and somebody had then dumped her on the bed and tossed the rough blanket over her body. She felt her left arm. Where the veins ran close to the surface of the skin, in the crook of her elbow, it was sore, and she guessed that she'd been given an injection to knock her out.

But this didn't explain why she, too, hadn't been raped and her lifeblood drained. Had the men been interrupted? That was pretty unlikely, because they were on a remote island in the Venetian lagoon, where the only access was by boat or possibly helicopter. There was almost no chance, she knew, of anyone appearing there unexpectedly.

In fact, she could think of only one reason why she was still in the cellar and still alive: the hooded men must have gotten enough blood from Benedetta to satisfy their repulsive desires and hadn't needed hers as well. In which case, Benedetta must surely be dead.

Marietta shuddered. She'd been granted a temporary reprieve, but her prolonged and violent death would surely follow, as inevitably as night follows day. In fact, she guessed she had less than twenty-four hours to live.

The realization hit her hard. Ever since she'd been abducted, she'd been clinging to the hope that somehow she'd be able to escape. But what she'd witnessed just hours before had finally extinguished even this faint comfort.

Shaking with fear, Marietta curled up into a ball underneath her coarse, damp blanket and squeezed her eyes tightly shut, sobs racking her body as she gave way to the utter despair that overwhelmed her.

33

In the mortuary, the three men stood in a rough circle around the trolley, staring down at the violated body lying on it, but their thoughts and feelings very were different. Bianchi was professionally distant and reserved, concerned only with the proper identification of the young woman whose death he would now have to investigate. The attendant was bored, if anything. But Bronson was trembling with emotion, so much so that he barely heard Bianchi's next words, and the inspector had to repeat himself.

"So you can confirm that this is the body of your wife, Angela Lewis?" he again asked softly.

"No," Bronson said, a lot more firmly than he felt. "I can confirm that I've never seen this woman before in my life. This is definitely not my wife."

"But I thought . . . I mean, your description? Her hair, eyes, skin color?"

"It's a good match, but this is definitely not Angela."

Again Bronson looked down at the body lying in front of him; then he reached forward, toward the neck of the corpse, around which a padded bandage had been placed, and tugged down on the material. Immediately, the mortuary attendant pushed him back and started smoothing the bandage back into position, but by then Bronson had seen enough.

The girl's neck bore a large oval wound, the flesh cut and bruised around it, the blood faded to a dull red-brown color.

"Signor Bronson," Bianchi snapped, "kindly remember where you are. Do not try to touch the corpse."

Bronson looked at him levelly. "Her skin's very pale," he said. "Was she killed like the others? Her blood drained from that wound in the side of her throat? Is that why you've put that dressing there?" He pointed at the bandage the attendant was still repositioning around her neck.

Bianchi stared at him in a hostile manner. "What are you talking about?"

"I was the man who found the three bodies dumped together in the tomb on the Isola di San Michele, the corpses you were sent out there to investigate," Bronson replied. "I'm a policeman, and when I smelled rotting flesh, I took a photograph through the hole in the slab covering the tomb. When I looked at the picture afterward, I could clearly see a mark just like that"—he pointed down at the sheeted corpse—"on the neck of each of those girls. And I saw the same thing on the body

of the other girl your men found out on San Michele. I
didn't find her, but I was out there, watching, when her
body was removed from the scene."

Bronson paused, looked again at the corpse on the
trolley, then back to Bianchi.

"What you've got going on here, right now, in Venice,
is the work of a serial killer." Then he shook his head.
"No. In fact it's much more complicated than that. I
think there's a gang of people who are snatching girls off
the streets, sucking the blood from their necks, and then
dumping the bodies."

By now Bianchi had recovered his composure. "What
you just said is a complete fantasy, a fabrication, Signor
Bronson. We have had some missing girls, it's true, and
we have unfortunately discovered some bodies, but all
this stuff about bloodsucking is complete nonsense."

The mortuary attendant reached out and started to
pull the sheet over the dead girl's face once more, but
again Bronson stopped him.

"Then take off that bandage so we can all see this girl's
neck," he snapped. "If I'm making all this up, then you'll
be able to tell me exactly what she died from, and you'll
be able to show me that her neck is unmarked."

"I don't have to show you anything, Signor Bronson,"
Bianchi responded sharply. "I asked you here because I
thought this body might be that of your missing partner.
I'm relieved for you that it's not her, obviously, but I still
have to try to identify this young woman and break the
news to her family. I'm certainly not prepared to discuss

how she died with you or with any other civilian. And here in Venice, that's what you are, Signor Bronson, just a civilian, a tourist. I suggest you remember that."

"I know exactly what my status is in Italy," Bronson said. "But I also know that if this poor girl didn't have a gaping wound on her neck, you'd be only too pleased to show me, just to prove me wrong." He pointed at the sheeted figure. "I saw her wound; I know that she died at the hands of these lunatics. And that makes at least five victims who have all been killed in the same way: massive blood loss from some sort of incisions made in the side of their necks, just like the sort of wounds supposedly inflicted by the vampires of fiction."

Bianchi raised a warning finger. "Signor Bronson, I suggest you refrain from repeating anything you've said here to anyone in Venice. If the newspapers start printing lurid stories, I'll know exactly where they got the information from, and I'll take great pleasure in arresting you."

"On what charge?" Bronson asked mildly.

"I'll think of something. Now, I suggest you get out of here, before you say anything else you might regret."

An hour later, Bronson was back in his hotel room. The diary Angela had taken was the key to her abduction, he was certain, and he was keen to get back to it. Locking the door firmly behind him, he switched on Angela's computer again, and opened up the scanned image of the final section of the book, the part that obviously hadn't been written in diary format. Then he opened Angela's translation of the first part of the text, and read it again. He remembered that one word seemed to be repeated over and over again, a word Angela had rendered as the "answer." That seemed to sit rather oddly in some of the sentences that she'd already translated into English.

But she'd obviously done more work on the book the previous evening, and had transcribed more of the Latin text, although none of this seemed particularly helpful. She'd also revised the translations that mentioned the "twin angels" tomb, and had clearly decided that a more accurate meaning of the "answer" would be the "source."

Bronson again read the passages Angela had translated. The text was specific about only one thing: that the tomb of the twin angels, the grave they thought they might have located in the cemetery on the Isola di San Michele, held the "answer" or the "source" or whatever the Latin word actually meant to the woman who'd written the diary.

It was odd, Bronson thought, the way the Island of the Dead seemed so intimately connected with the events they'd become involved with in Venice. The shattered tomb and the mutilated corpse had started the puzzle, and the cemetery had also been chosen as a dumping ground for the bodies of the girls once the group of killers had finished with them. And, of course, the vampire's diary itself had come from the first tomb, and contained references to at least one other burial on San Michele.

One way or another, the island and its ancient graveyard were inextricably linked to the events of the present day. Maybe, Bronson thought, he should go back there, take another look at that tomb of the twin angels, and see if he could work out anything useful from the inscriptions on the old stone. It wasn't much of a plan, and he wasn't sure it was even worth doing, but it was, he reflected, probably better than sitting in the hotel room trying to translate an old Latin text.

He shut down the computer, checked he had his camera and his binoculars, took his leather jacket out of the wardrobe, and walked down to the reception desk.

Half an hour later he was again sitting at the controls of his small red boat, and steering the small vessel northeast across the choppy waters of the Venetian lagoon.

34

Apart from a few visits to the restroom, each time accompanied by one of her silent and unsmiling guards to the door of a ground-floor lavatory—which had a barred window and no internal lock or bolt—Angela hadn't left the elegant room in the house since she'd arrived. Early in the evening, a tray of food had been put in front of her, and around midnight she'd eventually tried to get some sleep on the wide sofa in front of the fireplace.

But she hadn't been idle that evening. The suave but indescribably menacing man had seen to that. He had finally introduced himself as "Marco," but she had no idea if that was what he was actually called or just a convenient name he'd pulled out of the air.

As soon as he'd shown her the appalling collection of "souvenirs," Angela had realized that cooperation with her captors was hardly a choice: it was an absolute necessity if she was to avoid the agonizing mutilation that the group was so obviously capable of inflicting. So when Marco had asked if she was prepared to complete the translation, she'd simply nodded her agreement.

She'd been led across to a large oak desk set in one corner, and been told to sit on a leather swivel chair right in front of it, an incongruously modern piece of furniture in the elegant and old-fashioned room. Even those few steps across the polished wooden floor left her feeling as weak as a kitten; presumably she'd been pumped full of a cocktail of drugs to keep her quiet while they transported her to the house—wherever it was—and her body was still feeling the aftereffects. She knew that trying to fight her captors or run out of the room would be completely futile. Before she could do anything to try to escape, she would have to wait until she'd regained her strength. And she also needed to find out a lot more about the house in which she was being held prisoner, and its location. And especially what lay outside the windows.

On the desk was a selection of reference books of various types, the majority clearly written in English, about half a dozen pencils, roughly half a ream of white paper, the battered leather-bound diary itself, and two separate piles of pages, which she saw immediately were photocopies of the diary entries.

Marco had pointed to those two sets of pages. "Ignore the one on the left," he said. "Those are just records of Carmelita's life: interesting but not important for us. The other section is the one we're interested in. You can start translating that right now."

Angela shook her head. "I'll need a Latin dictionary," she said. "I don't have the vocabulary to translate this. Can you find one on the Internet for me?"

Marco laughed shortly. "We're not going to let you anywhere near a computer," he said. Then he searched quickly through the pile of books at the back of the desk and selected a Latin-Italian dictionary.

Angela opened her mouth to point out that she didn't speak Italian, but before she could say anything, he had found another dictionary, this time a Latin-English version, and the words of protest died in her throat.

"And when I've finished?" Angela had asked. "What then? You'll shoot me? Is that it?"

Marco had shaken his head. "I think we can find a more interesting way to usher you into the next life," he'd said. "But I do have some good news for you."

"What?"

"If you do a good job, you'll still be alive tomorrow. But after that, I can't promise you anything. And before you start work, let me point out that we've already translated some of the text ourselves, so we'll know if your version is accurate."

"If you've done that, then why do you need me at all?" Angela had asked.

"You English have an expression about a gift horse. If we don't need you to do the translation, then we don't need you at all, so just be grateful. But it's not just translating the Latin. There are some unusual aspects of the text that we haven't been able to make sense of. That's the real reason why we want you to work on it."

Without another word Angela had pulled the dictionary in front of her, picked up a pencil and looked at the first sentence.

35

Sometime that morning—Marietta had no idea exactly when—the upper door to the cellar rumbled open and the light snapped on.

A few moments later, the guard appeared in the room, carrying a tray of food exactly as he'd done on previous occasions, and a plastic bag that contained her clothes. He walked across to Marietta, tossed the bag onto the mattress, placed the tray on the floor in front of her, and turned to leave.

"Please," Marietta pleaded with him. "Please leave the lights on. And what happened to Benedetta? Where is she? And who was that man—the one with those horrible teeth?"

"So many questions," the guard said mockingly. "But you needn't worry about Benedetta. We got what we wanted from her."

"So where is she now? Did you let her go?"

"In a manner of speaking, I suppose we did. We sent her to San Michele," he added.

For a moment, Marietta didn't understand the expression. Then it dawned on her that he meant the "Island of the Dead," and the confirmation of what she'd feared hit her hard.

"You killed her," she said flatly. "That foul ritual last night. You raped her and bled her to death. You bastards."

"You catch on quick," the guard said. "But at least she died for a good reason. There was a point to her death, just as there'll be a point to yours."

"What point could there possibly be in snatching girls like me off the streets of Venice and then killing us?"

The guard looked at her carefully for a few moments. "You're not just any girl," he said. "You and Benedetta were both special. That's why you were chosen. We've traced your bloodline."

"My bloodline?"

"You and Benedetta are descended from someone who is vitally important to our society."

"And you're going to kill me because of one of my ancestors? That makes no sense at all."

"It does to us," the guard said simply. "You'll have company soon."

"Who?" Marietta asked, though she dreaded hearing the answer.

"Another girl. We've got her in the house at the moment, but she'll be brought down here soon enough. But she won't be able to talk to you. No girly chatter with that one."

"Why?" Marietta demanded. "What have you done to her?"

The guard smiled slightly. "Nothing at all," he said. "It's just that she doesn't speak a word of Italian. But don't worry. You won't be on your own for too long. Soon you'll be reunited with your friend."

For a moment Marietta sat in silence, eyes downcast, guessing what he meant but hardly daring to ask the question that would confirm her fears. Then she looked at him directly.

"What do you mean?" she asked.

"You'll be back with Benedetta," the guard replied. "It's your turn on the table tonight."

36

Bronson maneuvered the boat through the water along the northwest side of the Isola di San Michele, past a tall greenish sculpture, probably made of copper, which depicted two figures standing on a small boat that rose from the waters a short distance from the Cimitero vaporetto stop. That side of the island was delineated by impressive walls formed from white stone and brown brick, with a large gateway in the center and smaller towers spaced at intervals on either side of it.

He continued around the northern edge of the island to where his map showed a small inlet, lined with jetties.

He'd hardly even been aware of how the boat handled on his short trip to and from the police station in the San Marco district, but he'd gotten the feel of the craft on the journey out to the Isola di San Michele, and it had proved quite easy to control. Not quite as simple as driving a car, but not that difficult either. As he entered the inlet he pulled the throttle back, slowing the boat to little more than walking pace.

There were perhaps a dozen similar boats already moored at various points on the jetties, but there was still plenty of space left for him to use. He swung the boat in a half circle, so that the bow pointed back out toward the lagoon, then eased it into a stop beside the jetty. He stopped the engine, climbed out of the vessel and secured both the bow and the stern mooring lines. A few moments later, he was making his way toward the center of the old graveyard.

As he walked, Bronson tried to recall exactly where they'd found the tomb that Angela had believed was the one mentioned in the vampire's diary. The problem was that many of the sections of the cemetery looked fairly similar, and he was also approaching the area from a different direction, which meant it was difficult to get his bearings.

The good thing was that today the place wasn't crowded with tourists and locals, although on the far side of the graveyard he could see three separate funerals taking place. That morning the weather was clear, with unsullied blue skies, and the brilliant sunshine imparted a warm glow to the memorial stones, and even seemed to have breathed fresh life into the bouquets of cut flowers that decorated most of the graves. For the first time, the Isola di San Michele seemed a friendly, almost welcoming place to walk and explore.

Bronson remembered that the tomb he was looking for lay in one of the older sections of the graveyard, so he made his way to the spot where he thought the grave should lie, then stopped short as he reached the end of a line of trees and looked over to his right. He had reached a section of the graveyard with numerous ancient tombs of the type he was seeking, but what had caused him to stop was the sight of two men standing beside a familiar-looking carved statue.

Bronson eased back into the shadows cast by the trees, took his compact binoculars from his pocket, and stared through the instrument at the intruders. He adjusted the focus, and immediately confirmed one thing: the men were right next to the tomb of the twin angels.

For a few seconds, Bronson studied the two figures, noting what he could of their physical appearance. Both were wearing casual clothes, jeans and white shirts, but each also wore a Windbreaker, one blue and the other dark gray, which suggested to Bronson that they'd most probably arrived on the island by boat. Driving a power-boat at speed over the water could be quite chilly, and he'd been glad of his leather jacket on his own journey. Not that that deduction actually helped him in any way. The two men could easily be workers sent out to San Michele to do maintenance jobs, or even a couple of bureaucrats counting the graves or something equally mundane.

Bronson moved the binoculars slightly so that he

could see the tomb itself. From the angle he was looking at it, he could see one side of the structure, while the two men were on the far side, both of them looking down at the ancient stone. Then one of the men bent down beside the grave, and was lost to sight.

Bronson wondered if he should simply stroll through that part of the cemetery toward the grave he was interested in, playing the part of an innocent tourist, because he was still unsure about who the two men were. If they were just workers, he would be able to examine the grave without any problems, and if they were in some way connected with Angela's abduction, he might see them clearly enough to provide a photofit for the carabinieri. Or perhaps he could even follow them when they left the island. Either way, getting closer to the tomb seemed like a good idea.

He slipped the binoculars back into his pocket, stepped out from behind the tree, and started making his way across the grass that carpeted the area between the graves. He'd gone only half a dozen steps when he heard a sudden noise from behind him, and glanced back to see another man walking swiftly toward him through the graves. Instinctively, Bronson stepped to one side to allow the man to hurry past.

The new arrival nodded his thanks and stepped past Bronson. And as he did so, he abruptly turned and swung his right arm toward Bronson's head. But something in the way the man moved must have triggered some subliminal warning, because as he did so Bronson realized two things simultaneously: first, that the figure beside him was one of the men who'd attacked him in the street when Angela was abducted, and, second, that he was trying precisely the same technique again, swinging a heavy blackjack with the intention of smashing it into the back of Bronson's skull.

37

Angela had woken stiff and aching from her fitful sleep on the sofa, and had been allowed to wash in a bathroom adjacent to the lavatory she'd used the previous day. Her breakfast had consisted of a plate of pastries and coffee, and as soon as she'd finished it, Marco had told her to carry on working on the translation.

She had acquired her knowledge of Latin over the years that she'd worked at the British Museum, building on the lessons in the dead language she'd enjoyed at school, more years ago than she could now contemplate with any degree of comfort. But try as she might to concentrate on the words in front of her, her thoughts kept returning to the awful reality of her situation and, inescapably, to Chris. She had no idea whether he was alive or dead. If he was alive, if he'd survived the attack on the street, she knew he'd be trying to find her, and would be frantic with worry. But how on earth would he be able to track her down?

She had no idea how long she'd spent in a drug-induced state of unconsciousness, but it must have been several hours, perhaps even days, and it was entirely possible that she was no longer in Venice at all. Her only reassurance was that her captors spoke together in Italian, which presumably meant that she was still in Italy. But even that, she had to acknowledge, was actually pure conjecture. It was just as possible that she'd been snatched by a gang of Italians, and then taken to some other country entirely.

And she'd found the coolly dispassionate attitude of her captors enormously alarming. She really believed that any one of them could kill her with as little compunction or concern as he would exhibit if he swatted a fly. As far as she could see, the only reason she was still alive at that moment was because they needed her translation skills, and Marco—or whatever his real name was—had implied that they wanted only to see her version of the ancient text to check that whoever else they had employed to decipher it had gotten it right.

That meant they already had a good idea of what the Latin text said, which in turn meant that she had to do a reasonably good job herself. But not a perfect job, she decided. Perhaps she would make a handful of trifling errors in the translation—errors that she could explain away because of her unfamiliarity with Latin, and which might mean they would keep her alive for a bit longer while they ensured that she'd done the best job she could, and that the text she'd produced was accurate.

That was the only thing she could think of doing to make her abductors think twice before killing her. And the longer she stayed alive, Angela knew, the better the chances of her finding some way of getting out of the house—wherever it was—and escaping. And maybe somebody, Chris or the police or even the occupants of a neighboring property, if there was one, might discover where she was being held prisoner. It was a cliché, obviously, but it was just as obviously true: while there was life, there really was hope.

Angela dabbed her eyes angrily with a tissue, cleared her mind of all extraneous thoughts, and again focused on the task at hand.

Quite a lot of the Latin words were familiar to her. One of the advantages of learning Latin was that it had an essentially finite vocabulary, unlike English and other modern languages in common usage, which acquire new words, new meanings and new variants of existing words on an almost daily basis. Once you knew the meaning of a Latin word, you knew it forever, because it would never change.

She remembered most of the declensions and many of the conjugations of verbs, and she was able to jot down the general sense of several of the sentences quite quickly, leaving just a handful of blanks for the words that she was either unfamiliar with or unsure of. Then she'd open the dictionary and flick through the pages until she found the first word she needed to check. Then she'd fill in the meaning, and move on to the next word. When she'd finished each sentence she paused for a moment to read it in its entirety, to make sure that it made sense, then rewrote it in modern English.

The translation itself had proved to be relatively straightforward, but she soon realized what Marco had meant when he referred to "unusual aspects" in the text. Although the references to the tomb of the twin angels still seemed fairly clear, other passages in the Latin were ambiguous at best, and she was increasingly unsure whether or not she was getting it right. In some passages, Carmelita had referred to the Isola di San Michele as the *insula silenti*, the phrase translating as the "island of the dead," but there were several occurrences of an entirely different phrase—*insula vetus mortuus*—which puzzled her.

Her literal translation rendered this as the "island of the ancient dead" or "old dead," which she really didn't understand. It wasn't clear to her whether Carmelita was using the expression as a synonym for San Michele, or if she meant somewhere completely different, possibly a more ancient graveyard located elsewhere in Venice.

And there was another phrase that sent a chill through her. The pages referred to *planctus mortuus*, which translated as the "wailing dead" or the "screaming dead." "Dead," as far as she was concerned, meant exactly that: death, the cessation of life. The dead could neither scream nor wail. But the same expression appeared in several places in the text, and the context suggested that Carmelita was referring to a specific place where the dead had screamed.

Angela shook her head and continued working through the text.

38

When anybody asked him if he knew any of the martial arts, Bronson normally told them he had a black belt in origami—it amused him to see the conflicting emotions this statement usually produced. In fact, he'd trained to an intermediate level in aikido.

Perhaps the most unusual, and certainly the least known, of the oriental fighting techniques, aikido is purely defensive. No master of aikido could attack anyone using the art, because no offensive moves exist. But once an aikido practitioner is attacked, his or her response to that attack can easily prove fatal to the assailant. It relies heavily on unbalancing the opponent, essentially using the attacker's own weight and speed and aggression against him.

Bronson's tutor, a Japanese man barely five feet five inches tall and aged sixty-three, had told him years before that an aikido master could take on as many as three masters in any of the other martial arts, at the same time, and still expect to be standing when the dust settled.

Bronson frankly hadn't believed him, but one evening when the two of them had left the dojo and were walking over to where Bronson had parked his car, a gang of six scarf-wearing football supporters, high on alcohol or drugs, had streamed out of an alleyway directly in front of them, looking for trouble, and ideally searching for a soft target.

Bronson had stepped forward to face them, but with a courteous bow the old Japanese man had motioned him back, taken two paces forward and just stood waiting. His harmless appearance and placid stance had seemed to enrage the youths, and they'd spent ten seconds shouting abuse before launching themselves at him.

What happened then had had all the appearance to Bronson of magic. It was as if each youth encountered something akin to a catapult: the faster they slammed into the old man, the faster they were tossed aside. In a little less than twenty seconds, the six youths were lying broken and bleeding on the ground, and throughout the entire time the old man barely seemed to have moved, and when he stepped over the legs of the nearest youth to rejoin Bronson, he hadn't even been breathing hard.

"Now do you believe me, Mr. Bronson?" he had asked, and all Bronson had been able to do was nod.

And now that training was going to save his life. Bronson swayed backward, and the blackjack whistled viciously through the air a bare inch in front of his face. Then he stepped toward his attacker, turning as he did so, and seized the man's right arm. He pulled him forward so that he was off-balance, and continued to turn his body so that his back was toward his assailant. Then he bent forward, still pulling on the man's right arm, and his attacker flew over his back to land—hard—on the ground directly in front of him.

Bronson hadn't practiced aikido for some time but, much like riding a bike, his brain still retained the moves and his body responded with the actions he'd practiced so many times in the past. The throw he'd just completed was one of the first and most basic of the moves he'd learned, and he finished it off in exactly the way he'd been taught, by tugging on the man's arm at the instant before he landed, dislocating his shoulder.

The man screamed in pain as the bone was wrenched from its socket, the blackjack tumbling from his hand onto the ground. He was hurt, but Bronson knew he wasn't immobilized, not yet, and this was something he needed to attend to. He snatched up the blackjack, and swung it as hard as he could against the man's skull. His attacker flinched and raised his left arm in a futile defense, but there was no way he could avoid the blow. The impact jarred Bronson's arm, but had the desired effect on his target. The man slumped backward, instantly knocked unconscious.

Bronson was certain he recognized his assailant—and this meant that the two men by the tomb, only some twenty yards away, were surely part of the same gang.

Standing up, he turned toward the tomb of the twin angels and took a couple of steps forward. Then he dropped down, because one of the men had just swung round to face him, and was brandishing a semiautomatic pistol in his hand.

The sound of the shot was shockingly loud amid the tranquillity of the ancient cemetery, echoing off the walls of the church and the tombs all around him. The bullet just missed Bronson as he dived for cover, smashing into a tall stone cross behind him and sending stone chips flying in all directions.

The pistol added a whole new dimension to the situation. Bronson would have had no qualms about tackling the two men. As he'd just demonstrated, he was proficient in unarmed combat, and his whole body burned with fury against the men who'd snatched Angela. Taking on two Italian thugs and beating them to a pulp might well have helped him find her, but no level of anger or competence in hand-to-hand combat would help against a man carrying a gun. This radically altered the dynamics of the situation.

For perhaps a second, he remained crouched down behind another of the tombs, weighing his options and figuring the angles. He couldn't run, not even if he'd dodged and weaved from side to side, because nobody can outrun a bullet. And he couldn't hide, either, because the other men knew where he was.

He had exactly one chance, and it all depended on the unconscious man lying on the ground a few feet behind him. Keeping as low as he could, he scuttled over to the unmoving figure, and crouched down beside him. He pulled open the man's jacket, searching desperately for a shoulder holster and a weapon he could use to save his life. But there was nothing, no sign of a pistol under either arm.

Bronson looked over to the tomb of the twin angels. The two men seemed to have separated: one had ducked back behind the tomb, and was keeping low, but Bronson couldn't see the second man, the one who'd fired the pistol.

Then another shot rang out, the bullet again missing Bronson, but only barely. The second man had moved around to the east, to get a better shot at him, and was standing only about fifteen yards away in the classic target-shooting stance: feet apart, the pistol held in his right hand, and his left hand supporting his right wrist.

The next shot, Bronson knew, would probably be the last thing he would know in this world, because from that range the man couldn't possibly miss him.

39

Almost despite herself, Angela was finding the task she'd been given quite fascinating. The dictionary was very comprehensive, and she had no difficulty in rendering the Latin expressions and sentences into modern English, albeit sometimes lengthy and rather convoluted modern English.

She knew that the grave on the Isola di San Michele dated from the early nineteenth century, and she still believed that the diary had been written by the woman who was buried there, and that the book had been interred with her by her family as a mark of respect. Indeed, the sections of the diary that she'd already translated back in the hotel room showed the unmistakable cadences of the kind of Latin she would expect to have been written by a well-educated person—male or female—of that period.

But the section at the back of the book, the text she was now being forced to translate, was very different. Although Angela was fairly sure that it had been written by

the same person who had authored the diary sections—
the handwriting was quite distinctive—apart from the
first few sentences, which seemed to act as a kind of introduction, the remainder of the text shared none of the
characteristics of the earlier pages.

The more she read and worked on, the more sure she
was that this Latin had been copied from a much older
source, which would confirm what Marco had told her—
most of it was a copy of a far more ancient document,
interspersed with comments and additional material presumably supplied by Carmelita. Some of the language
was medieval, she thought, maybe even older than that.
She could find no explanation anywhere in the text to
suggest what exactly the source book had been, but there
was something faintly familiar to her about some of the
phrases and expressions the unknown author had used,
and Angela began to wonder if what she was looking at
was a passage taken from a medieval grimoire. That might
actually tie up with Marco's apparent belief that the
source document dated from the twelfth century.

Whatever the source, the Latin text made for grim but
fascinating reading. The passage began with a long paragraph, almost messianic in its fervor, which baldly asserted that vampires were a reality, and that they had
existed since the dawn of time. These creatures were
older than the rocks and the stones that formed the con-
tinents.

They had, the text claimed, been known to all the
great writers of antiquity; and it even listed the names of

a handful of ancient Greek philosophers who had explicitly mentioned them.

Angela had snorted under her breath when she translated that particular section. She was reasonably familiar
with the works of two of the philosophers named in the
book, and couldn't recall either of them ever mentioning
anything quite as bizarre as vampires. And, she noticed,
the author of the text had conspicuously failed to mention where these explicit references might be found,
which was a sure sign that the references were simply a
product of the writer's imagination.

Having established, to the author's satisfaction, at
least, that vampires existed, the text continued with the
unsurprising claim that these creatures were not human
in the usual sense of the word. They looked human, the
writer stated, and were extremely difficult to identify, but
they were actually superhuman because of their immortality, their great physical beauty, and the enormous depth
of knowledge gleaned over the ages that they had walked
the earth.

Angela could see that, if this belief had become accepted by the general population in the days when it had
been written, almost any reasonably attractive and well-
educated man or woman could have been suspected of
being a vampire. And, at the height of the various anti-
vampire crazes that had swept Europe at intervals during
the late Middle Ages, it was likely that many people
would have suffered the consequences.

In the final section of what Angela was mentally calling

"the introduction," the writer set out the ultimate purpose of the treatise. In the following paragraphs, it was stated, fully detailed instructions would be provided so that mere mortals, *if seized with a true and honest wish and desire to achieve a state of sublime perfection*, might be elevated to a higher plane and actually join the legions of the undead.

She'd been right: what she was translating was a do-it-yourself vampire kit. Angela finished the introduction, read the Latin text and her English translation once more, then placed the page on one side of the desk.

Marco, who'd been sitting in a chair a few feet away from Angela while she worked on the text, stood up and walked over to the desk. He picked up the English translation she'd prepared, and nodded to her to continue working.

The next section of the text provided a stark reminder of the life of Carmelita Paganini, and of what she had tried to achieve. One sentence in particular served as a hideous confirmation of her apparent attempts to join the ranks of the undead, and even offered other people the opportunity of trying to join her. It also served as a further confirmation of Marco's contention that there was, indeed, an older source document that Carmelita must have seen.

This sentence read: *I now know the truth of the deeper realities that have governed the actions and conduct of my ancestors, and of the gift of eternal life that only the most dedicated adepts can enjoy, and I have had sight of the rules*

governing the conduct of those sacred rituals and measures
which will enable seekers after this most exquisite of gifts to
benefit to the fullest possible extent, to achieve immortality
through the mingling of new blood with sacred relics, to be-
come a sister of the night, a member of the holy brotherhood
and sisterhood of blood, as I have done.

Angela read the sentence again a couple of times,
changed a few of the phrases to make it read better, and
then put the page aside. The meaning seemed absolutely
clear to her. Clear, but senseless. The woman who'd kept
the journal and written those words had believed that
she'd found the secret of eternal life, by becoming a vampire. Granted, the actual word "vampire" didn't appear
in the sentence, but the last few phrases seemed to be
clear enough. Carmelita Paganini had believed she was
going to live forever, by feasting on a diet of blood and
sacred relics—whatever they were.

There were only two problems with her belief, as far as
Angela could see. First, vampires don't exist. They are a
myth, a premedieval legend, with no basis in reality whatsoever. Second, Angela had found the woman's diary in a
grave on the Isola di San Michele, lying underneath what
was left of a wooden coffin, which contained the bones of
the woman herself, the presumed author of the book, and
she'd looked pretty dead to her.

Belief was one thing, reality quite another.

Angela turned round in her seat and looked across the
room at where Marco was sitting in a comfortable easy
chair. She knew what she was reading was rubbish and

then she made the mistake of telling Marco precisely what she thought.

"I know exactly what this is," Angela said. "This book is some kind of do-it-yourself vampire kit. It's bullshit."

The slight smile left the Italian's face and he stared at her in a hostile manner. "I'm not interested in your opinion," he snapped, "only in your skill as a translator."

Angela tried again. "Look," she said, "the bones of the woman who wrote this are lying in a two-hundred-year-old tomb on the Isola di San Michele, crumbling away to dust. I think that's a fairly compelling argument to suggest that she didn't live forever."

"How do you know she wrote it?"

The possibility that the book had actually been authored by somebody other than the occupant of the old grave hadn't occurred to Angela. But it didn't change anything.

"I don't, but it was a reasonable assumption. But whether she did or not, I know—and I hope you do too—that vampires don't exist. They're a myth, nothing more."

Marco didn't respond for a moment; then he shook his head. "I already told you," he said coldly, "I'm not interested in your opinion, ill informed though it obviously is. Just get on with that translation."

He stood up and walked across to where Angela was sitting. "Have you found any references to the source yet?" he asked.

Angela nodded and pointed at the last sentence she'd

translated. "This says that she'd seen some other document, but I haven't found any mention of when she saw it or whereabout it was."

Marco scanned her translation swiftly and nodded. "Good. Keep going. Let me know as soon as you find a mention of where the source might be hidden."

In fact, the very next section of the Latin text seemed to provide a clue. An obscure clue, granted, but the first indication she had seen of where the other document, the mysterious "source," might be concealed.

Carmelita had again referred to the ancient dead and the screaming dead, neither of which made very much sense to Angela, but the next sentence did provide what looked like a location. Once she'd translated it and rendered the words into readable English, it read: *Our revered guide and master has graced us with his sacred presence, and has instructed us in the ancient procedures and rituals, these being recorded by him for all time and for all acolytes in the Scroll of Amadeus, and then secreted beside the guardian in the new place where the legions of the dead reign supreme.*

She didn't like that last expression, though it could obviously just refer to a graveyard somewhere; and the idea of a "guardian" really troubled her. But, despite her unshakable conviction that vampires were nothing more than a premedieval myth, it was the first part of that sentence that sent a chill down Angela's back.

It suggested that Carmelita had actually met, or at least seen, the person—Amadeus?—who had authored the source document. But that made no sense. Carmelita had died in the third decade of the nineteenth century. Whoever had written the source document must have died some seven hundred years earlier. Maybe she meant that there had been a succession of "masters" through the ages, each acting as the head of the "Vampire Society" or whatever name had been given to the group that Carmelita had been a member of.

But that wasn't what the Latin said. And Latin was a peculiarly precise language.

40

Behind the tomb on the island of San Michele, Bronson spotted a glint of metal from one side of the unconscious man's belt. Risking a closer look, he saw a dull black shape: the lower end of the magazine for a semiautomatic pistol, tucked into a quick-release leather pouch. There was no reason why a man would carry a magazine unless he also had a pistol, which meant he must be wearing a belt holster, not a shoulder rig.

Bronson looked up again at the man with the pistol. He was taking a couple of steps closer to him—shortening the range to ensure that his next shot would be the last he would have to fire.

The unconscious man was lying faceup, which meant the weapon had to be tucked into the small of his back; otherwise Bronson would already have seen it. Jerking him over onto his side, he rammed his other hand behind the man's back, inside the Windbreaker he was wearing.

His fingers closed around a familiar shape and, as the

approaching man stopped and took aim, Bronson rolled
sideways behind a vertical gravestone. As he moved, he
racked back the slide of the automatic pistol with his left
hand to chamber a round.

His movement took him just beyond the gravestone
and, as he emerged from that fragile shelter, he aimed the
pistol straight at the approaching figure, who swung his
pistol toward him and fired two rapid shots.

Bronson flinched as a copper-jacketed nine-millimeter
bullet slammed into the gravestone right beside him, but
he held his aim and squeezed the trigger.

During his short career as an army officer, Bronson
had become quite proficient with the Browning Hi-
Power semiautomatic pistol, then the standard officer's
sidearm, but he also knew how inaccurate such weapons
were at anything other than very close range. So he
wasn't surprised when his shot went wide.

But his target was clearly shocked to be under attack
himself. He turned and ran, dodging around the gravestones as he fled.

Bronson rose cautiously to his feet, the pistol he'd
grabbed—which he now saw actually was a nine-
millimeter Browning, the weapon he'd gotten so used to
firing in the army—still pointing toward the fleeing figure. The second man had also taken to his heels, and was
a few yards ahead of his accomplice, a bulky bag clutched
in his left hand.

Bronson glanced down at the man lying on the
ground. He was obviously unconscious, and no doubt

would remain that way for some time. The noise of the shots had echoed around the island, and Bronson knew that people would start heading toward the area very soon, which would add to the confusion. He looked over at the tomb, at the two fleeing men, and made a decision.

What he should do was call the police, hand over the thug he'd knocked out and explain that he was one of the men who'd attacked him and Angela the previous evening. The problem was that he had absolutely no proof. And he knew only too well how the corporate police mind works: the most likely result of such actions would be that he—Bronson—would face a charge of assault or the Italian equivalent of grievous bodily harm.

No, that was never going to work. Even if by some miracle Bronson managed to avoid being arrested, it would be hours before his assailant would be in a fit state to answer questions himself. The best chance of finding Angela lay with the two men who were now about seventy yards away from him and running hard.

Bending over the unconscious man, Bronson unsnapped both the belt holster and the leather pouch containing the two spare magazines for the Browning, and put them in his pocket.

Then he sprinted after his quarry.

41

Angela shook her head, and moved on. A second, much shorter, sentence followed, but two of the words in it were not listed in the Latin dictionary she was using. The translated sentence read: *There the open graves yawn ready where the fires burned in ages past, in the place where a little man once strutted and postured, and where a little* veglia funebre *once held sway.*

For a few moments, she stared at what she'd written. It sounded like directions to a specific place, and she had a vague idea what at least one of the two non-Latin words might mean, because it wasn't that different from a familiar English word. She looked at the desk in front of her, and at the other books and dictionaries stacked on it. One of them was a pocket-size Italian-English dictionary. She picked it up, flicked through the pages until she reached the letter "V," and read the entry for *veglia*. She didn't need to look up *funebre*, because the combination of the two words was listed in that entry.

A *veglia funebre* was a wake, or a vigil for the dead. Angela had guessed at the possible meaning of *funebre* because it looked so similar to the English "funeral," or at least it probably had the same root.

Something else puzzled her about the way the sentence had been constructed. From what she knew of Italians, she doubted that any vigil for the dead could be described as "little," and the repetition of the same phrase, the three Latin words that translated as "little"— *parvus, minor, minimus*—so close together in the same sentence seemed to provide an unusual degree of emphasis, as if the writer was trying to convey some additional information.

Then there was the "little man." Angela didn't know a huge amount about Italian, and especially Venetian, history, but she did know that Napoleon had conquered Venice in the last decade of the eighteenth century, ending eleven hundred years of independence. His troops had sacked and virtually bankrupted the city; they had seized many of its most valuable treasures, shipping them off to Paris, where many remain to this day. He'd even stolen the Triumphal Quadriga—or Horses of St. Mark—the famous bronze statues that for some time had graced the top of a triumphal arch in the French capital before the Venetians managed to have them returned.

When anybody spoke about Napoleon, the expressions "petty tyrant" and "little man" were often used as pejorative terms, though in reality the Emperor was of about average height for the time. The Venetians loathed him, for perfectly obvious and understandable reasons, and the expression Carmelita had used—*where a little man once strutted and postured*—could well refer to somewhere in Venice where Napoleon had spent some time—a district in the city, perhaps, or one of the islands. She couldn't think of any other historical figure who was likely to have been referred to as the "little man."

Then she had another thought, picked up the Italian-English dictionary again, and turned the pages until she reached the English word "little." The Italian equivalent was *po*, *poco*, *pochi* and other forms, depending on the noun being qualified, with *poco* probably the commonest. Angela wrote down all the variants at the bottom of the page she was working on, and added the two Italian words—*veglia funebre*—as well. Maybe there was a district of Venice called Poca Veglia or something similar.

There was a tourist map of the Venetian lagoon in the pile of books in front of her. She unfolded it and checked the names of the six districts, or *sestieri*, of the city, but none was even slightly similar to what she was looking for. Then she expanded her search to the islands of the lagoon, moving outward from Venice itself. Even then, she nearly missed it, because she was expecting to see something like "Isola di Poca Veglia," and she was already checking the names in the southern end of the lagoon, near Chioggia, when her subconscious mind raised a flag. Her glance snapped back to the area between Venice and the Lido and there, due south of Venice itself, well away from any other islands and fairly close to the Lido, she saw it: Poveglia.

In fact, it wasn't an island: it was three islands, shaped like an inverted triangle, with the point to the south. There was a small, regularly shaped, possibly even octagonal, island to the south, with two much larger landmasses, separated by a narrow canal that cut the island in two, directly to the north of it.

Angela looked back at the text she'd translated, and then again at the map of the Laguna Veneta. That had to be it. "Po" and "veglia" combined in a single word. That must be the place that Carmelita was referring to in her very simple and basic textual code.

But what about Napoleon? Was there any connection between the emperor and the small island in the lagoon? One of the books stacked on the desk in front of her was an English-language guide to the history of Venice. She pulled it out of the pile, checked the index and then opened it to a section about midway through.

"Yes," she breathed as she read the entry. During the Napoleonic Wars, the emperor had used Poveglia as a storehouse for weapons, and there had been several vicious battles fought on and around the island. Napoleon definitely had a connection to the place, and might well have "strutted and postured" there.

Angela was sure she'd identified the right island. But there had to be more to it than that. Just stating that the long-lost document was secreted on Poveglia was not enough; for a search to succeed, much more information was needed. Although the island looked reasonably small, she guessed it would still take a large team of people several days to search it.

She continued with her translation. The next line contained the word *specula*, which Angela had to look up. The dictionary suggested a number of translations, but a "tower" or "watchtower" seemed the most likely, and the Latin word *campana*, or "bell," seemed to confirm it. On the map of the lagoon it looked as if there was a tower of some sort at the southern end of the largest of the three islands.

She felt her excitement growing as she realized she might be close to identifying the exact place where the ancient document was hidden, but then her thoughts tumbled back down to earth with a bump when the further realization struck her. Marco would keep her alive only as long as she was useful to him, and the moment she had identified the hiding place and the old documents had been recovered, she didn't think he would have any further use for her.

Could she delay completing the translation? Or would Marco guess what she was trying to do and impose a brutal punishment in retribution? Angela shuddered as she remembered the jar and its collection of hideous relics, and bent forward again over the pages.

She heard a soft footfall on the wooden floor behind her and glanced round to see Marco looking over her shoulder at the work she was doing.

"You've found something," he said, more a statement than a question.

Angela nodded. "I think so, yes."

"Show me."

She pointed to the last sentence she'd translated. "The author of this section of the text employed a fairly simple word code, but it looks to me as if she was referring to an island called Poveglia. Have you heard of it?"

Marco nodded, almost sadly. "Every Venetian knows about Poveglia," he said quietly.

42

When the guard arrived with her midday meal, Marietta stared at him listlessly. She absolutely believed what he'd said to her that morning, and she'd resigned herself to the fact that she was going to die, painfully and unpleasantly, in that damp cellar within a matter of hours. There was no point in even attempting to establish a rapport with the man, of asking for mercy or anything else. His callous attitude toward her, and toward Benedetta, had become obvious. As far as the guard and the other men were concerned, Marietta and all of the other nameless victims of the bizarre cult were simply animals who would be slaughtered when their time came.

The guard followed his usual routine and placed the tray on the floor close to the wooden bed, then picked up the other tray he'd brought down that morning. Despite the terror that bubbled inside her, Marietta had eventually eaten all the food he'd supplied, just as she expected she would finally eat whatever meal she had now been provided with.

"This is your last meal," the guard said, glancing at her, "so you might as well make the most of it. I'll bring warm water and a towel for you to wash yourself later this afternoon, to get ready for the ceremony tonight."

"And if I refuse? If I simply tell you and your revolting friends to go to hell, what then?"

The guard shrugged. "That's your choice," he said, "but if you don't do what we want, you'll taste the Taser again. And if you still don't cooperate, I'll ask a couple of the men to come down here and have a bit of fun with you before the ceremony. They'll enjoy it, but I don't suppose you will. It's up to you, really."

Marietta held herself together until the man had walked out of the cellar; then she dissolved into tears.

43

Bronson sprinted across the graveyard after the fleeing men. He paused for a few seconds beside the tomb of the twin angels, staring at it with a sense of déjà vu. The stone side of the grave had been smashed open—a hammer and chisel were lying on the ground beside the shattered stone—and what was left of the ancient coffin was scattered about. The grave itself was obviously very old, and most of the wood had long since disintegrated to reveal the skeletal remains of the tomb's occupant. This corpse had also been decapitated, but this time the head was nowhere in sight. Could that explain what was in the bag that one of the men had been carrying?

Bronson shook his head and set off in pursuit of the two men. He wasn't concerned about them getting too far ahead of him, because they must have used a boat to get to the island. From the direction they were running, this boat was moored in the inlet at the northern end of the island, where Bronson's own vessel was tied up.

The last thing he wanted to do was storm onto the jetty and start a firefight. He needed the two men to make their getaway, so that he could go after them.

Instead of following right behind the two men, he angled over to one side and did his best to increase speed, though having to dodge around gravestones and tree trunks hampered his progress somewhat. The sound of a powerboat engine starting close to him—just a few yards away—indicated that he must be right by the jetty. He stopped and made his way cautiously in the direction from which the sound had come.

In a couple of seconds he reached the edge of the jetty, but remained out of sight as he surveyed the scene in front of him. A blue powerboat was already about ten yards out from the water's edge, and gathering speed. The man who'd shot at him was sitting in the bow staring back toward the island, his pistol held low in his right hand, clearly waiting for Bronson to show himself, while the other man concentrated on getting the boat away from the jetty as quickly as possible.

Bronson memorized what the men were wearing and the color and type of the boat, and waited until they turned right out of the inlet, and the craft was lost to view. Then he stepped onto the jetty, ran down to where his own boat was moored, released the line and climbed aboard, starting the engine as he sat down on the padded seat. He opened the throttle and the boat surged forward. He pulled it around in a tight circle and headed for the entrance to the inlet, then swung the wheel to the right, to follow the other craft.

As he emerged into the open waters of the Venetian lagoon, he looked ahead. The blue boat was already perhaps a hundred yards in front of him, heading more or less east. But, as he turned in the same direction, the man in the bow pointed urgently back toward him. The other man glanced behind as well, and immediately turned the boat to the right.

Bronson knew he'd been spotted, and cursed. Wherever the two men had been heading, they were obviously not going that way any longer. They had turned southwest, toward Venice, and Bronson guessed their intentions. If they'd stayed out in the open waters, he'd have been able to follow them even at a distance. No doubt they were now heading into the city so that they could try to lose him in the notorious maze of Venice's canals and waterways.

44

Angela looked up at Marco. He seemed strangely subdued by her mention of the island.

"What is it about Poveglia?" she asked.

He stared at her for a moment, then shook his head. "You really don't know?" he replied. "Your ignorance staggers me."

He reached forward, plucked a book out of the pile on the desk and slammed it down in front of her. "It's all in here," he snapped. "Read it and educate yourself."

Pulling a mobile phone from his pocket, Marco stalked across to the other side of the drawing room and held a brief conversation with someone. It sounded as if he was issuing orders.

Angela glanced after him, then down at the book. It looked like a fairly typical multilanguage tourist guide to Venice, but the title promised that it would reveal the hidden stories of the Venetian lagoon: "the Venice that tourists never see," as the author claimed. The introduction pointed out that the city hosted around three million tourists every year, although most of them never got beyond Venice itself and the islands of Murano and Burano. There was a short chapter that dealt only with Poveglia, and by the time she'd finished reading it, Angela knew exactly why Carmelita had talked about the "ancient dead" and the "screaming dead."

The dead on Poveglia greatly outnumbered the living in Venice. The island was covered in plague pits, a legacy of one of the most terrible periods in Venetian history. In the outbreak of 1576 alone, it was estimated that fifty thousand people had died from the bubonic plague. Fifty thousand was only about ten thousand less than the total population of the old city today. And there had been at least twenty-two attacks of the plague before that one. According to some calculations, the bones of more than one hundred and sixty thousand people lay in shallow graves on Poveglia.

The island had been used as a lazaretto, a quarantine station, in the fifteenth and sixteenth centuries, in an attempt to prevent the spread of infectious diseases to Venice. The city was a maritime republic, almost entirely dependent upon trade for its survival, and visiting traders who wished to step ashore in Venice would first be required to undergo a lengthy period of isolation. In fact, it was the Venetians who invented the concept of quarantine, the word deriving from the Italian *quaranta giorni*, or "forty days."

But even this procedure clearly hadn't protected the

city from the ravages of the Black Death, as the sheer number of deaths throughout that period bore witness. The city authorities had been ruthless in their attempts to keep Venice clear of the plague. Anyone displaying the slightest signs of infection would be shipped out immediately to Poveglia or one of the other lazarettos in the lagoon. One island was actually named after this function: Lazzaretto Nuovo.

According to the author of the book, it was popularly believed that weak but still-living victims of the plague were either tossed on the burning funeral pyres or thrown into the plague pits among the decomposing bodies, and then buried alive. Angela thought that the expression "screaming dead" barely even hinted at the horrific events that must have taken place on Poveglia some half a millennium earlier.

And the horrors apparently hadn't stopped there. Much later, in the early twentieth century, a mental hospital had been built on the island. Some of the inmates had reportedly been subjected to inhuman tortures, mutilated and then butchered by a notoriously sadistic doctor. This man had apparently then gone mad himself, and had climbed to the top of the old bell tower and jumped to his death.

It was no wonder that the island was hardly ever mentioned in the guidebooks, and was almost never visited. In fact, the book stated that Poveglia was officially off-limits to everyone, locals and visitors. Angela couldn't think of a single reason why anyone could possibly want to go there. And that, of course, meant that it would provide an excellent hiding place for the ancient document Marco was seeking.

She put the book to one side and turned back to her translation, but the text didn't seem to provide any further details of where the source document might be hidden. Angela looked at the detailed map that was included in the chapter on Poveglia, jotted down a few notes, principally dates and events, and then sat back.

She didn't think it would have been buried in the ground somewhere, not least because of the plague pits that were the dominant feature of the island's soil, so that left one of the ruined buildings on Poveglia. The document couldn't possibly be hidden in the lunatic asylum—part of which had apparently also been used as a retirement home for senior citizens, a thought that made Angela shudder again—because the building hadn't been erected until 1922. Several of the other structures were also comparatively recent, certainly built after Carmelita's death.

The oldest structure on the island was the bell tower, the only surviving remnant of the twelfth-century church of San Vitale, which had been abandoned and then destroyed hundreds of years earlier. The translation Angela had completed was quite specific. It stated that after the source document had been prepared it had then been *secreted beside the guardian in the new place where the legions of the dead reign supreme.* Apart from the reference to the "guardian," which still bothered her because she didn't fully understand it, the meaning was perfectly

clear. The document had originally been hidden somewhere else but, after Carmelita had seen it, for some reason it had then been concealed in a different hiding place.

If her reading of the Latin was correct, and assuming
the document still existed, that meant there was only one
place it could possibly have been hidden on Poveglia: it
had to be somewhere in the bell tower.

45

Marietta lay on her back on the thin and uncomfortable mattress, eyes wide-open and staring at the cracked and discolored plaster on the ceiling above her. The food tray sat untouched on the floor beside the bed.

When the guard had casually, callously confirmed her worst fears, when she had finally realized that there really was no hope, it had driven all other thoughts from her mind. The idea of eating or drinking didn't even occur to her. Her mind was filled with vivid images of the horrendous events of the previous evening—of Benedetta strapped on the stone table, struggling futilely against her bonds, her screams reduced to muffled grunts and moans as she was violently raped and her blood drained from the wound on her neck.

Now Marietta knew what fate awaited her, knew that sometime—sometime soon—the guards would appear in the cellar and instruct her to wash her body. Would she resist? And, if so, how? There were no weapons she could use against her captors, no arguments or persuasion that would do anything to alter the events she knew would take place in the next few hours.

The choice was stark. Marietta was a fighter. But she was also a realist. If she refused to obey orders, she knew the guards would simply rape her or beat her into submission, or just strip her naked and then hose her down. Her best, and in fact her only, choice was to do it the easy way: do her best to detach her mind from the awful reality of what was going to happen to her and hope it would all be over quickly.

She thought again of her family, of her father and mother, and of the mental anguish she knew they would be feeling after her disappearance. When they'd read reports in the newspapers, or seen television programs about the other girls who had vanished from the streets of Venice, her mother had always said that the worst part was the uncertainty. For a mother, not knowing if her daughter was alive or dead was a burden not many could bear. At least if a body was found, the grieving process could start; the news would be devastating, in the proper sense of that word, but the family would be able to make their farewells, and then try their best to move on.

But when a person vanished, leaving no trace behind, every waking moment would be a torture. That could be the day where two grim-faced police officers would knock at the door to bring the final, dreadful news. Or—and this was the hope that Marietta was sure every mother would cling to—perhaps that would be the day when her daughter would at last walk back through the door.

Marietta closed her eyes again, but still the tears came, coursing down her cheeks, because she knew, beyond all reasonable doubt, that her own mother would never, ever find out what had happened to her. And she felt her heart breaking as she realized this.

She took a deep breath and tried to get herself back under control. She knew she was going to die, but she was determined to do her best to die with dignity, not to scream, not to shout. And, above all, not to cry. She rubbed angrily at her cheeks with her free hand. She would show them.

She was a Venetian, after all, descended—so she'd been told—from important, perhaps even noble, blood. No matter what they did to her, she would cling to what shreds of dignity she could during her ordeal.

46

Angela was so engrossed in what she was doing that she didn't see or hear the drawing room door swing open. She was just suddenly aware of a pungent and acrid smell, and of Marco jumping to his feet.

She turned round in her chair to look behind her and saw a figure clad in an all-enveloping black cloak, the hood covering his face, moving silently across the wooden floor toward her. She started to rise, but immediately Marco shouted out to her, "Sit down and face the wall."

The smell grew stronger as the figure approached, and Angela was seized by an overwhelming feeling of horror and dread, made worse by the uncanny silence with which the man moved. Even though she couldn't see him, because she was obeying Marco's commands to the letter and staring fixedly at the wall behind the desk, she knew that the man had stopped directly behind her.

Marco strode across toward her as well, and stood beside her.

"We may have it, Master," he said, pointing down at Angela's translations of the Latin text.

"Where?" The voice was little more than a whisper, a sibilant hiss.

"Poveglia," Marco said.

There was a short silence as the new arrival apparently digested this information, and then Angela heard his quiet voice again. "Get the boat ready," he said, "and bring her as well."

47

Bronson pushed the throttle all the way forward to the stop, and the bow of the speedboat lifted in response to the increased revolutions of the outboard engine's propeller.

Ahead of him, the blue powerboat had also increased speed, and was now clearly heading directly toward the square inlet on the northern side of Venice that was known as the Sacca della Misericordia. There were two canals that opened off the inlet, and any number of smaller canals that connected with those two. Bronson knew that once they got into the canal system, he would have his work cut out for him trying to keep track of them, so he kept up his speed, heedless of the increasing number of boats maneuvering in the water around him.

The blue powerboat swung left into the Sacca della Misericordia, weaving around vaporettos and gondolas and launches and various other types of craft, the driver pushing the boat much too quickly in the congested waters.

Behind him, Bronson was starting to close the gap, simply because he wasn't yet in the thick of the water traffic. But as he, too, entered the inlet, he was forced to reduce speed considerably. A vaporetto was heading straight for him, probably aiming for the Fondamente Nuove vaporetto stop down to the southeast, and Bronson was forced to turn the boat hard to the right to avoid a collision. He straightened up and steered around the passenger craft, the driver shaking his fist angrily at Bronson and mouthing expletives as he, too, took evasive action. Bronson ignored him, his attention still fixed on his quarry as he instinctively maneuvered the boat around all the other vessels in the congested area.

The blue powerboat steered to the left of the Sacca della Misericordia and, still traveling quickly, started heading down the Rio di Noale canal, which would lead them directly to the Grand Canal and its myriad tributaries. Bronson knew that if his quarry managed to reach there, they could vanish into any one of the smaller canals, and he would probably never see them again. At all costs, he had to keep them in sight.

He increased speed as much as he dared—smashing the boat into the sidewall of the canal or into another vessel would absolutely ensure that his pursuit would end prematurely—and powered into the canal after them.

A short distance down the canal the waterway split in a Y-junction, the wider Rio di Noale veering to the right, while a slightly narrower canal, the Rio di San Felice, lay straight ahead. That was the quickest route straight through to the Grand Canal, Bronson guessed, as the blue boat kept to the left of the stone breakwater that marked the junction.

Then he saw something that made him smile. At the end of the canal, where it narrowed still further, was a veritable logjam of gondolas, all maneuvering either in or out of the Grand Canal at the junction ahead. The blue powerboat would have to slow down to a crawl to get through the melee. Either that, or they'd have to take a different route.

In fact, the blue boat did both: it slowed and turned. Bronson saw the wake diminish markedly as the driver pulled back the throttle, slowing down, and then accelerated again as he steered the boat into the entrance to another canal on the left-hand side.

Bronson eased back the throttle, ensuring that he was traveling slowly enough to make the turn, then accelerated again once he was inside the other canal. The sound of the two fast-revving engines on the boats echoed off the walls of the surrounding buildings, and the waves from their wakes slapped hard against the stones that lined the canal.

The waterway ran straight for a short distance, but at the end it swung through about ninety degrees to the left. There were also two other canals that had junctions with the one they were in, both on the left-hand side and leading away from the Grand Canal. Bronson had managed to keep up with the other boat so far, and he knew that he could go on chasing the two men through the canals of Venice until he ran out of fuel or miscalculated some corner and smashed up the boat, but this wouldn't help him to find Angela. Instead, what he needed to do was convince the men he was chasing that he'd given up. He knew they wouldn't head for home until they were sure he was no longer on their tail.

But how could he convince the two men that he was a spent force? At that moment he could think of only one way to do this. It was a risky maneuver, and if it went wrong, he'd be dead in minutes. It all depended on timing, and the inherent inaccuracy of semiautomatic pistols, especially when such pistols were being fired from an unstable platform, like a boat traveling at speed.

The driver of the blue boat turned the wheel hard to the left, steered the vessel into the first of the subsidiary canals and increased speed again. This canal was slightly narrower than the one they'd just left, and there were only a few other boats in it, mainly moored at various landing stages and jetties along the sides. There were no gondolas in sight. It was as good a place as any.

Bronson pulled the Browning semiautomatic pistol from his pocket, pointed it in the general direction of the boat in front of him, and pulled the trigger twice. The shots boomed out, deafeningly loud in the narrow canal. As far as he could see, neither bullet went anywhere near its target, but that wasn't his intention. He wanted a reaction. A reaction he could use to his own advantage.

The driver of the blue boat obliged him.

He was just coming up to the entrance to another

canal on the right, and swung the boat into it. As he did so, the man in the bow of the boat raised his own pistol and fired off a shot toward Bronson.

That was what he'd been waiting for. Pulling back on the throttle, Bronson spun the wheel hard to the right, to make sure that the boat would circle in more or less the same place. Then, rising in his seat, he clutched at his chest and slumped down out of sight, the Browning still in his hand, just in case the two men decided to come alongside his boat for a closer look.

From his position on the floor of the powerboat, Bronson could see nothing except the sky and the tops of the buildings that lined the canal, so he was relying entirely on his ears to deduce what was happening. He heard the sound of the engine of the other boat fade away sharply, which meant the driver had chopped back the throttle. Then the engine noise—and Bronson was sure it was the same engine—increased again, and appeared to be getting closer, though it was difficult to be certain of this because of the way the noise echoed from both sides of the man-made canyon. It certainly sounded as though the two men were approaching to make sure he was dead.

Bronson checked the Browning was ready to fire, and waited as the sound of the other boat's engine grew louder.

48

About an hour later, Angela was taken out of the main door of the house into the pale watery light of a cloudy afternoon in the Venetian lagoon.

After the hooded man had left the drawing room, Marco had instructed her to make a complete translation of the rest of that section of the diary as quickly as possible, obviously hoping that the remainder of the Latin text would provide details of the precise location of the source document. It didn't. The only reference Angela found was to the "campanile of light," which just served to confirm her assumption that the document must be somewhere in the ancient bell tower. From her reading of the chapter dealing with the history of Poveglia, she knew that the bell tower had for a time been converted into a lighthouse. But she still had no idea exactly where to start looking.

Marco and another of his men hustled her down the path toward the jetty at the end of the island, where two men were already waiting, standing in the stern of a powerboat, the rumble of the engine clearly audible.

"Why do you want me to go with you?" Angela asked, as Marco pushed her inside the small cabin.

"You've read and translated the Latin," he replied. "We don't know what we'll find when we get there, but there might be something, some clue, that you'll see and understand but we won't. That's why you're here."

"What happens if you don't find what you're looking for?"

"You'd better pray that we do. Finding the source document is the only thing that's keeping you alive right now. If it isn't there, then we have no further use for you."

The casual, almost conversational, tone of his voice scared Angela even more than the words he'd used, and she sat in silence as Marco handcuffed her wrists together, looping the link between the cuffs behind a handrail, immobilizing her. Then he left the cabin.

A few moments later the door opened again and the hooded man entered, the now-familiar stench preceding him. Angela shrank back in her seat as the figure passed right beside her, and then took a seat at the opposite end of the cabin.

Moments later, she felt the boat start to move, and soon the bow was cutting through the choppy waters of the lagoon, the waves thumping rhythmically against the hull.

She had no idea how long the journey would take,

because she didn't know where she'd been imprisoned, and the view through the side windows of the boat was so restricted that she could see almost nothing of her surroundings. And in truth, her thoughts were dominated by the hooded man she was sharing the cabin with. He had said nothing to her, and gave no sign that he was even aware of her presence, but the all-pervasive smell of rotting meat seemed to fill the air, and she was simply terrified in case he came close or, worse, touched her.

A few minutes later, Marco returned to the cabin and sat down opposite Angela, which actually made her feel safer and slightly more comfortable. At least the menace Marco represented was clear and tangible. The hooded man inspired only feelings of horror and revulsion, which were far worse than any physical threat.

"Who is that man?" she asked quietly, nodding toward the silent figure. "He terrifies me."

Marco smiled bleakly. "He should."

49

Bronson tensed as the sound of the boat drew closer, and a moment later he felt a slight bump as some part of the other craft touched his boat. He kept his eyes half-open, and lay as still as possible, the Browning held loosely by his side but ready to fire.

He could hear the two men talking as they maneuvered their boat alongside his, their efforts hampered by the fact that the engine of Bronson's craft was still running, and the boat was describing a small circle at the junction of the two canals.

"I can see him," one of the men said. "He's not moving."

"He must be dead, then," the other replied, "or at least he's badly wounded. Let's get out of here before a police launch comes along."

Bronson heard the noise of another boat's engine approaching, he thought from the opposite direction, though it was difficult to tell. But what he was quite certain about was that the blue boat was moving away. That sound was unmistakable.

For about thirty seconds he did nothing; then he eased himself up cautiously, and risked a quick glance over the side of the vessel. There was a slight bend in the canal to the east and, as he looked in that direction, he saw the blue powerboat disappear around it. The moment it was out of sight, he sat up, centered the steering wheel to stop the circular motion of the boat, grabbed his map of the Venetian waterways, and quickly worked out where he was.

He'd ended up in a canal called the Rio della Racchetta, and the men he'd been chasing would have to continue down the adjoining waterway until they reached the larger Rio del Gesuiti, because they'd already passed the only other canal entrance. What he didn't know was which way they'd turn when they reached it. Left would take them the shorter distance, out into the Canale delle Fondamente Nuove, the open water that lay on the northeast side of Venice. If they swung right, they'd have a longer run down the canal until they reached the Canal Grande—the Grand Canal—itself.

A wooden launch—its engine had been what Bronson had heard—swept down one side of the powerboat, the driver staring at him with some curiosity as he passed. He had obviously seen the pirouettes that Bronson's craft had been describing in the water, and probably thought he was drunk.

Bronson ignored him. His only concern was to try to

second-guess the men he was following. The trouble was, he had very little to go on. When the blue powerboat had pulled away from the Island of the Dead, the driver had headed southeast. If his destination had been one of the islands at the northeastern end of the Laguna Veneta, somewhere near Burano, for example, Bronson would have expected them to head in that direction. The fact that they'd continued along the north side of Venice suggested that they were going to sail around the eastern end of the island, and perhaps then turn southwest, toward the other end of the lagoon, where he knew there was a scattering of small islands.

It was a long shot, though, and for perhaps half a minute, Bronson sat at the wheel of the boat, his mind racked by indecision. He had just one chance. If he guessed wrong, he'd never see the blue boat again, which would mean he'd lose Angela. He had to get it right.

His mind made up, he spun the wheel and opened the throttle, sending the boat speeding south down the Rio della Racchetta, retracing the course he'd followed just minutes earlier. At the end of the canal, he turned the boat right and almost immediately left, back into the Rio di San Felice, where he'd seen the jam caused by the gondolas. As he made the turn, he prayed that this time the waterway would be clear.

It wasn't, but there were far fewer boats in the way. Bronson kept the speed up as much as he dared, then pulled the throttle back as he reached the nearest gondola. He started to weave his way through the jostling boats, his passage attracting a torrent of abuse in high-speed Italian, all of which he ignored.

A couple of minutes later he was through, and swung the boat to the left, into the Grand Canal itself. As he did so, he glanced to his left and saw a long wooden-hulled launch bearing down on him, just yards away. Bronson knew immediately that if he continued turning toward the boat, he'd never miss it. He reacted instantly, spinning the steering wheel to the right and pushed the throttle forward, sending his boat straight across the bow of the oncoming vessel.

There was a bang from the rear of Bronson's boat, as the bow of the much larger launch hit the left-hand rear of his powerboat, cracking the fiberglass and scattering paint flakes across the water. But the outboard motor was undamaged, and he was certain that the impact had been well above the waterline, so there was no danger of him taking in water. And in fact fiberglass boats of the type he was in were so full of air pockets that they were virtually unsinkable.

The driver of the launch immediately reduced speed, obviously intending to do the Italian marine equivalent of exchanging names and addresses. But Bronson had not the slightest intention of stopping or even slowing down. His boat's throttle was still wide-open and the outboard engine roaring, so he twitched the steering wheel to the left and sped away, heedless of the angry shouts echoing from behind him.

The Grand Canal in Venice follows an S-shaped course

from the Stazione Ferrovie dello Stato Santa Lucia, the railway station, to its southern end near the Piazza San Marco, where it opens out into the Bacino di San Marco and the much wider *canale* of the same name. Bronson had joined the canal about a third of the way along, so he knew he would have to contend with the fairly heavy water traffic for some time before he could get into the clearer and more open waters to the south of the city. And then, of course, he would have the even more difficult task of spotting the blue powerboat carrying the two men, among the hundreds of similar craft that plied the waters in and around Venice. And that assumed that he'd been right in his guess that the boat would be heading into the waters of the lagoon somewhere to the south of the city.

He also knew that although the men he'd been following now believed that he was dead or badly wounded, they would still be keeping their own eyes peeled for any sign of pursuit, and paying particular attention to anybody who looked like him. There was nothing he could do about the design and color of his boat, but Bronson realized that there were things—three things, in fact—that he could do to try to change his own appearance.

He was wearing his black leather jacket, so he took this off and dropped it on the floor of the boat beside him. Underneath, he had on a plain white shirt, which would give him an entirely different appearance to anyone viewing him from a distance. And in his shirt pocket he had a baseball cap and a pair of large sunglasses with impenetrable mirrored black lenses. He took out the sunglasses and slipped them on as he powered the boat down the Grand Canal toward the open water at its end, then settled the cap on his head, ensuring that it completely covered the dressing over the wound on his scalp.

Unless he got so close to the other boat that the men in it could actually see his features, Bronson guessed that he now looked quite different. Rolling his shoulders to ease away some of his tension, and trying hard not to think about what could be happening to Angela, he focused on the task in hand: spotting the other vessel, a challenge that made finding a needle in a haystack seem easy by comparison.

50

Marco released Angela's handcuffs, and led her out of the cabin. The boat was already moored, a bow and stern line attached, and it was easy enough to step from the side of the vessel onto the landing stage. She looked around. The boat was positioned a short distance down the channel between the small octagonal island that lay at the southern tip of Poveglia and the middle island. In the distance, looking south, she could make out buildings on the Lido.

The octagonal island looked like a flat-topped fort, the inward-sloping sides made of stone, and mooring alongside that would have been difficult. But that wasn't their objective. A short distance along the level stone landing stage that marked the southern end of the larger island was an impressive-looking building. It reminded Angela of a typical Venetian palazzo, and must, she thought, have been part of the retirement home on the island, before being abandoned in the 1960s. The facade was covered with a weblike exoskeleton of rusting scaffolding. That, Angela knew from her research, was not part of some renovation project, but had been erected almost a quarter of a century earlier simply to stop the buildings from falling down.

She looked over to the northeast, and there, beyond the trees, rose the imposing stone bell tower, looking something like a church steeple, its tall red-tiled roof supporting a large metal crucifix at the very top. All the openings in the tower appeared to have been bricked up, possibly when the scaffolding was put in place. A chill wind blew in suddenly from the waters of the lagoon, bringing with it a swirl of mist, and from somewhere nearby Angela heard the faint sound of a bell ringing.

She glanced at Marco. "Did you hear that bell?" she asked, and pointed toward the tower. "I thought it came from over there."

He looked at her dismissively. "Impossible," he said. "The bell was removed in nineteen thirteen."

"I know what I heard," Angela insisted, but her voice lacked conviction. She'd read in the guidebook that the sound of a bell was still sometimes heard on the island.

The hooded man emerged from the cabin of the boat and began moving silently—his feet never seemed to make a sound—toward the derelict building that lay closest to the tower.

Marco checked that Angela's handcuffs were still secured, and then pushed her in the same direction, two of his men following behind.

The short procession entered the building through an opening that had obviously once been a doorway, but that now gaped open to the elements. Inside, it was a scene of almost total devastation. Garbage and debris lay strewn across the floor. Plaster had fallen off the walls and ceiling, and in several places the floor timbers of the story above had broken, and pointed downward into the ground-floor room like long, blackened and jagged teeth. On many of the pieces of surviving plaster, graffiti had been scrawled. Cast-iron radiators stood forlornly against the walls, rust covering the areas where the paint had flaked off. In one corner, two windows had disappeared, and a heavy growth of vegetation had forced its way inside and was beginning the long, slow process of reclaiming the building.

Angela was not of a nervous disposition, but she knew absolutely that if she had had any choice in the matter, she would have walked out, climbed back onto the boat and never, ever returned to Poveglia.

The very fabric of the building seemed to echo with the cries of the dying, and the knowledge that the thin soil on the island covered the bones of tens of thousands of plague victims weighed heavily upon her. If there was any place on the face of the earth where the dead could speak, this, this island of Poveglia, was probably it. She could so easily imagine the giant fires consuming piles of smoldering bodies, and the shallow graves tended by workers who were themselves diseased. Through it all would stalk the bizarre and otherworldly figures of the doctors, trying vainly to fight a contagion that they didn't understand and could not cure, their only protection against the disease being the hook-nosed masks they wore, filled with peppers and spices they believed might filter out the infective elements. These men must have looked like massive predatory birds as they tried in vain to bring some relief to the sufferers.

Suddenly, a movement caught her eye and Angela gave a little cry of alarm. A shadow played across the wall as a beam of sunlight entered the building, and she could almost swear that she saw the shape of a man wearing a beaklike mask somewhere outside the building. Then the wind blew again and the shape dissolved and re-formed, as the branches of the tree shifted.

"Come on," Marco ordered, tugging at Angela's arm.

Following the hooded man, they stepped over and around the debris to the far end of the room and made their way carefully over to the bell tower.

Inside, little light penetrated because the windows and other openings had been bricked up. The tower extended above their heads, a vertical well of darkness. In the gloom, they saw the first few steps of a rusting spiral staircase that ran around the walls of the tower.

"So where is it?" Marco demanded.

For an instant, Angela didn't realize that he was talking to her; then she pulled herself together.

"The text doesn't say," she replied. "It just seems to suggest that it's hidden somewhere here, in this place. There's nothing else I can tell you, and I did translate all the rest of the Latin."

Marco looked at her for a long moment, then switched his glance to the stairs before turning to one of his men and issuing a crisp order in Italian. The man turned and strode swiftly out of the tower.

"We need flashlights," he said. "I don't think the document is hidden anywhere down here. People still come to this island—you can tell that from the graffiti they've scrawled on the walls—and if it had been found already, we would have known about it. So it's probably hidden somewhere that people wouldn't normally visit or explore." He looked again at Angela. "I hope you're not afraid of heights," he said, "because my guess is that Carmelita, or whoever hid it, probably put it right at the top of the bell tower. You're going up there to find it for us."

When the man he'd sent back to the boat returned, half a dozen flashlights of different sizes in his hands, Marco stepped across to Angela and unlocked her handcuffs. Then he picked up the biggest flashlight, a squat, gray and clearly heavy instrument with a rechargeable battery, and shone a powerful beam directly upward, tracing the course that the spiral staircase followed until it reached a level platform.

"That can't be the top of the tower," Marco said. "It's not high enough. There must be another staircase above that."

"I don't want to do this," Angela murmured. "I really don't want to go up there."

Marco shrugged. "You've got two choices. Do this and you'll live, at least for a little while longer. Refuse, and I'll have one of my men strangle you right now and dump your body here. It's up to you."

For a few seconds Angela stared at him, but she knew she had no option. She was quite certain that Marco would order her death with as little compunction as he would order a cup of coffee. She grimaced, reached down and picked up two of the smaller flashlights; then she strode across to the foot of the spiral staircase.

She switched on one of the flashlights and shone the beam at the metal treads in front of her. There was little dust or debris visible on them, and even the banister appeared to be intact and in reasonably good condition. She guessed that some of the infrequent and illegal visitors to the island probably climbed at least some distance up into the tower out of idle curiosity, if nothing else. That was good news, because it meant that the staircase should support her weight. Cautiously, she rested her left foot on the lowest tread, then began to climb.

Behind her, she heard the sound of footsteps and glanced back: Marco was following, flashlight in hand.

"Keep going," he snapped. "I'm just here to make sure you do what you're told."

The staircase wound up the inside of the tower. For the first few steps, it felt extremely solid, but the higher she climbed, the more unhappy Angela felt, realizing she was relying on bolts and fittings that had been in place for a very long time, without the benefit of any kind of maintenance or repair. She moved as close as she could to the wall, where she hoped the old metal might be stronger, and tested each step before she put her full weight on it.

The climb seemed endless, but eventually she stepped onto a platform that she guessed was virtually at the top of the main part of the tower, and looked around. Again, there was graffiti on the walls, which meant that other people had made the same climb fairly recently. There was no obvious hiding place at that level.

Marco appeared beside her within seconds. "I told you the bell had been removed," he said, pointing at a substantial beam that ran from one wall of the tower to the opposite side, and which had clearly been designed to support some heavy object.

"I did hear something," Angela insisted.

She looked at the walls of the bell chamber, and at the bricked-up openings in the sidewalls, and shivered.

"I suppose this was where he jumped from?" she said quietly.

"Who?" Marco asked.

"The mad doctor. If the story about him in that book was true, I mean."

"Nobody knows, and I don't care." Marco looked all around them, quickly reaching the same conclusion as Angela. "There's nothing here," he said. "We need to get to the very top."

Another short flight of stairs brought them to a second level, above the old bell chamber. And the stairs stopped there. Attached to one wall was a steel ladder, around which metal hoops had been bolted to prevent anyone climbing it from falling off. Like the spiral staircase, the metal looked old and rusty, and none too safe.

"Keep going," Marco ordered again.

Angela swallowed hard. Heights didn't particularly bother her, but she had a horror of falling, and even the metal hoops around the ladder weren't much of a safeguard against that happening. But she knew she had no option. She tucked both the flashlights into the waistband of her trousers, because she'd definitely need both hands free to make the climb, then reached up and began the ascent.

It wasn't a long climb, perhaps twenty steps in all, and at the top she was faced with a wooden trapdoor set into the underside of a narrow platform. There was no bolt or catch, and the trapdoor swung open fairly easily as she pushed up on it. As it swung back against the wall with a dull thud, she took out one of the flashlights and shone the beam into the void above. Apart from an old broom, it appeared to be completely empty.

She reached up and placed both flashlights on the floor of the small platform, then heaved herself through the hole and stood up.

Angela could see that Marco was just beginning to make the same climb, and for a fleeting instant she debated dropping some heavy object down onto the top of his head, but then dismissed the thought. Even if she succeeded in hitting him, she would still have to contend with the men waiting on the ground floor down below, and if Marco didn't reappear, she guessed that she wouldn't leave the tower alive.

The platform was about eight feet long and three feet wide, and the walls appeared to be just as solid and featureless as those on the two platforms below her. As far she could see, there was nowhere here where anything of any size could be concealed.

Marco pulled himself through the trapdoor and stood next to her. "What now?" he demanded. "Where is it?"

Angela shook her head in despair. "I have no idea," she said. "I can only tell you what I translated from the Latin text. That didn't give any indication of where the document might be hidden, apart from mentioning this tower, and even that was far from explicit." She looked around at the featureless walls of the platform. "If it was ever here, maybe somebody found it and removed it, years ago."

"I've already told you: if it had been found, we would know about it. It must be here somewhere."

"But there's no possible hiding place here."

Then a thought struck her and she walked back to the trapdoor and peered down the square-sided shaft up which they had both climbed. She turned back to Marco.

"How high do you think we've climbed?" she asked.

"Why?"

"Because the walls are square," she replied. "At the top of this tower is a tall steeple. If we'd climbed to the very top of the tower, the walls would meet at a point above our heads. There must still be a space somewhere above us."

Marco glanced down through the trapdoor, then looked around and nodded. "So where's the access?" he asked.

The ceiling of the space they were standing in was only about seven feet above their heads. Angela didn't reply, but simply picked up the broom and began gently tapping its handle against the ceiling. It didn't take long to cover the small space, and in one corner this technique generated a hollow-sounding thud.

"Here," she said, and shone the flashlight beam at the ceiling. Almost invisible in the grubby whitewash that covered the ceiling was the outline of an oblong shape. If they hadn't been looking for it, there was no way they would ever have seen it. At one end of it was a small hole, inside which a few strands of frayed material could be seen poking out.

"What's that?"

"I think it's the end of a length of rope, probably used to pull the trapdoor closed from here. And then they cut the rest off to hide the fact there was an opening in the ceiling. Just hold this," Angela snapped, the spirit of the quest taking over, despite the circumstances. She passed the flashlight to Marco, who looked surprised, but did as she had told him and aimed the beam where she indicated.

She pressed her hands firmly against one end of the oblong mark and pushed upward. There was a creaking and tearing sound, the noise of old dry wood moving against a solid object, and the section of ceiling lifted a fraction of an inch. She changed position, and pushed again, but the panel wouldn't budge.

"You hold the flashlight and I'll lift it," Marco told her.

Angela took a few paces backward and aimed the beam of her flashlight at the ceiling. Marco raised his arms and shoved against the wood. Nothing happened, so he stepped back a few inches and tried again, his face contorted from the effort. With a final snapping sound, the panel suddenly gave way and flew upward.

A cloud of dust and small pieces of wood cascaded down over his head. Angela looked on in horror as a skeletal arm, held together within a carapace of leathery skin, swung down, the bony hand seeming almost to grab for Marco. Above his head, framed in the dark opening, she found herself staring into the sightless eye sockets of a partially fleshed human skull.

51

Bronson steered the powerboat out of the end of the Grand Canal and swung the bow around to the south. Directly in front of him, on the opposite side of the Canale della Giudecca, lay the long and narrow, almost banana-shaped, island of Giudecca, with the much smaller triangular island of San Giorgio Maggiore to the left.

If he *was* right, and the men were heading for the southern part of the lagoon, a good place to wait for them to pass would be near the end of Giudecca. He stopped his turn and aimed for the Canale della Grazia, which separated the two islands in front of him. Once he'd motored through the gap, he steered the boat over to the right, stopping alongside the southern coast of the island just below Campiello Campalto.

Like almost everywhere else in Venice, the island of Giudecca was bordered not by a wall but by a level walkway perched only two or three feet above the surface of the virtually tideless Adriatic. The edge of the walkway was interrupted by sets of shallow steps to allow people to disembark from boats, and by substantial lengths of timber driven vertically down into the seabed to act as mooring posts. A line of old-fashioned metal streetlamps marked the seaward side of the walkway, and on the opposite side of it were the front walls and doors of the houses and shops.

Several powerboats and launches were already secured alongside the walkway, but Bronson had no trouble finding a vacant mooring post. He looped the bowline of the boat around it and secured it with a quick-release knot, so that he would be ready to leave at a moment's notice. He shut down the outboard motor to conserve fuel, and checked to see how much he had left. It looked like about half a tank, which he hoped would be enough.

Then he pulled his binoculars out of his jacket pocket and climbed up onto the walkway using the nearest set of steps. He sat down, dangling his legs over the edge of the walkway. He could have begun his surveillance of the water traffic around the island from his boat, but the boat was bouncing and rolling in the waves that continuously washed against the shore of the island, and in the wake of every passing vessel; focusing on anything through the binoculars would have proved difficult. It made much better sense to use his binoculars from the stable platform that the walkway offered.

He had carried out numerous surveillance operations

in his short career as an army officer, and later in the police force, but in those tasks he had been part of a large team, both static and mobile, and the target had usually been a particular individual to be followed and watched. If he'd been covering a building, it had generally been a single dwelling with only one or two entrances, and one team would be assigned to cover each. The emphasis had always been on team operations—a large number of people blanketing a small target—never would one man cover even a single location with any degree of success.

But out here, in the choppy waters of the Venetian lagoon, Bronson was going to try to do exactly this. He intended to look at every boat heading south that passed on either side of his position. If he'd been right in his guess, and his attackers had originally intended to sail around the eastern end of Venice, and they'd left the canal system on the north side of the city after their confrontation with him, then they would have to pass fairly close to him now to reach the same area. But he was also keenly aware that if the blue powerboat had managed to reach the Grand Canal before him, his attackers could already be well beyond his reach.

He started by checking all the small boats he could see out in the lagoon, and which were already a good distance away from him.

As he'd expected, there was a huge number of boats and launches in a variety of shapes and sizes and types and colors. Blue seemed to be quite popular, and twice he saw

vessels that looked remarkably like the one he was searching for, but in both cases he was able to reject the sight-
ings. One of the boats had three people in it and the
other one at least four, possibly five, and he was fairly
certain that the men he was chasing wouldn't have
stopped to pick up passengers. What was more, these two
boats were a long way to the south of where he was sitting, and whatever route the two men had taken, he
doubted if they could possibly have gotten that far ahead
of him.

Although he was concentrating on checking the vessels at the far end of the lagoon, Bronson was also watching those passing much closer to him. He knew that if he
was to stand any chance at all of spotting the boat, he
would have to establish a pattern for his surveillance, and
not get fixated on watching just a single part of the lagoon. In fact, he knew he ought to use the binoculars as
sparingly as possible, because it would be a fairly unusual
thing for someone to be doing on the island, and he definitely didn't want to draw attention to himself. If this
was going to work, he had to look pretty much like any
of the other people going about their business on Giudecca.

So Bronson relied largely on his eyes, and quickly
worked out a kind of pattern search that he thought
would give him the best chance of spotting the boat and
its occupants before they saw him. The most likely area
for them to enter the southern half of the lagoon was, he

believed, over to the east, so he concentrated most of his attention there. He looked that way for about thirty seconds, then looked down to the south of the lagoon for fifteen seconds, and finished his one-minute scan by looking over to the west, then back to the east again. It was boring and repetitive, but Bronson didn't care. It offered the best chance he was going to get to find Angela, and for that he could endure almost anything.

So he sat on the walkway, beside his powerboat, and watched, and kept watching, never letting his concentration flag for an instant, as the hull of his vessel rose and fell gently beneath him. Fifteen minutes passed. Then twenty, and then twenty-five. After half an hour, Bronson began to feel desperate. Either his guess about the destination of the two men was completely wrong or they had slipped past him somehow. Or maybe they'd just been much faster than he'd expected. In any case, he'd blown it.

Bronson sat there, following the pattern search that he was now convinced was a waste of time, and wondering what the hell he could do next. He toyed with the idea of simply getting back into the boat and motoring around the islands scattered about the lagoon in the hope that he might catch a glimpse of the blue powerboat that way. But even as he considered this course of action, he realized it would be a complete waste of time. There were more than one hundred islands out there, and almost every one would have a powerboat secured to its jetty, and there was a fair chance that quite a lot of them would be blue.

He picked up the binoculars to check out another flash of blue he'd spotted some way down to the south, then muttered in irritation. That particular boat was blue and white, a completely different color scheme. He lowered the binoculars again and for a few seconds just sat staring vacantly across the glistening blue waters of the Laguna Veneta, trying to work out his next move.

And then, almost without him being aware of it, he found himself looking directly at the blue boat with the two men on board. It had just emerged from around the east end of the main island of Venice, as part of a group of perhaps half a dozen other small boats and one larger launch, all of whose courses then began to diverge as they headed for their individual destinations.

Bronson didn't react in any way at all. He just sat on the walkway, looking back toward Venice while his eyes, invisible behind his mirrored shades under the peak of his baseball cap, remained locked on the vessel. The men in the boat appeared to be looking around casually as they headed south, but gave no sign that they were in any way suspicious of the man wearing sunglasses sitting by himself on the southeast side of the island of Giudecca.

Bronson waited until the boat was a couple of hundred yards distant. Then he climbed casually down the steps into his craft and started the outboard engine, which immediately rumbled into life. He released the bowline, and swung the boat around to follow the other vessel, keeping his speed well down, to ensure that he wouldn't get close enough to attract attention.

Then, as if linked by an invisible tether, the two powerboats, now almost three hundred yards apart, headed south across the Laguna Veneta, away from the city and toward the scatter of outlying islands.

52

Angela couldn't help it. She squealed in fright and stepped backward, away from the horrendous apparition that had just appeared. But in seconds she'd recovered her composure. She was no stranger to old bones, and ancient corpses interested, rather than frightened, her. It was just the shock, and the unexpected appearance of the old body.

Marco had jumped back with a yell of fear, lashing out with his torch at the dangling corpse.

For a few seconds, neither of them moved, the beams of their flashlights shining across the open space toward the trapdoor, and illuminating the grisly body that had partially fallen through it.

"I didn't expect that," Marco said, brushing dust from his clothes.

"Nor did I."

Angela moved forward and shone her flashlight upward. The skeleton—or what she could see of it—appeared to be largely articulated, skin and desiccated muscle still clinging to the bones. It looked old.

"There's a story," Marco said, "that the mad doctor from the lunatic asylum didn't jump from the tower, but was actually walled up here. Could that be him?"

Angela shook her head. "I don't think so, because that was a hundred years later. The Latin text referred to a 'guardian' for the source document. I think this body was placed up here to act as a kind of warning to anyone who wanted to get into the space above us. I think this is what Carmelita meant."

"You mean this corpse was once a member of her group?"

"Not necessarily. From what I've read, finding a dead body on this island wouldn't be difficult. I think they just dug one up and positioned the corpse above the trapdoor before they closed it."

It took a moment for the implication to hit them both.

"A plague victim?" Marco asked, his voice hushed as realization dawned.

"It's possible," Angela said. "We both know this island is covered in plague pits. But that doesn't mean that the corpse is still infectious. I'm not a doctor. I don't know how long the bacteria can survive once the host is dead."

"But it could still be carrying the disease?"

Angela shrugged. "I don't know. Maybe. But these days there are treatments available for the plague," she added reassuringly.

She was silent for a moment before she voiced the

logical conclusion. "If I'm right—and the corpse was positioned there as a form of protection for the source document—my guess is that the people responsible probably thought the body was infected. That's why Carmelita referred to a 'guardian.'"

"So you think the document might be up there?" Marco asked, pointing upward.

"That would seem likely, and I really hope so."

"Well, we'll soon find out. Or you will, to be exact."

There was an old broom, almost all the bristles long vanished, standing in one corner of the space. Marco picked it up, placed the head under the skull of the corpse and pushed upward. The skeleton vanished from sight, the dangling arm disappearing as quickly as it had materialized.

Angela shone her flashlight through the trapdoor. In the void above her, it was surprisingly light, the daylight spearing in through gaps between the tiles, and she could clearly see the pointed shape of the top of the tower.

She turned to Marco. "If you want me to climb up there," she said, "you're going to have to give me a hand."

He nodded, put his flashlight down on the floor so that it illuminated that end of the platform, then walked across to Angela. Unceremoniously, he wrapped his arms around her waist and lifted her straight up through the open trapdoor.

Angela used her arms to lever herself completely through the opening, and shone the flashlight around her. The skeletonized remains of the body lay just a couple of feet away, but she ignored it completely. She wasn't entirely sure what she was looking for but, if her deductions had been correct, the lost source document that Marco and his cronies were seeking had to be somewhere nearby.

The sides of the steeple sloped gently toward one another, to meet at a point perhaps twenty feet above her head: it was difficult to estimate the distance exactly. She doubted if the hiding place would be that inaccessible. It was more likely to be within reach of her at that moment, somewhere on the floor or the walls nearby, simply because of the difficulty of getting to the top of the steeple. Even maneuvering a ladder into the void would have been a virtual impossibility, and the sloping walls were unclimbable.

If the document—this scroll or codex or whatever it was—had survived, and was still hidden somewhere in the old bell tower, it had to be close by.

Angela moved the beam of the flashlight slowly around her in a complete circle. She was standing on what appeared to be a solid stone floor, pierced only by the open trapdoor. It seemed unlikely that there could be a cavity anywhere within it. She shifted her glance to the walls. Formed from solid timbers, with horizontal braces every few feet, they didn't look too hopeful either. She ran the flashlight over the walls from floor level up to about eight feet, the maximum height that most men could reach, but saw nothing that looked like a box or other kind of container.

Then she stopped. Among the pinpricks of light filtering through the gaps between the tiles, she thought she'd spotted something else. A glint. Something shiny. Without altering her position, she moved the flashlight back in the opposite direction, the beam of light illuminating the opposite wall. As it passed over one of the vertical timbers, she spotted something reflective.

She strode over to the upright, her sense of excitement mounting. The glint she'd seen was slightly to the right of the old timber, on one of the horizontal braces about five feet off the ground. The odd thing was that there seemed to be nothing on the wood that could have reflected the flashlight. Then she saw a long split that ran along the length of the brace. She bent slightly forward to peer into the crack, and discovered that the object that had attracted her attention was actually inside the timber. That really didn't make sense.

Angela looked at the top of the brace, and noticed two deep cuts running across it. Immediately after she saw those, she guessed the reason for the wide longitudinal crack: over the years, the wood must have dried out and warped slightly. Somebody had fashioned a kind of box out of the timber, cutting off the top section and cutting out a hollow underneath it.

She took hold of the top of the brace and lifted the wood, which came away quite easily. Lying in a shallow depression underneath was something metallic. It was that that had reflected the flashlight, the metal glinting in the darkness.

Angela reached up and lifted it down. It was a metal cylinder about ten inches long and three inches in diameter, one end sealed by a cap. Originally it had been painted dark brown, presumably to match the color of the wood, but much of the paint had flaked off.

The cylinder was too small to contain a codex or a book, but it was easily big enough for a scroll or a rolled length of parchment.

"What is it?" Marco asked. He had levered himself up so that his head and shoulders were inside the void, and he was watching her closely.

"A steel cylinder," Angela replied. "Do you want me to open it?"

"No. Give it to me."

She walked across the floor to the trapdoor and looked down at Marco. He'd dropped back to the floor below, his hand raised up ready to receive the object. Angela passed him the metal cylinder and then lowered herself back down through the trapdoor. By the time she'd dropped the last couple of feet, Marco had already twisted off the steel cap and was examining a length of parchment, a cruel smile on his face.

"Is that it?"

Marco nodded. "Yes. We'll need your translation skills again," he added as he carefully rolled up the parchment and replaced it in the cylinder. "Get back down the stairs. You've just bought yourself another few hours."

53

The trick with shadowing a car was for the driver of the pursuing vehicle to remain far enough away that the man under surveillance didn't realize anyone was following him, while at the same time keeping so close to him that he couldn't—deliberately or accidentally—get lost in traffic. This was why surveillance operations normally used a minimum of four vehicles, including at least one powerful motorcycle able to keep up with any car, and whose rider could cut through even the heaviest traffic. And all these vehicles would swap positions at frequent and irregular intervals so that the target would never be able to see one particular vehicle in his mirrors for long enough to register it.

Bronson, of course, was by himself, but the good news was that all he now had to do was keep his target in sight and avoid being spotted himself, a comparatively easy task in the open waters of the Laguna Veneta. There wasn't enough boat traffic for him to lose sight of the vessel, and

Bronson knew that if it vanished behind an island and didn't reappear, it would have reached its destination. And that was what he was interested in, nothing else. Following the boat was simply a means to an end.

Once they'd cleared the quite heavy water traffic to the south of the island of Giudecca, the two men in the blue powerboat appeared to focus on the water ahead of them. But still Bronson was cautious and, once he'd established the direction in which the other boat seemed to be heading, he changed his own course slightly so that he was following a parallel course and heading more toward the center of the Venetian lagoon.

Under other circumstances it would have been very pleasant, sitting in the powerboat in the bright sunshine, steering the vessel across the blue waters of the lagoon, the area dotted by picturesque islands, some of which had tall and elegant houses standing on them, others with low buildings, some quite dilapidated, while still other islands appeared deserted. Behind him, the bulk of the city dominated the northern end of the lagoon. In the clear afternoon light, over to the northwest, due to one of those freak atmospheric conditions that occasionally occur, he could quite clearly see the impressive snowcapped Dolomite mountains, looking as if they were only about ten miles away, though in fact they were actually about a hundred miles distant.

But Bronson was in no mood to appreciate the aesthetics of the situation. All his attention was focused on the blue powerboat that was still heading southwest, toward the islands that lay near the Italian mainland. The number of other boats heading in the same direction had diminished considerably the farther away they'd traveled from Venice, and now there were perhaps only a dozen or so craft within about half a mile of Bronson's boat.

As the other vessels moved away, he began to worry that the men he was following would become suspicious of him. He couldn't afford to let this happen, so when another three boats swung west and out of his sight, he realized he was going have to do something.

Easing back the throttle slightly, he picked up the chart of the Laguna Veneta and studied it for a few moments. He was getting close to the southern end of the lagoon, and he knew that the men he was pursuing couldn't go very much farther. He looked ahead at the blue boat, which now seemed to be heading toward a loose group of small islands, quite well separated from one another.

Over to his right was a very small island, only about fifty yards across, which appeared to be uninhabited—or at least, he could see no sign of any buildings or other structures on it—but which looked as if it could provide a reasonable view of the island group toward which the other boat was heading. Making a decision, he eased back still further on the throttle and turned the wheel to the right. The boat heeled over as it changed direction, and Bronson aimed it toward a gently sloping muddy mound, fringed with bushes and a handful of trees, where it looked as if he could beach the boat safely.

A few moments later, he felt the fiberglass hull make contact with the seabed in the shallow water. Immediately, he switched off the outboard motor and pulled his leather jacket back on. He wanted to avoid the white of his shirt being seen on the island, which might alert his quarry that they were being observed.

He clambered forward to the bow of the powerboat, seized the line and vaulted over the side of the vessel to land with a splash, up to his calves in water. He jogged a few feet up the muddy beach, took a firm hold on the bowline and heaved the boat a few feet farther up the beach, then threw the rope around the stem of a large bush and tied it securely: the one thing he couldn't afford to do was lose the boat.

He checked that the binoculars were still around his neck, then ran a few dozen yards until he reached the southern side of the tiny island, found a vantage point where he could see across the water that lay beyond, and dropped flat on his stomach. In seconds he had located his target.

The two men were looking around, apparently checking out the handful of boats nearby, and Bronson congratulated himself on having hidden his boat from view. As he watched, the boat altered course slightly and headed directly toward one of the islands. Adjusting the focus of his binoculars, he switched his attention to their destination. Another small island, though probably at least ten times bigger than the islet he was lying on, it was dominated by a large, gray stone house.

As he watched, the boat decreased speed slightly and moved around the back of the island and out of sight. Bronson remained motionless for a few minutes and continued studying the scene. But the boat didn't reappear, although several other powerboats passed to and fro. Finally, he stood upright again and jogged through the undergrowth back to his own boat. There, he picked up the chart of the lagoon, identified the islet he was standing on, and the island behind which the boat had vanished, and marked them both on it.

Now he had something he could take to the Italian police, because he knew there was no way he could tackle the people on the island by himself. Even armed with the pistol, which was still a heavy and comforting weight in the pocket of his leather jacket, he would be outnumbered and outgunned if he tried any kind of a solo attack. What he needed to do was to get a bunch of heavily armed carabinieri out to the island as quickly as possible.

Bronson released the rope, gave the bow of the boat a hefty shove to refloat it, then splashed through the shallows and climbed aboard. As the boat drifted backward, he started the engine, and swung the wheel to aim the vessel back toward the city of Venice. If this was the island where Angela was being held, he needed to get help. Fast.

54

The descent from the bell tower was noticeably quicker than the climb up, because Marco was clearly in a hurry, eager to show what they'd found to the hooded man who seemed to inspire such fear in everyone, not just in Angela.

On the ground floor Angela was again handcuffed by one of the men while Marco unrolled the parchment so that he and the others could examine it more closely. It was obviously old, stained by the passage of years, the edges frayed and torn, but the men handled it as if it were pure gold. Then Marco carefully slid it back into the steel cylinder and secured the end cap.

Within minutes, Angela was back in the cabin of the powerboat, her wrists again secured to a handrail as the boat picked up speed across the waters of the Venetian lagoon.

This time, the hooded man didn't share the cabin with her; instead he remained at the rear of the boat with

Marco and the others, and Angela was able to stare out of the window, back toward Venice. The afternoon was bright, but patches of mist drifted across the water, giving the lagoon a ghostly and ethereal appearance. Her view was partially blocked by the island of Giudecca, lying just to the south of Venice, but what she could see of the eastern end of the old city seemed almost to float, the mist obscuring much of the lower levels of the buildings. But even over the bulk of Giudecca, she could still make out the top of one of the most enduring images of Venice: the Campanile di Marco, the huge bell tower in the Piazza San Marco.

She remembered when she and Chris had joined the thousands of other tourists and walked around the square, looking up at the huge brick structure. The original, she remembered, had been built in the sixteenth century, but then collapsed unexpectedly in 1902. The people of Venice had rejected every new design produced by hopeful architects, and simply had the tower rebuilt to exactly the same plan as the original.

They'd been happy, that afternoon, despite the crowds milling around them, and had even thrown caution to the wind and ordered a coffee in one of the cafés that lined the piazza, wincing at the price but reveling in the atmosphere. Now, Angela pondered, as she stared back through the small cabin window toward Venice, she had no idea where Chris was, what had happened to him, or even whether he was alive or dead. And Marco had made it perfectly clear that her own life span was now measured in hours rather than years. She had no future, but without Chris beside her she realized she wasn't actually sure she wanted one.

For a moment, she felt like giving way, letting the tears flow, tears of utter and complete despair, but she steeled herself. If Chris was alive, she knew that he'd be tearing Venice apart looking for her, and she owed it to him, as well as to herself, not to give in without a fight.

There was nothing she could do in the bouncing speedboat, no way to attract attention, but once they got back to the island, maybe she could escape from the men, perhaps even try to swim to another island. She shivered at this prospect, not from fear, but at the simple realization that if that really was her last, desperate resort, then she'd be far more likely to die from hypothermia in the cold waters of the lagoon.

But even that might be better than whatever fate Marco had planned for her.

55

Bronson made good time getting back to Venice. Water traffic in the lagoon had thinned out considerably, and he was able to hold the boat at more or less top speed for most of the way. And time, he knew, really was of the essence.

He moored the powerboat as close as he could to the police station in San Marco, remembering his meeting with Bianchi there and the body of the young woman he'd been asked to identify. As his thoughts returned to that scene, Bronson once again gave somewhat guilty thanks that the pale and lifeless body had been that of someone he'd never seen before, and not Angela. If it had been, Bronson knew he would never have been able to forgive himself.

But now, finally, he thought he knew where she might be. And even if she wasn't on that particular island, he was quite convinced that the people there would know something about her, and might have been involved in her abduction. All he had to do was to convince the police to take action.

At the desk inside the station he asked to speak directly to Bianchi, but was told that the senior inspector was unavailable, which Bronson knew could mean almost anything. But he needed action quickly, and he certainly wasn't prepared to be fobbed off by the Italian equivalent of a truculent desk sergeant.

"That's a shame," he said in Italian, "because I think I know the whereabouts of the men who've been killing all these girls in Venice."

The sergeant told him to wait, picked up the internal phone and held a very brief conversation. Less than two minutes later, Bianchi strode into the station's reception area.

"Oh," he said, his step faltering as he recognized Bronson, "it's you again. You have some information for us, I believe?"

"Yes," Bronson said, and he began to explain how he'd seen two men vandalizing a grave on the Island of San Michele, and how, when he'd approached them, they'd shot at him.

Before Bronson got even halfway through his highly edited account of what had taken place on the Isola di San Michele, Bianchi began looking at him in what could only be described as a suspicious manner. But he waited until Bronson had finished—describing how he'd followed the men to an island out in the lagoon—before he responded.

"And I suppose you know nothing about a man we found out on San Michele?" Bianchi said. "He's now in hospital, suffering from a severe concussion, because somebody smashed him over the head with a lead-filled blackjack."

"I only saw the two men I've told you about, nobody else." Bronson held Bianchi's unblinking stare until the policeman looked down at the notes he'd made.

"Very well," he said at last. "And are you sure you can identify this island again?"

Bronson nodded and showed Bianchi the chart of the lagoon he'd brought from the powerboat, on which he'd drawn a distinct circle around one of the islands at the southern end of the lagoon. He'd wisely left the pistol and the spare magazines locked up on the boat, having concluded that walking into a police station carrying an unlicensed semiautomatic pistol probably wasn't the sharpest of ideas. But he definitely wanted to hang on to the weapon in case he did have to take matters into his own hands in order to rescue Angela.

And Bianchi's immediate reaction when he looked at the chart suggested that this might be a possibility.

"I know this island," he said. "Are you absolutely sure this is where the two men went?"

"Yes," Bronson replied. "I didn't actually see them moor their boat or get out of it, because they went around to the opposite side of the island, behind the house."

"You're mistaken," Bianchi said flatly. "That's a private island owned by a senior Italian politician. It's inconceivable that a man of his stature and standing in the community could possibly be involved in anything like this. And," he went on remorselessly, "I still do not see any evidence of the link you're suggesting between the men you followed out to the island and the abduction of your wife or, for that matter, the deaths of young women in this city. What, exactly, would be the connection between a vandalized grave on San Michele and either of these two crimes?"

Bronson just looked at him. "We've been through all this, Inspector. Even if you won't admit it publicly, you know perfectly well that there's a gang of people operating in Venice who've been snatching girls off the street and bleeding them to death. The men I saw earlier today were vandalizing tombs on the Isola di San Michele that contain the bodies of people who they believe were once vampires. Those are the facts as I see them, and that is your link."

"And your wife? Why was she had abducted? Does she think she's a vampire as well?"

Bianchi's face wore a slight smile as he asked the question, and Bronson resisted the temptation to plant his fist firmly on the man's jaw.

"No, Inspector. Like me, and I hope like you, she knows vampires don't exist."

"Then why was she abducted?"

"Because when we examined the first grave on San Michele, she spotted an old book at the bottom of the tomb, underneath the remains of the body, which she removed. That's why our hotel room was burgled, and that's why Angela was abducted."

"Why didn't you mention this before?" Bianchi snapped.

Bronson shrugged. "It didn't honestly seem that important at the time. Now I wish we'd just walked away from that first broken tomb and never spoken to a soul."

"Yes," Bianchi murmured, "hindsight is a wonderful tool."

"So this island . . ." Bronson continued. "Are you going to send somebody to check it out?"

Bianchi nodded, somewhat reluctantly. "You've made a report, and I am duty-bound to respond to it, no matter how unbelievable your statement is, and despite my personal misgivings. I will order one of our police patrol boats to go out there now and make inquiries."

This wasn't quite the response that Bronson had been hoping for, but it was better than nothing.

"Can I go with them?" he asked. "That way I can make sure they go to the right place."

"Certainly not," Bianchi said. "If they find anything—which I doubt very much—I will call you at your hotel. You will be there, won't you?"

The inference was obvious. "I might be out and about," Bronson said, lightly, "so it would probably be best if you called me on my mobile instead."

Bianchi looked at him in silence for a few moments, and then nodded. "Very well, Signor Bronson. Just ensure that you stay out of trouble. I wouldn't want our patrol officers to visit that island and find that you were already there. Do you understand what I mean?"

"Of course," Bronson said. "I can promise you that they won't see me anywhere near the island." Which wasn't quite the same as saying he wouldn't go there, of course, but it seemed to satisfy Bianchi.

Ten minutes later, Bronson was walking quickly back through the crowded streets to where he'd moored the powerboat. He started the engine, cast off the line, and motored slowly away, deep in thought.

The first thing he was going to have to do, he knew, was top off the boat's fuel tank, to ensure that he had enough gas for whatever the night might bring.

He was also worried about Bianchi's apparent reluctance to take his claim seriously. The island might be the property of an Italian politician, but Bronson couldn't think of a single country anywhere in the world that didn't have a large and successful crop of corrupt politicians—and in Italy being corrupt seemed to be a part of the job description for a career in government.

His second worry was that Bianchi was apparently only going to send a single patrol boat over to the island, where the officers would presumably ask politely if anybody in the house knew anything about the bunch of murdered girls. He could guess the probable answer. And that was assuming that Bianchi actually sent anyone at all.

Bronson had seen the fast, blue-and-white patrol boats

in the Venetian lagoon—normally crewed by about three or four officers apparently armed only with pistols, though it was possible, Bronson guessed, that they might have heavier weapons inside the vessels. Even so, they were obviously more concerned with minor crimes, essentially traffic offenses, committed on the waters of the lagoon rather than anything more serious.

But the thing that concerned him most wasn't anything Bianchi had said. It was actually something the inspector *hadn't* said. Specifically, it was a question the man hadn't asked. It was, of course, possible that Bianchi had simply missed it, in which case it just meant he wasn't a particularly good policeman, but Bronson doubted this. In his short acquaintance with Bianchi, the inspector had never struck Bronson as a particularly likable character, but he had always seemed competent.

The other explanation was that Bianchi hadn't needed to ask the question because he already knew the answer, and this was a real worry.

56

Angela heard the engine note of the powerboat die away to nothing a few seconds after it reached the jetty. Moments later, Marco opened the door to the cabin and stepped inside.

Angela tensed, wondering if she dared try to escape right then but, even before he unlocked the handcuff, she realized any attempt was doomed to failure; another one of the men stood waiting by the cabin door, clearly ready for trouble. She doubted she could tackle Marco with any degree of success, and she certainly couldn't cope with the two of them. So she meekly allowed her wrists to be handcuffed in front of her, and was led along the path from the jetty and back toward the house.

She was almost at the door when an unearthly howling noise echoed from somewhere nearby. Angela froze in midstride, her eyes wide as she stared around her. She couldn't pinpoint the location of the sound, but she was certain it was very close.

"What on earth was that?" she asked.

Marco didn't bother to reply, just led her through the front door of the house and into the drawing room. Only when she was standing beside the desk were the handcuffs finally removed.

"So what now?" Angela asked.

"I would have thought that was obvious. One of my men is making a photocopy of the scroll. As soon as he's done that, you can start translating it. And then we'll find the answer."

"The answer to what?"

But before Marco could reply there was a double knock on the door and one of his men appeared carrying half a dozen sheets of paper. Marco took them, glanced at each in turn, and then placed them on the desk in front of Angela.

"Right," he said. "Get started."

Angela knew she had no choice. She picked up the first sheet and looked at it. She'd already seen that the writing on the scroll was indistinct, the ink a faded gray against the brown of the parchment, but the photocopies were actually fairly clear. She nodded and reached for the Latin-English dictionary she'd been using previously.

Within minutes it was clear that what she was looking at was not a piece of text like those she'd worked on before. The first two pages appeared simply to contain a list of names, divided up into groups and interspersed by a number of Latin words that she had not encountered before. Words like *agnatus, abdormitus* and *cognationis* appeared frequently, and it was only when she translated these expressions that she realized what she was looking at. *Agnatus* meant a "blood relative in the male line"; *abdormitus* translated as "died"; and *cognationis* referred to a "blood relationship," a meaning that she'd guessed even before the dictionary confirmed it. The list was simply a genealogy, one section of a family tree.

The first name on the list was familiar to her, because she'd seen it somewhere in the very recent past, though it still took her a few seconds to place it. The genealogy that she was transcribing traced the blood relationship of a number of Italian families back to a single royal source: the Princess Eleonora Elisabeth Amalia Magdalena of Lobkowicz, Princess of Schwarzenberg, the woman who was also known as the Vampire Princess.

Angela sat back from the desk and stared across at Marco, who was sitting in his easy chair on the opposite side of the room. He was looking in her general direction, and when she met his glance, he nodded.

"Do you know what this is?" Angela asked.

"Yes. But you don't have to list all the members of the family. We're only interested in the names of the people who died here in Venice in the late eighteenth century. In fact, it's only one of those names that we need you to check, just to confirm his link to the princess."

"Which is?"

"Nicodema Diluca."

The name meant nothing immediately to Angela, though again the surname had a slightly familiar ring to it. She turned back to the photocopied sheets, quickly found what she was looking for and painstakingly traced the names of Diluca's forebears back to the Princess of Schwarzenberg. If the names and relationships listed were correct, then Diluca was undeniably one of her blood descendants.

"He's a descendant, yes, according to this," she reported to Marco. "Why is it important?"

He looked at her for a moment, then shook his head. "You really don't understand, do you? It's all in the blood. There's nothing quite so important as the bloodline. That's why you won't find the name Carmelita Paganini listed anywhere on those pages. She wasn't part of the sacred family, though she obviously wished she had been. But she did do one useful thing. She—or rather, her diary—pointed us toward the correct grave on San Michele."

Then the penny dropped. "The tomb of the twin angels?" Angela said. "We found it, but I thought the name inscribed on it was Delaca."

"You were nearly right. I have men out on the island now, recovering what we need."

Angela didn't know what he meant by that remark, unless there was some other document or relic they needed hidden in that tomb as well.

Then there was an urgent double knock on the door.

Before Marco could even get out of his seat, the door swung open and a man Angela hadn't seen before stepped into the room. Obviously agitated, he strode over to

Marco and held a brief but animated conversation with him. Partway through, they both paused to stare across at Angela for a few seconds. Then Marco smiled. The other man pointed back toward the door, and then left the room.

"What?" Angela demanded, conscious that Marco was staring at her again.

"I have good news and bad news for you, I suppose," he said. "The good news is that your ex-husband wasn't killed when my men attacked him on the street, because he's just been spotted chasing around the lagoon in a powerboat. The bad news is that he encountered two of my men in one of the canals in Venice and they shot him."

Angela's face displayed the turmoil of emotions flooding through her body as she absorbed Marco's matter-of-fact statements, and for several seconds she found she couldn't speak.

"Is he . . . ?" she finally managed.

"Dead?" Marco supplied for her. "I've no idea. Probably. But whether he's alive or dead makes no difference to you, here and now. The important thing is that he's no longer of any concern to us. We now have both of the things that we needed, the scroll and the relic, and that's all that matters. And we'll be keeping you alive for a little while longer."

Angela was starting to recover her composure. She knew Chris, and knew he had a habit of bouncing back. Just because he'd been shot at didn't mean he was dead. At least, that was what she would cling to. She turned slightly to face Marco.

"You're letting me live?" she asked.

Marco nodded. "At least until you've finished the translation," he said, and walked across to her. "This scroll," he continued, pointing at the photocopied sheets on the desk in front of her, "is the most important document you'll ever see. This is the source, the sacred record. This is what we've been seeking all these years. Forget Carmelita Paganini's diary; this scroll contains the answers to every question we've ever wanted to ask. Translating it will keep you alive, at least for a few more hours."

He paused and smiled. "In fact, if everything works out as we hope, whether you live or die might not matter one way or the other."

57

Despite the veiled threat Bianchi had made for Bronson to stay away from the investigation, he had absolutely no intention of sitting around in his hotel room waiting for the phone to ring. Angela had to be on that island, and he was determined—after all he'd been through—to stay close to her.

This time he knew exactly where he was going, and steered a direct course from the mouth of the Grand Canal across the waterway and through the gap between the islands of Giudecca and San Giorgio Maggiore. Once he was clear of the water traffic around the islands, he opened the throttle and accelerated toward his destination. He kept his eyes open, looking for any sign of the police launch that Bianchi had said he'd be sending to the island to investigate. He saw several of the distinctive blue-and-white craft in the lagoon, but none appeared to be heading in the direction he was going.

After several minutes of traveling at almost full speed,

Bronson reached the small islet where he'd beached the boat previously. He throttled back, bringing the power-boat to an almost complete stop about fifty yards away from the shore of the islet, and for a few moments con-sidered his next course of action. The problem he'd had previously was that the bulk of the house on the larger island to the south of him obscured his view of the jetty where the two men must have landed. It would obviously be far better for him to find a position from which he could see this part of the island, if only to observe the arrival of the police launch—assuming, of course, that one was going to turn up.

Finally he made a plan. He would head south, toward the end of the lagoon, just like any other tourist exploring this part of Venice, then turn around and come back. That way he would achieve two things: he'd get a far bet-ter look at the island itself, and, with any luck, he'd find another island from which he'd be able to watch. At all costs he had to avoid alerting anybody on the island of his interest in them. In other words, he had to play the tour-ist card.

Steering the boat around the islet, he meandered south, sitting on the plastic seat in the powerboat and looking all around him, exactly as an innocent tourist would do. But behind his mirrored sunglasses, he was focusing on the island to his right.

As he'd observed earlier, the island was a reasonable size—big enough for the house to look comfortable in its setting—and as he steered the boat farther south, a small inlet came into view. Within it, he could see a wooden jetty and beside it a launch, quite a bit larger than the powerboat Bronson had hired. The inlet wasn't very big and as far as he could see, there wasn't much room for any other vessels if the launch was moored there.

Then he noticed something else. Behind the house, and about midway between the property and the inlet, was an area of level ground that appeared to have been tarmacked, and on it he could just about make out something painted in white. Playing the tourist again, Bronson looked casually around him, then turned back to look once more toward the island. And now, from his slightly altered perspective, he could see exactly what was on the tarmac.

It was a large white circle, inside which was painted a letter "H": a helicopter landing pad, which made perfect sense. Bianchi had told him that the island was owned by a senior Italian politician, so traveling to the island by boat would probably be a last resort. It would be so much more impressive, and cater to the politician's inevitable sense of his own importance, to arrive there by helicopter.

Bronson continued ambling gently south, past the island and toward a handful of others in the same loose group, most of which had houses built on them. Again, he tried to look like a tourist as he steered the craft around and past these islands.

About two hundred yards from the politician's island was another very small island, upon which was a simple structure that looked something like a carport—just a flat roof resting on four vertical supports with a rough wooden table underneath it. Bronson guessed that was probably a picnic spot, the roof providing some shade from the heat of the midday sun. He looked closely at the island, trying to see if there was anyone ashore there. He glanced at his watch. It was now late afternoon in November, and the island was unlikely to be in use. Certainly, it appeared to be deserted.

Bronson spotted a narrow bay where he thought he could easily beach his craft. He took a quick look around, but there were no other boats near him, and less than ten minutes later, he was hauling on the bowline to pull the powerboat a few feet farther up the muddy beach. He turned off the outboard motor, tied the rope around the trunk of a small tree that was growing near the beach, checked he had his binoculars and the pistol—just in case—and made his way quickly across the small island until he could see his target.

He had quite a good view of the front of the house, and of the small inlet with its wooden jetty, and the launch moored against it. He lay down, resting on his elbows, and peered through the binoculars. There was no sign of life around the house so he switched his attention to the lagoon that lay beyond the island.

And then, perhaps a quarter of a mile away, he saw an approaching police launch, its distinctive color scheme making it quite unmistakable. It looked as if Bianchi had done what he had promised, and had dispatched a police patrol to check out the island. Bronson was glad that both he and his powerboat were well out of sight.

He moved the binoculars again, and looked back at the house. It was, like many of the other properties he'd seen on the outlying islands, built of a kind of gray stone, the windows fitted with wooden shutters and the roof covered in terra-cotta tiles. But as he looked at it again, he was struck by something else. All the shutters on the windows were firmly closed, and the house seemed to exude an indefinable sense of desolation, of emptiness. If he hadn't known better—if he hadn't seen the two men in the powerboat arrive with his own eyes—he would have assumed that it was deserted.

But then, bearing in mind the activities of the group that had snatched Angela, they would hardly be likely to advertise their presence.

The police launch was now much closer. It had slowed down, and the bow wave was about half the size it had been previously. As Bronson watched, the boat swung around the end of the island and slowed even more, finally coming to a halt beside the entrance to the inlet, where the driver of the vessel reversed the direction of the propeller in a short burst to bring the boat to a stop. He didn't steer the boat into the inlet, which puzzled Bronson for a moment until he focused the binoculars more carefully and saw a substantial chain locked across the seaward end of the inlet, preventing the launch from entering.

Two police officers leaped nimbly onto the jetty from the cockpit of the launch and walked unhurriedly along a gravel path toward the house. At the front door they paused and then one of them pressed the doorbell. But the door remained firmly closed and there was no sign of life whatsoever from the house. Eventually, the officers stepped back from the door and looked up at the house. Even from the distance he was watching, Bronson saw one of them give an expressive shrug of his shoulders; then they walked back to the police launch and got back on board. The driver gunned the engine, turned sharply in a sudden spray of white water and accelerated away from the island.

For a few seconds, Bronson just lay there staring through the binoculars at the departing vessel. As searches went, the most accurate description of what he'd just witnessed would be "pathetic." The officers had made no attempt to look around the island, to try opening the main door, or even to try the other entrance to the house—there would certainly be a second and maybe even a third door into the property.

He sighed. If the Italian police weren't prepared to search the place, he would just have to do it himself.

With a deep sense of foreboding, he stood up, took a final look toward the house on the island, and strode back to the small bay where he'd left his boat.

58

Angela sat at the desk and stared down at the text she was translating. In her work at the British Museum, she had quite often had to translate passages of Latin, usually sections of very old documents or inscriptions that dated back almost two millennia to the height of the Roman Empire, and she'd become familiar with the syntax and sentence construction of writings from that period.

But she'd also worked on documents that were much more recent, everything from documents produced at the height of the Byzantine Empire at the end of the first millennium through medieval texts and all the way to passages that were only a couple of hundred years old. It had always fascinated her the way that Latin, though essentially "dead" and unchanging, had been adapted by its users to the changing patterns of speech and writing over the centuries. It was sometimes possible to estimate the age of a piece of text simply from the way the Latin had been written, by the words that were used.

And what she was working on now was clearly much more ancient than the bulk of the diary that she'd seen before. The syntax suggested it was probably late medieval, dating from between the tenth and fourteenth centuries, hundreds of years before Carmelita Paganini had started keeping her journal. That suggested that Marco had been right in the date he'd ascribed to the scroll.

On one level, Angela was quite enjoying what she was doing, working out the meaning of the Latin sentences and transcribing them into clear and understandable English. But even as she worked, a growing sense of foreboding was creeping over her, a foreboding that gave way to a kind of numb resignation as she understood the full implications of the information contained in the scroll. Even the title of the text was disturbing, though not entirely a surprise: *The Noble Vampyr*.

Once she'd completed what Marco had told her to do with the genealogy, just confirming the link, the bloodline, that existed between Nicodema Diluca and the so-called Vampire Princess, she'd started working on the next page. But she hadn't needed to translate the initial section, because within a few minutes she'd realized that it was almost exactly the same as the Latin she'd already seen in the leather-bound diary, and had presumably been copied from the same source. This part of the scroll appeared to be essentially an introduction to the topic and included the attempt to justify the ridiculous claims that the author had made and which Angela had already translated.

But the second section of the manuscript was highly specific about vampires. It explained at some length about the way vampires were supposed to live, and, according to the unidentified author, the reality was a far cry from the romantic images of suave, well-dressed vampires of the twentieth century drinking the blood of their willing victims. Clearly, none of the more contemporary writers had referred to this text or to any other ancient source documents that might have contained similar descriptions.

According to this treatise, vampires were both cannibalistic—which was hardly a surprise, given that their favorite diet was supposed to be blood drunk from the necks of nubile young girls—and scavengers. In fact, according to the translated text, the favorite hunting grounds of vampires were graveyards, where they would break into the tombs of recent burials and feast on the decaying flesh of the bodies they found there. The only inviolate rule was that the bodies of former vampires—the discarded hosts, as it were—were considered to be noble, and were never to be consumed.

The most reliable way to identify a vampire, the author of the text asserted, was by the smell of rotting meat that they invariably exuded, and which normally caused them to be shunned by mere mortals. But this, the author then explained, was a small price for the vampire to pay in exchange for the priceless gift of eternal life.

As she finished translating this particular sentence, Angela shuddered at her recollection of the hooded man and the appalling smell that seemed to surround him like a miasma. Whoever he was, he was clearly the leader of this group of deranged men, and had presumably decided to make himself seem as much like an authentic vampire as he could. She guessed that somewhere under his black robe he was carrying a piece of decaying meat to produce the odor she had smelled.

She shook her head and returned to the translation.

The next few sentences dealt with the misguided and usually futile attempts to kill vampires, attempts that the text stated were frequently mounted by people who simply failed to appreciate the inherent nobility of the vampire. Then the only guaranteed ways by which the death of a vampire might be achieved were specified in some detail. The most effective method was for the heart of the creature to be removed from the body and buried separately—as far away from the vampire as possible.

Decapitation also worked, but driving a wooden stake through the heart was, in the opinion of the author, useless because the heart remained in place, and the heart of a vampire was so powerful that nothing short of its removal from the body would guarantee death. Similar derision was reserved for the idea of placing some object—a brick or a length of timber—in the mouth of the vampire, and the author cited two cases that he had known of personally where a body had been buried with a brick driven into the jaw, and where the vampire had risen effortlessly from the grave after biting through the offending object. Again, he failed to be specific about where and when these alleged events were supposed to have occurred.

What bothered Angela the most about the text was the author's matter-of-fact acceptance of the existence of vampires. From the tone of his descriptions, he could have been talking about any natural phenomenon with which he would have expected most of his readers to be familiar. It was as if, at the time the author was writing, vampires were regular and accepted members of society who simply lived very different lives from most of the people around them.

Angela found such an attitude impossible to accept, and she repeatedly checked the text for any sign that the author was being less than completely serious. But there was no indication that this was the case. Whoever had created the original text was apparently absolutely factual in what he was describing—or, at least, he appeared to believe he was being absolutely factual. He was certainly convinced of the reality of the vampire as a living and breathing—albeit undead—member of the society in which he lived.

Again, Angela wished she had some idea who the author had been, and where and in which period he'd lived. She was still certain, from the Latin syntax, that the time period was roughly medieval, but beyond that she hadn't been able to pin it down.

She read the English translation she had prepared for a second time, then held it up to Marco, who walked over to the desk and took it from her with a nod.

Then she sighed deeply, and read the first sentence of the Latin text that formed the third part of the treatise written on the scroll: the section of the document that she now understood contained detailed instructions on how anyone who wished to do so could become a vampire himself.

59

Bronson cut the motor as he approached the entrance to the inlet. There was, he realized, no point in trying to sneak ashore. The island was too open to make any sort of covert approach feasible, so he allowed the boat to coast gently forward until it just nudged the end of the jetty, then stepped ashore, tying the rope around the heavy chain that barred the entrance to the inlet. As he did so, he noted that the chain itself was rusty, as was the padlock that secured it, and for the first time since he'd followed the two men, a scintilla of doubt entered his mind. It didn't look to him as if anyone had unlocked the padlock or moved the chain for quite a long time; otherwise at least some of the rust would have flaked off.

He looked at the launch that was secured to the jetty. The water was quite clear and he could see the curve of the hull where it vanished beneath the surface. The dark paintwork was liberally covered in marine growth, which suggested that the boat had been sitting there for some time—boats that were used regularly tended to have much cleaner hulls.

But that, of course, might also mean that the owner tended to commute by helicopter. It was an alternative explanation, but didn't do much to quell the doubts that were now nagging at him. The island really did look deserted.

He took out the Browning semiautomatic, removed the magazine and checked it, then replaced it in the pistol, pulled back the slide to chamber a round and cock the hammer, and set the safety catch. Then he walked slowly along the gravel path that led from the jetty and past the helicopter landing pad to the house, looking all around him all the time as he did so.

He didn't ring the bell, just pressed his ear to the wooden front door and listened. There was absolutely no sound from inside the property. With the pistol held ready in his right hand, he walked all the way around the house, checking each window as he went, and listening at both of the other doors. Finally he accepted the sickening truth: he'd gotten the wrong island.

He couldn't understand it. This was definitely the place where he'd seen the two men in the blue boat disappear, although the restricted size of the inlet and the state of the chain that barred it suggested that the boat couldn't have been tied up at the jetty.

At that moment, his mobile phone rang. It was an Italian number, and when he pressed the key to answer it, he wasn't entirely surprised to hear the cool and indifferent voice of Inspector Bianchi in his ear.

"I did as you requested, Signor Bronson," he said. "I sent a launch to the island where you think your wife is being held, and the officers found absolutely nothing. There was nobody on the island, and the house is shuttered and barred. All you've achieved is to waste valuable police time, which is an offense in Italy just as, I believe, it is an offense in Britain."

"I'm sorry," Bronson said. There really wasn't anything else he could say. "I was certain that you would find her there."

"Well, we didn't, and I suggest that now you stop interfering and leave the business of investigating this crime to the professionals."

And with this, the phone went dead. Bronson looked at it for a moment, then slipped it back into his pocket. The one thing he wasn't going to do was stop looking for Angela.

He replayed the sequence of events in his mind. He visualized the pursuit across the lagoon, and his decision to watch from the smaller island. He'd seen the blue boat slow down and then disappear from view. Then he remembered something else: there had been several other craft in the area, buzzing around the islands. Perhaps the men he'd been following, who'd clearly been checking around them as they approached the island—he remembered seeing them do this—had simply stopped the boat beside the chained-off inlet and waited there for a few minutes until the other tourist boats had cleared the area. And then they would have continued their journey, careful not to let anybody see their final destination.

Bronson groaned as the realization struck home. If these men were part of the gang responsible for the deaths of half a dozen young women in Venice, their caution was merited. The only encouraging fact was that there were so few islands any farther south: their hideaway had to be somewhere nearby.

All he had to do now was find it.

60

Angela had thought that the second section of the Latin treatise was bizarre enough, but the contents of the third and final part of the text were shockingly brutal.

It began simply enough with a declaration that it was possible for anyone who so wished to join the ranks of the "favored immortals," as it described vampires. But, the author cautioned, the process was lengthy and required the utmost dedication and commitment. As she translated the next few lines, Angela realized that dedication and commitment were only a part of it. The aspiring vampire also had to be prepared to become a genealogist, a grave robber and, finally and most shockingly of all, a rapist and murderer.

First, she read, it was essential to identify one of the most important of the vampire families. That concept seemed bizarre enough on its own. It suggested that vampires could breed just like normal people, and sparked a whole new line of thought for Angela. Would it be enough, she wondered, if just one parent was a vampire? Would that be sufficient to convey immortality and unpleasant dietary requirements on the children? Or did it have to be both parents? She shook her head. She'd become so immersed in this ridiculous piece of medieval fantasy that she wasn't thinking straight.

The reason for identifying a vampire family was then explained. Vampires, the author went on, had the ability to discard the body they were inhabiting and take over another one when the first body became infirm or so well-known that continuing to live the lifestyle of a vampire became impossible.

When she'd translated that, she sat in thought for another minute or two. What could it mean exactly? And then it dawned on her. This was the crux of the matter. This was the explanation—both the reason and the justification. This was how people who believed in the reality of vampires were able to reconcile the claim of immortality with the fact that alleged vampires did actually grow old and die. It wasn't that they died, in the usual sense of the word. Rather, the author was suggesting, their essential life force was able to move from one body to another, and they simply discarded their previous bodies when it was convenient for them to do so.

Quite how you reconciled the completely different personality of the new host for the vampire's spirit with that of the previous person, Angela didn't quite understand, though perhaps the explanation was a lot simpler than that. Maybe people just looked for similarities in behavior or appearance or anything else, and made the assumption that the vampire's spirit now inhabited a new host. And, as proving a negative is always virtually impossible, any protestations of innocence made by the new alleged vampire would be dismissed.

The important thing, the author then explained, was that once a human body had been inhabited by the immortal spirit of a vampire, a part of the vampire's essence would be retained in the flesh and bones, and especially in the skull.

There were two reasons for identifying the family of a vampire, he went on. The first was so that the corpse of a former vampire could be located and part of the skeleton, ideally the skull, obtained for the ritual. That was the first mention of any ritual or ceremony, but Angela was quite sure it wouldn't be the last.

So the first thing the aspiring vampire had to do was find a tomb belonging to a person who had been a vampire, break into it and remove the head. That was distasteful enough, but it was only the beginning.

A section of the skull then had to be removed and ground up into a powder, as finely as possible, so that the essence of the vampire's spirit could be released from the bone. But this operation would be carried out only once the other essential component of the formula had been identified and obtained.

This was the other reason for identifying the vampire family, because in order for the essence of the vampire's spirit to be released from the bone and then recaptured, the ground-up skull had to be mixed with the fresh blood of a female descendant of that same family.

The author digressed slightly at this point to explain, using quasi-scientific reasoning, how the female line retained the spirit of the vampire more strongly than the male line. The explanation frankly made no sense—like almost everything else Angela had translated—but it seemed to involve a woman's periods, when she *voided her excess of blood to summon a noble vampyr and signify her willingness to be taken*. The blood of a female child was of no use, *for the essence is not yet sufficient strong in her*, and nor was the blood of a woman past childbearing age, or even that of a woman who had given birth. *She should bleed but be without child*, as the author succinctly put it.

The unknown author then moved on to the details of the ritual itself. First, a section of the skull was to be *ground exceeding fine* and placed in a suitable container. Only then was the girl introduced to the proceedings. Her body was to be washed thoroughly and she was to be immobilized in a *position convenient for all*. At least two people had to take part in the next phase of the ritual, for one would have to rape the girl, *to ensure her blood would flow sufficient free*, while the other person would bite into her neck to open the veins and allow the bleeding to start.

The text recommended allowing the blood to flow until *the heart could pump no more*—which would obviously mean that the girl would die as part of the ceremony—*for her sublime ecstasy in surrendering her soul and spirit* would help guarantee the success of the proceedings.

The blood was to be collected in a suitable receptacle and mixed with the powdered bone of the skull, and the mixture then drunk by the participants. The author cautioned that it might be necessary to repeat the process several times before success would finally be achieved.

At this point, Angela put down her pencil and sat for a few moments just staring at the Latin text. The document, ludicrous though its suggestions undeniably were, was essentially a recipe and, to a certain extent, a justification for repeated rape and murder, enshrouded in a quasi-religious ritual.

Then she started translating the final section dealing with the ritual, and found herself totally engrossed in the text. There was, the author asserted, a further refinement that was essential if success was to be achieved. As well as the ground-up bones of a long-dead vampire and the fresh blood of one of the creature's lineal descendants, the mixture also required the addition of blood taken from another woman, from someone who had never had any connection with any of the vampire families, but who otherwise met the same criteria. This infusion of blood, the author said, would give added strength to the mixture, and was to be extracted from the subject in the same way, by multiple rapes and severing the blood vessels in the neck.

When Angela read that, she closed her eyes and shook

her head, wondering how she could subtly alter the translation to avoid the inevitable conclusion from being drawn.

But as she reached for her pencil, she realized that Marco was standing directly behind her, and had already read exactly what she'd written.

"I knew that we'd find a more entertaining way to kill you than just a bullet," he said. "You'll be able to take your turn on the table tonight."

61

Bronson tucked the Browning pistol into the waistband of his trousers and stared out across the still waters of the Venetian lagoon. Afternoon was steadily turning into evening, and the gray light of early dusk was deepening the aquamarine of the waters around the island.

There were two islands directly in front of him, both about the same size as the one he was standing on, and both inhabited. He could see lights shining through the windows of the small properties that had been erected on them. They looked homey, welcoming, and were also quite close together. That juxtaposition argued against either of them being the location of any kind of illegal activity, simply because anything that happened on one of the islands would be clearly visible to the people who lived on the other. The only way that either could be the place he was looking for was if the residents on both were involved in some kind of joint conspiracy. And that was a stretch.

Bronson scanned the islands through the binoculars, but saw nothing out of the ordinary. Then he looked over to the left, where another small island was visible in the fading light. As far as he could see, there were no buildings of any sort on that one. It was a similar story when he searched the lagoon farther to the west: just a couple of small islets without any sign of habitation. So where, exactly, had the two men vanished to earlier that afternoon?

He lowered the binoculars and stared out across the lagoon, despair clutching at his heart. He'd been so convinced that he'd found where Angela was being held, so sure that he'd be able to rescue her. But the cold hard reality was that he was no further forward than he'd been the previous day. All he could think of doing was climbing back into his boat and carrying out a visual search of all the islands in the vicinity, and just hoping that he spotted the blue powerboat—the right blue powerboat.

He was about to reach down to release the bowline when a tiny gleam of light attracted his attention. It was coming from the area between, and obviously behind, the two inhabited islands he'd already looked at. At first, it looked as if the light might actually be on the mainland, but when he brought the binoculars up to his eyes he could see that there was another island in the lagoon, quite some distance to the south, which he'd never noticed. He'd been so fixated on the island owned by the Italian politician that he hadn't thought to check any farther south.

He studied it carefully through the binoculars, and noticed right away that it was reasonably isolated. The only thing anywhere near it was a tiny patch of reeds and scrubby vegetation about a hundred yards away from its western shore. Bronson wasn't even sure that he'd find any solid ground there, but it was absolutely the only possible vantage point from which he could see what was happening on the island.

There was another gray stone house there, and some kind of outbuilding nearby. The light he'd seen was coming from a downstairs window, and was a mere sliver escaping through the gap between two shutters. Other than that, he could see no sign of life.

Bronson took a final look at both the island, where the thin vertical line of light still marked the position of the house, and the tiny clump of reeds, fixing their relative positions in his mind. Then he unhitched the rope, climbed down into his boat, started the engine and moved slowly away. At least the gathering darkness might help conceal him from anyone who might be watching from the island.

He steered the boat well out to the west, then turned the bow so that it pointed directly toward the reeds, closed the throttle still further and approached at little more than walking pace. He kept as low as he could in the vessel, knowing that the silhouette of a man sitting in a boat was very distinctive, and that by lying almost flat, his craft would hopefully just look like another shadow on the water in the gloom.

He turned off the engine when he was still a few feet clear of the reeds, and allowed the boat to drift into them. At the very least, they would hold the boat reasonably steady while he looked at the island through his binoculars.

But in fact, a few moments later the hull grounded, probably on mud, and the boat shuddered to a stop. That was better than he had hoped. Bronson climbed out of the vessel and pulled it farther into the reedbed. The ground, such as it was, was soft and spongy underfoot, and several times his feet plunged into holes several inches deep, soaking his shoes and trouser legs. But he didn't care. His search for Angela was back on course.

Making certain that the boat was wedged tightly in place, Bronson stepped back on board and resumed his scrutiny of the island through his binoculars.

62

Marco hadn't finished with her. Despite his bleak statement to her that she would be dead—dying screaming in agony—within hours, there was still the final section of the text to be translated. And Angela knew she had no option but to comply.

Tears clouding her eyes, she again bent forward over the photocopied pages.

After describing in graphic detail the appalling ceremony designed to turn a human being into a vampire, and that would, almost incidentally, necessitate the rape and murder of not one but two young women, the author of the work had concluded by describing how an initiate would know if the process had been successful.

This section of the text was perhaps the least detailed of the entire corpus of work. The author admitted that there was no definitive proof, but suggested that an increasing dislike of consuming the meat of animals, of the beasts of the fields, and an aversion to daylight, were positive indicators. And if the initiate eventually found that he could be sustained only by the flesh of the recently dead, then it was certain that he would live forever.

And now she even knew the name of the lapsed monk, as Marco had described him, and where he'd lived, because the very last section of the Latin text contained a single sentence that identified him, clearly written by the member of the society who'd copied down the words of the author. The translation read: *Inscribed by my hand this fourteenth day of the month of August in the year eleven hundred and twenty-six, from the sacred words of our most sacred and illustrious Master, the noble and revered Father Amadeus of Györ, Transdanubia.*

Angela had actually heard of Györ—it was one of the counties of what became known in the eighteenth century as the Districtus Trans-Danubianus, that part of Hungary which lay to the south and west of the River Danube. It was one of the twelve counties of Transdanubia whose boundaries had been established by Stephen I of Hungary, and which remained unchanged until 1920.

But if ever a monk—lapsed or otherwise—had been misnamed, it was Amadeus of Györ. His name meant "lover of God," and what Angela had read had convinced her that she'd rarely read anything more evil, more contrary to the essential goodness preached by most religions and especially by Christianity, than the treatise in front of her.

She shuddered slightly, and handed the page to Marco,

who retreated to his chair, where he read slowly through the rest of what she had transcribed.

"So what happens now?" Angela asked nervously.

Marco smiled coldly at her. "The good news," he said, "is that you get to keep all your fingers. But you already know the bad news. You'll take part—in fact, you'll have a starring role—in the ceremony tonight."

The slight smile left his face, and he nodded at her, his eyes traveling up and down her body appreciatively.

"It would have been helpful if you'd had your passport in your handbag," he continued. "But even so, we've managed to initiate some inquiries in Britain, and on the Internet, into your family history, and as far as we can tell there's no evidence that your bloodline—any of your ancestors, I mean—have ever been linked to one of the noble families of the immortals. So you're an ideal candidate for the ceremony. You're here on the island, and we need to dispose of you anyway, simply because you've seen our faces and you know too much about us. And, to look on the bright side, having you here means we don't have to snatch another girl off the streets of Venice. So your death will actually save the life of a stranger."

Angela felt a chill of pure terror sweep over her. She opened her mouth to speak, then closed it again. Nothing she could say would make the slightest difference to her fate. She had fallen in with a group of people to whom the sanctity of human life meant absolutely nothing, and who would kill her without the faintest flicker of remorse or regret. The only thing that would concern them was whether or not her death could assist them in their pointless and horrendous activities.

Tears filled her eyes, and she dropped her head into her hands. That something like this could happen to her—to anyone—in a civilized country like Italy, in the twenty-first century, was simply appalling. She wondered where Chris was, whether he was even still alive, or if he was now lying on a slab in some mortuary in Venice. It had been a disaster and it was all her fault, she thought bitterly and inconsequentially. The holiday to Italy had been her idea. Everything had been her idea, even the visit to the Isola di San Michele, which had started everything.

"Let's go," Marco said. The door of the drawing room now stood open and two burly figures were waiting in the hall outside.

"Where to?" Angela managed, her voice barely audible.

"We have a convenient cellar. It's where we hold our ceremonies, in fact. And until tonight you'll have a bit of company, because the other girl is already waiting down there. But there's no point in you trying to get friendly with her," he added. "You'll both be dead before midnight."

Angela snapped. She grabbed one of the pencils—the only thing she could see that even slightly resembled a weapon—and swung it as hard and as fast as she could toward Marco's face, aiming for his eyes.

But it was as if he'd been expecting it, and he effortlessly blocked the blow with his left arm, simultaneously swinging his right hand toward her, catching her a stinging blow with his hand against her cheek.

"You've got some spirit; I'll give you that," he said. "It's a shame you have to die tonight. If we'd had you here a little longer, we could have had some fun with you. Taught you a little humility, perhaps. Take her away."

63

Bronson had studied the island closely, trying to glean as much detail as he could in the fading light about the terrain and the buildings. It appeared to be quite large, the landscape dominated by another big house built of light-colored stone, while behind that was what looked like a ruined outhouse of some sort. Most of the walls were still standing, but the roof had vanished. And a little way behind that was another, much smaller building, apparently made of wood. At the front of the house, just about visible from where Bronson sat, binoculars glued to his eyes, was quite a large inlet with ample mooring spaces. He could see at least two boats there, both with dark paintwork, but the light had now faded to the point where he could no longer make out colors.

He completed his visual survey of the island and then sat back in the seat in his boat. Then he looked away, because a distant sound was becoming steadily more audible. A powerboat was approaching the area, and Bronson swung round in his seat to try to spot the vessel as it drew near. He assumed it was simply a tourist enjoying an early-evening boat ride, or possibly a police launch sailing through the area as part of its normal patrol route.

In fact, the boat was actually a reasonable-size launch, and within seconds of spotting it, Bronson realized that it was heading directly for the island in front of him. The obvious conclusion was that the owners of the property— perhaps an Italian family—were returning home after a day out in Venice. And if this was the case, then Bronson knew he'd gotten it wrong yet again.

He focused his binoculars on the vessel as it approached. There were clearly several people on board the launch, their bulky shapes just visible in the twilight, although it was now too dark for him to be able to see their faces. He watched as the vessel slowed down, and then nosed gently into the inlet. In a few seconds, the sound of the engine died away to nothing, and Bronson watched expectantly for the passengers to alight from the craft.

But before this happened, the main door of the house swung open and two men and a woman stepped out, their figures briefly illuminated by the light streaming out of the property. Could it be Angela? His heart thumping, Bronson ignored the figures who were now walking from the jetty toward the house, and concentrated on trying to see the other three people more clearly.

He couldn't. The light was very poor, patches of mist were drifting across the water in front of him, and their faces were invisible because they were walking away from him. Even through the binoculars all he could really be sure of was that there were two dark-haired men flanking a blond woman. Bronson tensed. Angela was blond, but so were a lot of other women in Venice. The reality was that they could have been anybody, but he kept watching all the same.

They were walking along a path that ran down the side of the house toward the back of the property. It looked as if the woman was having trouble walking—the men seemed to be supporting her on both sides. Perhaps, he wondered, she was physically disabled in some way, or possibly even drunk. The idea of a party going on in the house hadn't occurred to him until that moment, but it was a possible, perhaps even a probable, explanation for what he was seeing.

The three figures now seemed less important to Bronson than the new arrivals, and he switched his attention back to the area that lay between the jetty and the house itself, and concentrated on the people who were walking toward the front door of the property. And his idea about a party seemed to be supported by what he saw. In the light that streamed out of the front door, he could see that the new arrivals were all men, and all appeared to be dressed elegantly, white shirts and ties in evidence underneath the coats they were wearing against the chilly crossing of the lagoon.

It looked to Bronson as if he was watching a group of early arrivals turning up for a dinner party, out to enjoy an entirely innocent evening. He knew he had to be in the wrong place—again. He lowered the binoculars and stood up. He'd head back to Venice, grab something to eat and get an early night, and then start his search again in the morning.

He was actually standing in ankle-deep water beside the bow of the boat, ready to push it back, when a scream rang out across the lagoon.

64

Angela struggled as the two men hustled her out of the house and along the path that led to the ruined church, but she was as helpless as a child between the two heavily built men, and her frantic attempts to escape achieved nothing. Out of sheer desperation, she released a single scream, a howl of terror that echoed off the building beside her.

One of the men raised his hand to strike her, but the other one stopped him.

"Don't do that," he said. "We don't want her bleeding everywhere. I'll give her a jolt instead."

He pulled a Taser from his pocket, held it in front of Angela's face, and then pressed it against her blouse.

Angela hadn't understood what the man had said, but she knew what a gun looked like.

"No, please, no. Please don't."

Her voice rose to a crescendo, but was then abruptly cut short as the Italian squeezed the trigger. The current that slammed into her was like being hit by a truck, and she jolted backward and then tumbled unconscious to the ground.

"Now we'll have to carry her," the man with the Taser said.

They each took one of her arms and looped it over their shoulders, and continued their short journey into the ruined church.

65

The scream galvanized Bronson. It was almost feral in its intensity, a primeval howl of anguish and fear, the sound of a woman pushed to her breaking point. And somehow, he simply knew it was Angela. He hadn't been able to recognize her through the binoculars, but the instant he heard the piercing scream he knew exactly where she was.

If he'd needed any confirmation, what happened next supplied it. There was a confused babble of voices, too far away for him even to tell what language they were speaking, and then he saw a faint but distinct blue flash, and the woman just seemed to collapse onto the path.

Bronson knew immediately what had happened to her: they'd used a Taser. Then he looked on in horror as they unceremoniously dragged her into the ruined building behind the house.

For a few moments, he considered his options, limited though they were. He didn't know how many people were on the island, but he'd already seen the two men

with the woman he was sure was Angela, and at least four
men had arrived in the launch, so he was severely outnumbered. He remembered the old Clint Eastwood line:
"the three of us—that's me, Smith and Wesson"; but even
with the Browning Hi-Power as a force multiplier, he was
still unsure if he could take on that many people, some of
whom must be armed.

He definitely needed backup. He took out his mobile
phone and dialed the number Bianchi had given him at
the police station in San Marco. His call was answered
in a few seconds, but not by the inspector, who was now
off duty. For a moment, Bronson considered trying to
persuade the duty sergeant to send a couple of boatloads
of armed police out to the island, but after the fiasco of
the earlier "investigation," he doubted if he would be
taken seriously. He really needed to speak to Bianchi
himself.

"I've found my wife," Bronson said, "and I need urgent help to rescue her. It's essential that I speak with
Inspector Bianchi as soon as possible. Can you please give
me his mobile number?"

Bronson could almost hear the thought processes of
the sergeant at the other end of the line, as he weighed
up the possible consequences of giving a civilian—
Bronson—Inspector Bianchi's cell number, with the even
more dire consequences of *not* giving him the number if
it turned out that Bronson really had located the kidnappers and the woman then died.

"Very well," the sergeant said. "But if anyone asks,

you got his number from the phone book, not from me. You understand?"

"Whatever you want," Bronson agreed, and wrote down the number in his notebook, using the light from the mobile phone's screen to see what he was doing.

Still worried sick about Angela, he scanned the island again through the binoculars: the two men were walking back from the ruins. Then he heard the sound of another boat approaching, and looked over to his left. He could just about make out a launch—it looked slightly smaller than the other boat—heading for the island, and a couple of minutes later that boat, too, edged its way slowly into the inlet and stopped beside the jetty. Even more people were arriving, increasing the odds against Bronson still further.

He dialed the number he'd written down, pressed the button to complete the call and lifted the phone to his ear. He heard the ringing tone, and simultaneously the shrill sound of a mobile phone rang out over the lagoon. Bronson couldn't believe what he saw next: one of the figures walking from the jetty toward the house stopped and pulled a phone from his pocket. Bianchi was himself a member of the group that had abducted Angela.

66

"Yes, Signor Bronson?" Bianchi asked, his tone resigned. "What do you want now?"

Obviously the inspector had recognized Bronson's mobile number or had stored it in his contacts list.

The one thing that Bronson wasn't going to do, now that he knew of Bianchi's involvement with the gang, was to reveal anything of what he knew. If the inspector realized that Bronson was only about a hundred yards away, he was sure that he'd be dead within minutes. They'd send out half a dozen men in a couple of boats, and they'd run him down in the dark and shoot him.

"I hope I haven't caught you at a bad moment, Inspector," Bronson said.

"Not really," Bianchi replied smoothly. "I'm just about to sit down to dinner with my family."

A blatant lie, obviously, as Bronson could see the man through his binoculars, standing on the path right in front of him.

"I just wondered if you had any more news."

"No, I'm afraid not. Let me assure you again that the moment I learn anything I will tell you. Now, good evening, Signor Bronson."

Bronson kept his eyes fixed on the distant figure, and saw the man snap his phone closed. That was the final confirmation—if any was needed—that it really was Bianchi who was standing on the island in front of him.

Bronson nodded to himself. That also explained something else. When he'd told the inspector about the book Angela had recovered from the desecrated tomb on the Island of the Dead, and described the subsequent burglary at their hotel, Bianchi hadn't asked how the burglars had known where to look for the diary. The only people who knew that Bronson and Angela had been in the graveyard that night, and who also knew where they were staying in Venice, were the two carabinieri officers. Bianchi had not asked the obvious question, because he'd already known the answer. Somebody in the Venetian police force—most likely Bianchi himself—must have given the information to the men on the island.

Bronson knew then that he was entirely on his own.

Pulling the Browning from his waistband, he removed the magazine and, working by feel, ejected all the cartridges from it. He repeated the process with the spare magazines he'd taken from the man in the graveyard on the Island of San Michele, and then carefully reloaded each magazine again. It was a technique he'd learned in the army. Stoppages—the pistol jamming—were far more likely if the magazine had been left loaded for some time. Emptying it and then refilling it helped avoid the problem. And the one thing he could not afford was the possibility that the weapon would jam.

Until that point, Bronson had been keeping the pistol purely for his own protection. But venturing onto that island meant he was taking the fight directly into the enemy's camp, and for that he needed all the help he could get. That included carrying the pistol in its holster instead of simply stuffed into his waistband, where it might snag on his belt or shirt.

Bronson clipped on both the holster and the magazine pouch, on the right- and left-hand sides respectively of his belt, and then did it up again. The pouch held the two magazines slightly separated so that each of them could be grasped easily. He inserted the magazines so that they faced in the same direction, with the forward lip pointing behind him, so that when he pulled out one of the magazines to reload the weapon, it would be the right way round to slide into the butt of the Browning. A fast and fumble-free magazine change could make the difference between life and death in a close-combat situation.

He loaded the last magazine into the Browning, pulled back the slide to chamber the first cartridge and ensured that the safety catch was on. Cocking any semiautomatic pistol makes a very distinctive sound, and he didn't want to risk doing it on the island—anybody hearing it would know immediately what it was. He slid the Browning into the holster, and ensured it was held firmly. Then he switched off his mobile phone and slid it into his pocket.

His preparations complete, Bronson climbed over the side of the boat onto the swampy vegetation, and pushed the vessel back into the water so that it floated free; then he stepped back on board.

67

Angela's eyes flickered open and she looked around her. Or rather, she tried to, because wherever she looked she could see absolutely nothing. Impenetrable stygian blackness surrounded her. For a moment, she wondered if she was actually blindfolded, if somebody had put something over her head or her eyes to block out the light. She lifted her right hand to her face and felt her cheeks and eyelids and mouth, and realized that wasn't the case.

She sucked in a deep breath through her mouth. She knew she was in a very, very dark room, and for several seconds the confusion in her mind almost overwhelmed her, and she had no idea where she was or what had happened to her, or what had caused the dull ache she could feel in the center of her chest between and below her breasts. Her nerves seemed to be screaming at the aftereffects of some trauma and her whole body was trembling in shock.

And then she remembered Marco's instruction to the

two men, to put her in the cellar. And with a sudden rush she also remembered fighting them every inch of the way, outside the house and along a gravel path, until one of the men had pulled out some kind of a gun and shot her. Instantly, her hand flew to her torso, her fingers probing for the bullet hole that she fully expected to find there. But that made no sense. If she'd been shot in the chest, she'd be dead, wouldn't she?

"What happened to me?" she muttered. She lifted her hands to her face, and only then heard the clanking of a chain next to her and felt the pressure of the handcuff that had been secured around her left wrist.

Then, from somewhere quite close by, she heard a voice and realized she wasn't alone.

"Hello? Who's there?" Angela called out.

"I speak only a little English. My name is Marietta. They probably used a Taser on you. They had to carry you down the stairs. You'll be sore all over, but it will pass."

That helped a little. At least Angela now knew why she felt the way she did. And not being alone in the dark was a huge comfort.

"My name is Angela, and I don't speak any Italian. What are you doing here?" she asked.

The only response was a snuffling sound, as if the girl was crying. And then Angela realized that that was exactly what she was doing. Marietta—whoever she was— was sobbing her heart out, and for a few minutes she didn't say another word. Then the girl seemed to pull herself together and spoke a single sentence that chilled Angela to the bone.

"I've been brought here to be killed," she said quietly.

There really was no adequate answer to that statement and for a few seconds Angela just lay on the bed, stunned into silence. Then she spoke again.

"You can't be sure of that. You can—"

"I'm very sure," Marietta interrupted. "Last night I watched them do it."

Angela wasn't quite certain what the girl meant. She was obviously alive so she had to be talking about someone else, unless Angela had completely misunderstood what she was saying.

"What do you mean?"

"There was another girl down here. Her name was Benedetta." Marietta's voice was fracturing under the emotional strain she was feeling, the words indistinct.

"Just tell me, Marietta. Take your time."

"There's a ceremony. They made me wash and put on a robe. But they took Benedetta first and I watched." Marietta's voice broke again, and for several minutes she sobbed uncontrollably before she regained some semblance of composure.

In a shaking voice, she hesitantly described the rest of the ceremony she'd witnessed. As she did so, Angela's terror increased. What the other girl was describing was an almost exact match for the ritual that had been described in the scroll—the *Noble Vampyr* document.

Until that moment, Angela had harbored the faint and

completely irrational belief that what she was experiencing was somehow unreal, an elaborate charade or something of that sort. But Marietta's words, as she described the brutal rape and murder of another girl in that very room the previous day, completely destroyed even that tiny hope.

She shuddered when she heard Marietta's description of the ritual rape, but it was the very last part of the ceremony, the last acts that Marietta had witnessed, which frightened her the most.

"Please tell me that again," Angela asked.

"The man who killed her, the man who bit into her neck, he was a vampire."

Before she'd arrived in Venice, Angela would have unhesitatingly countered such a claim with a calm and reasoned statement of her own. Vampires, she would have said, do not exist and have never existed. Belief in such creatures is a premedieval legend with no basis whatsoever in reality.

She was tempted to say something like that to Marietta, but for a moment she didn't. Because, whatever the truth or otherwise of the vampire legend, she knew beyond any doubt that the group of people who were holding them believed absolutely in the reality of the undead. For them, vampires were undeniably real.

And, though she wouldn't even admit it to herself, the hooded man, the apparent leader of the group, bothered her more than she could say. His ability to move in complete silence, the fact that she'd never seen his face because it was kept permanently in shadow under his hood, and above all the stench of rotting flesh that clung to him all seemed so totally nonhuman that she was beginning to doubt her own mind. Her rational brain still rejected utterly the concept of the existence of vampires, but at that moment, in those circumstances and in that place, she was no longer certain that she was right.

But she tried to persuade the girl anyway. "Vampires are not real, Marietta," she said soothingly. "You must have seen something else."

"You didn't see him. He had huge teeth, long and pointed, and he drank the blood from her neck."

Angela let it go. "So what happened then?" she asked.

"I don't know. I screamed and one of the men hit me with the Taser and knocked me out. When I came round, the cellar was empty and Benedetta was gone. One of the men told me they'd taken her to San Michele, so I know she was dead."

For a few moments, Angela sat in silence, wondering if she should share what she knew about the group, about the lapsed Hungarian monk Amadeus, about Nicodema Diluca, the Venetian who had claimed descent from the Princess Eleonora Amalia von Schwarzenberg, and who both Marietta and the dead girl had unfortunately been related to. But she knew that wouldn't help, wouldn't help either of them, and so she held her tongue.

There was just one last question she needed to ask, though she already knew the answer: "But how do you know they're going to kill you as well?"

Marietta sobbed out her reply. "Because they told me it's my turn on the table tonight," she said.

68

The last group of men who had arrived by launch—including Inspector Bianchi—had now disappeared inside the house, and there was no sign of anyone moving about on the island. But that didn't mean that nobody was watching, so Bronson wasn't going to drive his boat into the inlet and moor it there. Instead, he decided that his best option was to steer a course that would take him well away from the island and allow him to approach it from the southern end, the shore opposite the jetty and farthest away from the house.

Bronson started the engine of his boat and immediately closed the throttle almost fully, muting the outboard's exhaust note as much as he could. Then he steered away from the island, out to the west, before starting a gentle turn that would take him on a semicircular course around to the south of his objective. The boat was moving at little more than walking pace, but that suited him fine. He knew that silence and stealth were both far more important than speed.

Keeping the boat moving slowly until he estimated that he was directly behind the gray stone house on the island, he turned the wheel to point the bow of the craft toward his objective. When he estimated that he was probably about fifty yards from the shore, he cut the engine completely and let the boat drift on in silence. A lot of the water in the Venetian lagoon was very shallow, and he guessed he might well be able to wade ashore, pulling the boat behind him. He should have checked the chart before the light faded, he realized, but it was too late to try to do so now. At worst, once the boat stopped moving forward, he might have to swim ashore and pull it.

In fact, he wouldn't have to do either, because the shore of the island was looming up in front of him out of the murk, and the boat still had enough forward speed to reach it without any difficulty. The bow of the powerboat ran through a clump of reeds, and then grounded on something solid. Immediately Bronson stepped over the side, trying to be as quiet as he could, strode forward and tied the bowline around a projecting tree stump. With the boat secured, he crouched down to avoid being seen in silhouette, and studied the ground around him.

Over to his left was an old jetty, much smaller than the large landing stage he'd seen at the front of the house, and tied up to it was a small powerboat.

As he'd already established from his survey of the island before night fell, the land was reasonably flat, and projected only a matter of a few feet above the water level in the lagoon. There were no fences or barriers that he could see, and the most distinctive feature was the bulk of the house that stood at the northern end of the island and was blotting out the night sky directly in front of him—a massive, featureless gray monolith, its shape relieved only by the lighter gray outlines of the shuttered windows.

Between Bronson and the house were the walls of the ruined building, which he now thought might be the remains of another house, or possibly a chapel or small church. The light wasn't good enough for him to tell for sure. And a short distance over to his left was the other structure, which looked like a wooden stable or a farm outhouse.

Bronson sniffed the air. He'd never thought he had a particularly sensitive nose, but he'd detected an unusual smell. He sniffed again. Whatever it was, it seemed to be emanating from the wooden structure.

He checked around him, then ran across to it. There was a single door on one side, and a window to the right, through which he looked cautiously. The interior was completely dark, but he had the strange sense that there was something, something large, moving around inside. He pressed his ear against the wooden wall, and quite clearly detected a rubbing, scuffing sound from the interior. The door was secured by a large new padlock and a substantial hasp, and he knew he wouldn't be able to unlock it or force it without tools. He could probably shoot off the padlock with the Browning, but that was hardly an option.

For a few moments, he wondered if Angela might be held captive inside the building, and if he should tap on the glass or the door, to attract her attention. But something stopped him—some visceral feeling that told him whatever was imprisoned in the shed was not human. His heart thumping, he stepped backward, away from the door.

Instead, he switched his attention to the gray stone house and the ruins behind it. Choosing his path carefully, every sense attuned to any signs of life, he walked as quietly as he could toward the stone wall that marked the end of the tumbledown building.

As he approached, he realized that his earlier guess had been correct. It was a small church. A few of the roof trusses were still in place, but the battens, tiles and joists had long since vanished. What was left were the four stone walls, a couple of windows and the original door. The windows were above his eye level, and the door closed, so he was unable to see what was inside.

Bronson did a full circuit of the building before pausing beside the door, the only entrance to the ruined interior. He checked all around him, looking and listening, but the night was dark and silent, the only sound the distant lapping of waves against the shore. Lights twinkled all around, principally from the city of Venice itself in the northeast, and from the mainland, which extended in an arc around to the north, but none of the other islands at this end of the lagoon appeared to be inhabited.

He made a final check, then took hold of the ring that formed the handle of the old church door and very slowly turned it. There was a faint squeak as the old metal moved, and then he felt the door give slightly. He pushed gently against it, and the door swung inward almost silently. Looking round again, he stepped through the opening into the ancient building.

Dotted here and there across the old stone floor were piles of stones and lumps of wood. Grass and other plants were starting to grow in the cracks between the paving slabs that composed the floor. There had clearly been no attempt made to restore the building. Whoever owned the island was apparently quite happy to let the place fall apart, and for nature to reclaim the site. And yet Bronson felt uneasy. Why had the entrance door opened so easily? It was almost as though the hinges were kept lubricated, and that the door itself was well used.

Then he heard a door opening and closing somewhere beyond the ruined building. Footsteps of at least two people sounded from outside, heading toward him, and Bronson knew that he didn't have time to get out of the church.

He was trapped inside the building.

69

Before Angela could reply, the cellar lights clicked on and she was able to look at her prison for the first time. Seconds later, a guard strode down the stairs and walked across the stone floor to Marietta's cell. He was carrying towels, two buckets of warm water and a pair of white robes.

"It's time," he ordered. "Get ready; and be quick about it. The first members have already arrived, and we don't want to keep them waiting."

He tossed a towel and a robe onto the bed, gave Marietta a malicious grin, and left her to wash. Next, he stood at the entrance to Angela's cell. Stepping forward, he threw the robe and towel onto her bed, said something to her in Italian, then turned and left the cellar.

"What did he say to me?" Angela asked, once the cellar door had rumbled closed.

For a few moments, Marietta didn't respond. Then she gave a heavy sigh. "He told you that the show was about to start," she replied, "and we'd both have starring roles. I think they're going to kill us both."

The girl's voice sounded flat and resigned, as if she'd somehow managed to come to terms with the inevitability of her fate.

"I know," Angela replied, her voice choked with emotion. "They told me we'd die together tonight."

For a minute or so there was silence in the cellar; then Angela spoke again.

"What are you going to do?" she asked. "Will you cooperate with them?"

Marietta's voice broke into sobs. "I'm going to do exactly what they tell me," she said finally, and Angela could hear her starting to wash in the adjacent cell. "What else can I do? If I don't obey their instructions, that bastard guard will send a couple of his men down here to rape or beat me. If I do as I'm told, I'll only get raped during the ceremony itself. And I've seen what happens down here, so I suggest you cooperate as well. In the end, it'll make it easier for you."

"Dear God," Angela murmured, as the appalling inevitability of their situation hit home.

70

Bronson knew that if he tried to leave, they would certainly see him. He had to stay where he was.

He ran toward the door, his sneakers making almost no sound on the stone floor, and flattened himself against the wall beside it. Pulling the Browning pistol out of the belt holster, he held it in a two-handed grip, the muzzle pointing down toward the floor. He clicked off the safety catch, and waited.

But the footsteps didn't stop at the door. Instead, Bronson heard the two men—and he guessed from the snatches of conversation that there were only two of them—walk past the church and on—or so he guessed—to the wooden stable.

Easing the door open a crack, he peered out and crept forward to the corner of the wall where he could see the stable. Two shadowy figures were standing beside the door, both apparently looking down. One held a flashlight, the beam shining downward to illuminate the padlock while the other man unlocked it. There was a faint metallic clicking; then they opened the door and stepped inside.

For a few moments, Bronson didn't move. If Angela was in the stable, he would be able to tackle the two men with his Browning, get her into the boat, and return to Venice before anybody could stop him. But this seemed way too easy. No, wherever Angela was, she'd be in a much less accessible location.

On the other hand, whatever was in the shed was clearly of some importance; otherwise why would the door be kept locked?

He turned back, intending to walk around the opposite side of the ruins of the church, where he would be invisible to the men in the stable, but he'd taken only three or four paces when an unearthly howl tore through the night.

He froze instantly. It sounded like a huge dog, and for a brief, terrifying moment, Bronson thought that the island might be protected by attack dogs. If it was, the dogs would pick up his scent wherever he went and whatever he did. The Browning would dispose of them—he wasn't worried about that—but the men in the house would know immediately that they had an intruder, and he would stand no chance against half a dozen armed men. He'd be lucky to get off the island alive, and there'd be no chance of finding and rescuing Angela.

Then he relaxed slightly. Guard dogs, or those trained to attack intruders, either worked silently or would bark or growl. The sound he had just heard was neither. It had been more like an animal in pain, and it had sounded close by. Bronson's thoughts spun back to the wooden stable. There had definitely been something alive inside it.

And that was where the two men had gone.

Bronson ran swiftly around the old stone walls of the church, a moving shadow in the deeper blackness of the night. Before he'd covered more than a few feet, he heard the howl again, echoing from the stones around him, and filling the air with a sense of mournful and impending doom. He reached the end of the ruined building and crouched down beside a bush. The door of the stable was open and a dim glow came from the window that he'd tried to look through before.

Keeping well to one side of the building, Bronson made his way stealthily back toward where he'd left the boat, then circled around to approach the stable from behind. As he did so, the animal howled again, the sound dying away to a threatening growl. Then there was silence broken only by a faint whimpering noise. Bronson edged his way along the rear wall of the stable, turned the corner and stopped beside the window. For a few seconds he just listened, relying on his ears to warn him of the approach of anyone through the darkness. But apart from the noises emanating from the shed, the night was silent.

Slowly, carefully, Bronson looked through the small window. Inside, the walls were unadorned, just plain wood. The men were still out of sight, somewhere over to his left, but beside the door, which was wide-open, he saw a long wooden table, a number of tins and packets placed on it, together with several metal bowls, a handful of forks and spoons, and a couple of metal jugs that possibly contained water. It was fairly obvious what he was looking at: the table was where they prepared food for the dog.

Bronson moved slowly, infinitesimally slowly, to the right, steadily bringing more and more of the interior of the stable into view, until at last he could see the whole building. Breathing in sharply in shock, he stepped back. The occupant of the stable was not the dog he'd expected. And what the men were doing to the animal made no sense at all.

71

Bronson shrank back into the undergrowth beside the old church and waited. About fifteen minutes had passed, and the men had just left the stable and were walking back toward the ruins. For an instant, he thought they might have seen him, but their posture was wrong: they were too relaxed, too casual.

They were still talking together as they passed him, and then, stepping slightly in front of the other, one of the men seized the ring handle on the church door and pushed it open. They both stepped through into the ruins and disappeared, leaving the door wide-open behind them.

Bronson stood up slowly. For a few seconds there was total silence, and then he heard a distant rumbling that seemed to come from somewhere close by. It sounded like one heavy stone being moved across another.

Bronson reached the open door, looked inside—and shook his head in astonishment. The two men had simply disappeared. He'd walked around the entire interior of the building, just half an hour before, checking for any other way out, and had found nothing. But now, as he stared across the weed-strewn interior, piles of stone and wood faintly illuminated in the moonlight, he realized that there had to be a hidden door, or trapdoor, or something, somewhere in the building, and he had obviously missed it.

And wherever that door was, and whatever space it gave access to, it had to be the most likely place for Angela to be imprisoned.

If he'd seen where the two men had gone, he would have been able to wait outside and tackle them. One man armed with a semiautomatic pistol facing two unarmed men was no contest. He'd missed that chance but, he rationalized, sooner or later they would have to come out. And when they did, he'd be ready.

It was a simple enough plan, and almost immediately it started going wrong.

Marietta looked up when she heard the cellar door swinging open. "Not so soon, please, no," she whispered.

Shaking with fear, she looked with terrified eyes toward the stairs, and almost wept with relief when she realized that she still had a little time left. The two men were dressed in normal street clothes, not the hooded robes they would wear for the ceremony itself. One of them was carrying a small metal jug, which he placed on a ledge on the wall behind the stone table. Then they walked across the stone floor and peered at both Marietta and Angela, presumably making sure that they had obeyed their instructions and were wearing their robes in preparation for the ritual.

One of the men nodded toward Marietta and smiled; then they both turned and walked back to the spiral staircase.

Bronson stepped silently into the ruined church. Most of the debris littering the floor comprised individual lumps of stone and lengths of wood or small piles of rubbish, far too small for him to use for concealment. The only option he could see was about halfway down the wall to his left, where somebody had made an effort to clear some of the timber and building materials. The result was a heap of debris about two feet high and eight feet long, positioned quite close to the wall. It was just about big enough for him to hide behind, at least lying down, and would keep him invisible to anyone entering through the church door, though if somebody stepped across to the sidewall of the building, they would see him immediately. It was a chance he was going to have to take.

The Browning in his hand, he crouched down behind the collection of old timbers. The only sound he could hear was the wind sighing through the branches of the handful of trees on the island, the branches creaking and groaning faintly as they moved. Even the animal imprisoned in the shed seemed to have fallen silent.

Then there was a click and a faint rumble, and a black oblong shape appeared at the far end of the church. Beyond it he could see electric lights illuminating the top of a staircase that was set into the wall. It was obviously a door that led down to a cellar.

Two figures—the men he'd seen in the stable—stepped out and into the church. Bronson tensed as he prepared to run toward the hidden door and down the steps. But then he relaxed again. The men had left the cellar door wide-open, which meant that they could be going back down again. It would be better to wait until they'd left the church completely, and then make his entrance.

But then he realized there was another possibility. They could have left the door open to allow other people to enter the cellar, and this changed the odds once again.

As the two men reached the main entrance to the church, Bronson heard another noise. From over to his right, from the house itself, he heard the sound of shoes on gravel. It was clear that several people were now approaching the old church.

By now, the two men were still clearly visible at the church doorway, presumably waiting for the arrival of the approaching people. Bronson glanced over at the secret door, but knew that if he left his hiding place, he'd be seen well before he reached it. He would have to wait, and pick his moment.

There was a brief instant of silence, and then the first of the new arrivals stepped into the church. Bronson stared across at the figure, disbelief clouding his mind.

The man—and Bronson knew the figure was male sim-

ply by the way he walked—was clad in a dark, possibly
black, hooded robe, his face completely hidden. He
looked like a caricature of a monk, though without any
doubt Christian thoughts and prayers were a long way
from his mind. Bronson had guessed from the few clues
he had been able to find that the deaths of the girls might
well have involved some kind of ritual. What he hadn't
anticipated was that the ritual might involve a quasi-
religious ceremony. But this was what seemed to be about
to take place, because the hooded man was followed by
others, all clad in the same all-enveloping robes.

The figures made their way in single file across the old
stone floor, the hems of their robes just brushing the
ground. Bronson counted eleven, plus the first man, who
appeared to be the leader of the group. He seemed to
remember that thirteen was supposed to be the number
of witches in a coven, and wondered if that was significant, if there was another man already waiting down in
the cellar.

Then he heard a faint click, and saw that the lights on
the stone staircase had been extinguished. A new light,
faint and flickering, had sprung to life just inside the hidden doorway. Obviously the leader of the group had lit a
candle.

As the man started to walk slowly down the staircase,
Bronson heard something else: a single scream of anguish
from deep within the chamber below. Could it have been
Angela? One way or another, he was going to find out.

Bronson knew he was heavily outnumbered, and he

had no idea if any of the group were carrying weapons under their robes, or if there were firearms stored in the cellar. Whatever the case, he had to get down to that cellar.

And suddenly he saw a way of achieving just that. The men filing down the stairs were walking slowly, but they were too close together for him to tackle one without the person in front seeing what was happening. Each man paused inside the secret doorway to light a candle before descending out of sight, which meant several of them were now clustered outside the doorway, waiting their turn. But then the last man in the group stopped and turned back to the church entrance. One of the two men outside the ruined building had said something— Bronson didn't catch what—and had attracted his attention.

The man walked swiftly back to the church entrance, muttered something to the men outside, and closed the door. Then he turned and walked back toward the hidden doorway, through which the last of his companions had just disappeared. At that moment Bronson holstered the Browning and made his move.

He ran across the debris-strewn stone floor after his target. The moment he did so, the hooded man turned toward him, obviously having seen some movement in his peripheral vision. When he saw Bronson, a sudden expression of panic clouded his features, and he opened his mouth to shout.

But Bronson didn't give him the chance, as he dived

forward and slammed his left shoulder into the man's chest. The impact drove every vestige of breath from his target's body, and he fell backward, gasping for air.

The two men tumbled to the ground together, Bronson cushioned by the body that had fallen beneath him. The other man caught his breath and started to rise, but Bronson had anticipated his movement. He punched him—hard—in his solar plexus, and followed it up with a vicious short-arm jab to the chin. The man's head snapped backward, the rear of his skull crunching onto one of the flagstones. His eyes rolled backward and his body went limp.

Bronson stood up and looked all around him. He knew he had only seconds to act before somebody in the group noticed that the last man hadn't appeared.

He seized the man's right arm and pulled him into a sitting position, then wrapped his arms around his chest and lifted him upright across his body, like a bulky sack. Moving awkwardly across the ground to the pile of debris behind which he'd hidden before, he simply let go. The man's limp body crashed to the ground, his head again cracking onto the old stones. At best, Bronson guessed that he would have a concussion and a blinding headache for a few days. At worst, he might already be dying from cranial bleeding. Either way, he didn't care.

With some difficulty, he removed the man's robe. Underneath it, he was naked apart from a pair of sandals, confirmation, if it was needed, of the sort of ritual that was about to take place. Bronson didn't bother about the sandals, but swiftly pulled on the robe over his street clothes and then ran across to the door in the church wall.

Pulling the hood down over his features to conceal his face as much as he could, he picked up one of the large yellow candles lying on a shelf just inside the doorway, lit it from the box of matches that was also on the shelf, and began to make his way slowly down the stone spiral staircase.

72

The moment the light went out, Marietta gave a shriek of terror. She knew what the sudden darkness meant. For them, there was no more time. The ceremony was about to start, and within minutes she and Angela would be dying in agony.

She screamed again as the first hooded figure appeared at the base of the stone staircase, his features fitfully illuminated by the flickering light of his candle.

In almost complete silence, the remainder of the group appeared one by one at the bottom of the staircase and stepped into the cellar, the only noise the faint slapping of their leather sandals against the stone floor. As before, they moved slowly around the stone table, taking up their prearranged positions in what looked like a ghastly parody of a religious service.

Angela watched with mounting horror as the figures, all dressed in identical black robes, strode silently and menacingly across the cellar. Marietta had explained what had happened the night Benedetta had died, and it was obvious that the ritual tonight was going to be almost identical.

For a few moments, the men stood in unmoving silence around the stone table, apparently waiting for something. A couple of them turned slightly and looked back toward the entrance to the staircase. Then everyone in the cellar clearly heard the sound of another set of footsteps descending toward them, and seconds later a twelfth hooded man stepped into the room. There was only one space in the circle of figures, and the man stepped confidently forward and took his place within it.

The leader nodded his satisfaction. The circle was complete and, once the Master made his appearance, the ceremony could begin.

Bronson stood near the foot of the stone table, his head bowed respectfully, trying his best to emulate the stance of the other men in the cellar. Like them, he held the candle in his left hand but, unlike the others, his right hand was hovering close to the vertical seam that joined the two halves of his robe together at the front.

The garment had only one small pocket, nowhere near big enough to conceal the Browning pistol, and he'd had to leave it tucked into the belt holster. With the heavy robe over the top, the weapon was fairly inaccessible, and he knew that if—or rather, when—he had to draw it, he'd have to be quick and get the robe open as fast as possible.

But his prospects were bleak. He knew that when he

pulled the weapon, he might be able to shoot down two or three of the men, but in this confined space he would soon be overpowered. He would have to wait, and choose his moment carefully.

He was aware that there were other people in the cellar besides the dozen men near him. He could hear faint movements, and the sound of sobbing, coming from somewhere in the darkness over to his left. Convinced it was Angela, he resisted the temptation to rush to her aid.

The scene Bronson was witnessing was bizarre in the extreme. Aboveground, and away from the isolated island, life in the twenty-first century continued unabated, but what he saw in front of him was medieval both in its appearance and, he was sure, in its objective. In that cellar, at that time, the modern world had simply ceased to exist, and the ritual about to take place was designed to produce a result that wasn't even medieval in scope. It was far older, and far more evil, than that.

Suddenly he detected a change in the atmosphere. A sense of anticipation, of barely controlled excitement, filled the air.

And then he heard something: a soft, sibilant sound, coming from the stone staircase behind him. The noise could be caused only by the hem of one of the robes rubbing on the stone steps as someone else descended into the cellar. All the other hooded men who were now surrounding the stone table were wearing sandals, and he'd clearly heard their footsteps as they crossed the floor of the ruined church. Perhaps the new arrival was barefoot?

He detected a new and unpleasant odor, and then the thirteenth man entered the cellar. He moved silently to the opposite side of the stone table, his hands and face invisible in the folds of his black robe, and all the other men, including Bronson, bowed low in supplication.

For a few seconds, nothing happened; then the new arrival—the person Bronson now assumed was their leader—gestured to the man on his left, who bowed in acknowledgment and produced a small box that he raised above his head while the other men looked on with reverence. Bronson tried to keep his face in shadow as much as he could, but he knew he had to act just like one of the other acolytes in order to remain safely anonymous. So he moved the candle slightly to one side, so that its light no longer fell directly on his face, and looked up.

The man lowered the box, opened it and removed a skull, the bone dark brown and cracked with age, the lower jaw and parts of the cranium missing. There was a soft collective intake of breath at the sight of the relic.

"Behold the skull of Nicodema Diluca himself," the man said, "the legitimate descendant of the Princess Eleonora Amalia, the relic for which we have searched for so long."

What happened next made no sense to Bronson. He watched in fascination as the man used a pair of modern pliers to snap off a section of the cranium, and then proceeded to grind it up using a pestle and mortar, his movements slow and deliberate, almost ceremonial.

The operation took several minutes, because the man

clearly wanted to reduce the fragment of bone to dust, but eventually he appeared to be satisfied and placed the pestle to one side. He lifted the mortar above his head, and again this action seemed to inspire a kind of rapture in the group around the table, the dozen men raising their heads to stare reverently at the stone container.

Finally, the man lowered the mortar and walked slowly around the table to show the contents to the leader; then he returned to his place in the circle and put the mortar to one side, on another, very much smaller, stone table behind him.

For a few seconds, nobody moved. Then the leader made another gesture, this time to the man on his right, who nodded and pointed toward the two men who were standing on Bronson's left. They both bowed slightly, then stepped away from the stone table and walked slowly away into the darkness that shrouded the other part of the underground room.

As they did so, a scream ripped through the oppressive silence, and Bronson could sense an almost palpable ripple of excitement coursing through the men around him. Working by feel with his right hand, through the thick material of the robe, he checked the Browning, trying to make sure that the hammer was cocked and the weapon ready to fire.

Then he heard another voice from the darkness, laced with fury and yelling in English, which he recognized immediately. Angela was somewhere in the room, together with at least one other young woman.

The leader of the group turned his head slightly to look toward the sound of her voice, as did several other men around the table. Bronson stared in that direction as well, trying to build up a picture of the layout of the room, so that when he moved, he wouldn't slam into a wall or trip over anything. As far as he could tell, in the fitful illumination provided by the candles, it had a low ceiling and no doors apart from the one leading to the spiral staircase. Along one side of the room were short dividing walls that formed small, doorless, internal rooms. Possibly they'd once been storerooms but now, even in poor candlelight, he could see that they were being used as cells.

He could just about see Angela, who was still shouting her defiance at the men. Bronson tensed, ready for action. And then he heard a sudden sharp crack and a brief flare of light from the darkness, and she fell silent. He didn't know for sure, but it looked as if one of the men had used a Taser on her. He would pay for that, Bronson vowed, his hands clenched, blood pounding in his temples.

The leader of the group held up his hand, and immediately the attention of all the men around the table snapped back to him. He whispered something to the man on his right, who'd been acting as his assistant during the first part of the ceremony. This man nodded and then he, too, lifted his hand.

"Our Master has made a decision," the man said, his Italian smooth and educated. "We have two subjects available to us tonight. As you know, one of these shares the holy bloodline of Nicodema Diluca, and she will enjoy the rapture of giving her lifeblood freely while two or three of our number offer their unworthy seed to her sacred womb."

For a moment, Bronson didn't understand what the man meant. Then it dawned on him: despite the almost literary expression he had used, what he was actually talking about was multiple rape. Bronson felt his whole body tense with loathing and disgust.

"Our second subject," he continued, "has no direct connection with us, but has accidentally proved to be of enormous value to our quest. She was responsible for removing the diary of Carmelita Paganini from its resting place in her tomb. She has provided a translation of a part of that book, and this information in turn led us to the island of Poveglia, where we recovered the source document, the *Noble Vampyr* treatise written by our ancient and revered master, Amadeus. This holy text has confirmed the validity of our quest and the accuracy of our rituals, except in one important respect."

There was a sudden silence in the chamber, and Bronson could tell that every man there was totally attentive, waiting for the explanation.

"What we did not know until now was that, for the ritual to be successful, we needed to combine the blood of the descendant of Nicodema Diluca with that of a woman without connection to any of the sacred families. Our leader has decided that this Englishwoman, whose usefulness to us is now at an end and whose spirit must be released to the void for our own security, will fill that role. So this evening we will celebrate the passing of both spirits."

The chill Bronson felt as he heard those words and understood what the man meant had nothing to do with the cool and clammy air of the cellar. Angela, it was clear, was also destined for multiple rape, and was then to be murdered. As if that wasn't horrific enough, the man's next statement showed the hideous depths of the cult's brutality.

"Afterward, in accordance with the tenets of our quest and our sacred knowledge, we will then enjoy her directly, consuming her blood and her still-warm and ripe flesh in the manner prescribed by our sacred guide and master in spirit, the venerable and inspiring Amadeus."

Several of the men appeared to nod, though the voluminous hoods that covered their heads and faces largely concealed any movement, and Bronson heard a faint murmur of approval.

"Now let us begin. Bring forward the first subject."

There was a howl of outrage and anguish, and then the two men walked back toward the circle and the stone altar, each gripping the arm of a dark-haired girl in her early twenties who was struggling violently, trying desperately to get away. They stopped a short distance away from the stone table and held her as still as possible.

Two other men then left their places in the circle and stepped over to her, one in front and the other behind her.

His features invisible beneath the hood covering his head, Bronson glanced toward the girl, stark terror written all over her face, and then at the silent figures of the men surrounding the stone table. He knew he would have to make his move soon—he would not permit the men around him to do harm to this girl or to Angela. Or he would die trying.

73

But right then wasn't the correct moment. When the bullets started flying, Bronson wanted the innocent parties—the girl standing a dozen feet from him and awaiting her fate and, of course, Angela—to be as far away from the firing line as possible. It looked to him as if the ceremony would require the girl to be tied down on the table, and that would probably be as safe a place as anywhere in the cellar. So his best option was to wait until she was immobilized, because then she wouldn't panic and run into a stray bullet. And she would also be the focus of everybody in the room. That might give him time to step back to a suitable vantage point and cover the dozen men with his pistol. Quite how the scenario would pan out after that, Bronson didn't know. He would just have to think on his feet, and play the cards he'd been dealt.

He switched his attention to the four men who now surrounded the dark-haired girl. The two who had dragged her from the cell by the wall were still holding her bare upper arms, keeping her in position. Bronson couldn't see what the other two men were supposed to be doing. Then he found out.

Simultaneously, they both reached out, seized the material of her white robe and pulled violently on it. The Velcro seams ripped apart, the robe separating into two halves, front and back, which the men casually tossed aside before stepping backward a couple of paces.

The girl emitted an even louder squeal of terror as her nakedness was revealed to all, and redoubled her struggles to get free. But it was an unequal contest, and the two men had no difficulty in keeping her still. They looked toward the leader of the group, and when he beckoned them, they strode forward, forcing the naked girl toward the end of the table almost directly in front of Bronson.

They turned her round so that her buttocks were resting against the old stone, then simply pushed her off her feet. The two men who'd removed her robe stepped forward and seized her legs, lifting her up and placing her writhing body flat on the table. In moments, the men had buckled the leather straps around her wrists and ankles, while another man tied a strap around her head as well.

He knew that it was time to stop this, before anything else could happen to the girl.

The men who'd been lashing the girl's body to the table stepped back and resumed their places in the circle, and waited expectantly. Bronson knew without a shadow of doubt what the next act in these bizarrely medieval and simply monstrous proceedings was going to be. Somebody, one of the men around the table, was going to climb up onto the table, force himself onto the girl's body and rape her. And he knew absolutely that he wasn't going to stand by and let that happen.

Surreptitiously, he took a couple of steps backward, moving slightly out of the circle, and took a firm hold of the Velcro seam of his robe, preparing to act.

Then the leader of the group spoke again to his assistant, and Bronson caught the faint sound of his voice, though not the words he spoke. The voice was weak and rasping, as if he hadn't used it for a long time or was simply unused to talking. The assistant nodded, then looked up and extended his hand, pointing directly at Bronson. And suddenly, every man in the room was looking at him.

As he stared across the table at the figures opposite him, Bronson could just make out the glint of the leader's eyes under the hood, and below that the shine of his teeth, a faint horizontal bar of white in the gloom. But there was something else, something that sent a chill through Bronson's soul and literally raised the hairs on the back of his neck. It looked as if the canine teeth in the man's upper jaw were at least twice as long as they should have been, the ends sharply pointed.

But before he could react to the sight, the leader's assistant spoke directly to him.

"You go first," he murmured. "Give her something to scream about."

74

Bronson knew that he was the focus of everyone's attention. He assumed that there was some kind of sick prestige in being the first one chosen to violate the girl strapped down on the stone table, the girl whose desperate screams and moans were still echoing around the underground room. He had hoped that as soon as this part of the ritual began, he would be able to step farther back, away from the group, and use the nine-millimeter persuasion afforded by the Browning to stop the action even before it started.

Clearly, that wasn't going to work. He had to act immediately.

He had just started to pull apart the seam of his robe when the man who had been assisting the leader raised his hand and spoke to him.

"Wait," he said. "You are eager enough, brother, but don't forget there is one more step we have to complete."

Bronson relaxed a little and eased his grip on the material.

The assistant gestured behind him, and two of the men left the circle and stepped across to the end wall of the cellar, returning in moments with a small jug and a funnel. As soon as he saw these two utensils, Bronson guessed what they were going to do, and knew he had a few more minutes.

The two black-clad figures walked across to the girl. One of them pulled down on her chin to force her mouth open, then pushed the end of the funnel between her teeth. He held it in position and nodded to his companion, who began dribbling a white fluid into the top of the funnel, forcing the girl to swallow it. She choked and coughed, but to no avail; the two men continued with their actions until the jug was empty.

As soon as Bronson could see that they'd finished force-feeding her the milk, he stepped slightly away from the circle, as if he was preparing to remove his robe and carry out the rape as he'd been instructed by the leader of the group.

The assistant saw that he was moving out of the circle, and called across the table to him: "Now we can begin. Prepare yourself, brother, for your appointed task, so that we may release the lifeblood from this willing subject— the blood that will allow us to fulfill our destiny."

Bronson nodded, the movement barely perceptible because of his all-enveloping hood, and turned away from the table. Out of the corner of his eye, he could just make out the shadowy form of Angela climbing slowly to her feet as she recovered from the assault by the Taser.

His plan was simple enough. He had to get out of the robe, because the garment was heavy and would restrict his movements, just as the robes would hamper the other men in the cellar. Being told to rape the girl actually provided him with an opportunity to dump the robe without arousing the suspicions of the rest of the group. Once he'd done that, he had the Browning and the spare magazines to control and, if it came to it, shoot down, the other men.

75

But before he could remove the robe, there was a sudden bang from somewhere behind him, and a hoarse shout echoed down the stone spiral staircase, followed immediately by the staircase lights coming on and the sound of somebody pounding down the steps. Then the single electric bulb over the stone table snapped on, flooding that end of the room with light. Seconds later, one of the two men Bronson had seen outside the church ran into the cellar, his face flushed and his breath coming in short gasps.

He blurted out something that Bronson didn't catch, though he did make out the words "naked" and "robe," and in that instant he knew they'd found the man he'd attacked in the church.

Immediately, all the men standing around the stone table looked at Bronson, identifying him as the impostor.

In a single movement, Bronson pulled open the front of his robe, pushed the hood back off his head and grabbed for his Browning.

In that instant, Angela called out his name, a single shrill syllable that echoed around the room. But two of the hooded men were already reaching for their own weapons, and Bronson knew he'd be outgunned in seconds.

There was only one thing he could do to save the situation and buy himself some time. Taking rapid aim, he pulled the trigger. But his target wasn't one of the menacing hooded men advancing toward him. Despite the circumstances, Bronson still wasn't prepared to shoot down a man in cold blood—at least, not until he had absolutely no alternative. Instead, he raised the pistol higher, aiming it toward the ceiling, and the single lamp dangling there, and squeezed the trigger.

The sound of the nine-millimeter cartridge firing in the confined space of the cellar was deafening, the noise of the explosion echoing from the walls. The copper-jacketed bullet missed the lightbulb, smashed into the concrete ceiling and ricocheted onto the back wall. Still carrying a lot of kinetic energy, it then bounced off the stone and hit one of the robed figures. Bronson heard a man call out in pain and fall to the ground.

He fired again, and again, the crashing blast of each shot deafeningly loud, the bullets ricocheting off the walls and ceiling, fragments of stone and red-hot copper from the bullet flying everywhere.

The last bullet hit either the lightbulb itself or, more likely, the lamp holder, because as well as extinguishing the single light in the cellar, there was a sudden flash and the staircase lights went out. Bronson guessed that the bullet's impact had blown a fuse somewhere.

Instantly, the cellar was plunged into darkness, the only illumination being the candles held by the hooded figures, several of which had already been blown out.

But there was still enough light to see the men around the stone table, and two of them were already aiming pistols directly at Bronson. He shifted his aim, bringing down his weapon until the sights lined up with one of the two men. As he squeezed the trigger, the other man fired, and Bronson felt a tug on the left-hand side of the heavy robe he was wearing as the bullet plowed through the material.

The shot may have missed him, but Bronson had taken an extra half-second to make sure he didn't miss his target. The man gave a shriek of pain and fell backward, clutching at his shoulder while his weapon cartwheeled uselessly from his hand to clatter onto the stone floor.

One down, but eleven men were still facing him in the room. The second man fired, but Bronson was already moving. He ducked down and took a few steps over to his right, moving deeper into the shadows that danced around the far end of the cellar. He heard the impact of the bullet somewhere in the darkness behind him, took rapid aim at the armed man and squeezed the trigger.

His shot missed, and his target dived off to one side, finding cover behind the stone wall that marked the end of one of the cells built along the side of the cellar.

Then Bronson heard a sharp command, and almost immediately all the candles were extinguished.

For a few moments, the only sound in the room was the moaning of the man Bronson had shot. Angela, after her one yell of recognition, had said nothing else, and even the girl on the stone table had fallen silent.

The blackness was stygian, impenetrable. Bronson took two silent steps to one side, so that he was no longer in the same spot where he'd been standing when the candles were put out. He slid out of the heavy robe and tossed it to one side, a few feet away from him, the garment landing with a muffled sound on the stone floor. Instantly, another shot crashed out, the bullet slamming into the rear wall of the cellar several feet away from him.

OK, Bronson thought. His assailants would fire at any sound they heard because he was a single vulnerable target: if he made a noise, he would die. The only advantage he had was that the men were probably still clustered near the stone table, so at least he knew where they were. But he couldn't fire at them, not in the darkness without any point of reference—the risk of hitting the girl on the table was too high.

For the moment, it was a stalemate.

Making no sound at all, Bronson stood up and started to ease his way along the wall beside him, touching it with his left hand—he needed to feel the old stones to ensure that he was going in the right direction. All he hoped to do was put a little more distance between himself and the other men. And if he could get as far as the back wall of the room, he could try to work his way across to the cell where Angela was being held and try to free her.

There was another sharp command from the other end of the room. The voice was quiet and he couldn't make out the words, but the effect was immediate. Bronson heard the sound of movement—someone was cautiously crossing the floor toward him, their robes rustling and their leather sandals slapping faintly on the old stones. He guessed that two of the men, both no doubt armed with pistols, had been ordered to move apart so that they could catch him in the cross fire.

Still he didn't dare fire blind. He might hit the girl. He could even hit Angela. And if he did shoot, the muzzle flash from his pistol would instantly give away his position, and he knew exactly what would happen if he did that.

He moved infinitely slowly, backing away from the sound of movement. Then he stopped and crouched down with his back to the wall, making himself as small a target as possible. He held the Browning ready in his right hand, his left pressed against the wall behind him, prepared to move or to shoot as events dictated, listening hard and desperately trying to make sense of what he was hearing.

Then, through the darkness, he heard another muttered command, and almost immediately two shots blasted out from opposite sides of the cellar, the bullets smashing into the wall where he'd been standing just moments earlier, then ricocheting away. The muzzle flashes illuminated the shooters for a split second, just long enough for Bronson to see where they were.

He fired once, at the figure on his right, then dived sideways, changing his own position.

Two more shots deafened him, and he knew immediately that his own bullet had missed.

Then the man spoke again, and this time he was close enough for Bronson to hear exactly what he said.

"Stop. That's far enough," he said in Italian.

Then another man spoke from the opposite end of the cellar.

"Drop your weapon, Bronson." The voice was familiar, and Bronson immediately recognized the hostile tones of Inspector Bianchi. "You have no chance. Give up, and we'll kill you quickly. But if you don't surrender, I can promise that you'll take a very long time to die, though probably not as long as your interfering wife. We'll make sure she dies first, and we'll make you watch."

Bronson didn't move or respond, figuring the angles. It's a basic rule of close combat that you never, ever surrender your weapon. He knew that as well as anyone who'd ever served in the military of any nation, and he also knew that if he spoke, if he responded in any way at all, the men in front of him would open fire immediately.

But there was one thing he could do. He pressed the button on the left side of the Browning and slid out the magazine. Then he extracted a full one from the carrier on his belt and slid it into place in the weapon, the faintest of clicks confirming it was locked home. He replaced the half-empty magazine in the carrier.

"Very well, Bronson. It is your choice," Bianchi said.

Then the sound of loud, angry shouts filled the air, followed by the clattering of shoes on the stones of the spiral staircase. Dancing flashlight beams illuminated that end of the cellar.

At the moment, Bronson knew he'd reached the end of his rope. Reinforcements had obviously been summoned from the house; they would pick him out in an instant with their flashlights and, no matter what he did then, he would die. The best he could hope to do was take a few of them with him.

Then, from somewhere over to his left, he heard a sudden movement. There was a faint snap, like the sound of a distant whip-crack, and a flare of dim blue light so transient Bronson wasn't sure he'd actually seen it. It was followed, an instant later, by a dull sound, like something heavy dropping onto the floor, from that side of the cellar. And then someone started to scream.

76

Reacting instinctively to the screams, Bronson took a couple of steps to his left. Then he stopped. The danger was right in front of him, the men still coming down the stone staircase. He stood up, raised the pistol in his right hand and braced his wrist with his left, waiting until he could identify a target. He would make every shot count. That was all he could do.

But something was wrong. The men in the cellar weren't reacting the way they should be, the way he expected.

In the flickering flashlight he could see that the men around him were moving quickly back toward the stone table and the foot of the staircase, the only exit from the room. And then he finally understood what the people coming down the stairs were shouting.

A dark figure appeared in the opening to the staircase, a powerful flashlight attached to his weapon illuminating the scene in front of him. But the moment he stepped into the cellar, a shot rang out, and he fell backward out of sight. A second man took his place, and immediately opened fire, a burst of three shots from his submachine gun taking out two of the hooded figures, who tumbled to the ground screaming.

But another shot from one of the men in the cellar threw the man to the ground before he could fire again.

Another figure appeared, clad in dark combat clothing like the first two, and Bronson realized that—somehow—the Italian police were here. What he was witnessing was an assault by the Italian equivalent of a SWAT team.

The problem the police had was getting into the cellar. Normally, an assault would be mounted through multiple entrances and using the maximum possible number of officers. But the only way into this room was down the staircase, which put the assault team at a tremendous disadvantage. And the men in the cellar obviously had nothing to lose.

The third police officer had clearly seen what had happened to his two companions and tried a different tack: he aimed his submachine gun around the end of the wall, the beam of the attached flashlight seeking a target. But the hooded figures had scattered, some taking refuge behind the stone table, others in the cell nearest the staircase.

Bronson ran over to the wall on his right, getting as far away as possible from both the police and their targets. No bullets followed him as he moved.

The girl lashed down on the table screamed in terror.

Bronson stared through the gloom, and what he saw spurred him into immediate action.

One of the hooded men down at that end of the stone table had reached up, a blade in his hand, feeling for her neck, presumably so that he could permanently remove one witness to their activities. Bronson took a couple of steps forward to shorten the range, raised his pistol and aimed at the center of the dark shape, squeezing the trigger as he did so. The Browning kicked in his hand, and the man tumbled sideways, his knife clattering to the floor.

Then more shots crashed out as the armed men in the cellar fired at the police officer. He replied with two short bursts from his weapon, the bullets striking stone. One hit the ancient skull sitting on the small stone table, sending shards of old bone flying as it disintegrated.

The cellar filled with the smell of cordite, and the stabbing beams of the flashlights attached to the submachine guns of the two men sheltering in the stairwell—another officer had just appeared there—erratically illuminated different parts of the room as the officers looked for targets.

Bronson shrank down, trying to make himself as small and insignificant as possible. He knew there was only one way this was going to end, because the hooded men were ludicrously outgunned, but the fight wasn't over yet. And he really didn't want to get taken out by a bullet from either side.

Suddenly, in the flickering light from the flashlights,

he saw a round object hit the floor just to one side of the stone table, and knew exactly what it was. Immediately, he placed the Browning on the ground, shut his eyes and pressed his hands over his ears as hard as he could.

Half a second later, the stun grenade exploded, the blast obscenely loud in the confined space. Bronson opened his eyes, then closed them again as another stun grenade rolled across the floor. Once again, the cellar rocked with the massive blast. And then there seemed to be flashlights everywhere, as the rest of the assault team ran into the chamber.

Most of the hooded men were still in a state of shock after the two blasts, and offered no resistance. One of them, who'd been carrying a pistol but had dropped it on the floor, made a grab for it. But one of the assault team reached him before he could pick it up and smashed the butt of his submachine gun into the side of his head, instantly knocking him unconscious.

Bronson stood up, leaned back against the wall and raised both his hands high in the air. Frantically, he looked about him. Where was Angela? He guessed she'd dived for cover at the back of her cell as soon as the bullets started flying, and if she hadn't covered her ears when the stun grenades went off, she was probably still disoriented. She had to be somewhere near, but right then he couldn't see her.

Two members of the assault team walked over to him, their weapons pointing steadily at his stomach.

"Are you Bronson?" one of them asked him in Italian.

That was pretty much the last thing he expected them to say. Once he'd realized the men coming down the stairs were police officers, Bronson had presumed that he would be arrested with all the other people in the building and taken back to Venice.

He nodded. "Yes. How did you—"

"Passport," the second officer snapped. "Now."

Bronson reached around with his left hand, pulled the document from the hip pocket of his jeans and passed it over. One of the Italian policemen flicked it open, looked at the photograph inside it, then raised his weapon so that the beam from the attached flashlight shone straight into Bronson's face. He nodded, handed back the document and lowered his submachine gun.

Bronson tried again. "How did you know who I was?"

Another figure, still wearing his black robe, strode over to the three men and pushed back his hood.

"They knew," Inspector Bianchi said, "because I told them."

"But I thought—"

"I know exactly what you thought. You almost managed to wreck our operation. It's taken me nearly six months to get close enough to this group so that they would trust me. I only found out tonight, when they brought me here, to this island, where they were based."

"So how did the assault team know where to come?"

"There's a tracking chip in my mobile phone. As backup, I had six police boats out in the lagoon watching where I was taken. If you'd just done what I told you, and left this operation to us, we might have managed to take them all alive. As it is, now I've got corpses to identify as well."

"I saw two of your men shot when they tried to get in here. Are they OK?"

"Yes. They're just bruised. They both took chest shots, but they were wearing Kevlar jackets." Bianchi smiled for the first time since he'd walked across to Bronson. "Now, I have to get this situation tidied up. Don't leave the island until you've made a full written statement, and keep your schedule clear. We'll probably want you to come back out here as a witness when these bastards go on trial."

Sighing with relief, Bronson picked up the Browning pistol, clicked the safety catch on, and slid it into his belt holster. Nobody had asked him to hand it over, so he thought he might as well hang on to it. Then he walked across to the cell where Angela had been imprisoned.

She was nowhere to be seen. Bronson rubbed his eyes as he took in the roughly fashioned bed and mattress, and the chain and handcuff that had secured her to the wall. The handcuff was open, so he knew somebody—one of the policemen, perhaps—must have freed her. He stepped back into the middle of the cellar and looked round.

The injured members of the cult were sitting with their backs to the wall opposite the cells, their wrists handcuffed behind them. Some were receiving basic medical treatment, but there was little the assault team members could do for them. Bronson assumed that an ambulance boat was on its way. The dead men were still lying where they'd fallen, waiting for the arrival of a forensics team.

The girl who'd been strapped down on the stone table had been released. She was wrapped in a blanket and was clinging to one of the Italian police officers as if she never wanted to let him go. Bronson could only imagine the turmoil of emotions that were coursing through her body.

But he still couldn't see Angela. Perhaps she'd already been taken up to ground level. Perhaps. But a knot of anxiety was forming in Bronson's chest. He strode across the room to where Bianchi stood, issuing orders and directing his men.

"Where's Angela?" he demanded. "Where's my wife?"

Bianchi pointed back toward the other end of the cellar. "She's in the last cell."

Bronson shook his head. "No, she isn't. Are you sure none of your men took her upstairs?"

"Nobody has left here apart from some of my officers. She must be here."

Then Bronson noticed something else. "One of them is missing," he said, pointing to the robed men.

"Who?" Bianchi demanded.

The cult members had had the hoods pulled clear of their faces. And as Bronson stared at each one in turn, he realized that the man who'd been directing operations wasn't there.

"The leader," he said. "Where is he?"

Bianchi snapped an order and two of his men immediately started to search the cellar.

Bronson stood there, thinking furiously. If Bianchi was right, and nobody had left the cellar up the spiral staircase, then there had to be another way out.

Somehow, the leader had managed to slip past everyone in the confusion of the police assault, and had grabbed Angela as he left.

Bronson groaned. He'd been so close, so sure that he'd managed to save her. But again she'd disappeared. And this time he had only the haziest idea where to start looking for her.

77

Bronson leaned against the wall of the cellar as he re-played the events that had just taken place. He'd seen Angela, seen exactly where she was, standing at the open-ing of the end cell. He'd heard her calling out his name.

Nobody had gone anywhere near her from that mo-ment on. The attention of the hooded men had been entirely concentrated on the girl who'd been lashed down on the stone table. Then the shooting had started, and people had been moving all around the cellar, trying to take cover from the bullets, or firing themselves.

As Bronson recalled each of these events, he remem-bered something else: just before the screaming started, there'd been a noise like something heavy falling to the ground. But could it have been something else? Could it have been the sound of a stone door closing?

"I think there's another way out of here," Bronson said to Bianchi.

Bianchi looked doubtful. "An underground chamber

is rare enough in the Laguna Veneta, and this is quite a big room on a small island. It's very unlikely there are any other spaces down here."

Bronson reached out and grabbed a flashlight from the assault vest of a police officer who was standing next to Bianchi. The officer tried to take it back, but the inspector stopped him.

"Very well," he said, sighing. "But if you find a door, call me, and then we'll assess the situation."

Bronson ran over to the cell where Angela had been imprisoned. That was the obvious—in fact the only—starting point. But all that was there was the crudely made wooden bed, a thin mattress and a single pillow. Under the bed was a rusty metal bucket and a partially used roll of toilet paper. The only other object he could see was the steel chain lying across the mattress, one end attached to a large eyebolt screwed into the stone wall, the other end dangling down, the open handcuff resting on the floor.

Bronson turned to his right, toward the opposite end of the cellar from the stone table. If there was a hidden door—and this was the only explanation that made sense—it had to be somewhere beyond the line of cells.

He gave the outside wall of the cell a cursory glance, then directed the beam of the flashlight at the solid wall of the cellar as he walked across to it. The old stones looked damp and cold; and none showed the slightest sign of movement when he pressed against them. Bronson used both hands, pushing his palms firmly against each stone at about chest level as he worked his way slowly toward the back wall of the cellar. He reached the corner of the wall, glanced back briefly and then resumed his steady and methodical progress. Using the same technique, he crossed the back wall of the cellar with exactly the same lack of result. Every stone he'd pushed had seemed absolutely solid.

But Angela had been in the cellar, and now she wasn't. She hadn't gone up the spiral staircase, so there definitely had to be another exit. He'd tried the walls without result. Now he had to look at the floor.

Bronson directed the flashlight beam downward and stared at the old flagstones, worn down by countless feet over the years. It didn't look as if any of them had been moved in decades, possibly for centuries. He studied them anyway, looking for any sign of movement, of suspiciously clean edges or anything of that sort. Nothing.

He had to have missed something, some clue that would show him where the hidden entrance was located. Then he slowly became aware of something gnawing away at his subconscious. He'd seen something, or felt something—something that wasn't quite right, something out of place. Bronson jogged back to the sidewall of the cellar, and started walking slowly along the wall, staring at the stones and touching each one that he'd pressed against before. He reached the end, then started on the back wall. And then it struck him.

The stones on the sidewall had looked and felt damp, as had those on the back wall, all except three of them in a horizontal line, about five feet from the junction of the two walls. Those stones were solid and cold, but not quite as cold as the stones on either side of them, and his fingers could detect no trace of damp.

He felt the stones above and below the three he'd detected, and they all showed the same characteristics: they were solid and cold but not damp. He'd found the hidden door. All he had to do now was work out how to open it.

Bronson shone the flashlight at the stones. Now that he'd identified the door, its shape was fairly obvious. He looked closely at the spaces between the stones. In an almost vertical line, from floor level up to about five feet above the ground, there was a straight edge where no mortar was visible.

But what he still couldn't see was how to get it open. He ran his fingers up and down the vertical edge, feeling for a catch or lever. He pushed against each of the stones in turn, in case one of them would work a hidden catch, but again without result.

There had to be a way of getting the door open. Almost in desperation, he pressed his left shoulder against the stones, braced his feet on the floor and started to push. His right foot started to slide, and he changed position. As he again put his weight on his right foot, he felt rather than heard a click under the sole of his shoe, and the stone door swung silently outward.

Caught completely unawares, Bronson tumbled through the opening, and crashed to the ground on the other side. Immediately, powerful springs swung the door closed again, the solid structure clicking back into place with a muted thump, the same sound he had heard minutes earlier.

He scrambled to his feet, reached down and drew the Browning from his holster. Then he replaced the weapon. It was pitch-black in the chamber, and if he couldn't see, he couldn't shoot. He needed light.

The flashlight had fallen from his hand as he'd tumbled through the doorway, and he crouched down and felt around on the floor, searching for it. His probing fingers touched something shriveled and furry, and he recoiled. A dead rat, probably. In a few seconds, his hand closed around a cool metal tube, and he gave a sigh of relief.

But that feeling didn't last long. When he pressed the switch on the end of the flashlight, nothing happened. He shook it, and could hear a faint rattling sound inside it. The bulb or something else had obviously broken when he fell.

He would have to find his way around by feel. Having made sure his pistol was properly seated in the holster, because if he dropped it, he might not be able to find it again, Bronson extended both arms in front of him and started walking forward.

Then he stopped dead. Somewhere in the darkness ahead of him, he could hear the faint sound of movement.

*   *   *

"What happened?" Inspector Bianchi demanded.

The black-clad police officer shook his head. "I don't really know, sir. One minute the Englishman was standing close to the back wall of the cellar. Then I looked away for a few seconds. I heard a noise and—"

"What kind of a noise?"

The police officer shook his head again. "A kind of thump, I suppose. And when I looked back to that end of the room, he'd disappeared."

"Right." Bianchi called out to a pair of police officers who were manhandling a battery-powered floodlight into the cellar. "Get that light on, and aim it at the back wall. We need to find where Bronson has gone—right now."

78

Bronson was desperate for even the faintest scintilla of illumination that might allow him to see his surroundings. But there was nothing, no light at all. All he had to go on was what his ears could hear, or his probing hands could touch. The only possible good news was that if he couldn't see anything, then neither could anyone else.

What he could hear sounded like something moving cautiously over a stone floor, a kind of swishing, pattering noise that didn't seem to be very close. He swung his left arm around in a semicircle in front of him, then did the same with his right, and took a cautious step forward. Then he repeated the sequence of movements, making very slow, and very cautious, progress.

He estimated he'd covered about fifteen feet in total darkness before the faint noises he was hearing stopped altogether. Whoever—or whatever—was ahead of him was no longer moving.

*   *   *

Inspector Bianchi strode across the flagstone floor to the back wall of the cellar. The two officers had already positioned the battery-powered floodlight a few feet away and, as Bianchi approached, they switched it on. Instantly, that corner of the chamber was brightly illuminated, the white light bouncing off the old stones.

For a few moments, the handful of police officers stared at the wall. Then Bianchi turned to his companion. "Tell me again what you saw," he instructed.

Once more the officer explained the sequence of events.

"And he couldn't have left this room by the staircase?"

The officer shook his head.

"OK, you two, examine this corner of the cellar. Don't stop till you find the doorway."

Then he went over to the group of handcuffed figures still sitting with their backs to the wall at the other end of the chamber. He looked at each in turn until he found the man whom he'd cultivated in order to join the group.

"Stefano," he said, crouching down in front of him. "You're going to jail, probably for a very long time. I'm not going to offer you a deal, but if you answer my next question correctly, then I will at least tell the judge at your trial that tried to help us when you were arrested. Now, we know that there's a hidden door at the other end of this room. How do we open it?"

The man named Stefano spat. "Judas," he snapped. "I should have guessed you were too good to be true. A senior policeman wanting to learn our secrets and share in our triumph? A man who could misdirect any inquiries and provide us with some protection from the law? We should never have even talked to you."

"I'll take that as a no, then, shall I, you contemptible piece of shit?"

Bianchi motioned to two of his officers. "As soon as you've got the wounded men out of here," he said, "get this lot upstairs. Before you do that, separate them and ask them individually about a hidden door and a secret chamber. They probably won't talk to you, but I suppose it's worth a try."

Then he walked back to the other end of the cellar, where his men were still examining the wall. "Have you found anything?" he asked.

One of the officers turned around to face him. "We think we've spotted a doorway, sir. There's a vertical line, here, between the stones, which could be the edge of a door, but we've still no idea how to get it open."

"There should be some tools in one of the boats. One of you, go out and see if you can find a hammer and chisel or a crowbar. If we can't work out how to open it, maybe we can break it down."

Bronson took a deep breath and then held it to minimize the sound of his own breathing, the better to hear what was happening.

There was a scuffling sound from his left, a noise that rose and fell erratically. He heard an angry squeal from the same direction, and guessed he was probably hearing a family of rats moving about. Then there was another noise, from somewhere to his front. Not loud, but unmistakable. He could hear the sound of beating wings, and then his ears, the only sense organs that were of any use to him at that moment and in that place, detected several faint squeaks.

Bronson relaxed slightly. As well as the rats, it sounded to him as if he was sharing the space with bats. And that was actually good news, because it meant there had to be a way out of the cellar to the open air, though how the hell he was going to find it in the pitch darkness was another matter.

And then he heard a noise that electrified him. A yell of pain, suddenly cut short, sounded through the cellar, not close but very clear. In that instant Bronson knew that Angela was somewhere in the darkness ahead of him.

His every instinct told him to run, to find her as quickly as possible, but instead he stayed where he was, trying to pinpoint the exact direction from which the sound had come. Then he started moving, just as slowly and carefully as he'd done previously, because in the blackness that was the only way to ensure that he didn't run headlong into a wall or trip over something.

Bronson stopped again. He'd sensed movement, somewhere near him. It wasn't something he'd heard so much as a subtle change in the air, a faint waft across his face. And then he smelled something rancid and deeply unpleasant that appalled him. It took him a moment to place it amid the other smells of damp and decay that filled the air. Rotting meat. The smell of decomposing flesh. He was sharing this chamber with a dead body.

But what he didn't understand was why the smell was getting stronger. He'd stopped moving, so the foul odor should have stayed more or less constant. But it wasn't. It was definitely increasing, which made sense only if he was getting closer to the corpse.

A horrifying thought struck him. Bronson took a couple of steps backward, but still the stench grew stronger. Something—something foul—was near him, and getting closer.

He could still see nothing, but the feeling of revulsion was growing stronger by the second, and he knew he had to do something.

Almost without thinking, Bronson drew the Browning from his holster, aimed the pistol toward the roof of the chamber, and pulled the trigger. The noise of the shot was deafening, and the bullet ricocheted off the concrete ceiling and smashed into the floor a few feet away from him.

Bronson flinched, but his reaction had nothing to do with the firing of his weapon. What stunned him was the sight that had been illuminated for the barest fraction of a second by the muzzle flash of his pistol. Less than six feet in front of him, he'd seen the appalling specter of the leader of the group who had abducted Angela, his arms outstretched and his hands formed into clutching claws as he felt around for his prey. The hood of his robe was thrown back to reveal his totally bald head, black

eyes sunk deep into their sockets, and his mouth open
to reveal a row of pointed teeth, the two canines so long
they extended beneath his lower lip.

It was an image that burned itself into Bronson's
brain.

He lowered the pistol, aimed it where he thought the
figure should be, and pulled the trigger.

On the other side of the stone wall, Inspector Bianchi and
his men clearly heard the shot. He now had four men
inspecting the wall, probing for a catch, and pressing on
the old stones, all without result.

"Find that bloody lever," Bianchi shouted, "and
quickly. If Bronson could find it by himself in the dark, I
can't think of any good reason why the four of you can't
do the same thing. At least you can see what you're
doing."

This time the muzzle flash of the Browning revealed
nothing apart from the darkness of the cellar. Bronson
stepped backward, turned to his right and fired the pistol
again, with exactly the same result. The nightmare figure
had vanished. And the stench, the rotting corpse smell,
was now little more than a disgusting memory in his nos-
trils.

There was a sudden creaking sound from somewhere
ahead, and almost immediately a faint light illuminated
the oblong shape of a doorway perhaps thirty feet in
front of him. A door to the outside had obviously been

opened. And almost simultaneously, Bronson heard a dull thud from behind him as one of the Italian police officers finally stood on exactly the right stone in the cellar. Instantly, light from the battery-powered floodlight poured in, and for the first time he could see his surroundings.

He was standing in a chamber about half the size of the one used for the ceremonies, but this one was devoid of all structures and furnishings. Rats, frightened away by the sound of the shots, were now reappearing, scuttling around the perimeter of the chamber, and a handful of small bats wheeled and banked near the ceiling.

Now that Bronson could see what he was doing, he ran forward, straight toward the doorway in the opposite wall. He could hear Inspector Bianchi calling out for him to stop, but that wasn't an option.

Bronson slammed to a halt beside the doorway. Ahead of him was a short, empty passage, two doors opening off it on the left-hand side, and a heavy wooden door, half open, at the end. He guessed that the leader had probably gone through that door to the outside of the building. With Angela.

He wrenched open the outside door. In front of him, the waters of the Venetian lagoon, black in the moonlight, lapped at a small muddy beach. He glanced quickly in all directions, but there was nobody in sight. A path, little more than flattened grass and compressed earth, led away to his right. On his left, an almost vertical bank rose, blocking his way.

Bronson turned right, the only way out, and ran up the path. The moonlight cast a pale white glow over his surroundings, and was sufficiently bright for him to see exactly where he was. The house was over to his right, and the ruined church almost directly in front of him. Near the house he could see several figures, clad in dark clothes and carrying weapons: obviously other Italian police officers, so he knew that his quarry wouldn't have gone to the main landing stage in front of the house. In fact, the only place the leader could possibly have gone was to the old jetty, at the other end of the island, where Bronson had seen the small speedboat. It was his only viable avenue of escape.

Turning away from the house, Bronson started to run, but after only a few seconds he saw a dark shape lying to one side of the path.

Bronson stopped in his tracks and aimed the pistol directly at it. He took a couple of tentative steps forward, then muttered an oath. The police officer had obviously had time to draw his weapon, because Bronson could see a Beretta nine-millimeter pistol lying on the ground beside him. But the weapon had clearly done him no good at all, because he was dead, his throat ripped apart, his head resting in a huge pool of blood.

Fearing for Angela, his blood pounding in his ears, Bronson ran on, checking left and right as he did so, and occasionally glancing behind him, just in case his quarry had decided to double back. He heard a commotion some way back, and guessed that Bianchi and his officers had followed him out of the chamber, and had just found the dead policeman.

Then, perhaps fifty yards ahead, he saw a figure, a blacker shape against the darkness of the sky. He caught a sudden whiff of decaying flesh, and knew he'd guessed right. The man was making for the jetty and the speedboat.

Bronson stepped off the path and onto the grass at the side. The man was still much too far away for him to use his pistol, and he couldn't see whether or not he had Angela with him.

Making maximum use of the moonlight to pick his route over the tussocky grass, Bronson ran on, closing the distance as quickly as he could. Then he saw a tumble of blond hair on the right-hand side of the dark robe the figure was wearing, and knew the man was carrying Angela. She seemed to be unconscious or at least, as far as Bronson could see, her head appeared to be hanging limply.

He'd gotten within about twenty yards of them when the man clearly sensed his presence and glanced back at him. Bronson saw his face, saw the blood staining his mouth and chin. He brought the Browning up to the aim, wondering if he dared risk a shot. The moon disappeared suddenly, almost instantly, it seemed, behind a thick cloud, and the figure vanished. The path in front of him appeared completely empty.

Bronson shook his head in disbelief, then carried on. He saw nothing for another hundred yards or so and then, as he approached the inlet that contained the old jetty, he heard the rumble of an engine and saw the man again. He was already standing in the bow of the power-boat and releasing the painter. Angela was lying in the center of the boat, her body draped over one of the seats.

Bronson stopped, took careful aim at the standing figure and squeezed the trigger.

79

The Browning recoiled in his hand, but it was too late. The man had ducked down, stepped to the stern of the boat and opened the throttle. Bronson didn't dare fire again, because the man was now too close to Angela. He holstered the weapon and ran for his own boat, beached only about fifteen yards away.

Bronson pushed on the bow of his craft, but for several agonizing seconds it remained immobile. Then he changed his grip, lifted the bow slightly and pushed again, and this time the boat moved. He scrambled on board and, gasping for breath, started the engine and swung the craft around in a tight circle and set off in pursuit of the other boat.

Inspector Bianchi had just ordered his men to begin a line search of the whole island when he heard the rising scream of a boat engine fairly close by. He looked in the direction of the sound and saw two powerboats carving white wakes through the dark waters of the Venetian lagoon. As far as he could see, each boat contained a single figure, and it was immediately obvious to him what had happened.

"You four," he ordered, "take a police launch and catch those two boats. You three, come with me. We'll use the other boat."

A couple of minutes later, the deep rumble of the marine diesel engines of the launches echoed around the landing stage, as the two boats set off in pursuit.

Bronson had pushed the throttle as far forward as it would go, and as he swung around the end of the island, he saw the other boat about seventy yards ahead of him. From over to his right, he heard the sound of another engine starting, and guessed that at least one of the police launches was following them.

Within moments he knew that his craft was faster than the one he was chasing. Only a little faster, but enough. Inexorably the distance between them closed: fifty yards, forty, thirty . . .

Then a police launch powered across the water directly in front of him, the driver obviously intent on reaching the fleeing craft first.

Bronson cursed and swung around the stern of the launch, then turned the vessel back in pursuit. He'd lost some ground, but he was still gaining on the other boat. The police launch was almost matching speed with him, and running parallel.

Bronson took one hand off the steering wheel, pulled the Browning out of the holster and aimed it at the boat in front of him, waiting for a clear shot.

Twenty yards . . . ten. The leader obviously knew that Bronson and the police launch were behind him, but there was nothing he could do to get away from the faster boats.

As Bronson's boat closed to a matter of a few feet, the leader swung his wheel hard over to the right, diving straight across his bow. Bronson reacted instantly, mirroring the man's actions, so that his vessel turned just as sharply. But it was too late—there was a screech of tearing fiberglass as the two boats collided, the port side of Bronson's boat smashing into the starboard side of the other vessel.

The two boats jammed together, the gunwale of Bronson's slightly smaller craft riding up over the side of the larger vessel. Instinctively, he reached out and pulled back the throttle. As he did so, he lost his grip on the Browning, which fell from his hand and clattered to the floor.

Just feet away, the hooded man stared at him, his face white in the moonlight, the streaks of blood down his chin clearly visible. He obviously saw that Bronson didn't have a weapon in his hand, and rose up from the boat, his arms outstretched as he reached for his next victim.

And at that moment Angela recovered consciousness, and screamed.

Bronson looked in sheer terror at the appalling specter looming over him, then bent down, both hands scrabbling desperately to try to find the pistol. The stench of decomposition rolled over him in a nauseous wave as his hand closed around cold metal. He snapped off the safety catch on the Browning, pointed it straight in the center of the dark shape in front of him, and squeezed the trigger.

Once, twice, three times, he fired, the sound of the shots rolling across the dark waters. As he fired, Bronson knew that the nine-millimeter copper-jacketed bullets couldn't possibly have missed the target. Not at less than six-feet range.

But still the figure came on, his black robe blotting out the moon, as he reached for Bronson.

80

Bronson was never quite sure what happened next. He fired again as he was enveloped by the dark shape, then tumbled backward, the back of his head cracking sharply against the seat as he fell.

When he came to, Angela was beside him, cradling his head in her hands in the stern of the boat.

"Wake up, Chris, damn you. Wake up," she muttered. Then, as his eyes flicked open, she bent down and kissed him on the lips. "Thank God," she said simply.

In the distance, Bronson heard the rumble of another boat's engine. A police launch was just drawing alongside, Inspector Bianchi standing in the stern and staring at the two boats, still locked together and rocking in the chop disturbing the surface of the lagoon.

"Where is he?" Bianchi called over to them.

Bronson looked up at Angela. "Where did he go?"

"I don't know," she replied. "I saw him jump at you after the boats collided, and then you shot at him. He seemed to fall right on top of you, but when I reached the end of the boat he'd gone, and all I could see was his robe. There was no body, and no blood. I didn't hear him fall into the water, but he must have."

Bronson sat up, ran his palm over the tender bruise on the back of his head—it was already noticeably swollen and bleeding—and looked across at the inspector.

"I don't know," Bronson explained in Italian. "I banged my head when he leaped onto the boat so I didn't see. Angela says he must have jumped into the water and got away."

"Right," Bianchi snapped, and turned to the police officer driving the boat. "Tell the other crew to start quartering the area. We're probably looking for a body, but it's possible the man is still alive. Either way, I want him found."

With a throaty roar from its turbo-charged diesel engine, the second police boat swung away, two searchlights snapping into life as the crew started their search.

"You shot him," Bianchi said, a statement rather than a question.

"I shot *at* him, Inspector," Bronson replied, "and that's not quite the same thing. He dropped his robe," he added, passing it over to the police officer.

"You'd better get back to Venice, Signor Bronson. That looks like a nasty wound on your head, and you need to get it checked. We'll stay out here until we find the body, and I'll send somebody round to your hotel to take a statement in the morning. It's been a long night for all of us. Oh, before you go, you'd better give me that pistol, unless you've managed to acquire a license for it in the last twelve hours. And any ammunition you might have picked up as well."

Bronson handed over the pistol, holster and spare magazines, then spent a couple of minutes separating his powerboat from the one the cult leader had been driving. Once he'd freed the gunwale, he waved a hand at Bianchi, started the boat's engine again and motored away.

As they headed back toward the lights of Venice, Bronson slipped his arm around Angela's shoulders and she nestled her head against him.

"How's your head?" she asked.

"I'll live," Bronson said. "It feels like a bad bruise, but I don't think it needs stitches. All I really want to do is get back to the hotel and lock the door against the world. It's been a hell of a night for us all, and especially for you."

Angela shivered. "Thank God it's all over. I really thought I was going to die in that bloody cellar. I couldn't believe it when I saw you there—and carrying a gun."

"Well, we're safe now. Just don't think about what happened tonight."

Angela was silent for a few moments, then looked up at Bronson again. "Are you sure he's dead? That foul creature?"

Bronson nodded. "At that range, I couldn't possibly

have missed. I fired four or five shots into him at a range of about six feet. If that didn't kill him outright, he'd have bled to death in minutes. He's dead—that's for sure. Tomorrow, Bianchi will tell us he's recovered the body, and that'll be the end of it."

81

Bronson and Angela walked into the hotel dining room the next morning only a few minutes before breakfast stopped being served. Angela had bathed and dressed the wound on his head as soon as they'd gotten back to the hotel the previous night and then they'd fallen into bed. They'd talked for a few minutes about the traumatic events of the previous few days, and especially the last frantic hours out in the lagoon; then exhaustion had overtaken them both and they'd quickly fallen asleep.

Bronson collected a coffeepot, a couple of cups and the last remaining basket of bread and croissants from the serving table and took everything over to the table by the window where Angela was sitting. She fell on the food as if she was starving.

"God, I'm famished," she said, between mouthfuls of croissant.

"I'm not surprised." Bronson poured her a cup of coffee, then sat back in his chair and looked at her.

"What?" she said, smiling.

"I just like looking at you; that's all," Bronson replied, "and for a while there I really didn't think that was something I was ever going to be able to do again."

Angela shuddered. "Don't remind me," she said. "I never thought I was going to get out alive. You know, I still can't believe you managed to find me."

Bronson had explained about his visit to the Isola di San Michele and the events that had followed it the previous evening.

"I don't think I could have lived with myself if I'd lost you a second time," he said, taking her hand. "You know, I was certain that Inspector Bianchi was one of the bad guys, but now I'm really glad I was wrong, because if he had been, my guess is we'd both be dead now."

Angela nodded, and in a halting voice described in more detail the code-breaking she'd been forced to do.

"It was appalling stuff," she finished. "That scroll I found in the bell tower on Poveglia—which is a severely creepy place, by the way—was neither more nor less than an authorization to go out and commit multiple rape and mass murder. But what really bothered me about it was the whole tone of the text. It was so matter-of-fact about vampires, as if they were simply another sector of society that everyone would have known about. Oh, and by implication everyone could become one if they really wanted to, and were prepared to follow the rituals."

"I had a question about that," Bronson said. "They had a female wolf chained up in a stable, and before the ceremony started I saw two men go into the building and milk her. And then they forced the milk down poor Marietta's throat. What the hell has that got to do with becoming a vampire?"

Angela's face was pale and strained as she remembered what she'd been through. "That was something they got completely wrong. My guess is that the members of the vampire group had studied all the ancient literature. They would certainly have read about the eighteenth-century Vampire Princess of the Schwarzenbergs—Eleonora Amalia. Almost every contemporary source agreed that she was a vampire, and her body was autopsied after her death, something that was only very rarely done in those days, and almost never on a member of the aristocracy. It's now thought that the procedure was performed not to find out why she died, but simply so her heart could legitimately be removed from her body. Because she was of royal blood, they couldn't decapitate her or burn her corpse. Wrenching out a vampire's heart was supposed to make sure it stayed dead.

"But one of the other odd things about Eleonora Amalia was that she drank the milk of wolves, and my guess is that the members of the group discovered that and thought it was just something else they—or rather their victims—should do. But, according to other sources, Eleonora Amalia didn't think she was a vampire, and she drank the milk for an entirely different reason, though it was based on another old legend—Romulus and Remus. She was trying to increase her fertility."

Angela stopped talking and looked across at Bronson. Then she voiced the unspoken question that was uppermost in both their minds.

"Last night . . . the leader of that group . . . was he really a man, do you think?"

Bronson shook his head helplessly. "I don't know," he muttered. "What I do know is that he was the most terrifying thing I've ever seen."

"When I came round after that Taser hit me, he was carrying me, and I'll tell you this: he was incredibly strong. For part of the time he literally held me in one arm. You're strong, Chris, and I'm sure you could pick me up fairly easily, but I very much doubt if you could carry me very far, especially not over such rough ground." Angela paused, and Bronson noticed her hand was shaking. "There's something else about it that bothers me. I know it's not definite proof either way, but there is one consistent factor that seems to crop up in all the records about—"

She broke off as the door to the dining room opened and Inspector Bianchi walked in. He crossed over to their table, pulled up a third chair and sat down.

"Good morning, Inspector," Bronson greeted him in Italian. "Would you like a coffee?" Without waiting for an answer, he picked up an unused cup from the next table, poured coffee into it and slid it over.

"Good morning. I think we've wrapped up almost everything on the island," Bianchi said, sticking to English so that Angela could understand what he was saying. "The forensics people are still out there, and will be for a while, but I'm pretty certain we've got all the evidence we need, including the pistol that was used to kill my superior officer here in the city. I hope this means an end to these disappearances and murders." He paused for a moment to taste his drink. "But I'm afraid we've still not found a body in the lagoon."

Bianchi glanced at Angela, then continued. "But it's only a matter of time. The currents in the lagoon can be fierce. We think that man's corpse probably sank below the surface soon after he fell into the water, and simply drifted away. Trying to spot a body in the water at night is very difficult."

"But you are *sure* he's dead?" Angela asked.

Bianchi nodded. "We would certainly have spotted that man if he'd been swimming away from the scene. And there are bullet holes in his robe, in both the front and the back, so clearly your shots must have badly wounded him, at least. If his corpse doesn't turn up over the next couple of days, it will probably have washed out into the Adriatic, and we'll never find it."

Bronson opened his mouth to object, but Bianchi held up his hand to forestall him. "No doubt you have your own views about this, Signor Bronson, but what I've just described seems to us to make logical sense, and will be what our final report into this matter will say. We already have his accomplices in custody, and the circumstances of their arrest mean that their trial should be almost a formality."

Bronson nodded slowly. "Perhaps you're right," he said. "That's probably the best way to handle this. Stick to the facts, produce the bodies, line up the suspects and then let justice take its course."

"And Marietta?" Angela asked. "How is she?"

Bianchi finished the last of his coffee and smiled. "She's fine. Well, she's obviously still very traumatized by her experience, as I'm sure you are, too, but she's back with her family, and her boyfriend."

"Send her my love," Angela said, a tremor in her voice. "She was so brave in that cellar."

"I will." Bianchi stood up. "Make sure you come to the police station in San Marco before you leave Venice, please," he said. "You are both material witnesses in this case, and the prosecution may well decide that we need you here when the trial finally takes place, so it's essential that we have your full contact details. Other than that, enjoy the rest of your holiday in Venice. And if I might make a suggestion, please try to avoid going near any other graveyards or churches while you're here."

Bianchi extended his hand and Bronson shook it. Then he kissed Angela on both cheeks, turned and left the room.

Bronson sat down again and looked across at Angela. "So they've got the killers," he said, "and they'll prosecute them for the multiple murders. They might need us as witnesses, but we'll have to wait and see. That means we might just get another trip out here to Venice, all expenses paid."

Angela looked at him for a moment. "You were going to say something to the inspector? Something about the body?"

Bronson nodded. "Two things, in fact. I know it was dark last night, but I took a quick look at that robe when I handed it to Bianchi. He was right about the bullet holes, but I didn't see any blood. And dead bodies don't sink—they float."

"So what are you saying? That he's still alive?"

"No. He can't be. That's simply impossible. It's just a bit odd, the way it all happened at the end. And you were about to say something when Bianchi arrived?"

"Oh yes," Angela remembered. "It's only a small thing. If you look back through all the accounts of vampires, from every country that has a tradition relating to the undead, you'll find a mass of contradictions. Some say you can only kill them by beheading them, others that they're terrified of a crucifix, or held at bay by garlic. In some countries, sunlight kills them. As far as I know, there are only two things that seem to be consistent everywhere. First, and most obviously, vampires live on human blood." She paused for a second, and glanced at Bronson. "And the second thing is that vampires have a very distinctive smell. They reek of decay, of decomposing flesh."

Bronson caught his breath as he remembered his experience in the secret chamber, and what he'd smelled in those moments when the leader of the group attacked him. "I'm not sure I'm hearing you right," he said, trying to smile. "Is this really my precious, logical, scientific Angela? Are you saying that you think we really did meet a vampire out on that island?"

Angela shook her head slowly. "Vampires don't exist," she said. "Everybody knows that. But we have been in contact with a very strange person, someone I never, ever want to see again." She got up and stretched. "We've got one more day left in Venice. I'm not visiting any of the islands, and definitely no churches, but do you think we'd be safe if we did some shopping? I've always fancied some handmade gloves."

Bronson stood up too, and put his arms around her. "After what happened yesterday," he said, "I'll happily buy you ten pairs."

Epilogue

Venice is a maze of narrow streets and canals, lined with old buildings. Because of the continuing problems with flooding and subsidence, many of the older properties and especially a number of the early palaces, the palazzi, have been abandoned because water damage to their lower floors has fatally weakened the entire structure. Sad, crumbling and in some cases too dangerous to enter, these ancient buildings endure mainly because they are supported by adjacent properties. Without this, most of them would have collapsed decades or even centuries ago.

Beside one small canal at the southern end of the Cannaregio district stands a tall and narrow building that dates almost as far back as the founding of the city. Last inhabited in the early nineteenth century, both its doors—the canal and the street entrances—are locked and barred and the windows shuttered, as they have been for decades. It is beyond repair, the foundations slowly crumbling away into the waters below. Occasionally, the occupants of properties nearby can hear the rumble and splash as yet another piece of masonry falls away and tumbles down the interior of the building.

They have grown accustomed to these sounds, and rarely even remark on them. But these are not the only sounds that have recently been echoing through the old building.

Sometimes, late at night, the family who live next door can hear a faint slithering and swishing sound from one of the rooms on the very top floor of the doomed building, a room that they know has not been occupied for many years. Sometimes, the noises are loud enough to wake their children. And neither of their cats will even enter the rooms on the side of their house that abuts the deserted property.

They don't know exactly what is making the noises, but they have their suspicions, because of the smell. Faint, but all-pervasive, the ruined house is beginning to smell distinctly of rotting flesh. Obviously something has gotten in there and died, they tell one another. And maybe the other noises are rats feeding on the remains.

Recently, the noises have started getting louder, and the smell stronger.

AUTHOR'S NOTE
THE REAL VAMPIRE
CHRONICLES

Vampires in History

Many people think that belief in vampires is a comparatively recent phenomenon, but in fact the myth of a bloodsucking creature of the night can trace its roots back for thousands of years, and there is one school of thought that suggests that perhaps the most famous murder of all time was the result of an attack by a vampire.

The Bible is strangely silent about the weapon used by Cain to kill his brother. In Genesis, it only says that "Cain rose up against Abel his brother, and slew him." Over time, numerous objects were suggested as the likely murder weapons, typically rocks or lengths of wood of some kind, though another theory stated that it was the jawbone of an animal, the teeth specially sharpened. Shakespeare made reference to this as the weapon in *Hamlet*.

But the Zohar, the group of books that provide the foundation of the Jewish Kabbalah, offers another suggestion entirely. In that work, there is no doubt whatsoever about the circumstances of Abel's death—it states explicitly that Cain bit his brother on the throat. So it could be argued that the world's first known vampire was actually the biblical Cain.

Unlike most other monsters and demons, in which belief is often restricted to a particular geographical area or linguistic group, the vampire legend appears to have roots in nearly every country of the world. In Iran—ancient Persia—a vase was found that depicted a man being attacked by a huge creature apparently trying to suck his blood. The mythical Babylonian deity named Lilith, possibly the woman who was supposed to be the first wife of Adam, was reputed to drink the blood of babies. Some sixth-century Chinese texts refer to so-called "revenants" or the living dead. Other cultures around the world, from the Aztecs to the Eskimos, and from India to Polynesia, have legends that refer to creatures that are remarkably consistent and eerily similar to the vampires of European fiction.

Blood, and especially the blood of virgins, became an important cure for ailments in the eleventh century, being prescribed by both witches and doctors, and even the Catholic Church recognized and latched onto the symbolic importance of this belief, offering wine as the "blood of Christ" as a part of Holy Communion.

Belief in vampires gained ground during the Renaissance, but reached almost epidemic proportions in central Europe in the fourteenth century. The Black Death, the plague that decimated the population of Europe, was popularly believed to be caused by vampires. According to one theory, in their haste to dispose of corpses, it is quite possible that many people were buried in plague pits while they were still alive. Their frantic efforts to free themselves from the earth above them could have fueled stories about the vampire myth, as the dead would literally seem to be rising from their graves. And there were documented cases of suspected vampires being symbolically killed before being buried, often by beheading.

Then there were the real-life vampires. Or people who just about qualified for the title. In the mid-fifteenth century, a man named Gilles de Rais, a respected French military officer, began torturing and killing children to use their blood in various experiments. He was believed to have killed between two hundred and three hundred children before he was caught and brought to trial.

Farther to the east, Vlad Tepes Dracula—the "Tepes" meant "impaler" and "Dracula" the "son of Dracul," while "Dracul" itself meant "devil" or "dragon"—the Prince of Wallachia, now a part of Romania, was also bathed in blood, though by an entirely different mechanism. As the name "Tepes" suggests, his particular speciality was impaling, and he killed literally thousands of his own people as well as every enemy of his country whom he could get his hands on. His particular speciality was eating meals outdoors surrounded by newly impaled victims, who might last for hours on the stakes before finally expiring. And he was, of course, at least in name, the inspiration for the villain of Bram Stoker's novel.

Still in Eastern Europe, the sixteenth- and seventeenth-century Countess Elizabeth Báthory von Ecsed (later known as the "Blood Countess" or "Blood Queen") is said to have become obsessed with preserving her youth and looks and, according to some sources, resorted to a study of alchemy and the occult to determine a method that would work. Once again, the answer was "blood," and she began the systematic kidnapping and killing of young girls—the "virgin" concept again—allegedly to obtain their blood, which she would then either drink or bathe in.

As time went on, the social status of her chosen victims began to rise, because the countess apparently believed that the blood of the nobility would be more pure and effective than the blood of the simple peasant girls who were her first victims. Suspicion eventually fell on her because of the sheer number of unexplained deaths of young girls in the area, but she was spared trial and execution because of her status. In 1610 she was sealed up in a windowless tower room in her home—Cseite Castle, then in Hungary, now part of Slovakia and today known as Čachtice—for the rest of her life. Her four accomplices, the servants she had employed to select, kidnap and torture her victims, were all swiftly tried and three of them executed. According to some reports, the countess and her servants were responsible for some 650 deaths altogether, though they were convicted of only eighty.

The stories about her bathing in blood first surfaced considerably later, in the eighteenth century, and it's now believed that, although the countess and her cohorts were certainly responsible for a large number of killings, her motive may have been simple sadism, as many of the bodies of their victims bore the unmistakable signs of torture, including beating, mutilation and burning.

Superstitions about both vampires and werewolves began to gain ground in Eastern Europe around this time. There was a persistent belief that *vrykolakas* (the Slavic word for "werewolves") would become vampires when they died, which linked the two legends firmly together. And the wolves—the ordinary kind—that roamed the forests of Europe at the time also became associated with the vampire legend.

Among the largely illiterate population of Europe, the vampire was more than a legend. For many people, the creature of the night was as real as anything else in their lives, a monster to be feared and killed whenever possible. And the results of that fear, and of the steps taken to prevent a vampire from ever rising from its grave, can still sometimes be seen today.

Excavations that took place during 2000, in one of the older cemeteries of Český Krumlov in Bohemia, uncovered an eighteenth-century graveyard containing eleven bodies, three of which had been buried in an unusual fashion. Bodies are normally laid to rest east–west, but these were lying north–south. One skeleton had been decapitated and its skull placed between its legs, and also had a stone forced between its jaws. It was believed that moving the head well away from the neck would prevent the vampire from replacing the head on its shoulders, and the stone would stop the jaws from being able to chew, an essential first step in turning a dead body into a vampire. All three of these skeletons had been pinned down with flat, heavy stones, to immobilize the bodies.

The remains were taken to Prague for anthropological examination, where it was ascertained that all three were male, and nitrogen analysis confirmed that the skeletons dated from between 1700 and 1750, the height of the anti-vampire craze in central Europe. The sternum of one body revealed a hole consistent with the left side of the chest, above the heart, having been impaled with a sharp object.

The identities of the three corpses have not been ascertained, and almost certainly never will be because of the paucity of records. But other "vampires" were much better known, even notorious.

Princess Eleonora Amalia

The prologue of this novel describes the burial of Princess Eleonora Amalia of the Schwarzenberg dynasty, and is factually accurate in almost all respects. Eleonora became sick in about 1740, and her health declined rapidly. In those days, about the only known treatment for any serious illness was bloodletting, which was believed to flush out evil spirits. She was moved from Krumlov to Vienna to get better medical treatment, but she died at about six in the morning on 5 May 1741 at the Schwarzenberg Palace in the city.

The empire's leading physicians assembled for a post-mortem, an unusual step as such examinations weren't usually performed on aristocrats. She apparently had a large tumor in her lower abdomen that had metastasized, invading her lungs—cancer, in short—but the outward signs were as if her body was being drained of blood from day to day, not helped by the bloodletting, obviously. Her preferred physician was Dr. Franz von Gerschstov, who also headed various commissions charged with investigating vampires, and who believed that vampirism was contagious. The probability is that the postmortem—which was extremely expensive—was actually an intervention, intended to stop the vampire rising from her grave. The autopsy allowed the heart to be legitimately removed from the body to avoid the indignity of impaling or decapitation.

But if the princess was a vampire, that meant there must be another, very powerful, one in the area, who had infected her. Anti-vampire fever swept the land, with the corpses of suspected vampires being dug up and burned, decapitated or impaled. The Schwarzenbergs were traditionally buried in the family tomb in St. Augustine's Church in Vienna, but the princess's body was returned to Bohemia the same night she died for burial, apparently by her own wish in an addition to her will, made a few days before her death. This may have been a forgery, and an attempt to avoid Vienna having a potential vampire buried in the heart of the city.

At the castle in Krumlov, one life-size portrait of her has revealed under X-ray examination that the princess's head had been removed and a new section of canvas sewn in its place—a symbolic beheading, perhaps?

The Milk of Wolves

Eleonora had found it difficult to conceive after producing her first child, Maria Anna, in 1706, and had finally resorted to an old remedy to enhance her fertility—she drank the milk of wolves. Their milk was believed to strengthen the female reproductive system and encourage the birth of male babies, and was based on the legend of the twins Romulus and Remus. She had cages built at the castle in which captured wolves were bred, and where the females were milked—a difficult task, and one that caused the animals to howl, an eerie and penetrating sound that could be heard for miles around. At that time, wolves were greatly feared and reputed to be both in league with the devil and friends to vampires.

In 1722, aged forty-one, Eleonora finally gave birth to a son. In 1732, the same year that the word "vampire" first appeared in the German language, her husband was shot dead in a hunt near Prague, accidentally killed by a bullet fired by Emperor Charles VI. Her son was taken from her to live in the emperor's court near Vienna, while she spent her remaining days roaming the corridors of Krumlov Zamek, the family castle.

Contemporary Vampires

After the superstitions and legends that characterized the medieval and Renaissance periods, the Age of Enlightenment followed in the eighteenth century. Various attempts were made by scholars, priests and others to debunk the vampire myth, as well as other superstitions that were prevalent at the time. But the legend of the vampire proved to be almost as immortal as the creatures it described, and the stories and beliefs persisted.

Vampires started to migrate from the graveyards and forests of Eastern Europe to the pages of Gothic novels and the verses of Romantic poets. *The Vampyre* by John William Polidori is mentioned in this novel, and that was followed in 1847 by *Varney the Vampyre*, the longest novel ever written on the subject to that date. To some extent, the popularity of vampires in fiction then declined somewhat, but enjoyed a sudden revival when Bram Stoker's *Dracula* was published. Since that time vampires, in one form or another, have always been with us.

Nosferatu in the Printed Word and on the Silver Screen

The origin of the word "nosferatu" is obscure. The first recorded reference in print was in a magazine article in 1885, and three years later in a travelogue entitled *The Land Beyond the Forest*, both written by the British author

Emily Gerard. The travelogue described the country of Transylvania (its Latin name translates as "the land beyond the forest"). In both she stated that "nosferatu" was the Romanian word for "vampire," but there is no known and identifiable corresponding word in any form of the Romanian language, ancient or modern. The closest are *necuratul* ("the devil") and *nesuferitul* ("the insufferable one").

An alternative explanation, which has been accepted by many writers, is that "nosferatu" is derived from an old Slavonic word *nesufur-atu*, which was apparently itself derived from the Greek *nosophoros* (νοσοφόρος), meaning "plague-carrier" or "disease-bearing." The obvious objection to this etymology is that Romanian and other Slavonic languages are Romance in origin and contain very few words from the Greek. It's also significant that, though the word *nosophoros* is a valid compound word in the Greek language—meaning that the two parts of the compound word are individually valid and are correctly combined—there's no evidence that the word ever existed in any phase of the Greek language. So this suggested etymology relies on an unknown Greek word that somehow gave rise to an unknown Romanian word, which seems fairly unlikely.

It has also been suggested that *nesufur-atu/nosferatu* was a technical term in Old Slavonic that had migrated into common usage, but never appeared in a Romanian dictionary. That is a somewhat difficult argument to sustain, given that the sole purpose of a dictionary is to record words in common usage, and it would be reasonable to expect that it would have been recorded somewhere.

So we'll probably never know exactly where "nosferatu" originated, but the balance of probability is that Emily Gerard either misheard a Romanian word or was misinformed.

Bram Stoker, of course, used the word in his novel *Dracula*, but his usage suggests that he probably believed it meant "not dead" or "undead" in Romanian, not "vampire," and he used it as a calque or loaned word.

The silver screen showed the world the face of the vampire for the first time with the 1922 film *Nosferatu: Eine Symphonie des Grauens* (*Nosferatu: A Symphony of Horrors*), starring Max Schreck as the vampire, his appearance taken straight from the descriptions in folklore: batlike ears, hairy palms and sharp pointed teeth. In 2010 the film was ranked number 21 in *Empire* magazine's list of the 100 best films of world cinema, and was basically an unauthorized movie version of Bram Stoker's *Dracula*. The word "nosferatu" was popularized by it because the studio hadn't obtained the rights to the novel, and so several changes had to be made. "Count Dracula" became "Count Orlok," and they used the word "nosferatu" as a synonym for "vampire," and this has essentially remained its meaning until today.

Bela Lugosi then took over the vampire role as Hollywood latched onto the character, while in England a few decades later, Christopher Lee strutted his stuff as the suave, handsome, almost romantic, antihero. Since then, vampires seem to have appeared almost everywhere, and in a bewildering variety of forms, from the leather-jacketed stars of *The Lost Boys* through the almost tragic hero of the Anne Rice novels, to the extreme violence of *From Dusk Till Dawn* and the sexy lighthearted exploits of *Buffy the Vampire Slayer*.

At least in one sense, then, the vampire does seem to be truly immortal.

Why Venice?

Venice is a beautiful, romantic and mysterious city, with a fascinating and extremely colorful history. And vampires—in both fiction and reality—feature in that history. The 1988 film *Vampire in Venice* starred Klaus Kinski in the title role, and more recently *The Vampires of Venice* was an episode of the *Doctor Who* television series.

That's the fiction, but this is reality.

The skull of a sixteenth-century female and supposed vampire was discovered in a mass grave—a plague pit—in Venice in March 2009. The brick jammed into her jaw was intended to stop her from feeding on the other plague victims buried with her.

So Venice seemed an ideal location for this novel. There are more than one hundred islands scattered around the Venetian lagoon, some with busy, populous settlements, others far too small to live on, and still others on which ancient ruined houses stand as stark reminders of the difficulties of establishing a viable habitation in the salty, marshy waters.

Venice itself can be spooky enough on a fine day. When the mist rolls in from the Adriatic, even small figures can cast giant shadows in the narrow streets and across the canals. Out in the lagoon, the islands become isolated worlds of their own where, in my imagination, almost anything could—and in this novel did—happen.

James Becker
Principality of Andorra, 2011

James Becker

NATIONAL BESTSELLING AUTHOR OF
THE FIRST APOSTLE

THE MOSES STONE

An ancient code...
A sinister secret...
A deadly chase for the truth.

In Morocco, an English couple discovers a clay tablet covered in ancient writing. One day later, they are dead.

Called to North Africa to investigate, detective Chris Bronson follows a trail of clues that plunge him into a mystery that has gone unsolved since biblical times. For the stone he must find is older and far more dangerous than he could ever have imagined...

Available wherever books are sold or at
penguin.com

THE NATIONAL BESTSELLER

FROM

James Becker

THE FIRST APOSTLE

An ancient inscription...
A dangerous secret...
An explosive debut thriller.

Chris Bronson is devastated when his best friend's
wife—the woman he was secretly in love with—
dies in a tragic accident. But when Bronson
heads to Italy to console his friend, he finds the
evidence of a break-in—and a strange Latin
inscription on a stone above the fireplace.

To decipher the stone, Bronson enlists the help
of his ex-wife, an antiques expert, sending them
on a treacherous path of clues across Europe—
and leading to a truth so dangerous it could
destroy the very foundations of the Christian faith.

**Available wherever books are sold or at
penguin.com**

New York Times bestselling author

Paul Christopher

THE SWORD OF THE TEMPLARS

A mystery that spans the past.
A conspiracy that lives on in the heart of
an ancient order.

Army Ranger Lt. Col. John Holliday had resigned
himself to ending his career teaching at West Point.
When his uncle passes away, Holliday discovers a
medieval sword—wrapped in Adolf Hitler's personal
battle standard. But when someone burns down his
uncle's house in an attempt to retrieve the sword,
Holliday realizes that he's being drawn into a war that
has been fought for centuries—a war in which he
may be the next casualty.

Available wherever books are sold or at
penguin.com

The *New York Times* bestseller

THE TEMPLAR CROSS

Paul Christopher

Retired Army Ranger Lt. Col. John Holliday has reluctantly settled into his teaching position at West Point when young Israeli archaeologist Rafi Wanounou comes to him with desperate news.

Holliday's niece—and Rafi's fiancé—Peggy has been kidnapped. Holliday sets out with Rafi to find the only family he has left. But their search for Peggy will lead them to a trail of clues that spans across the globe, and into the heart of a conspiracy involving an ancient Egyptian legend and the darkest secrets of the Order of Templar Knights.

Secrets that, once known, cannot be survived...

S0077